P9-DBY-868

Berkley books by M. K. Wren

THE PHOENIX LEGACY

BOOK I: SWORD OF THE LAMB
BOOK II: SHADOW OF THE SWAN
BOOK III: HOUSE OF THE WOLF

BOOK ONE OF THE PHOENIX LEGACY

SWORD OF THE LAMB

M.K. WREN

BERKLEY BOOKS, NEW YORK

SWORD OF THE LAMB

A Berkley Book / published by arrangement with
the author

PRINTING HISTORY
Berkley edition / February 1981
Second printing / July 1982
Third printing / March 1985

ISBN: 0-425-07587-7

This book is dedicated in gratitude to Dwight V. Swain, a man with a rare talent for teaching well an art that defies teaching.

Contents

SWORD
OF THE
LAMB

PHOENIX MEMFILES: DEPT HUMAN SCIENCES: HISTORY
(HS/H)
SUBFILE: WAR OF THE TWIN PLANETS (3208–3210): PELADEEN
REPUBLIC: LETTAPE #61: FROM
LORD ELOR USSHER PELADEEN
TO DR. ANDREAS
RIIS 1 JANUAR 3210
DOC LOC #819/8–232016–1618–122016 #61: 52116/118–113210

My dear Andreas,

I'm touched by your appeal to join you "underground," and I admit I was tempted; it isn't easy to face the prospect of one's imminent death. But I took the Crest Ring of Peladeen from my father's dead hand, and I swore the Oath of Allegiance to the Republic. These are both life vows, and I will not betray them.

I must also decline for another reason. The Concord cannot let me live. The House of Peladeen must be destroyed or the memory of the Republic will continue to be a thorn in its side. The Directors will demand my corpse. If they don't find it, they'll hunt me down even into the remotest parts of the Centauri System, and they might discover your existence in the process. The survival of the Society of the Phoenix is too important for me to justify that risk.

I considered sending the Lady Manir and our son, Predis, to you for sanctuary. I have no secrets from Manir, and she knows about the Phoenix. However, she refused this alternative as she refused to seek sanctuary of her relatives in the House of Kalister on Terra, which, as she said, would necessitate a public repudiation of me and the Republic. I would urge her to do so if it would save her life, but she's a proud woman, and beyond that knows full well that the Kalister aren't likely to risk the ire of the other Lords of the Concord to protect a very distant cousin so unfortunate as to be my wife.

Manir might have considered the sanctuary of the Phoe-

nix if she thought our son could be saved, but she sees no
hope for him. The Concord can't let Predis live for the
same reasons it can't let me live. He's only a child, and
it seems doubly cruel, but he might grow up to become the
focus of future revolt, and so he must die, as I must, for
the Concord's peace of mind.

I speak too much of death, but you'll understand that.
The end is closer than I thought when I last 'taped you.
Pollux is lost, and by the time this reaches you, I'll have
retreated to the Helen estate on Castor. That planet is less
hospitable to human life, and invading armies, than Pollux.
This may be my last opportunity to communicate with you,
Andreas. I have no solemn words to leave you, but I'm
offering something more useful—the pragmatic fuel of existence, money. My messenger will be carrying a case with
a lock keyed to your voice. Only part of this last bequest
is in cash; I've had no opportunity to gather much in 'cords,
and Republic drakos will soon be worthless. Most of this
bequest consists of jewelry and unset stones; its total value
is probably in excess of five million 'cords.

I'm relieved to hear that the installation of your facilities
is so near completion. It comes none too soon. I've assigned
my chief ministrator, Master Hamner, the task of checking
the Republic Archives to be sure no record of the original
geophysical station remains in the memfiles. I have complete faith in Master Hamner; he will not fail you.

Andreas, we won't meet again, but I face defeat without
despair knowing the Phoenix lives. I will be the last Lord
of the House of Peladeen, and if the Republic goes down
in history bearing the Peladeen name, I doubt the Concord
will let it be spoken with pride. The Society of the Phoenix
is my only hope. My hope for humankind, and my hope
for immortality. If the time ever comes, Andreas, when the
Phoenix rises from the ashes of this disaster like its namesake, let it be known that the Lord Elor had some part in
its birthing.

May the Holy Mezion and the All-God smile on this
fledgling. I live and shall die in that hope.

> Elor, the Lord Ussher Peladeen
> Leda, Pollux 1 Januar 3210

PART 1: APPRENTICESHIP

●II●II●II●II●II●II●II●II●II●II●II●II●II●II●II●II●II●II●II●II●II●II●

PHOENIX MEMFILES: DEPT HUMAN SCIENCES:
                    SOCIOTHEOLOGY (HS/STh)
SUBFILE: LAMB, RICHARD: PERSONAL NOTES
                12 SEPTEM 3250
DOC LOC #819/19208–1812–1614–1293250

I'm an old man in some senses; an old man because I'm so close to the end of my life, not because of the number of years that have elapsed since the beginning of it. Those total nineteen, although they seem more.

I thought I had come to terms with the myriad aspects of fear of death. I had learned to live with and in spite of the shadow of death. *Under* the shadow, the Shepherds say. Before the Selasid uprising in Concordia (in my mind it's always *the* uprising), I had feared most the *not being* of death, a state that defies the *being* imagination. But the uprising was the watershed of my life, and that was due in part to the fact that it expanded—explosively—my cognizance of death.

It introduced me to violent death.

On an overcast autumn day—it was last Avril—the Elder Shepherd Satva and I sat in his visitation room in the chapel in Compound B discussing the concept of free will over tamas tea. I remember that conversation with extraordinary clarity; in fact, I can repeat most of it verbatim, and I'm not usually a mnemonic adept. Two old men, one in a young but failing body, measuring the dimensions of a concept meaningful to the other only in theological terms.

When Satva's acolyte, Lukis, came tumbling into the room with the news of the "trouble" in the third quad dining hall, only his fear registered with me, but Satva reacted with the ready reflexes of a man trained by intensive drill,

3

although I'm sure he had never previously given any thought to how he would respond in such a crisis.

The All-God and the Holy Mezion will guide your hand.

He threw his brown and green Selasid Bond cloak over my shoulders, thrust my crutches into my hands, lifted me by one arm, ordering Lukis to take the other, and together they carried me out the rear door of the chapel. I translated "trouble" into "uprising" then as they swept me along, my feet dragging and bouncing helplessly in counterpoint to their hurrying, shuffling footfalls. Satva said something to indicate that our destination was the "door," but I didn't know what he meant.

They happen so abruptly, these uprisings, with the instantaneity of a chain reaction, and although this one was only minutes old when Lukis burst into Satva's visitation room, it had already engulfed most of the compound and would soon spread to the adjoining compounds, transmitted by the shriek of sirens, the disaster lights of fire, the massing of House guards, and, I'm convinced, by some subtle frequency emanated by the human brain in a state of terror.

This one began in the service alley behind the third quad dining hall where three Selasid guards entertained themselves with the sequential rape of a Bondmaid, one of the kitchen workers. Her fellow workers couldn't have been unaware of what was happening with only an open door separating them from her abject agony, yet none of them responded to it overtly. There would have been no uprising if the woman's husband hadn't entered the alley at that point.

He killed one of the guards with his bare hands—a superhuman feat that, if he hadn't been Bond, would have guaranteed him hero status in vidicommed legend—before he was cut down by the other guards' lasers.

But before he died, he tried to escape into the kitchen; the Bonds there panicked and ran into the dining hall, and in the melee a cooker exploded, adding impetus to the panic, which spread into the hall, filled to capacity—at least two thousand Bonds. They poured out of the hall (where the casualties were due primarily to trampling, not lasers), and out into the compound; the chain reaction was out of control.

The guards 'commed for reinforcements, and no doubt the word "uprising" was first spoken then.

The Lord Orin Badir Selasis later had submitted to him detailed reports on the "disturbances," which assured him unanimously that it all began with an unprovoked attack by a Bondman on a House guard, and when his fellow guards came to his defense, the Bonds in the dining hall "revolted."

I learned the genesis of the uprising from the Bonds who were present in the kitchen and hall at the time. Those who survived. Neither Lord Selasis nor his Fesh overseers questioned a single Bond.

But all that is in retrospect. I neither knew nor cared, any more than the Bonds, about the origins of the holocaust while Satva and Lukis carried me through the fetid baselevel passages. Above us the pedways swarmed with aimlessly fleeing Bonds oblivious to the ampspeaker orders demanding their immediate halt, pursued and overtaken by troops of guards firing—and using charged lashes or any other handy weapon—at malicious will.

In my memory color, sound, and smell are interfused. Blue. The laser beams. And charred black, and pinkish red, and osseous white. Hammering, pounding, booted footsteps; shouts, cries, pleas, and, constantly, screams of pain. And saturating it all, the ghastly—what other word suffices?—odors of burned flesh and fear.

My brother in his nightmares spoke of those odors. That was later after his personal Armageddon. He never spoke of that consciously; only in sleep when he couldn't know I heard.

The "door" toward which Satva and Lukis carried me was a hidden opening enlarged through a storm drain under the compound wall. That secret access surprised me; it suggested revolutionary intent and planning among the Bonds.

But it represented only a relative revolution. The purpose of the opening wasn't to offer Bonds a means of escape from the compound—and where would they escape to? The Outside, when the headprice on runaway Bonds is high enough to tempt any Outsider noddy or hound?—but a means of access *into* the compound for Bonds unfortunate enough to miss the curfew closure. The penalties for defying the curfew in Selasid compounds are inevitably painful and often maiming.

We weren't far from the "door," and I was panting as hard as Satva and Lukis, yet I hadn't run a step; I couldn't. I could only clutch my crutches to my breast, aware that I'd be helpless without them when I lost my human crutches. On the pedway above us, Bonds and guards clashed in the limited passage ten meters in the air, and three Bonds were forced, or thrown, off the 'way. I heard their descending shrieks, heard sounds I can't even approach in words as they hit the plasment, one no more than a meter in front of us.

The light was dim and erratic, and neither Satva nor Lukis paused before turning into an even darker side passage, yet every detail of that image is as clear in my memory as my theological discourse with Satva on free will.

It was a man, and his body seemed both to burst and to collapse on impact. Horrible, yes. I'd never considered the color of human entrails before.

But what was clearest in my mind was a sense of outrage, not for the man so much as for his body. I mean, his physical, living body. It had been in some way *violated*, and I was horrified that such a sacrilege—that seemed the only applicable term—was possible.

I saw death then as more than not-being, as a wanton violation of the infinitely complex, finely ordered mechanism that houses and sustains life.

And I *felt* that violation as I hope the man himself did not; felt the sudden disintegration of the physical system, its bursting implosion; felt the whole agony and terror of it as if it were my own.

Sometimes I wonder if we don't think with our cells, and if the brain is only a sophisticated data processing and storage center. If so, wouldn't every cell recoil from the dissolution of the order, the system, that gives it life?

And if—as Lemric and Kow Daws theorize—social units can be treated as living organisms, what of the agony of the individual cells, the individual people, within the sustaining mechanism of the *dying* social organism?

Whose pain did I feel?

Satva helped me through the storm drain and outside the compound wall, where I found myself in a 'way channel that led to a transit plaza. He took the Bond cloak from my shoulders, propped me against the wall on my crutches, and with a plea for my blessing—*my* blessing!—returned to the compound. The 'ways above me teemed with Selasid guards and Conpol reinforcements, but I was alone and unnoticed.

And I was Fesh, not Bond, and thus safe.

Satva returned to his flock. And died with ten thousand Bonds who died—violently—in those compounds that day. Izak succeeded Satva as Elder Shepherd of Compound B, but Lukis won't be Izak's acolyte. He died with his Shepherd.

Whose pain? Whose pain did I feel?

CHAPTER I: Octov 3244

●‖

1.

Theron Rovere walked with the cautious gait of the elderly, sedately dignified in his long lector's robes, gray-bearded chin resting on his chest. His robes were white with edgings of black denoting a lector/professor of the University, the gold stripe around the flared right sleeve of his surcoat indicated that he was a GuildMaster, and the badge on his left shoulder with the lion crest in gold and purple was a reminder that he was born allieged to the House of Daro Galinin. But he hadn't walked on Galinin ground for many years, and didn't now. For the last ten years, he had made his home here in the Estate of the House of DeKoven Woolf.

But that, like so many things, would soon be changed.

Lector Rovere sighed and clasped his hands behind his back, noting, as he always did, the faint indentations worn into the slate path by ten generations of DeKoven Woolf footsteps.

Minutiae. . . .

One would think that at a time like this such trivia would escape his notice. A pedantic habit. But even as he considered the irony of it, he was remembering that the dappled shadows on the slate were cast by the eucalypt trees planted by Konan Woolf, the third First Lord of the House, over three hundred years ago.

A light wind, warm with spring, swept the leaves; Octov, and beyond the grove Concordia lazed and buzzed in the crystal sunlight. The acacias were in bloom, their fluffy batons casting a sweet perfume into the wind. Rovere smiled, his eye drawn by a sharp chattering and a multihued flash in the branches above him. A rainbow lorikeet. But he was thinking of the

9

conversation concluded only seconds ago in the small salon off the grove, and remembering the spectacular fury of the Lady Elise Galinin Woolf. It was this memory that brought the smile.

Elise always made him think of spring, and perhaps it was appropriate, their parting at this season. He'd known her since she was a child, been tutor to her and her brother, Lord Evin Galinin. That he thought of her—even addressed her at times— as Elise was indicative of their long and close relationship. No other Fesh would dare address the Lady Galinin Woolf so familiarly, nor even many Elite.

And if she made him think of spring, her wrath could only be likened to a spring rainstorm, quick and turbulent: Elise in a silken, floor-length gown of pale green—a true spring green—drawn to her full regal height, gray eyes flashing, fixed on her husband, her red-bronze hair cascading over her shoulders, glinting as if fired by her angry impatience.

Elisean Titian. The color of her hair called to mind that term.

Minutiae. . . .

He wondered if she knew that women of the Elite and even upper-class Fesh throughout the Concord had among the choices offered by their coiffurers a hair color called Elisean Titian, an unnatural imitation of that candescent hue naturally her own. And he wondered how many of the women who availed themselves of that imitation knew who Titian was.

Elise knew. But Rovere's special field of study was Pre-Disasters history, and Elise Galinin had been one of his best students.

"Phillip, you wouldn't deny him an opportunity to tell the boys goodbye!"

Theron Rovere's gaze moved across the salon with its airy NeoMedit furnishings to the Lord Phillip DeKoven Woolf, who stood gazing out the windowall into the grove, a lean, dark figure clothed in rich, wine-colored hues, a summer night to Elise's spring day, calling to mind another Pre-Disasters artist. Rovere frowned until he pulled the name out of his memory.

Elgreco.

Phillip Woolf's countenance was as elegantly aquiline as those long-dead Espanish lords immortalized by a forgotten artist's hand; his hair was as raven black, his trim mustache and beard followed the contours of his mouth and chin in a similar manner, but his eyes weren't the limpid black of Elgreco's lords. They were the crystalline blue found at the heart of a glacier.

Woolf didn't respond to Elise's exclamation; he seemed too preoccupied to hear it. Instead, he turned on Rovere.

"Lector Rovere . . ." He paused, black brows drawn. "Damn it, Theron, I respect your scholarly ethics, but I cannot understand why you felt it necessary to take the defendant's stand on Quiller's thesis."

Rovere smiled gently, more for Elise than for Woolf. Mute sadness misted her eyes now, the quick anger passing like the spring rainstorm it evoked.

"My lord, Quiller was a student of mine; I was his sponsor when he entered the Academicians Guild. He's an excellent historian; a genius, in fact. His thesis may not have met with the approval of the Board of Censors, but it is impeccably researched and profoundly perceptive."

Woolf began pacing the small room, and Rovere was reminded of the leopards in the Galinin zoological preserve, rare survivors of a species nearly lost.

"Theron, I'm sure Quiller's thesis *is* perceptive, but why did he try to publish it under a Priority-*Four* rating? Why couldn't he be satisfied to let it circulate among scholars on a Pri-Three? For the God's sake, the Peladeen Republic is nearly forty years dead."

"True, my lord, but it existed for seventy-five years and functioned quite successfully."

"I'm well aware of that, but it's a matter of indifference to me at the moment. Even if you believed in Quiller, to take full responsibility for his thesis, to call it your own . . ." He stopped, searching Rovere's face. "You knew the inevitable consequences for you."

Rovere took a deep breath. "Yes, my lord, but I'm an old

man. Quiller, as I said, is a talented young man. We need such men; the Concord needs them."

"And what kind of man is he to let you shoulder the burden of *his* error?"

"An unhappy man, but I boxed him in very neatly. Don't blame him."

"Then I'm left with no one to blame but you."

"True. So was the Board of Censors."

Woolf returned to the windowall, his mouth a tight line as he looked out into the grove. A stray shaft of sunlight caught on the Crest Ring on his right hand, flashing crimson from the depths of the great Mogok ruby, its table incised with the Eagle Crest of the House. Only a First Lord wore such a ring. He took it from his father's dead hand and wore it for the remainder of his life until his first born son took it from his dead hand. Rovere thought of the thirteen Woolf Lords who had borne that blood-hued burden, and of Alexand, who would be the fourteenth.

Lord Phillip's thoughts were still on Quiller.

"*Independent* Fesh," he pronounced bitterly. "This is what comes of giving young zealots like Quiller too *much* independence. He hasn't the maturity to foresee the results of his enthusiasm." Then he turned and studied Rovere soberly. "I can't shield you now; it's out of my hands. If you'd come to me before the Board—"

"No, my lord. I made my choice, and my only regret is that it might reflect badly on you or Lord Galinin, to whom I'm still allieged, however 'independently.'" He looked at Elise, her spring-rain wrath now entirely dissipated. "No, I have *two* regrets. I'll miss Alexand and Richard. Serving as teacher to them has been both a privilege and pleasure."

She turned away, tears shining in her cloud-colored eyes. "Oh, Theron . . . Theron. . . ."

"Now, Elise, you mustn't worry about me. Please. I'll be treated well at the Detention Center. I'm sure your lord husband will see to that."

"Phillip, you *will* see to it? *Promise* me."

His glacial eyes seemed to thaw as he turned to her. Few

people saw that tenderness in Phillip Woolf's eyes; it was reserved for only three people: Elise and his sons.

He said quietly, "I *have* seen to it. He'll be treated with due respect. It was all I could do."

She sighed her relief, then a spark of anger revived.

"And can't you allow him a little time with the boys before he's . . . taken away? I doubt he can contaminate their minds in a few minutes. I've detected no hint of corruption in nearly ten years."

Woolf sighed and turned to Rovere. "They're waiting in the viewpoint pavilion. I intended to tell them myself that you'd be leaving them."

"Shall I tell them, my lord?"

He hesitated, then, "What will you say?"

"Not the truth. I've no intention of inflicting any gratuitous pain on them, particularly not on Rich." He saw the fleeting shadow of sorrow in Woolf's eyes. "I'll simply tell them I'm retiring."

Woolf nodded mechanically. "Very well, Theron."

"Thank you, my lord. Elise . . ." He waited until she looked around at him. "Goodbye, my lady. Waste no tears on this old man. You've given me so much happiness, I wouldn't like to think I repaid you with grief."

She mustered a smile that seemed to catch the spring sunlight and dispel the shadows in the room.

"Goodbye, Theron. Go in peace."

The windwheels hanging in the trees chimed softly with the quickening of the breeze. The slate path divided. Rovere stopped and looked down the narrower walk to his right. It crossed a footbridge over a stone-strewn white rush of water, then wound a few meters farther to the glass-walled wing that had been his domain for ten years: the school.

A single spacious room housing facilities for almost any endeavor from sculpture to biochemistry, with a comprehensive computer console, direct inputs to Concord University System and Archive memfiles—an array of education tools that would be the envy of any Fesh Basic School, and all for two students.

But these were very special students, and the Concord could be grateful that Lord Woolf was so deeply concerned with the education of his sons.

At least—Rovere sobered as he continued along the left-hand path—at least for Alexand.

Alexand was the first born, heir to the First Lordship of DeKoven Woolf with its commutronics franchises and its seat on the Directorate, a virtually hereditary position. And he was the grandson of Lord Mathis Daro Galinin, who held all Solar System energy franchises as well as the Chairmanship of the Directorate, the most powerful man in the Concord of the Loyal Houses.

And Richard, the second born . . .

Rovere pulled in a long breath. Rich would never take part in the grand games of power. Not that he'd have a large part to play as the second born, a VisLord. Still, any son of DeKoven Woolf could make his presence felt in the half-feudal world of the Concord.

But, at thirteen, Richard DeKoven Woolf was dying.

It began with the epidemic that ravaged the Two Systems nine years ago; an aberrant virus striking with the terrible democracy of disease, cutting down Elite, Fesh, and Bond alike. Most of its victims died with the initial viral invasion, but Rich had the best medical care available, and he survived.

His family's relief at that was short-lived when it became apparent that the disease had unexpected side effects: it disrupted the chemistry of his neural system so violently that the damage was irreversible and continuing. His body turned upon itself, a kind of chemical cancer gradually sheathing the spinal cord with inert sclerose tissue, cutting off the vital electric link between brain and muscle. It began with his legs and worked its way toward his heart and lungs, day by day, year by year. But with good medical treatment, Dr. Stel assured Lord and Lady Woolf, Rich might live to Age of Rights. Twenty.

The Woolfs took little comfort in that, either as loving parents or as First Lord and Lady of the House. It was a well kept secret, and Rovere was one of a trusted handful who knew the real nature of Rich's illness.

His measured tread brought him out of the grove onto a grass-covered hillock topped by a small, circular pavilion. Only here did it become apparent that the whole miniature forest, the streamlets, and the grassy hill were built on one of the roof terraces of the vast Home Estate of the House of DeKoven Woolf.

From this point one could look down on this sprawling, multileveled edifice that was a palace in the sense of being a lordly residence, the citadel of a feifdom to which six million Fesh and Bonds were allieged, and an administrative complex for an industrial empire encompassing every aspect of communications throughout the Concord, including the PubliCom System vidicom network. Rovere could trace the Estate's growth over three centuries in the materials comprising its sheer walls and jutting wings—from white marble to luminescent marlite—and in the variety of architectural styles, although it had a coherence of design that always amazed him in view of its long history.

The Estate occupied a ridge forested with eucalypts and fernwood like an exotic extension of rock, and overlooked a small city that was an extension of itself. Tiered up the flanks of the ridge were the apartments of the Woolf Fesh, their opulence increasing in ratio to their proximity to the Estate. At the foot of the ridge was the commutronics factory with its huge, blank-walled assembly buildings and warehouses dominated by three fifty-meter beamed-power receptors. DeKoven Woolf wasn't one of the landed Houses; it was an exclusively industrial House, and this factory complex was only one of fifty throughout the Two Systems.

Beyond the factory were ten compounds, each housing ten thousand Bonds, and beyond them, stretching south as far as the eye could see, lay Concordia, the city of lights, capital of the Concord, governmental nerve center of the Two Systems, lying in the shadow of, but too vast to be overshadowed by, snow-flecked Mount Torbrek. The Woolf Estate was sited at the city's edge, but was still part of it and only one of hundreds of similar minicities making up the grand whole; more than half the Houses in the Court of Lords had estates in Concordia, and many of them were Home Estates.

And at the white, shining center of the city, encompassing the blue-green scallop of Phillip Bay, was the Concord administrative complex; five million Concord Fesh and Bonds lived and worked there. On this clear day Rovere could pick out the towering Hall of the Directorate and even the slender triple spires of the Cathedron.

It was a vista to make one pause, and his pace slowed. It was the last time he would see it.

The sound of laughter drew his attention to the pavilion. Rich sat on one of the benches lining the perimeter, looking down at a small chessboard, while Alexand stood with one foot propped on the bench, a hand resting on a chess piece. They were too intent to hear Rovere approaching, and he didn't hurry his pace. He was thinking of a *Post*-Disasters artist this time. Kelly Song, whose portraits of Patric Ballarat assured his fame with the general public—or, rather, with the Fesh and Elite, who were exposed to Song in history textapes—but whose exquisite eye for composition assured his immortality among artists. Here was a composition for Song, these two figures arranged among the slender marble columns, the clear light casting barred shadows warmed with reflected colors, their shirts, with the full, gathered sleeves—the kind of sleeves worn by people who didn't have to concern themselves with practicality—making strong, graceful shapes in white, foils for their dark heads and the elongated brushstrokes of legs encased in dark velveen. Alexand was wearing boots, Rovere noted; he wore them more and more often now. The mark of the adult male Elite. Or their military and police minions.

Rovere was close enough now to hear their voices. Rich was saying, "Alex, you're bluffing. You think I won't trade queens with you?"

Alexand laughed, and Rovere thought how different the quality of it was from his brother's. Rich was still capable of the uninhibited laughter of childhood, but with Alexand there was a hint of constraint; it had always been there.

"I think your king will be in check in another move if you do." He studied the board a moment longer, then withdrew his hand.

"But I have you now. Rook takes bishop and check; then

queen takes queen and check again, and if your knight takes my rook, my pawn moves to the last rank and—"

"Oh, 'Zion!" Alexand straightened and threw up his hands in mock resignation. "All right, I'll concede, but don't—" He stopped, aware of Rovere, the brief hesitation displayed by both boys indicative of surprise; they were expecting their father.

"Lector Theron, good morning," Rich said. He hastily folded the board, which made a box to hold the pieces.

"Good morning, Rich. Alex, it sounds as if you were thoroughly outmaneuvered."

Alexand laughed and, like Rich, his surprise had given way to warm welcome. He asked, "Isn't Father coming?"

"No, he won't be coming after all. Please, sit down, Alex, and we'll get on with our lesson for the day."

Alexand moved silently to sit down beside Rich, while Rovere lowered his stiff-jointed bulk to the bench next to theirs. He studied them, feeling already the emptiness of loss. He'd never married or had children, and these boys were as dear to him as if they were his own.

Both had the Woolf coloring: black hair and intense blue eyes, although there was an echo of Elise in the sensitive curves of Rich's mouth and his deep-set, long-lashed eyes. He was slight for his age; that was the only outward manifestation of the disease when he was seated. But the nulgrav crutches were propped against the bench beside him, an ever present reminder.

And Alexand, fifteen, at that turning point on the verge of maturity, the remarkable resemblance he bore to Phillip Woolf becoming increasingly evident, the aquiline planes, evocative of the Black Eagle of the House crest, emerging from the gentler contours of childhood. He had Woolf's lean grace, too, even in the awkward midst of adolescence, this due in part to the rigorous physical training Woolf insisted upon as an integral part of his education. And already there was in Alexand's eyes a hint of Woolf's wary, aloof, faintly cynical cognizance of the realities of life.

Rovere sighed. He would miss these boys—Holy God, he would miss them. Especially Rich.

It had been his pleasure to make Rich's life, short as it must be, as full as possible with the joys of the mind, and Rich had responded beyond his expectations. He had long ago closed the two-year age gap between himself and Alexand and in many areas surpassed him. Both were a teacher's delight, curious and quick, a constant challenge. And he'd learned from them, learned something of the human potential for love in the sentient rapport between these brothers.

Finally Rovere said, "Today we'll have a short review of history; a verbal test of your understanding."

At that, Alexand frowned slightly. "I thought we were going into Drakonian physics today."

Rich laughed. "Alex has been doing extra work on that. He just wants to show off."

"Then he's probably outstripped me, Rich, on that subject. No, today we'll consider history."

Rich's eyes lighted with anticipation; he'd assimilated Rovere's interest in history and its sister study, sociology. To Alexand, all subjects seemed of equal interest, each a challenge to be overcome. But he was distracted now, more intent on his teacher's face than on his words.

He knew. Rovere sighed; somehow Alexand knew something was wrong.

"All right, boys," he began firmly. "I'll give you a date, and I want you to tell me why it's important." He took a scriber and lightpen from a pocket in the voluminous folds of his robes and at the top of the screen wrote their initials. "A point for every correct answer. That is, the *first* with the correct answer. Ready?"

Rich was leaning forward attentively. "I'm ready."

Alexand only nodded, putting his back against the railing, his smile fading when he was out of Rich's line of sight.

"Very well, then," Rovere said, "A.D. 1945."

Rich answered quickly, "The first controlled nuclear reaction. A nuclear bomb."

Rovere marked the point. "Very good. Which of the old 'nations,' as they were called, was that bomb used against?"

"Uh . . . the States of Noramerika?"

"Is that correct, Alex?"

"No. It was used *by* the States of Noramerika against—I think it was called Japan. The islands held by the House of Matsune."

"Alex gets the point. Now, another date: 2030."

Rich took this question. "That would be the beginning of the Decades of Disaster. The Great Drought."

"And how long did it last?"

"The Disasters or the Drought?"

Rovere smiled. "Both."

"Well, the ending date for the Disasters is usually given as 2060. That was the year the last Prime Minister of Conta Austrail died. And the Drought . . ." That trailed out in a sigh, and Alexand took advantage of his hesitation to offer the answer.

"The ending date for the Drought is 2040."

Rovere marked a point for him. "Correct. Of course, all Disasters dates tend to be rather arbitrary; we know so little about the period, really. One date we're fairly certain of, though, is 2044."

Rich put in, "That was the Nuclear Wars."

"Yes, and how long did *they* last?"

"I don't know. Some textapes say three weeks, others say three months."

Alexand looked out at the city and noted absently, "I guess it doesn't really matter. Weeks or months. With the kind of weapons they were using, days would be enough."

Rich nodded and added, "What a terrible time to have to live in. Or die in."

That was typical of both of them, that empathetic response, and something else that made them such remarkable students. Rovere had lectured for many University history courses, but seldom had he encountered students who so consistently saw dry history in terms of personal experience, and certainly few Elite students showed that capacity; their training so often tended to make them incapable of empathy.

"Yes, it was a terrible time," he said, "and the Nuclear Wars were only a small part of it. There was the Pandemic— some of the diseases we can't even identify today—and the mutant plagues and, always and above all, starvation. And, of course, the ultimate plague, anarchy. But humankind had only itself to blame for its suffering. You don't burden a small planet with ten billion people, or befoul it with lethal chemicals and just plain sewage, or squander its resources as if they were infinite, without paying the price."

Alexand turned his clear gaze on Rovere. "But there was no justice in it. The people guilty of most of the overproliferation and exploitation didn't pay the price. They were safely dead before the Disasters."

Rovere nodded. "True, but justice is a human invention—not a natural law—and it's rare even in human interactions. To be at all objective about the Disasters, you have to think of them in natural terms. Human beings forced a natural reaction to their excesses, and that reaction included the annihilation of seventy-five to ninety percent of the human population." He paused, lips pursed on a frown. "But it *was* a terrible time, and I can't help agreeing, Alex, that there was no justice in it. Now, on with history and our test. We'll skip over the depths of the Second Dark Age and stop at another date: 2560."

"Bishop Colona," Rich replied.

"Good, but what in particular about Colona?"

Rich raised an eyebrow. "The . . . well, vision, or whatever. *The Revelations*. He instituted Mezionism."

Rovere repressed a smile at that hint of agnostic skepticism. The Woolfs carefully maintained every appearance of religious devotion in public, but Phillip Woolf didn't expect—or want—his sons to accept anything on blind faith in private.

"All right. Another date: 2571."

A long pause. Both boys frowned, looking first at Rovere, then at each other. Finally, Rich ventured, "The Holy Confederation of Conta Austrail?"

Rovere didn't comment. "Alex?"

"No, that was later—2585; 2571 was probably a good year for fishing or potatoes."

Rovere laughed. "Alex gets the point, Rich."

Rich objected, "You didn't say you were putting in unimportant dates."

"But you should know whether a date has significance.

Now, the Holy Confederation united all the feudal enclaves and holds of Conta Austrail under two banners: that of Colona's Orthodox Church of the Holy Mezion and—a bonus point—what Lord?"

Rich responded quickly, as if to make up for his lost point, "Lord Even Pilgram." Then he added, "But the Holy Confederation wasn't exactly under *his* banner."

Rovere shifted his weight and rested one elbow on the railing. Old limbs seemed to become cramped so easily. Or perhaps it only became more noticeable with age.

"I stand corrected, Rich. Yes, the Holy Confederation was actually a rather loose alliance, but it provided a stable framework for societal development, and particularly technological development. Another date: 2761."

Rich hesitated over that, looking at Alexand, who answered, "The invention of the Darwin cell. It was an energy storage and amplification device that made surface-collected solar energy a really viable power source."

"Indeed, and powered the industrial renaissance, which led to . . . what?"

Alexand said in an oddly flat tone, "The Wars of Confederation."

Rovere studied him a moment, then nodded. "True, but not immediately. Rich—any comments?"

"Well, there was a long period of exploration and trade with cultures outside Conta Austrail. None of them were as advanced technologically, but the contacts and trade gave most of them a boost along that line before Ballarat appeared."

"You're anticipating me. I was going to ask who is regarded as the father of the PanTerran Confederation."

Rich laughed. "Lord Patric Eyre Ballarat, 2839 to . . . uh, 2920."

Rovere in turn laughed as he marked the point. "Exactly. The Wars of Confederation were a prelude to the PanTerran Confederation, of course." He glanced at Alexand as he added, "Large-scale political unions are inevitably spawned by war, and the PanTerran Confederation was certainly large scale since it included the entire planet. How long did the Wars last?"

Alexand had the answer to that. "Twenty-seven years: 2876

to 2903." Then he asked, "Why is Ballarat called the father of the Confederation? He didn't have much to do with it after he finished conquering the world."

"A figure of speech, I suppose. You're right; Ballarat retired in something of a huff after the Wars when the Lords of the old Holy Confederation balked at making him their emperor. But there's some justification for crediting him with paternity of the PanTerran Confederation. His Articles of Union, which were enacted at the beginning of the Wars, established the basic outlines of the Confederation and, for that matter, the Concord. That included the Directorate, for instance, and its power to tax, to maintain a police force and an army independent of the Houses."

Rich frowned introspectively. "I wonder why the Lords wouldn't make him an emperor. I mean, you'd think when he'd just conquered a world for them, the time would be right, that they'd give him almost anything he asked for."

From the grove came the sardonic laugh of a kookaburra, and it seemed appropriate. "Well, Rich, it seems that Ballarat was a better conqueror and administrator than politician. Basically, I think the Lords were afraid of him. Afraid of innovation, of losing their own power."

Alexand commented, "Some things don't seem to change."

Rovere hesitated, finding the cynicism underlying that disturbing.

"No, Alex. In fact, our power distribution systems haven't changed appreciably since Ballarat, and that was—what? Three centuries ago."

"Nor has the class system."

True enough, Rovere thought, although he recognized a tendency to generality there that glossed over subtleties of development. Alexand apparently sensed his reservations and added, "I mean, even the *names* of the three basic classes haven't changed since Ballarat: Bond, Fesh, and Elite. The only difference is that now there's no hope of advancing from one class to another; there *was* in Ballarat's time." Then he smiled faintly, as if to mask his emotional intensity. "Did they have the Outside and Outsiders in his time?"

Rovere gave that a laugh. "Of course, but those terms didn't become popular until the late PanTerran Confederation period. There are always those who live outside the laws and moral codes of any society. They seem to be a social necessity in some sense; at least, most societies have made room for them, left them an area of existence in one way or another. But let's return to the PanTerran Confederation. And I'll leave off the 'PanTerran.' That was generally dispensed with after the extraterrestrial colonization phase. It's been called the Golden Age. Now, what about the year 3000, the Trimillennium? What, other than humankind's survival through approximately six thousand years of recorded history, is special about that date?"

Rich was first with the answer to that. "The Lunar landing; the first since the Disasters."

"Good." Alexand, he noted, was showing signs of preoccupation. Rovere recalled his attention with, "Alex, a bonus point if you can tell me when humankind *first* set foot on Luna—before the Second Dark Age."

"About . . . 1970."

Rich put in, "It was 1969, to be exact." To which Alexand only shrugged, and Rovere smiled as he marked the point under Rich's initial.

"All right. What about 3052?"

Rich was ready with, "That was the year Ela Tolstyne's *Treatise on Matter/Anti-Matter Interactions* was published."

"Yes, and that led to what two key developments?"

"Nulgrav and the MAM-An drive."

"Yes. Let's consider nulgrav first, although MAM-An actually preceded it by three years. What was its primary effect? Alex?"

"It made interplanetary travel truly practical, but that was in conjuction with MAM-An. Of course, there were already colonies on Luna and Mars, but they were rather primitive at that point. The nulgrav–MAM-An combination made it easier to develop them further and go on to new colonies."

"True, but nulgrav had planetside effects, too."

Rich observed wryly, "Well, there were the Vinay follies in the late thirty-first century."

Rovere sent him a sidelong smile. "Yes. Master Vinay was

a talented architech, but he neglected to allow for the effects of a momentary power failure on his floating edifices. However, nulgrav had more profound results, such as the elimination of ground travel, and with it the street. It made possible our pedway systems, and every aircar, 'dray, 'bus, and 'taxi is powered by nulgrav."

Alexand noted, "It also made the House of Hild Robek."

"Indeed, and MAM-An in a sense made the House of Badir Selasis and certainly Drakonis. Why? And by the way, can either of you translate that acronym—MAM-An?"

Rich replied crisply, "Matter/Anti-Matter Annihilation." Then he added, before Alexand could get a word in, "And MAM-An made the House of Selasis because it not only made interplanetary travel in the Solar System faster and more practical, but it made the speeds necessary for SynchShift possible."

Rovere smiled as he shifted his weight on the hard bench. The light wind had turned into the south, carrying the rumbling of the factory and the pervading hum of Concordia with it.

"Again, you're anticipating me, but I'll give you the date anyway: 3060."

Alexand managed to get in first with the answer. "That was the year the Drakonian Theory was published."

"Since you've been boning up on Drakonian physics, that was easy for you. And I'm sure you can tell me why I said MAM-An also made the House of Drakonis."

"It made SynchShift feasible, and Orabu Drakon was rewarded for that with a Lordship and the power franchises in the Centauri System." Then, after a pause, "It was still possible for a Fesh to become a Lord in those days."

Rovere didn't comment on that. He marked a point for Alexand, taking pleasure in the aural rotundities of the name: "Orabu Drakon. I wonder what our world would be like if he'd lived to finish his time/mass field theory."

A rhetorical question, but Alexand offered an answer to it.

"We might have the matter transmitter," he said casually, then, noting Rich's curiously raised eyebrow, "That's something I came across in my boning. Some of Drakon's followers seemed to think such a device is feasible."

Rovere said, "Dr. Relsing assures me it *isn't* feasible, if you mean instantaneous transmission of objects from one point to another. I'd be delighted to have the evidence to prove him wrong at the next . . . Guild meeting." The hesitation came as he realized there wouldn't be a next Academicians Guild meeting—not for Theron Rovere.

Perhaps Alexand caught the pause, but he only shrugged and said, "I'm just repeating opinions I've read. The man who supposedly demonstrated—mathematically, at least—the feasibility of a matter transmitter was Andreas Riis. He was a Polluxian physicist." Then he eyed his teacher obliquely. "I also came across some opinions suggesting that Riis founded the Society of the Phoenix."

"You must've been doing some of your boning in Priority-Two memfiles." But of course any Elite of any age had access to Pri-Two 'files. One of the privileges of rank.

Rich asked impatiently, "What in all the worlds is the Society of the Phoenix?"

Alexand laughed. "I'm not really sure. The opinions on that were all a little vague, but I've heard Father talk about it. I guess it's one of the Outsider pirate clans. Lector Theron, do you know anything about it?"

"No, not really, but the opinions—or, rather, rumors—I've heard suggest the Phoenix is more than a pirate clan; it has definite revolutionary overtones. In fact, I believe the SSB lists it as a subversive group, which means membership is punishable by execution."

Rich's eyes widened. "Revolutionary? You mean political revolution—against the Concord?"

Rovere nodded, feeling ill at ease with a subject bearing on treason and the SSB. The Special Services Branch of Conpol, with its black-cloaked, face-screened, ominously anonymous agents was something he didn't wish to dwell on now.

He made a show of studying his students' scores and said lightly, "Now, back to history. I'm not so easily distracted, you know. We were talking about Orabu Drakon and his theory. Synchronal metathesis and chrono-spatial eversion. You see, I'm not entirely ignorant on the subject since I can pronounce that."

Rich put in, "That's why they call it SynchShift, I guess. It's easier to say."

"Fortunately. All right, when was the first SynchShift—or

SS, which is even easier—ship launched?"

Rich answered, "3078 The *Double Star,* under Commander Izak Samovi."

"Indeed. One of the few genuine heroes left us by history. Now, what about the year 3084?"

Both spoke in unison, but Rich was a split-second ahead of his brother.

"The first permanent colony in the Alpha Centauri A system. Leda on Pollux, in the Twin Planets."

"Very good." Rovere marked another point. "Why are they called the *Twin* Planets, by the way? Alex? A bonus point."

"Because they revolve around each other, or rather a common center of gravity, and when they were first seen they looked like—well, twin stars."

"And a welcome sight they must've been since they fall within the life zone."

Rich said, "Pollux does, but Castor's a vacuum colony."

Rovere smiled as Alexand reminded his brother, "It may not be comfortable for human life, but it does fall within the life zone limits because it has a thin atmosphere and—"

"All right, I know. And even some fairly advanced life forms. Still, I think Pollux was a lot more welcome sight."

Rovere said, "I'm sure it was; it's called Terra's twin. But back to Castor. When was the first colony established there?"

Rich was first with, "3084. The city of Helen."

"And the three Inner Planets?"

"Perseus in 3085, Dionysus and Pan in . . . 3087."

"And the remaining planets of Alpha Centauri A?"

Rich gave a short laugh, suggesting that Rovere should realize that he knew better.

"Tityus and Hercules are gaseous giants, and they'll never be colonized. Not by human beings. And none of their satellites has been colonized yet. But Tityus was *discovered* in 3085 and Hercules in 3086."

Rovere smiled at that. "Correct, Rich. Apparently I've done a good job with the two of you in history, at least. What are the dates for the Confederation extrasolar exploration phase and how many expeditions were there?"

"3078 to 3104," Rich answered, "and I think there were

eighteen expeditions to eight different stars. Let's see . . . well, the Centauri System, of course; Proxima and Alpha A and B. Then Barnard's star, Lalande, Sirius A, Epsilon Eridani, 61 Cygni A, Procyon A, and Kapteyn's star."

"Excellent, and in perfect order, I believe. All right, Alex, I'll give you a chance for a bonus point. What did the Confederation's stellar explorers find in those star systems?"

Alexand stretched his legs and crossed his ankles, his first response to the question a brief laugh.

"Enough information to keep astronomers and astrophyicists busy correlating it for decades, but not much in the way of habitable planets or satellites, and that's what the Lords of the Confederation were looking for. Three of the stars didn't have any planets at all. Barnard's star and Cygni had some gaseous giants, a couple of them protosuns. The Confederation had some luck with Sirius and Procyon. Ivanoi and Cameroodo set up outposts on the four inner planets of Sirius, and I think on one of Procyon's planets. But if they had ever actually been colonized, it would have to be with habitat systems. There weren't any new Terras like Pollux." He paused for a moment, his gaze turned up toward the blue morning sky as if he were seeing the stars behind it. Then he shook his head slowly. "The Concord hasn't fared any better with its expeditions."

Rovere nodded, recognizing the regret in that. "We haven't yet, at least. What stars has the Concord explored?"

Both boys had the answer, but Rich was a little faster. "Kruger 60 A and B, Van Maanen's star, and Altair."

Alexand added, "The Concord also sent expeditions back to Sirius and Procyon."

"That's right, Alex," Rovere said. "When was the last Concord stellar expedition?"

Again, the two were almost in unison with the answer, but Alexand let Rich take it.

"That was the Altair expedition. The *Felicity*. In 3241. That was only three years ago."

"Yes, and I don't need to ask what happened to the *Felicity*."

Rich shrugged. "I couldn't tell you if you did."

"No. No one knows what happened to her. Well, perhaps in the future, there will be more expeditions and the mystery of *Felicity*'s disappearance will be unraveled. But we've gotten a little ahead of ourselves. About a century and a half, in fact. Another date: 3104."

"Mankeen," Rich said, and the single word seemed self-explanatory and all-encompassing.

"Yes, but something particular concerning the Mankeen Revolt occurred that year."

"The Mankeen League was formed; the Three Hundred Rebel Lords signed the League Charter with Lionar Mankeen. Actually, it was 302."

"Mm. And the Thousand Loyal Houses are actually 1,006 at this time, but simplification often makes for more dramatic syntax. How long did the Mankeen Revolt last?"

Alexand seemed to be losing interest, and again Rich took the question. "Sixteen years: 3104 to 3120."

"And what happened in 3105? That should be easy, considering what day this is."

"The founding of the Concord by the remaining Houses of the old Confederation: the Loyal Houses. Of course, the Concord is really the Confederation under another name. Sometimes I wonder why everyone gets so excited about Concord Day."

Rovere laughed. "Well, Rich, there are some differences in structure. Minor, I'll admit. It was a unifying ploy, primarily, and it came at a crucial time. Who is credited with paternity of the Concord?"

"Arman Daro Galinin. He was Chairman of the Directorate then."

And Rich's great-great-great-grandfather; he didn't seem to find it necessary or relevant to mention that.

"The Concord defeated Lionar Mankeen... when, Alex?"

"What? Oh. In 3120. The Battle of the Urals."

"Correct. Now, the—"

"And the first Purge followed," Alexand went on dully. "Ten million Mankeen sympathizers were killed."

Rovere frowned at that uninvited piece of information; the Purges weren't the Concord's proudest moments. But it was the bitterness in Alexand's tone that brought the frown.

In the last year he'd become aware of something underlying

Alexand's cognizant cynicism; something related to the capacity for empathy that made him so unusual as a student of history. It was also undoubtedly related to his age. Adolescence is a process of disillusionment always, but especially so for the first born of DeKoven Woolf. The heir to the First Lordship couldn't afford the luxury of comfortable delusions.

Rovere concentrated on the scriber a moment, then, "Yes, Alex, the Mankeen Purge was ghastly in its casualties. So was the entire Mankeen Revolt. Nearly a billion lives were lost in those sixteen years, and all the extraterrestrial colonies were abandoned. Humankind retreated to Terra, and almost into a third dark age. The only colonies that weren't entirely abandoned were on Pollux, which didn't require habitat systems, but even Pollux—and Centauri—was abandoned in a sense; there was no communication between the Two Systems for half a century. The Concord was a long time recovering from Mankeen." He paused, then, "Who can tell me when the first extraterrestrial colony was reestablished?"

"3170," Rich answered absently; his brother's distraction hadn't escaped him. "That was the Ivanoi mine complex in Tycho on Luna."

"And when was the last of the Solar System colonies reestablished?"

"The last was Pluto. House of Shang. About 3200."

Rovere marked the points. The wind had died, and the spring sun was hot on his shoulders; the sound of the city seemed more distant.

"Let's backtrack a little. Another date: 3135."

Rich again took the question by virtual default.

"The founding of the Peladeen Republic in Centauri."

"Correct. Which of the Peladeen Lords was in power when the Republic was founded?"

"Let's see, that would be Quintin Ussher Peladeen."

"Why was the Republic named after the Peladeen?"

Rich glanced at his brother, but for the moment Alexand was apparently intent on the view of Concordia.

"Well, because the Peladeen were titular heads of the Republic. It was a sort of monarchal republic, really."

"Was Peladeen the only Lord in Centauri at the time?"

"No. There were a lot of VisLords from Terran Houses and one other resident House and First Lord—Drakonis. I think it was *Konrad* Drakonis. But I guess Quintin Peladeen was the strongest, the one who really ran things. Until the Republic, I mean."

"Anything to add, Alex?"

He looked around at Rovere, then shrugged. "The Peladeen were little more than figureheads in the Republic. Quintin was probably lucky the Republicans left him and the Lords any power at all. He didn't have Confleet to back him up, so he was in no position to argue with them."

"And Elor Peladeen, his great-grandson?"

"His argument was with the Concord. He *did* believe in the Republic, but he grew up with it—fourth generation. It was a long time before the Concord recovered enough from the Mankeen Revolt to take over the Centauri System again."

Rich asked, "Lector Theron, why did the Concord have to take over Centauri again? I mean, we had access to the resources; we were trading with them before the War."

Rovere paused. "Perhaps you'd like to answer that, Alex."

Alexand shifted restlessly, and Rovere almost expected him to rise and begin pacing; in that he was also much like his father. But he remained seated.

"I suppose the Concord was forced to tolerate the Republic at first until we recovered from Mankeen. But after that . . ." He frowned down at the ground. "The Republic was a bad example. Too many Fesh and Bonds were escaping allegiance and going to Centauri. And perhaps getting at the resources by trade wasn't good enough."

"Possibly, but I think the resources were less important than, as you put it, the bad example the Republic set. It was a constant threat to the Concord's stability. But bear in mind that the Twin Planets were colonies; the original population was seventy-five percent Fesh and only twenty-five percent Bond. What was possible there—a monarchal republic—was not possible in the Solar System with seventy percent of the population illiterate Bonds." Rovere paused, studying Alexand's precociously wary features. "And remember, at the time of the War of the Twin Planets, the Lords of the Concord were very conscious of the chaos Mankeen unleashed and they saw in the Republic the threat of a new revolution."

"Do you remember the War of the Twin Planets?"

Rovere laughed. Alexand made it sound like ancient history.

"Yes, Alex. It was less than forty years ago."

Rich put in, "3208 to 3210."

"Correct," Rovere said, "and a point for you."

"You didn't ask a question," Alexand objected.

"I got an answer. That should be worth something."

"And the date of the Peladeen Purge?" Alexand asked, that bitter edge in his voice. "3210. Three million killed."

Rovere hesitated, then marked a point under his initial. "True, Alex."

There was a brief silence, which Rich broke with an adroit shift of subject that seemed unintentional.

"Lector Theron, the Bonds call Lionar Mankeen *Saint* Lionar."

"Do they?"

"Yes. Alda—she's one of the hall maids—told me. She had leave to go to her compound chapel one day, and she said it was Saint Lionar's day. When I asked her who he was, she said 'Lionar Mankeen.' The Bonds have a lot of saints, don't they?"

"They do, indeed, and they take them more seriously than does the Orthodox Church. Their religious practices differ in many ways from Orthodox Mezionism. They're quite fascinating, actually, although very few sociotheologists have investigated them. What did Alda tell you about *Saint* Lionar?"

Rich shrugged irritably. "Nothing. When I asked her why he was called a saint, she got scared. I didn't care if she called him a saint; I just wanted to know *why*."

"Well, the Bonds are allowed religious freedom, if nothing else. That's Benedic Galinin—your grandfather Galinin's great-grandfather's—famous rule: the Galinin Rule. But I suspect Alda realized that the Elite refer to Lionar Mankeen as the Heretic Lord." He gave a short laugh. "It's a matter of point of view. One of Mankeen's avowed purposes was to free the Bonds, yet he nearly precipitated another dark age in the process, and only succeeded in leaving them in a worse state of subjugation than before, but to the Bonds he's a hero, a saint."

Alexand asked, "Did he really intend to free them?"

That cynicism. Rovere paused. It was of Lionar Mankeen that he particularly wanted to speak in this last lesson.

"Yes, I think he did. It's more acceptable now to assume he was only using them for his own ends, but I'm inclined to think he was sincere; he wanted to free them."

"I suppose the Concord couldn't tolerate that any more than it could the Republic."

"It wasn't a question of toleration, but of survival. Alex, consider a hypothetical question: What would have happened if Lionar Mankeen hadn't been defeated, if he had defeated the Concord?"

He thought a moment, dark brows drawn. "I think all the Loyal Houses would have been destroyed. I suppose that would leave the League Houses to govern the Two Systems."

"Do you think those 302 Houses could have kept the machinery of civilization running?"

"Possibly. It would depend on how many Fesh survived and how quickly the Lords of the League could take over the functions of the other Houses and of the Concord."

"And what if the Fesh population had been reduced to the point where the wheels of production and government came to a halt? What would happen then?"

"The Bonds wouldn't be able to keep the wheels turning, if that's what you mean."

"That's what I mean. The result would be anarchy—a third dark age. But why would the machinery of civilization stop if the Bonds were left to run it?"

"They aren't educated or skilled enough. They wouldn't know how."

"True." Rovere smiled, noting Rich's attentive interest in this dialogue. "Alex, I'm following this line because one day you'll have to deal with these problems. We live within the entrenched limitations of feudalism that grew out of the Second Dark Age. The class system, the subjugation of the Bonds, and the hereditary rule of the elite are our heritage from the Decades of Disaster. Mankeen tried to break the hold of feudalism. My next question is this: Grant that his motives were good, why was he doomed to fail, whether or not he defeated the Concord?"

Alexand met his gaze squarely and answered, "He was doomed to fail because he thought the Bonds *could* ... take over. Perhaps he hoped to establish something like the old Pre-Disasters republics, but the Bonds aren't capable of the responsibilities. They couldn't keep the wheels of civilization turning for a single day without the Fesh and Elite to tell them what to do. But *they* can't be blamed for that."

"No," Rovere replied softly. "Who must take that blame?"

"The Lords, I suppose, because they—we keep them illiterate and restricted. Or, rather, enslaved. Perhaps that's a more accurate term."

"Perhaps. But why do the Lords keep the Bonds illiterate and restricted—or enslaved, if you will?"

He replied dully, as if it were a rote lesson, "Because we depend on them for a labor pool, for one thing, and if we started educating them, it might foster dissatisfaction, and that could mean revolt."

"Revolt. Considering that Bonds make up nearly three-quarters of the population, a Bond revolt is a frightening prospect; it could lead to total anarchy. Do you agree?"

He nodded. "Yes."

"Then are the Lords to be blamed for maintaining stringent control over the Bonds?"

"No. I suppose not." Alexand was silent for some time, then he looked directly at Rovere. "But there are always mutinies and uprisings among the Bonds, especially in the more conservative Houses. They get worse every year. Last year there were fifty-two Bond uprisings serious enough to require Conpol or even Confleet intervention. Has maintaining stringent control really helped? Is that the answer?"

It was revealing that he had the statistics on Bond uprisings so clearly in mind. Rovere's gaze rested for a moment on Rich, who was still listening intently.

"Yes, Alex, there are always uprisings, and they're increasing in frequency; they're a symptom of instability within the system. Mankeen, however worthy his motives, didn't have the answer. One cannot 'free' the Bonds overnight. On the other hand, from your study of history, you know feudalism can't survive indefinitely against the tide of natural societal evolution. Feudalism is the first step out of anarchy. It provides a stable framework for civilization to develop within, but when anarchy is vanquished, feudalism becomes restrictive rather than stabilizing. Restriction is what breeds dissatisfaction and revolt."

Alexand's penetrating eyes were so much like his father's, Rovere was thinking, except that they lacked Woolf's coldness. He was already capable of that, but he would never turn it on his tutor.

"Lector Theron, what *is* the answer?"

"I don't know, Alex. I wish I did. I only know that the Concord, like the proverbial tree in the storm, must learn to bend with the winds of change, and you may be in a position one day to help it bend, rather than standing rigidly against the storm to face the inevitable toppling. The Concord is all we have, the matrix of our civilization. When it falls, we'll be plunged into another dark age." He paused, then, "I can give you no answers, only some advice: Study the past to understand the future, and perhaps you can change the course of history to some degree for the better."

A silence grew out of those words; they had a ring of finality, he knew, and both boys sensed it. Alexand seemed to withdraw, assuming a mask of detached containment; part of his training, Rovere thought regretfully. But Rich wasn't capable of that, and his eyes darkened with uncertainty.

Rovere methodically put the scriber and lightpen away.

"Our lesson is finished, and I have some . . . sad news. Sad for me, at least. This is our last lesson together—"

"Lector Theron!" Rich couldn't restrain that exclamation.

"Now, Rich, don't make it difficult for me. I promised your lady mother I'd spend ten years with her sons. You see, I had intended to retire before she asked me to tutor you, and now I . . . well, there's quite a lot of writing I want to do, several theses I haven't finished . . ."

Alexand didn't believe a word of that; still, he didn't challenge it.

But Rich asked, "You're going to retire? Why didn't you tell us?"

"Well, I . . . I guess I'm a coward in some ways; I don't like farewells. I almost didn't come today, but at the last minute

I changed my mind. For all the trouble you two have caused me—" He put on an expression of sternness that dissolved into gentle affection, "—I couldn't leave without saying goodbye."

"But where will you go?"

"Oh, I have a place . . . away from the city."

"Where is it? Can we visit you?"

Rovere closed his eyes briefly. That Alexand asked no questions was revealing.

"It's a . . . retirement compound. And perhaps—well, after I'm settled . . ." He had never before lied to Rich and it rankled. "At any rate, you can correspond with me. Your father will know where to send your lettapes. That is, if you don't forget me altogether in a week or so."

"Oh, Lector Theron—never! I'll 'tape you every week. Every day. We both will—Alex?"

Alexand's smile was quite convincing. "You won't be rid of us so easily. We'll 'tape you until you'll wish you'd never heard of us. All your writing will be to Rich and me."

Rovere met Alexand's gaze, and after a moment nodded.

"I'll look forward to that." Then he pulled himself to his feet, and Alexand rose with him. Rovere paused, feeling the incipient tears burning in his eyes. "Rich, the God bless you. And Alex . . ." Of the three of them only Alexand was entirely dry-eyed, and there was something symbolic in that. It was another luxury that would be denied him along with comfortable delusions. Tears. The very human act of weeping.

And this boy would be envied when he became a man.

"Alexand, you have a high destiny. Peace be with you."

There was a flickering shadow in Alexand's eyes, but his voice was still steady.

"And with you, Lector Theron."

Rovere turned away, moving as quickly as his aged joints would take him down the path toward the eucalypt grove. Beyond it, he knew, two black-uniformed, face-screened SSB officers waited, shadows among the shadows.

Behind him, he heard Rich's distant, "Goodbye . . ."

But Theron Rovere didn't look back.

2.

It was called the residential wing, but Alexand had never been sure why. Of course, one subwing did serve as a residence for certain Fesh employees and House officials, another for pages currently attached to the House, and another as a sometime residence for the Lady Morna Woolf Gray, Phillip Woolf's widowed sister, who divided her time between the Woolf Estate and the Manstine Gray Estate in Coben, depending on the season and her whim. And yet another subwing served as a residence for Woolf's only brother, VisLord Ives, his wife, Rosann, and their son, Delman, and daughters, Rosel and Kira. Alexand wondered absently if Delman would be sporting his Confleet uniform tonight; he seemed so inordinately proud of it and the rank of leftant, although he had no choice about Confleet, and the rank was only standard for any Confleet Academy graduate. Alexand wasn't even sure Delman was home on his holiday leave yet. The brothers Phillip and Ives Woolf might share the same roof but their relationship could not be called close, and the coolness extended to their families.

But this wing encompassed so much more than these residences. It also housed the Estate's entertainment facilities, which was why it was so crowded and bustling with activity today. There were ten banquet halls, six covered courts, a small auditorium, seven salons, two small ballrooms, and the grand ballroom with its twin promenades and domed entry court, an airy, elegant feat of engineering and design that had made its architech, Hespay Alakine, famous, preserving his name in textapes for two centuries. Another subwing provided guest facilities that could easily accommodate up to 150 Lords, VisLords, their Ladies, offspring, and entourages. Beyond that, the residential wing also housed the gymnasium complex, the infirmary and medical center, the House museum, gallery, and historical library, and on the ground level, the aquarium, greenhouses, aviary, stables, and riding park.

It did *not* include the residence of the First Lord and his family. That was a separate wing known as the family wing, and its exclusivity was carefully—and literally—guarded; privacy was hard come by for a First Lord and those nearest him.

The harried activity that made the halls of the residential wing so noisy today barely impinged on Alexand's consciousness. He could muster no enthusiasm for the Concord Day celebration in the face of Theron Rovere's departure. He felt an odd sense of isolation, as if he were surrounded by an invisible shell of silence within which he was insulated from all outside stimuli; insulated from regret, from pain.

He didn't wonder if he had purposely sought out his mother until he reached the doorway of the blue salon on the fifth level. There he stopped, watching unnoticed in the constant stream of servants and House officials. The salon had become a command post, as strictly efficient as any Confleet comcenter, despite its sumptuous Trimillennium period appointments, and although the Lady Elise Galinin Woolf, seated at a Shanidel rosewood desk, might seem far removed from a commander engaged in a complex and precisely timed logistics maneuver, she was exactly that.

Alexand wondered how she managed it. How did she maintain her efficient calm? Rovere had been her tutor, too, and a close friend.

But as Lady of the First Lord of the House, it was her duty to preside over all Estate social events, and the preparations for the DeKoven Woolf Concord Day ball were a staggering challenge in management and organization. There was no time for grief.

At least five thousand guests would spend some time at the Woolf Estate on their traditional tours of the Concordia House balls after the public ceremonies in the Plaza. Nearly a hundred would also be staying the night: Lords and VisLords and their families from outside Concordia and, in some cases, outside Terra or the Solar System. Their entourages added five hundred more whose needs must be met, plus the three hundred musicians, dancers, and theatrotechs who would entertain the guests.

Many of the guests at the House balls were Fesh; it was one of the few occasions on which the two classes mixed socially. Treasured éclats, those invitations, Alexand knew; he'd seen those received by Mistra Adith Thal, his mother's dance instructor, preserved in plasex and proudly displayed on her dressing room wall. They were extended by all the Concordia Houses to Fesh of special distinction—scholars, scientists, artists, writers, and performers. Ranking officers in Confleet and Conpol were generally tendered invitations, too, as well as high officials in Conmed and other branches of the Concord bureaucracy and, of course, the Church hierarchy.

Alexand smiled faintly as he leaned against the doorframe. His mother hadn't noticed him, which wasn't surprising with Estate Chamberlin Ernest Hayn, Entertainments Steward Martin Camil, and theatrotech Dedrik Sander hovering over her and voices coming intermittently from the three intercom screens before her on the desk.

Her attention at the moment was on VisSteward James Cordel and the three Bonds with him, each holding swags of delicate, sparkling chiffeen of varying shades of gold.

"The palest one, Fer Cordel," she said. "And tell Master Rawlin the drapery—*all* the decorations—must be kept out of the way of the guests, even if it disrupts his décor. Yes, Marco?" This in answer to an insistent voice from one of the intercom screens.

"My lady—disaster! It is terrible! We are undone!"

She only smiled tolerantly. "What is the nature of this disaster, Master Marco?"

"The champagne, My Lady! I asked for four thousand bottles of Shato Bord, and what do they send? *Cornielle!* An *inferior* wine!"

"Now, Marco, it isn't that inferior, and by the time our guests have made the rounds of the Estates tonight, I'm sure their palates will be too jaded to know the difference. What about the Mulier? You haven't forgotten to chill it?"

"Oh, my lady, of *course* not! Only once such an error should slip past me."

"The capons? Have they arrived? And the lobster?"

"Yes, my lady, and they're ready for the cookers."

"And the trays for the guest rooms?"

"All prepared, my lady."

"Very good, Marco. You have the checklist. I want you to go over it now."

"But, my lady, I know it by *heart*. Everything is—"

"Nevertheless, go over it again. Yes, Master Hayn?" She cut Marco off and looked up at the chamberlin.

"Master Demret and the musicians have arrived, my lady. They're checking the orchestron installation in the ballroom."

"Oh, marvelous. Is Master Demret satisfied with the arrangements?"

"He seems to be."

"Good. Give him my regards and tell him I'll talk to him as soon as possible. Oh—did you test the nulgrav levels on the dance stage? The ballet will be the finale of the indoor entertainment, and I want Mistra Liay and her dancers at their best."

"Mistra Liay hasn't arrived yet, but I'll certainly check the nulgrav setting with her."

"Thank you, Ernest." Then, as he departed, Camil and Sander began speaking at once. "A moment, Master Sander. Fer Camil, has the fireworks master and his team arrived?"

He bowed. "Yes, my lady. They're setting up in the ballroom court."

"They're late," she noted, with a glance at her watch. "Have the master consult with Demret on the timing. He's in the ballroom now." Then, when he departed, "Master Sander, the light display for the ballroom?"

"That's what I came to tell you, my lady. The installations are complete, and I've checked the sequences personally."

"Thank you. Oh—has Ernest left? I wanted him to be sure and check with Captain Sier about the landing roof guards. The first overnight guests will be arriving soon."

"I'll give him the message, my lady." Sander bowed himself out while Elise responded to a voice from one of the screens. Landin, apparently, about the flowers.

"Don't worry about the orchids, Fer Landin. Rawlin will need them for the tables, and roses and chrysanthemums will do very well for the garlands..."

Alexand slipped out in Sander's wake as three more House officials converged on the door. His mother would take time for him if he made his presence known; she was never too busy to welcome him. But he didn't want to talk to her except in private now, and that was impossible. And he wasn't entirely sure he wanted to talk to anyone at the moment. His retreat was further hastened by a glimpse of Lady Rosann Woolf riding down the corridor pedway, flanked, as always, by a Fesh waitingmaid and two Bondmaid attendants. She was coming to "help" Lady Elise, no doubt. Alexand struck off down the hall in the opposite direction.

The pedways and nulgrav lifts were swarming with Fesh and Bonds moving with hurried purpose, but he was hardly aware of them, still wrapped in his shell of silence. Once a flurry of awed comment aroused him. Lamino, Lady Elise's clothier, riding the pedway with his coiffed head held high. He was on his way to the Lady's salon with the gown she would wear at the ball. The gown followed, worn by Ana, Elise's mannequin. She was a Bond privileged to wear that resplendent gown by virtue of the fact that her physical measurements exactly duplicated Elise's.

Lamino might well be proud of his creation: iridescent blue-green satina, subtly draped, simple lines to emphasize the magnificent fanning train, which was covered with a mosaic of peacock feathers. Alexand smiled briefly, thinking that the clothiers of the Elite should prepare themselves for a rush of demands for feathered gowns.

He moved on, finding nothing more to hold his attention except one fleeting exchange caught in passing. Portly, red-cheeked Ferra Rona Hanly giving directions to a Bond with an armload of deep-blue delphiniums.

"Carlo, those go to the Eliseer suite. And check the linens. Make sure they're the blue with *silver* trim."

The concern for color arose from Elise's insistence on furnishing her guests' suites with the colors of their House crests. Alexand had to think a moment before he remembered the Camine Eliseer crest—a winged horse, blue and silver. Eliseer's Home Estate was on Castor, the less hospitable of the Twin Planets, where the House held a number of rare metals franchises, and the name caught his attention only because he'd heard his father speak of Loren Eliseer on several occasions lately. Phillip Woolf considered Eliseer a rising power, but

Alexand didn't realize that respect went so far as tendering him an invitation to be a guest of the House.

But Eliseer's status was of only passing interest. He moved through the bustling halls in his insulating shell, finding it a relief to reach the relatively quiet gymnasium complex high on one of the upper levels.

In the first room a formal karatt class was in progress under the direction of Fesh SportsMaster Ton Kosai, known for his fierce discipline, which showed no hint of laxness despite the holiday. He was offering terse comment on a practice match while the rest of the class observed. His young students, though they meekly toed his stern mark, were all Elite. Pages, sons of VisLords or heirs of First Lords of minor Cognate Houses, sent to enjoy the prestige of an education in the Home Estate of DeKoven Woolf.

Most of them were cousins of varying distance and, as Alexand passed, he exchanged the expected amenities, but he didn't stop until he reached the door on the far side of the room. The sound/vision screens were on, but the guard switched them off at his nod. He passed into the main gymnasium, a high-ceilinged chamber flooded with light from the south windowall; the S/V screens went on again behind him, and he stopped inside the doorway. His entrance didn't attract the attention of the only occupants of the huge room, his father and SportsMaster Fenn Lacroy; they were at the foils, totally preoccupied in a lightning-paced duel that was a game only by virtue of the soft tips and the low settings on the charged foils. Those blades, whip-thin tensteel, could kill with a touch if the charges were set at lethal maximum.

"A point, my lord! And accepted." Fenn Lacroy's booming laugh echoed in the sunlit expanse as he acknowledged a hit, raising the guard of his foil to his forehead, then bringing the blade down to his side as he bowed. "We're even, my lord, point for point."

Woolf laughed heartily as he reciprocated the salute and bow—the only occasion on which he ever bowed to anyone.

"Indeed, Fenn. Point for point, but not for long. Garde!" He took the guard stance; the foils sparked as they crossed. "Ready?" Then, at Lacroy's nod, "Allon!"

The mock battle resumed with the clashing and shivering

slither of metal on metal, the foils throwing off lightning flashes at every contact, the encounter circumscribed by a line of light in the resilient floor, a circle five meters in diameter. Both men were stripped to the waist, shod in soft-soled fencing boots, their faces protected with clear plasex masks. Their movements were almost too quick even for Alexand's experienced eye; feint and attack, parry and riposte, remise on riposte, counterriposte, then attack on a lunge, counterparry on retreat. They were a close match, and Fenn Lacroy, Fesh or not, never gave a millimeter to his Lord, but Alexand recognized Phillip Woolf as master here, not by title, but by skill and grace.

Lacroy going in with a quick flèche; he was good at the running attack, his footwork always a wonder of precision, but that aggressive approach too often left him open to a fast riposte. Alexand knew Fenn's weaknesses, but he had never bested him in a bout; the day he was capable of that he would call himself a true swordsman.

"Ah!" Lacroy loosed that exclamation as Woolf's foil struck his chest with a jolting shock on a coupé; the price of a split-second's loss of balance. "A point, and accepted—and the match is yours." He saluted and bowed, adding, "Well done, my lord!"

Woolf took off his mask; he was breathing hard, as was Lacroy.

"And well done on your part, Fenn. You keep me on my mettle."

"Then I consider myself a success. Another match—" He stopped and removed his mask when he saw Alexand at the door. "Ser Alex, good morning."

Woolf turned, studying his son's face as he approached, then absently handed Lacroy his foil and mask.

"Picking up a few pointers, Alex?"

"Just admiring, Father. A good match."

"So it was. I'll always be grateful to Fenn. Without him, I'd have succumbed to ulcers long ago. Tell me, Fenn, how is your student progressing?"

Lacroy put on a stern frown. "Well, passably, my lord. He thinks he's ready for a point of honor, but I have my doubts."

Alexand laughed and retorted, "I *would* be ready if you

didn't keep forcing me to fence left-handed."

"Good," Woolf said firmly. "You're too strongly right-handed. At any rate, calling points of honor is a game for VisLords."

"Oh? I seem to remember hearing about an encounter you had with the Lord Cadmon..."

Woolf raised an eyebrow, not quite succeeding in repressing his smile.

"That was when I was too young to know better." Then he glanced at his watch and his smile faded. "I suppose I must prepare myself for the guests."

Lacroy asked, "A shower and massage, my lord?"

"No, not here." He crossed to one of the benches against the wall where he'd left his shirt and street boots. "Send Chapman up to my suite, Fenn."

"Yes, my lord. And you, Ser Alex? Are you ready for a match or two?"

"All right. In a few minutes, Fenn."

Lacroy realized he was being dismissed. He hung the foils and masks in the racks on the wall, then started for the dressing room door.

"I'll find Chapman, my lord."

Woolf nodded. "Thank you. I enjoyed the match, Fenn."

"My pleasure, my lord."

Woolf sat down on the bench and stripped off his fencing boots, and Alexand waited in silence until Lacroy was gone, aware of his father's intent scrutiny.

"Alex, I'm sorry about Theron's... retirement."

He said tightly, "I'm sorry, too, Father."

"And Rich—where is he?"

"In the school."

"Alone?"

"He seemed to want to be alone for a while."

Woolf concentrated on pulling on his boots.

"Was he... upset?"

"Yes. But he's looking forward to corresponding with Lector Theron. He said you'd know his 'tape seq."

Woolf rose and shrugged on the full-sleeved shirt, still watching Alexand as he tied the laces at the neck.

"I'll go talk to Rich now. Damn this holiday. A hundred

House guests and half of them relatives. What about you? I mean, with Theron leaving."

Alexand didn't look at him. "I'll miss him very much."

"So will I, the old gadfly." He pulled in a deep breath, letting it out in a weary sigh.

"Father, what was the Quiller thesis about?"

Woolf's expression didn't change, but Alexand felt the sudden tension radiating from him.

"How did you know about that?"

"I heard you and Mother talking in the grove yesterday."

"You were eavesdropping?"

"Yes. I was there when you passed by. I simply didn't make my presence known."

Woolf gave a short laugh, then sobered. "Then you know Theron isn't retiring. Does Rich know?"

"No."

"Thank the God." He ran a hand through his hair distractedly. "Alex, you must understand I couldn't protect him. It was all I could do to keep him from being executed. I didn't tell Elise that; she's upset enough as it is."

Alexand felt a chill. It was incomprehensible, insane, that such a man might have met that fate.

"I know you did all you could, Father."

Woolf saw the pain hidden in his son's face, and his inclination was to reach out to him, to hold him as he had when he was a child. But Alexand was no longer a child. They grow up too fast, Woolf thought, realizing with a faint shock that Alexand was almost as tall as he.

"The Quiller thesis," he said finally, "concerns the inception of the War of the Twin Planets."

"Why was it classified as subversive?"

"For one thing, it was strictly factual. Quiller dug into old communiqués and Confleet orders, cross-checked dates and agreements. What he came up with doesn't put the Concord in a good light. It shows that we broke certain agreements, and in fact made the first overt move."

"But that's no great secret."

Woolf smiled bitterly, then began walking toward the windowall, Alexand falling into step with him.

"No, it's no great secret among the Elite, or even a few

upper-class Fesh, but that isn't the version taught in every Fesh Basic School. We're less than a hundred thousand out of four and a half billion, Alex. The Elite—and the Concord—can't survive without Fesh loyalty. So—" His shoulders came up in a quick shrug. "—we must be careful not to disillusion them, and that isn't easy these days."

At the windowall, Alexand stared bleakly at the sprawling glitter of Concordia. The pervading hum of the city, a sound as incessant as surf on the sea, didn't penetrate the ten centimeters of flexsteel-reinforced glass.

Woolf went on irritably, "Quiller is a young man enamored of the great god Truth—or, rather, Fact. He decided all this was so important, every literate citizen should know about it. He tried to slip it through with a Pri-Four rating, and that was his error. The Board of Censors wouldn't have objected so much to a Pri-Three."

Alexand looked at his father questioningly. "He wanted to publish it as a booktape on the open market? That falls under DeKoven Woolf franchises."

"If you're wondering if I had anything to do with it coming before the Board, the answer is no. I didn't hear about it until the judgment was passed."

Alexand nodded. The publishing branch of the House was run by his uncle, Ives, a man whose rigid morals always made Alexand question his ethics.

"Ives sent the thesis to the Board?"

"Yes. Then Theron stepped in claiming it as his own—*after* the Board passed judgment on it."

Alexand stared out into the midday glare, his eyes aching with more than the light.

"What about Quiller? What will happen to him?"

"Nothing. It's been assumed he laid claim to the thesis for exactly the reason Theron did: to protect a friend. He'll be reprimanded by the Board, but that's all."

"Lector Theron must have felt very strongly about Quiller to sacrifice himself for him."

"Apparently."

"I . . . suppose he did what he thought was right."

"I'm sure he did. Alex, I'm glad we had a chance to talk this over, and I'm bitterly sorry to lose Theron. But, as you said, he did what he thought was right. If he's caused us any pain, that must be forgiven."

"Forgiven." Alexand considered the word, gazing out at the sun-jeweled city, but seeing the lined face of Theron Rovere with his patient, cognizant eyes. "There's nothing to forgive. He did what he believed he had to do."

Woolf was silent for a moment, and Alexand was roused by that silence. One of his father's eyebrows came up almost imperceptibly.

"Unfortunately, Alex, an action taken out of one's convictions isn't necessarily good—or forgivable."

He replied levelly, "No, but one must consider the source of the convictions, the kind of person holding them."

"True." Woolf smiled. "A point, and accepted."

Alexand called up a smile in response, but couldn't hold on to it. He noted Woolf's glance at his watch.

"Father, I know you're busy now."

"At least I *should* be," he agreed with an annoyed sigh, but he made no move to leave. Apparently he had something more to say, but seemed uncharacteristically hesitant about it. He turned to face the windowall, hands clasped behind his back, then, "Alexand, you're fifteen, and it may seem premature, but the time is coming when we must consider your marriage."

Alexand studied him. "I know."

It was strange that his father seemed more uncomfortable with the subject of his future marriage than he. This wasn't the first time it had been broached, nor was it surprising that it came up now. The Elite were gathering in Concordia. The week of the Concord Day celebrations saw more economic and political agreements made and more marriages arranged than any other week in the year.

"Have you any specific candidates in mind, Father?"

"There are several possibilities; you know that. I hope you also understand that I'll make no commitments at this early date. Still, we must begin to study some of the possibilities more closely."

Alexand nodded, again feeling that curious sense of isolation. It was unlikely that any definite commitment would be made before he reached Age of Rights. There would be tentative explorations, and the promise of a union with DeKoven

Woolf would be useful as a bargaining lever. But Age of Rights was a comfortable five years in the future.

"Father, why haven't you and Mother had more children?"

He was a little surprised at the question himself: it seemed to come without conscious thought. Woolf's surprise was obvious, and it was more than surprise. Alexand saw him go pale.

"I suppose it's because Elise found it difficult to face having more children after . . . after Rich . . ."

"I'm sorry. I shouldn't have asked." The grief always waited; it crouched in ambush to spring at unexpected moments. He forced it back—he'd become adept at that—and brought out a smile. "Am I correct in assuming I'm to meet a potential bride?"

"Yes."

"What House? Desmon Fallor?"

"No, although Julia Fallor is still a possibility. You've met Julia." It was a question, even if it had no questioning inflection.

"Yes. She's . . . very attractive." The adjective was bitterly apt for the daughters of the Court of Lords. That was their function: to *attract* mutually profitable political and economic unions. "And Fallor *is* a Directorate House." This wasn't the time to comment further on Julia herself.

"Yes, but that isn't a prerequisite, although it might be desirable."

"You're considering a non-Directorate House?"

"Yes. Camine Eliseer."

Alexand frowned. The Lord of Castor must be a rising power indeed if Phillip Woolf was considering an alliance by marriage with his first born. Camine Eliseer was a young House, established after the Fall of the Peladeen Republic. Not a likely candidate for a union with DeKoven Woolf.

He turned to his father. "Is it a controlling influence in the Centauri System that attracts you?"

"That and keeping Orin Selasis *out* of Centauri."

Selasis. It was all but inevitable that Selasis would have a bearing even on this.

The House of Badir Selasis had held all extraplanetary transport franchises for eight generations and a seat on the Directorate for six, and, through all those generations, a bitter antagonism existed with DeKoven Woolf and Daro Galinin at one pole, Badir Selasis at the other, and the prize of the Chairmanship of the Directorate always in the middle.

And Alexand wondered for how many generations the name of Selasis had been universally evocative of fear and even loathing. Certainly it was true of this generation.

He couldn't think of Lord Orin Selasis without remembering the black eyepatch; it seemed to sum up the man somehow. He had lost his left eye in his youth in a point of honor duel with Kiron Woolf, Alexand's grandfather. What was revealing was that the patch wasn't necessary; an artificial eye would make the loss unnoticeable. But Orin Selasis chose to wear the patch, and for him it was a symbol of a pledge of retribution. That Kiron Woolf was twenty years dead now didn't diminish his fierce resolve. Only the downfall of the House of Woolf itself would satisfy that pledge.

"Then Selasis is trying for a foothold in Centauri?"

Woolf laughed caustically. "'Stranglehold' would be more apt, and the Selasids have been working at that since the Fall of the Republic."

"He already has something of a stranglehold over D'Ord Hamid."

"Yes, but Hamid can no longer claim to be the most powerful House in Centauri. Lazar isn't the man his father was."

Alexand restrained a smile. That was an understatement, particularly from Phillip Woolf.

"So Eliseer is putting Hamid in the shade?"

"And in the full light of Orin's attention, and he's been quite solicitous lately." Woolf's narrowed eyes were turned outward on the city, but his mental focus was inward. "There are some rather ironic aspects in that. Eliseer is a Cognate House of Camine, which has seen better days and never was a major House, but when the two new Centauran Houses were established after the Fall, Jofry Selasis backed Almor Eliseer for First Lordship of one of them."

"The Selasids backed him? Why?"

"Because both the last and present Lords Selasis underestimated the Eliseer. They had Hamid in their palm, and they didn't think Eliseer would survive. They were ready to pounce when the House collapsed and have Centauri all to themselves, except for Drakonis, who wasn't strong enough to offer them a real challenge."

"But that was thirty-four years ago."

Woolf gave him a wry smile. "It seems the Eliseer foiled the Selasids by flourishing. Loren Eliseer has done especially well for his House. Apparently he has an excellent intelligence system. At any rate, Camine Eliseer is in better shape financially than some Directorate Houses, and Lord Loren has put aside a respectable capital reserve and made good use of it. Lazar Hamid is deeply indebted to him at this point."

Alexand frowned slightly at that. "I'd think Hamid would go to Selasis for money."

"He would and has, but Loren Eliseer offered him loans at a substantially lower interest rate."

"I see. But what about Drakonis? Isador Drakonis seems to have flourished, too, and he's certainly not in the Selasid palm."

Woolf nodded. "For one thing, his income is derived from energy franchises; he isn't dependent on Selasis for freight. And Isador is a very adaptable man. But I think he owes his survival to some extent to Eliseer."

"What do you mean?"

"Ten years ago Drakonis was desperately in need of capital to enlarge the power plants on Perseus, and he made the error of borrowing from Selasis. The note came due a few months ago. It was a very secret transaction. I knew nothing of it, and our intelligence system is excellent. Nor did Mathis, and the Galinin intelligence system is second to none. But Eliseer found out about it. Drakonis had his back to a wall; he didn't have the liquid assets to meet the note, but, fortunately, Eliseer stepped in at that point."

Alexand nodded. "With another low-interest loan?"

"Yes. His profit margin on these loans is negligible, but the secondary benefits are incalculable. He blocked Orin's gambit with Drakonis, and has Hamid indebted to him. He has mineral leases on ten thousand square kilometers of Hamid holdings, and three smelter sites on Pollux at this point. Of course it's cheaper for him to put his smelters on Pollux; he doesn't have to maintain habitat systems there. And there are rumors of a marriage between one of Eliseer's sons and Hamid's youngest daughter."

Alexand understood now why his father considered Eliseer a rising power, and why the House wasn't, after all, such an unlikely candidate for a marriage alliance with Woolf.

"How many sons does Lord Loren have?"

"Two. Renay and Galen. They're only five years old now. Twins, by the way; appropriate for the Twin Planets. Actually, it's a Shang tendency, the twinning. Eliseer married Sato Shang's second daughter."

Alexand frowned absently. "Father, you didn't invite the Eliseer to the Estate to discuss a marriage."

"No, of course not. For public consumption, he's here to discuss an orthoferrite crystal synthesizing process his techs have developed. And it's not just an excuse for our meeting. That process has a staggering potential for commutronics and compsystems. If he can get it into production, it will make Eliseer a major House."

"If? What could stop him?"

"A conflict with Ivanoi's ytterbium franchises. He needs a special grant from the Board of Franchises."

"And he wants you to use your influence with the Board?"

"Yes. He's offering me a long-term contract on the processed crystals at a very attractive rate."

"Will you support him?"

"Certainly. He's hemmed in with freight costs—his major markets are in the Solar System—and Orin is putting pressure on him. If he doesn't get support from some of the major Houses, he'll be forced into an alliance with Selasis. Orin is already making the first overtures toward a marriage between Karlis and Eliseer's eldest daughter. The Eliseer are invited to the Selasid Estate this afternoon."

"The same daughter you're considering as my bride?"

Woolf laughed briefly. "The very same." Then he looked at his watch again. "I must go if I'm to have any time with Rich. At any rate, tomorrow morning your mother is entertaining Lady Galia Eliseer and her daughter in the rose garden salon, and of course this will be—well, very casual."

"Yes, Father, I know," Alexand said with a faint smile. "No doubt so casual as to seem accidental."

"No doubt. But I don't want you to feel under pressure. The choice of your bride is a vitally important decision both for you and the House. An Elite marriage is, after all, a lifetime commitment—: '. . . and unto death.' One doesn't enter that kind of covenant lightly or without a great deal of consideration."

Alexand nodded. "I didn't expect you to bind me in the chains of matrimony this early in the game."

Woolf gave that a brief, rueful laugh. "I think you're far more sensible about this than Elise and I. We haven't yet recovered from the realization that you've reached an age where we must consider such decisions at all." He paused, resting his hand on Alexand's shoulder. "We'll talk about it further, but now I must be on my way."

Alexand looked out at Concordia, listening to Woolf's retreating footsteps.

. . . and unto death.

Next year, after his sixteenth birthday, by hallowed tradition, he would make the tour of Concord Day balls as the escort of the Serras.

He wondered who it would be.

3.

Spotlights sent probing, multicolored shafts up from the Plaza of the Concord into the night sky, flashing on the firefly motes of aircars beading the invisible webs of the Trafficon grids. Alexand studied the scene through a flexsteel-reinforced window as the Faeton-limo sloped sedately down toward the Plaza. They were passing over the Cathedron, and Alexand, who had never stood in awe of the dogmas of Mezionism, was still awed by that magnificent structure. Its dimensions staggered conception, yet it was so elegantly proportioned, its reticulated arches and heliform buttresses leading so inexorably and perfectly to the culmination of its triple spires, that it seemed to rest weightlessly upon its massive foundations, especially when seen at night shining against the galaxy of Concordia's lights.

The Hall of the Directorate loomed ahead, a white shaft that bespoke power and solidity, while the Cathedron suggested the ethereal. Yet there was power in the Cathedron's soaring complexities, and grace in the Hall's seeking lines; they had been designed by the same architech, John Valerian, and Alexand always thought it unjust that he hadn't been rewarded with a Lordship for these creations of genius as Orabu Drakon had been for another kind of genius. But Valerian's only reward had been his Guild's title of Supreme Master—a title only he had ever held—and a solid niche in history.

The Faeton was descending over the Plaza now, a great rectangle five hundred meters long, one hundred wide, as light as day in the glare of helions, sparkling with floating banks of colored shimmeras, and brimming with close-packed humanity, the House colors of Bond tabards tending to broad, double-hued splashes interspersed with the more varied, and more conservative, colors of Fesh apparel. At least a hundred thousand Bonds and Fesh were gathered here—and, through the electronic eyes of vidicams, millions more at vidicom screens throughout the Two Systems—to see their rulers in splendid array, to hear the Lord Galinin himself speak, to partake in the blessing of the High Bishop, the Revered Eparch Simonidis, and especially to see the spectacular fireworks display that would culminate the ceremony.

The Hall and the buildings enclosing the Plaza's longest sides were faced in glowing white marlite, windowalls mirroring the multicolored lights, the first-level promenades garlanded with flowers, the rows of ancient ginkgoes crowned with light. At the north end of the Plaza, the Fountain of Victory sent its arching jets in everchanging patterns fifty meters into the air, and at the south end, the wide tiers of the Hall of the Directorate's steps served as a giant stage for the Court of Lords—the First Lords of the Thousand Loyal Houses—and their immediate families.

The cast was nearly all assembled, Alexand noted. The Woolfs would be the next-to-last arrivals; DeKoven Woolf gave precedence to no House but Daro Galinin.

On the second tier of steps at the front of this erstwhile stage, a podium was mounted, and from it hung a gonfalon bearing the crest of the Concord, the circled cross of the Mezion in gold on a background of black, with the constellation of the Southern Cross enclosed in the upper right quadrant. At one side of the podium, flanked by two lesser bishops, sat the Eparch Simonidis, dwarfed in a throne-like chair, weighted in jeweled miter and robes in the gold and white of the Church. Behind the podium was a short row of chairs, empty now, for the Lord Mathis Daro Galinin and his family; behind that a longer row for the remaining nine Lords of the Directorate and their families. They were filled, except for the four seats awaiting the Woolfs. Behind these, tiering up in rows of two hundred each, the families of the Court of Lords were seated, a sparkling mosaic of richly colored costumes. Behind them stood a rank of black-and-gold-clad trumpeters, instruments flashing like jewels, and lined against the white walls of the Hall were gonfalon bearers, whose bright banners bore the crests of all the Houses present. A glittering gathering, all the Lords and Ladies, Sers and Serras, in full panoply on this most important holiday of the Concord's calendar.

Merchant princes, Theron Rovere called them; masters of dynastic cartels; living fossils.

Alexand frowned, concentrating on the scene below, noting the incongruous patches of black among the colorful raiment of the Elite: dress uniforms worn by young Lords serving their traditionally mandated four-year tour of duty with Confleet. That was something he had to look forward to at Age of Rights. Or, rather, to dread.

The Faeton floated down toward the open area in front of the podium, which was cordoned off by Directorate guards, their golden helmets like bright beads on a necklace. The trumpets flashed, and dimly, through the thick glass, Alexand could hear the polyphonic *Salut*. He looked across the passenger compartment at his parents, both gazing out the windows, his father bored and impatient, his mother displaying a lively curiosity.

Elise Woolf was resplendent, her hair an intricate crown of burnished curls and braids, her gown—not the peacock gown; that was for the ball—pale green satinet shimmering with crystal brocade, complemented by a full-length cape of *lapis* blue trimmed in sable. Phillip Woolf was attired in umber and ochre, his cloak fastened with loops of gold, dress boots adorned with gold chains, the doublet under the open surcoat rich with gold-threaded brocade. The latter served a purpose beyond decoration: the flexsteel strands woven into the design could stop a light laser beam or deflect a knife thrust. Alexand and Rich wore suits similar in style, including the protective brocade, but with the shorter mantlets, rather than cloaks.

The lead 'car, with its complement of House guards and gonfalon bearers, landed in front of the podium, and a few seconds later, Hilding, their chauffeur, set the Faeton down as lightly as a feather. Alexand turned, feeling an indefinable chill.

Beside him Rich sat stiff and mute, trying hard to hide his misery, but Alexand felt it as if it were born in his own mind. Rich was well aware of the curious stares his crutches attracted and looked forward to becoming the focal point of those multitudes of eyes with nothing but dread.

No one would laugh, not at the son of Phillip DeKoven Woolf. But they would stare. The curiosity would be there, and the pity.

Alexand found his mouth dry, his eyes burning. It wasn't fair. Not Rich...

One of the guards opened the 'car door, and the blare of trumpets, the massed voices of the crowd, seemed to explode against his eardrums. Rich went pale, but when Elise paused to kiss his cheek before she stepped out of the 'car, he called up an uncertain smile. Woolf sent him an anxious glance as he followed his wife.

Alexand preceded Rich onto the landing area, restraining the impulse to close his eyes against the glare of light, and if he could, his ears against the onslaught of sound. From behind the barrier of Directorate guards, vidicam and imagraph lenses flashed avidly. Alexand didn't offer Rich a helping hand, but he was close enough to reach him in a split-second. The 'cars whisked away, and the Woolfs mounted the first tier of steps beneath the podium, then turned, standing side by side, the scarlet-clad House guards forming a line behind them with a gonfalon bearer at each end. The ampspeakers blared, *"The Lord Phillip DeKoven Woolf and the Lady Elise Galinin Woolf, with their sons, Ser Alexand and Ser Richard."*

A roar of applause and cheering followed, a concussive shockwave of sound. And Alexand wondered, as he always did, why they cheered.

Confetti and flowers thrown by the jubilant crowd showered the landing area and the tier of steps where they stood. Alexand saw his mother's radiant smile as she leaned down to pick up a blossom, kissed it, then tossed it back to the crowd, where it was hungrily fought over, and the volume of sound increased. He held himself erect, looking down at the shouting, ecstatic, grinning faces. What did they see? Something bigger than life, the stuff of legends: the Black Eagle of DeKoven Woolf, and his fair Lady, so exquisitely beautiful in the white light, and their handsome sons.

Of course, it was too bad about Ser Richard. . . .

Woolf offered his arm to Elise, and the roar began to subside as they turned to mount the steps to their seats. The guards hadn't yet realigned themselves, when Alexand heard a scream from the crowd behind him, and saw something small and dark fly past.

He ducked reflexively as the missile sliced close to his head, shouts of alarm and panic a meaningless assault on his senses. All he could think of was Rich.

He must not fall. Alexand reached out for him, dimly aware of a sodden smash and his mother's cry of surprise. Rich was off balance, staggering.

Alexand caught him, and at the same time, saw his father's face, dark with rage, and his mother's bewildered expression; not anger, only bewilderment and hurt. Rich was trembling, a tangible aura of fear emanating from him as he stared at the dripping stain on Elise's cape.

Black against the *lapis* blue. An ink bomb.

Alexand concentrated on getting Rich balanced on his crutches, his mind reverberating with the shock of realization.

An ink bomb. A childish prank, and harmless enough, but that the Lady Galinin Woolf had suffered such an indignity was incomprehensible.

He felt something of his father's rage then, and knew himself capable at this moment of violence against the person responsible for the hurt chagrin in his mother's eyes and for Rich's fear and embarrassment. The panicked crowd edging the landing area was on the verge of breaking through the cordon of guards. Reinforcements were moving in, some joining the House guards, and at Woolf's command forming a protective circle around his wife and sons.

But he didn't join them. He strode to the edge of the tier and, coldly, regally aloof, surveyed the crowd. Silence moved out from him, every eye fixing on the Lord Woolf, standing in magnificent solitude.

"Who is guilty of this outrage?"

Alexand heard his mother's quick intake of breath; fear for her husband standing isolated and unprotected.

An uneasy murmuring from the crowd, and again Woolf's commanding voice rang out.

"My patience runs thin—*I demand an answer!*"

At length, individuals within the crowd near the landing area began to shift. An opening appeared, growing slowly wider, until finally one man stood alone.

The guilty one, Alexand realized. The others accused him not with words, but with fear, drawing away from him as if his guilt were contagious. A Bond wearing a black-and-gold Concord tabard; a young man, not yet thirty. He stood alone now as Phillip Woolf stood alone. But the difference was infinite.

Alexand's breath came out in a long sigh. Seconds ago he'd been stifled with rage, but this man . . . what could he feel for this miserable human being awaiting his fate in a paralysis of terror except pity? It was a senseless, mindless act for which he stood condemned, something irrational in its triviality.

Woolf said not another word. He only glanced at the ranking Directorate guardsman and nodded. The officer bowed, gestured to another guard, and together they stepped into the crowd and seized the Bond.

"No—oh, no. . . ." The words were a whisper. Rich.

Woolf turned and rejoined his family, then, moving with calm deliberation, removed Elise's stained cape, tossed it to one of the House guards, and draped his own cloak around her shoulders. This done, he looked at his sons.

"Are you all right?"

Alexand answered; Rich wasn't capable of it. "Yes, of course, Father."

The trumpets burst into shimmering fanfares, the prelude to the Hymn of the Concord. Two aircars were slipping down into the landing area. The lead 'car was purple with a gold lion crest emblazoned on its side; the Faeton-limo following it was black with the Concord crest, but it sported double banners, black and gold, purple and gold.

The Chairman was arriving.

A collective sigh swept the Plaza, tension dissolving as the massed voices took up the words of the Hymn. The glittering rows of Elite rose to add their voices, their relief at the diversion as patent as that of the Fesh and Bonds. Alexand found the distraction especially welcome; it made Rich's passage up the steps to their seats less conspicuous. Finally, when the Hymn came to its end and the Elite ranks settled into their seats, Rich sank gratefully into his and put the crutches out of sight at his feet.

There was no cessation in the volume of sound. The Plaza reverberated with an ovation mounting to an awesome crescendo that nearly drowned the trumpet fanfares. On the first tier, Mathis Galinin, white-haired, white-bearded, a towering patriarch, accepted the deafening accolade with upraised hands.

The Chairman had arrived: the Lord Mathis, First Lord of Daro Galinin, Chairman of the Directorate, the ruling body of the Concord of the Loyal Houses.

But to Alexand—Grandser.

With him was his only surviving son, Lord Evin, Evin's wife, Lady Marcessa, and their son, Marc, and daughter, Camila.

Rich was still trembling, but it was easing. He leaned close to Alexand to make himself heard.

"What will happen to him, Alex?"

Alexand didn't have to ask whom Rich meant. The Bond. And he knew exactly what would happen to him.

"I . . . don't know."

"He'll be executed, won't he?"

"I suppose so."

"Why did he do that? He isn't even a DeKoven Woolf Bond. *Why*, Alex?"

Alexand looked down at the cheering crowd, and it occurred to him that it was an equivocal entity, and perhaps something to be feared.

But that Bond . . .

Why?

Some questions have no answers; at least, none the human mind is capable of encompassing. Those were Theron Rovere's words. Alexand closed his eyes against the threat of tears.

But the human mind must always keep asking questions if it is to remain human. And those were also Theron Rovere's words.

"I don't know, Rich. I don't know."

4.

One more gauntlet for Rich to run in the name of duty: the family's obligatory appearance at the Daro Galinin Estate ball. Alexand looked out the 'car window, not at his brother. It didn't require direct observation to know Rich's state of mind after the incident at the Plaza.

Incident.

Perhaps that was the word for it. A small event that would be noted by witnesses and reporters simply because the Woolfs had been involved, but would soon be forgotten.

Rich would never forget it because he didn't understand it. The inexplicable motives of the man who tossed the ink bomb would fix the incident indelibly in his memory.

The Galinin Estate was near the Plaza complex on a bend of the Yarra River. It was one of the oldest structures in Concordia, surrounded by parks and glades, its venerable, rose-hued stone walls garlanded with ivy, a sanctuary of calm, like Mathis Galinin himself. But tonight it was lighted and decorated for the festivities, and even though Hilding had the flashing clearance lights on, their approach was slowed by the tangle of traffic. Daro Galinin was traditionally the first stop on the Concord Day tour of the Concordia Estates, and the influx was at its peak.

That tradition was the reason for this last gauntlet for Rich. The Woolfs wouldn't find it necessary to tour the other Houses, but a stop at Daro Galinin was mandatory, and not because Mathis Galinin would be offended if they didn't put in an appearance tonight; he found social affairs on this scale tiresome and would much prefer to see his daughter and family in private.

Custom commands, according to the old maxim. To defy this custom would create speculation about the relationship between Daro Galinin and DeKoven Woolf. That the bond between the two Houses was generations old and cemented by personal affection and respect wasn't enough. Rumors could be disastrous in the games of politics; appearances were generally more important than truth.

The 'car was finally approaching the landing area at the foot of the entry stair below the ballroom. Alexand felt a change in Rich's posture; he was bracing himself.

Woolf had suggested casually that Rich might prefer to have Hilding take him home. Elise had seconded the suggestion, her tone light. But he refused. This duty call would be brief; it always was. There was nothing wrong with him.

Alexand recognized that decision as an error; Rich too often overestimated his strength, and emotional stress affected his muscular control. But he didn't argue with Rich, nor did his parents. At least there would be no stationary steps for him to contend with; the entry stair had moving ramps. And their stay *would* be brief; only long enough to pay their respects to Galinin and to Evin and Marcessa.

Alexand wondered if the Lady Camma would be at the ball. His grandmother's illness was seldom discussed, perhaps because it was hopeless. She hadn't accompanied her husband to the Plaza ceremonies.

The landing seemed to come with a lurch. Elise rose as the guard opened the door.

"Rich?"

"I'm fine, Mother."

The ramp carried them up into the crowd milling about the columned foyer off the ballroom, into the laughter and music, the silken rustlings, the murmuring of multitudinous footsteps. Alexand heard the change in the tone of voices, saw the faces turning in their direction.

The foyer level, the end of the ramp, and Rich managed it easily enough. But he was too pale.

"Ah, Elise! You're exquisite, my lady—as if you were ever anything less."

Elise laughed, extending her hand to the tall, golden-haired Lord Ivanoi.

"Alexis, you're the only man I know who can flatter without insult. Honoria, how are you?" This to Ivanoi's wife, a regal woman whose beauty was reason enough for her renown in the Concord, but it was overshadowed by her character; a woman of intelligence and outspoken conviction fortunate enough to marry a man who valued those qualities.

"I'm very well, Elise, except for an incipient case of boredom. I'm looking forward to Master Demret's symphalight concert at your ball to alleviate that."

"It's beautiful, Honoria, at least the little Demret would let me see of it."

The greetings extended to Alexand and Rich, and Woolf and Alexis Ivanoi took a moment for a *sotto voce* conference. Politics, Alexand knew. Ivanoi was a Director and a staunch ally of Galinin and Woolf.

Rich was still capable of smiles and polite responses. The Ivanoi drifted away to be replaced by the Robek, then the Matsune, the Reeswyck, and later Lord Charles and Lady Constanz Fallor with their daughter Julia in tow, all eyeing Alexand speculatively. The Woolfs moved steadily toward the ballroom, but their progress seemed unbearably slow; familiar faces that must be recognized, unfamiliar ones that called for introductions, seemed to expand in geometric progression. Alexand automatically made the expected responses, seldom looking directly at Rich, but keeping him always in the periphery of his vision.

And Rich was faltering. The trembling wouldn't be apparent to anyone else, but it was there, and his pallor was more pronounced. Rich had the will for this gauntlet, but not the strength, and he was beginning to realize it now.

Lord Cadmon, then the Cordulay, and the Zarlinska with three marriageable daughters on display; the Estwing, the Sharidar, the Delai Omer, the Cameroodo. . . .

"Alex . . ." Alexand had to lean close to Rich: he was nearly whispering. "Alex, perhaps I could wait near the ramp. . . ."

"We'll go to the car." Alexand caught his mother's eye; she only nodded, sending Rich a smile as they turned away.

But Alexand paused at the touch of his father's hand on his arm: that and the significant turn of Woolf's head focused Alexand's attention on a man standing near the ballroom doors.

The Lord Orin Badir Selasis, looming massively, his bulk draped, not disguised, by full-length robes heavy with fur, the black eye patch giving his swarthy features a sinister aspect against the background of festive decorations and costumes. Selasis was displaying a rare smile for the man with whom he was talking, a handsome man in his forties, tall and broad-shouldered. With his blond, Noreuropan coloring, he was a marked contrast to the woman beside him, who was slender and small with an oriental cast to her features.

"The gentleman enjoying Orin's attention," Woolf said, turning his gaze elsewhere, "is Loren Eliseer."

Alexand emulated his father's disinterest. "The Lady is his wife?"

"Yes. Galia Shang."

"Is their daughter here?"

Woolf glanced briefly toward the Eliseer. "I don't see her. At any rate, this isn't the time for—"

"*Rich*—" Alexand spun around, suddenly cold, his pulse leaden. Rich was gone. He'd started for the 'car, thinking Alexand was following him. But it wasn't Rich's absence in itself that brought that chill. It was a sound small in this pressing crowd, but one his ear was attuned to.

A metallic clatter. A crutch falling.

Alexand struck out through the crowd in a straight line toward the entry, veering slightly to one side of it. He couldn't see Rich, nor was there time to wonder why he moved so purposefully in this direction, how he knew exactly where Rich was. But he knew.

And he knew Rich needed him desperately.

He collided with someone, aware only of a mass of brocaded robes and cloying perfume. He didn't stop to apologize; he was oblivious to everyone around him, smiles and greetings meeting with silence and unseeing eyes.

An eddy off the mainstream, a transient gathering of young Sers and Serras. Alexand knew them all, knew their names and lineage; they were his peers. But only one of them registered in his consciousness.

Karlis Selasis.

Lord Orin's flawed Adonis, as fair as his father was dark, as handsome as he was sinister; Karlis attired in blood-red down to his gold-scrolled, sharp-heeled boots; Karlis with his Grecian mouth drawn in a languid smirk, bending his golden-curled head to a companion; Karlis laughing. The laugh was taken up on cue by the others, and Karlis was vain enough to think they followed his lead out of deference to him.

They laughed on his cue because all of them recognized behind him the shadow of Orin Badir Selasis.

Alexand plunged toward that psychic eddy, a circle shaped by an emotional current that would dissipate in a matter of seconds as it had formed in seconds, but those seconds were each eternities of pain. He was choked with it. It emanated from Rich and translated into blind rage in Alexand's mind.

Rich was at the center of that circle, isolated in that transient vortex like a trapped animal suffering the taunts of the closing hounds. One of his crutches lay gleaming on the floor, while he balanced precariously on the other. Under normal circumstances, he could retrieve the fallen crutch easily, but his nerves and muscles wouldn't respond now; even with the one crutch, he might fall in another second.

And Karlis Selasis laughed. The Sers and Serras laughed with him, and not one of them had the humanity or the courage to offer Rich a succoring hand. Again, Alexand knew himself capable of violence. He would stop that laughter with his bare hands at Karlis's throat if—

Rich was no longer alone. Alexand was only a few paces from him, but he stopped short, jarred as if he were confronted by an apparition.

There was one person here capable of compassion and possessed of the courage to defy the first born of Orin Selasis. She moved toward Rich silently, an eidolon materialized out of nothingness, a slight girl who seemed at first no more than a child. Yet she struck the laughter down.

She walked with regal grace that dispelled the impression of childishness; not yet a woman, but far more than a child, and Alexand had the irrational conviction that she'd never been a child. He thought at first she was dressed in white, but that was also a false impression. Pale blue velveen bordered with pearls. Strands of pearls decked her night-black hair like stars; oblique eyes, black as her hair.

Those weren't the eyes of a child, and the unmasked contempt in them didn't stop short of loathing. It was there to be read by anyone, and it was directed with no hint of equivocation at Karlis Selasis. He shrank under that gaze; his fair skin reddened, and no words came from his open mouth.

The girl stopped when she reached Rich, the contempt vanished, and in its place was a gentle smile that hardly touched her lips; it was all in her dark eyes. She sank in a graceful, formal curtsy.

"Ser Richard, if I may..."

Rich could only stare at her, dazed and silent, while she knelt to pick up his crutch, then steadied him as he took it and grasped the handgrip. Alexand roused himself and started toward Rich. The eddy had already dissipated; only Karlis was left, standing in livid humiliation, ready to vent his anger on the Serra, but the words died on his lips when Alexand appeared at Rich's side.

"Lost your nerve, Karlis?" Alexand asked softly.

His chin came up sullenly. "Are you calling me a coward?"

"That would flatter you." Then the rage surfaced in a rush. "Out of my sight, Karlis, or we'll settle this with a point of honor!"

Karlis glared at him, then turned and stalked away.

"We'll settle it," he said belligerently over his shoulder, but he didn't pause in his retreat.

"Alex..." Rich's faltering voice made that more a sigh than a word.

And the Serra was gone, like the eidolon she called to mind. But there wasn't time to think about her; Rich was shaking, on the edge of collapse.

"Rich, hold on." Alexand had long ago learned how to support him without making it obvious; his hand on his arm high under the shoulder; a grip Rich could lean on, that would cause him no pain. The crutches were on maximum lift; if he didn't lose his hold on the handgrips...

Elise Woolf appeared, taking Rich's other arm without comment, her smile still intact. But she stopped to speak with no one as the three of them moved toward the entry.

"Rich, your father 'commed Hilding. The 'car will be waiting. Phillip will stay to finish the socializing here."

The ramp, and Rich sagged as it carried them downward.

"Mother, I'm sorry...."

"Hush, love, none of that." She leaned down to kiss his forehead. "All you need is some rest."

Alexand's gaze was fixed on the scarlet and black banners on the Faeton waiting at the bottom of the ramp. He couldn't meet his mother's eyes now.

5.

Dr. Stel and Phillip Woolf were gone now. Rich lay quiet; the nearly hysterical bout of weeping he'd staved off until their return to the Estate was over. His mother sat on the edge of the bed holding his hand, and Alexand leaned against the canopy post at the head of the bed. The windowall framed a scintillant galaxy, the lights of Concordia, and the only sounds were Elise's soothing voice and Harlequin's music.

Alexand looked over to the corner by the windowall where the old Bond sat crosslegged on the floor, lined face tilted up, blind eyes focused somewhere in the blackness behind those unseeing sockets. An electroharp rested on his knees, and his blunt fingers moved deftly among the strings, sending out soft, bell-like tones. The lumensa wall behind him shimmered with amorphic light-shadows, violet to blue to green, with the pulse of the music.

Harlequin he was called, and Alexand didn't know his real name. Elise had dubbed him Harlequin when she was a child. He wore the gold-and-purple tabard of a Galinin Bond, but he had lived in the Woolf Estate since her marriage, his extraordinary talents her private delight. And Rich's. There the old man's loyalties were happily divided—and shared.

There were no words to this song. Only a graceful melody that turned upon itself in exquisite variations, a melody that would be Harlequin's own. A man who could neither read nor write, who could scarcely communicate in words, but the fire of genius burned behind those dead eyes. Yet only a handful of people would ever know it existed.

But Harlequin was happy. His genius was rewarded with the solicitous care of his Lady and the appreciation of those few people whose lives were enriched by his talents. Harlequin asked nothing more of life.

Rich was saying earnestly, "Mother, I'm all right now, really. The guests will be arriving, and you haven't even changed your gown."

She hesitated, studying his pale features. "Are you really feeling better now?"

"Yes, I *am* getting sleepy. Must be the sedative Dr. Stel gave me."

She nodded. "Rich, perhaps we'll go to the beach estate for a few days. Would you enjoy that?"

His eyes brightened. "Yes, I would—very much."

"So would I. All this celebration is exhausting." She leaned forward to kiss him and take him in her arms. "Good night, Rich. I love you dearly."

"I love you, Mother."

She rose and turned to Alexand, their eyes meeting in a shared understanding, a mutual pain. But her smile didn't falter.

"Alex, will you be joining us at the ball later?"

"If you wish."

"Only if *you* wish. You'll have enough of such affairs in your life, and you won't always have a choice." She turned, touching Rich's hand. "Rest well, darling." Then, as she crossed to the door, she smiled at the old musician. "Good night, Harlequin. It's a lovely song."

When the door closed softly behind her, Alexand brought a chair up beside the bed and slumped into it, then unlaced the brocaded doublet. Rich studied his brother silently. For some time neither of them spoke.

Finally, Rich shifted his gaze to the windowall and the wash of Concordia's lights.

"One day I'm going to find out *why*. I mean, that Bond. It was so senseless. An ink bomb. And why throw it at Mother?"

"It was probably intended for Father."

"That still doesn't make sense. What did Father ever do to him?"

"Nothing. It's just that he's the Lord Woolf."

Rich was quiet for a while; the sedative was pulling at his eyelids, but he was still fighting it.

"Alex, who was she, the Serra?"

Alexand didn't have to ask which Serra. Her image haunted his thoughts, that child-woman with her pearl-starred hair.

"I didn't know her, Rich."

"Aren't you curious about her? The mysterious Serra with the courage to defy Karlis Selasis?"

"I don't want to know who she is or anything about her."

"Why not?"

Alexand turned to look across the bed to the windowall. "Tomorrow I'm to meet a potential bride. Not the first such meeting, not the last, and one day the Contracts of Marriage will be drawn and signed. But that mysterious Serra..." His throat seemed to close on him. "One could love someone like that. I don't want to know her name."

Rich sighed. "Yes, one could love...oh, Alex—"

"Rich, it comes with the Crest Ring, with the name and the power. It's part of the price."

He nodded, closing his eyes; he could no longer stave off the sedative, and his words were slow and slurred.

"So...sleepy. Alex, thanks...."

Alexand didn't move until Rich was well asleep. The time moved past, paced by Harlequin's music. He would play without pause until asked to stop; the notes under his fingers were as essential and as effortless to him as his own heartbeat.

And Alexand sat motionless, listening. Why? So many whys: so many unanswerable questions. Tears moved unchecked down his cheeks. Harlequin couldn't see them.

6.

From an acacia near the terrace, windwheels spun out sporadic waterfalls of chimes in the light breeze. It was a gray morning, threatening rain, but Serra Adrien Camine Eliseer found the foreboding sky appealing, and she was pleased that Lady Elise chose to serve tea here on the open terrace overlooking the rose garden. Adrien looked across the tea table at her mother, noting the subtle light that always came to her eyes on these occasions.

They still called Galia Shang Eliseer a beautiful woman, and she was that, as all the Shang women were, her manner fastidious and restrained, her dress impeccably tasteful, her attitude outwardly serene. But she was worried. The Lady Galia was worried about her wayward daughter.

Adrien looked down at the bandage on her right wrist; a minor sprain, but it ached. Perhaps her mother guessed more than she'd been told.

And Adrien was wondering if her mother thought her so much a dupe. Tea with the Lady Elise. That was attractive enough, but there was more to it. Lady Galia had frowned at the pink gown Adrien chose with its high waistline and full sleeves. Couldn't she wear something more—well, dignified? And must she insist on letting her hair run wild?

Adrien had ignored that, but she'd also refrained from asking bluntly when Ser Alexand would appear. Lady Galia hadn't mentioned him, and no doubt would be quite surprised when he did appear, as she'd been yesterday at the Selasid Estate when Karlis put in his studiously casual appearance.

That was the way the game was played. Adrien didn't take exception to that, only to her mother's assumption that she was blind to the game. And she couldn't explain even to her own satisfaction her uneasiness at this carefully casual encounter. With Karlis it had been simple; she recognized him for what he was and loathed him for it.

But Ser Alexand . . .

Corinth Panatell, her tutor, said the true test of character is stress; a few seconds in a stress situation is more revealing than years of acquaintance without conflict. As usual, Corinth was quite correct.

In a few fleeting seconds last night she'd understood everything worth knowing about Ser Richard Woolf, for instance. She knew him to be as forgiving as he was vulnerable. He hadn't been angry, nor was there a trace of recrimination in his eyes for his tormentors, vile as they were. Only pain. Pain that cut to her soul.

The incident had also revealed a great deal about Karlis Selasis, but there was nothing new in the revelation. He was ready to laugh at a helpless cripple, even if he were a DeKoven Woolf, but not to face up to a whole-bodied son of Phillip Woolf with a reputation for some skill at the foils.

The incident had also revealed much about Ser Alexand, something that made him more than a face familiar through the PubliCom System screens, that made him intensely human. He wasn't as forgiving as his brother, and in his bearing was the stamp of pride almost synonymous with DeKoven Woolf, but what struck Adrien was the realization that this was a young man capable of deep and passionate love. He came to his brother's aid like an avenging angel; she had no doubt he would kill or die for him. She wasn't sure why, but she found that revelation disturbing, and she was vaguely apprehensive about the impending encounter.

Still, she would always treasure the memory of this morning for one reason: the Lady Elise Galinin Woolf. Adrien watched her as she nodded to the Bondmaid to refill their cups. A living legend even more beautiful and gracious in person than in imagraphs or on vidicom. She was discussing certain mutual friends with Galia now, but most of her conversation had been directed to Adrien.

Adrien knew she was being examined and assessed; she'd been through the process before. But most of the Ladies considering her as a future daughter-in-law limited their questions to matters of lineage, manner, House management, and etiquette. The Lady Elise was a pleasant surprise. She talked about music, art, poetry, history, and even politics, and without a hint of condescension for Adrien because of her age. And Lady Elise listened, not critically, but with curious interest, to what Adrien had to say.

"My lady, I must compliment you." Galia Eliseer lifted the

dainty cup to her lips and smiled. "This is perfectly brewed, which is rather rare with Black Shang."

"That pleases me. Master Marco isn't a fancier of tea, unfortunately, but he assures me he's willing to learn." Then she added with a quick laugh, "A little reluctantly sometimes, of course."

As the discussion of tea and the Woolfs' master chef continued, Adrien looked down toward the end of the terrace where Lectris, her Bond bodyguard, stood waiting near the salon door—all two meters and hundred kilos of him—staunch and stolid in his blue-and-silver tabard, endlessly patient. It was the turn of Lectris's head toward the salon, the wary narrowing of his eyes, that gave her warning. She put her cup down, wondering at the quickening of her pulse, wondering if he'd remember her, wondering so many things.

When she looked up, he was emerging from the salon, dressed with appropriate casualness, the wide-necked shirt loosely laced under an open vest of blue—the color of his eyes, she noted—with only a narrow border of decorative brocade; informal boots of the same pale gray as the slim trousers. He walks like a dancer, she thought. He'd lose some of that youthful grace in the next few years; he'd fill out and grow taller. But he would never lose it entirely. Phillip Woolf still had it.

He glanced curiously at Lectris, then when he saw her, stopped abruptly. He recognized her. He didn't expect her, but he recognized her.

And Adrien felt briefly afraid.

She was the daughter of a First Lord; certain things were denied her by her birth as they were denied him. Yet there was a Rightness here. That's what the Elder Shepherd Malaki would call it. Or perhaps a spirit weft.

At any rate, it was too late now.

"That's only Lectris," she said with a faint smile, noting Alexand's backward glance at the Bond.

"Only?" He laughed, offering his arm as they stepped down into the garden. Lectris loomed silently, a granitic pillar of a man with great, sinewy hands that would be nothing less than lethal weapons, and he was further armed with an X^2 laser, which was particularly unusual for a Bond.

"Lectris is my personal guard," Adrien explained. "He's really a very gentle soul. He's been looking after me since I was old enough to walk."

The winding path led them away from the terrace, and if not out of range of maternal eyes, at least out of range of maternal ears. No attempt would be made to escape visual observation; that would strain the bounds of propriety as well as the patience of their curious and attentive mothers. For some time they walked in silence, and the garden had never seemed so beautiful. The gray light contradictorily intensified the colors, the incipient rain heightened the scents.

Alexand looked down at her. The "mysterious Serra" was no longer a mystery. Serra Adrien Camine Eliseer, first daughter of the Lord Loren and the Lady Galia Shang Eliseer.

And a potential bride.

A cold warning sounded in his mind: in any human encounter, your best defense is doubt. His father's words. There was truth behind them, and bitter experience, yet they rankled. He'd told Rich that one could love a young woman like this. Was it asking so much, or was it so foolish, to want to find out if he were right?

He studied her face, in profile to him, shadowed by her black hair, which fell straight and unfettered to her waist. It asked to be touched, and he had to restrain the impulse. It had the same silken, blued sheen as Lady Galia's, their heritage from Shang. Adrien's features also reflected the Shang heritage: high cheekbones and dark, oblique eyes. Her hands were small and as delicate as finely carved ivories. A Selaneen doll; something so exquisitely fragile it should be encased in plasex as the finest Selaneens always were.

Yet she'd seemed anything but fragile last night when she silenced Karlis Selasis with that potent, unmasked contempt. This Selaneen had bones of steel. She was something entirely new to him in his experience with the daughters of the Court of Lords.

Your best defense is doubt. . . .

He frowned, aware that the silence was stretching too long, even if she showed no impatience with it.

"Serra Adrien, I'm grateful for this opportunity to talk with you, both for my sake and my brother's. Rich regretted very much that he didn't thank you last night. He'll be happy that I've found you so I can offer his thanks—and mine—for your kindness."

She seemed to freeze, but it was something behind her eyes; her pace didn't change, nor did her expression.

"Kindness." She pronounced the word almost coldly. "Holy God, it was his due, and not because of his lineage. A matter of simple courtesy that needs no special thanks."

"Serra, whether or not it was his due, you were the only one present who showed that simple courtesy."

"That changes nothing. Those simpering, gutless Lordlings try to bring *him* to his knees because he's so much—" She stopped, her shoulders sagging. "Forgive me, Ser Alexand. There's nothing new in this for you, I know, nor is it something that bears reiteration."

"No. It isn't new, and perhaps it doesn't bear reiteration, but understanding is another matter. And compassion."

She looked up at him intently, a gentle smile making shadows at the corners of her mouth.

"Tell Ser Richard for me, please, that I'm only sorry my small act of courtesy was necessary." Then her smile turned pensive and finally faded. "Your brother seems a very extraordinary person. There's a light about him. Lectris would call it a Beyond Light. Will he . . . always have to use crutches?"

Alexand tried not to think about the real answer to that.

"Yes, I'm afraid so."

"I'm sorry. But if that's the case, he's fortunate in having you as his brother."

It wasn't flattery; it was a simple statement of opinion; an observation.

"No more fortunate than I in having him as my brother."

She looked up as they passed under an arched bower heavy with climbing roses. "Is Ser Richard well this morning?"

"No, he isn't." He answered without thinking, then felt it necessary to qualify the answers perhaps because of the flash of alarm in her eyes. "He'll be all right. It's just that yesterday was a very tiring day, and an unhappy one for him, even without the incident at Grandser's. We lost our tutor. He . . . had to retire."

"Lector Rovere?"

"Yes, but how did you know—"

"He's a friend of my tutor's. Corinth has spoken of him often and insisted on my reading some of his theses. I can understand Ser Richard's distress. I'd be devastated if I should lose Corinth."

"It was especially painful for Rich; his studies are very important to him."

She paused, then, "And it wasn't painful for you?"

"Yes, of course."

"But you consider yourself more capable of bearing it."

He looked at her sharply, but she only smiled.

"Ser Alexand, we've been brought up in the same school." Then she turned away, as if to spare him the necessity of meeting her gaze directly.

After a moment, he said a little stiffly, "It's just that Rich is more vulnerable in some areas. But all he needs is some rest. Mother's taking him to our Barrier Reef estate tomorrow. He loves the sea."

"The universal balm, so they say." Then she added with a short laugh, "At least, so Terrans and Polluxians say. I'll envy you your holiday at the beach."

"Envy Rich this time. I'm going to Montril with Father tomorrow."

"Montril. Oh—Canadia. Lord Fallor's Home Estate is there, isn't it?"

"Yes, and DeKoven Woolf has a factory site there."

"Ah. A tour of inspection, no doubt."

"No doubt." He smiled, noting the ironic laughter in her eyes, noting irrelevantly the reflection of the pink of her gown in her cheeks. "There's also the problem of negotiating a new lease on the factory site; Fallor owns the land." And, he thought, the problem of Julia. Another potential bride, one he wasn't looking forward to meeting again.

Adrien was frowning thoughtfully. "I've caught a few unguarded remarks from my father about Charles Fallor. I suppose he exacts a high price for that site, and I'm sure he wouldn't consider selling it to your father outright."

"Not when he can pocket a nice profit on the lease."

"And it makes a good lever."

Alexand studied her curiously. "Yes, it does."

She nodded. "Fallor can use any extra profit now, with D'Ord Hamid cutting into his grain markets, and any levers.

But levers tilt both ways. Your father always has the option of giving up the factory site, which would put Fallor—you're laughing at me."

"I'm sorry," he said, immediately regretting the laughter than came so unconsciously. "I was only surprised to hear you speak of these business matters so casually."

"Why? Because proper Ladylings aren't supposed to know about such things?"

"I'm not sure what proper Ladylings are supposed to know, but I've yet to meet one who *is* aware of such things. Even among the Ladies, I know of only two who show any cognizance of business or politics: Honoria Ivanoi and my mother."

"You put me in impressive company, Ser Alexand."

"I think you'll belong there one day."

"Now, that does flatter me."

"I mean it."

"I know you do." She studied him and seemed to be weighing his words, then pushed her hair, caught in a light gust of wind, back from her face. The wind had the scent of rain in it.

"This is an error," she said softly.

Alexand stopped, wondering if he'd misunderstood her. But he hadn't, and he didn't have to wonder what was an error. He'd said it himself: One could love a young woman like this. And if she understood that, too . . .

It could only be a double error.

She smiled wistfully and continued down the path.

"Ser Alexand, you're a rare young man," she said lightly, "but I won't test your patience with further discussion of business and politics; they can be very tiresome."

He laughed with her, or perhaps out of relief that had nothing to do with business or politics.

"All right, but please spare me the 'Ser Alexands.' You'll find 'Alex' easier."

"If you'll spare me the 'Serras.'"

"Gladly. Ah—" He stopped at a bloom-laden bush and broke off a blossom and offered it to her as they walked on. "I knew there was a rose of that particular shade somewhere in this garden."

She took the rose, smiling as she breathed in its sweet scent. It was exactly the color of her gown.

"Thank you, Alex. Mm—what an exquisite fragrance!"

"That variety is one of Mother's favorites. But be careful, it has thorns."

"Malaki says the best roses always have thorns. He's Elder Shepherd in our Estate compound. He's also a practitioner of herbal medicine. Malaki says the fruits of roses have magical properties for curing illnesses. I've never had the heart to tell him about mundane matters like vitamins."

Alexand smiled, wondering at her casual attitude toward her apparently close relationship with a Bond Shepherd. They had reached the edge of the garden terrace, and beyond the factory complex and the compounds, Concordia lay resplendent even on this sunless day. To the southeast Mount Torbrek, still wearing patches of winter white, hid its head in cloudy veils. Adrien crossed to the bench against the stone balustrade and gazed up at the grayed ceiling of cloud.

"Adrien, I'd like to ask you a question."

She looked around at him. "Is it so serious?"

"I don't know. I wondered . . ." He sighed, frowning. "Perhaps it's not even a question. I was only thinking about last night. Of you and Karlis and Rich. Karlis could make a great deal of trouble for you."

"And couldn't I make trouble for him?" Her eyes seemed blacker and more oblique, then she laughed briefly and seated herself on the bench, watching Alexand as he sat down beside her. "No, I couldn't, really. I know that. For one thing, I can't antagonize Karlis too much for my father's sake; it's to his advantage to stay on Lord Orin's good side—if he has one. For another, I might find myself . . ." She stopped and looked out toward the city.

But Alexand saw her eyes rest on the bandage on her wrist, and saw a hint of something close to dread before she turned away.

"Adrien, you might find yourself *what*?"

She shrugged and laughed. "In trouble myself."

That wasn't the real answer, but he didn't ask again. His father had told him Orin Selasis was courting Eliseer—and Karlis was courting Adrien.

The sudden anger he felt at that brought him up short. An error. She was right. He didn't realize a silence was growing until she spoke.

"Do you know Karlis well, Alex?"

"Well enough. My father has to deal with Lord Orin on Directorate business all too often, and Karlis and I were born on the same day, by some sardonic quirk of fate. Supposedly that gives us something in common."

"Then that's the only thing you have in common. Karlis's mother died when he was born, didn't she?"

"The Lady Idris? Yes. After five daughters, the Seladis finally had a son, Lord Orin's pride and joy, and it killed his mother."

"I'm sure there's a moral in that. Or perhaps it was just expediency."

Alexand's eyes narrowed. There was a cynical irony in that, revealing an awareness again atypical of "proper Ladylings." Idris Svynhel Selasis had been as famous for her strong will and caustic tongue as for her beauty, and rumor had it that she had despised her husband and made no effort to conceal it from him or anyone else. Rumor also had it that once Idris had borne him a son, Orin Selasis had decided to rid himself of his intractable spouse in the only way possible in Elite marriages.

Adrien didn't pursue that, instead commenting, "They say Lord Orin lost his eye in a point-of-honor duel with your father."

"Not with my father. It was my grandfather Kiron. That was a few years before his death."

"Oh, yes." Then she added, with a sidelong glance, "His very untimely death."

"Yes, it was untimely. A hunting accident. He was thrown from his horse." He didn't add that Lord Orin, then first born and not yet First Lord of Badir Selasis, was also present on that hunt.

His restraint, however, proved bootless.

She asked, "Do you think Lord Orin had a hand in that accident?"

He laughed. "Yes." Then he added, "But I have no reason to think that."

"No proof, you mean," she countered.

He only shrugged for an answer, then, keeping his tone light, "Tell me, how long have *you* known Karlis?"

"Only one day. Lord Orin invited the family to his Estate yesterday afternoon, and you know how these things work out.

The men head in one direction to talk about affairs of state, the women head in another to talk about affairs—period—and the children are supposed to go out and play, or entertain each other one way or another."

She was omitting, he noted, the real reason for the visit to the Selasid Estate and for the "children" being brought together.

"Being entertained by Karlis isn't the best way to spend an afternoon."

Her laugh was cold and brief. "No, and I can't say I like his idea of entertainment."

Alexand stiffened. "Adrien, did Karlis offend you?"

"Yes, as a matter of fact. Does that surprise you?"

"No. May I ask the nature of his offense?"

"You certainly may ask, but you needn't be concerned—" She stopped, eyeing him curiously. "What would you do if it were a grievous offense, Alex? Call a point of honor?"

She was joking, but Alexand didn't laugh. "I might."

His seriousness seemed to embarrass her.

"Well, it wasn't all that important. Besides, I took care of Ser Karlis myself. He tried to kiss me, which I thought rather presumptuous of him." She smiled, more to herself than to Alexand. "I doubt you noticed last night, and I'm sure he used cosmetics to hide it. I gave him a black eye."

Alexand stared at her. Then the thought of this petite girl giving Karlis a black eye brought the laughter, heady and irrepressible, and she joined him, the laughter creating a wordless fountain of warmth in the gray day.

"Adrien," he said at last, catching his breath, "that's beautiful; absolutely amazing. Did anyone see you?"

"Lectris was there. If Karlis knew how close he came to getting himself killed—but fortunately I got Lectris under control in time, and Karlis left the salon in something of a rush. I don't know what he told his father about his eye, but I doubt it was the truth. It was quite satisfying, except I sprained my wrist in the process. Karlis has a very hard head."

Alexand was divided between amusement at that and concern for her injury, and finally the concern won out.

"I'm sorry for that. Is it painful?"

"Not really. But this bandage wasn't exactly an elegant accessory for the Concord Day balls."

"A badge of honor, Serra; wear it with pride."

She nodded, but her smile faded. "It was a foolish thing to do, really."

Foolish. It was astounding. And interesting that, except for the Bond, she and Karlis had apparently been alone at the time. Karlis had no doubt led her into that compromising position.

"Adrien, you can be sure Karlis won't divulge your secret. Did you tell your parents?"

"Holy God, no. I—ah, fell on some steps."

Yet she showed no hint of concern that Alexand might betray her secret. He looked down at her wrist because he couldn't meet her unmasked gaze. Why was it unmasked? Not because she was incapable of it; not this steel-boned Selaneen. It was a matter of choice.

"That wrist won't make for pleasant memories of your holiday in Concordia."

"Alex, I'm tough as a belnong. A little thing like this won't color my memories."

He glanced up at her questioningly. "A belnong?"

"A Castorian triped; a symbiont with the Marching Forests. It's a colloquialism—tough as a belnong. They're viturally indestructible, since they can regenerate themselves from ten percent of their bodies."

"Well, that's something I didn't come across in my study of Castorian flora and fauna, but if you can compare yourself to a belnong, it must be a delightful creature."

He kept his tone light, shaded with studied irony, and she responded with equal levity, "If you'd ever seen a belnong, Ser, you'd know I wasn't comparing myself to one; only to one of its more admirable characteristics. I'm surprised you didn't encounter the belnong in your studies. It's one of Castor's most interesting life forms."

"And how did you come to find it of interest?"

She laughed, her shoulders rising in a shrug. "Well, when I was a child I had quite a penchant for animals. I used to plague Dr. Lile—that is, Dr. Perralt, our House physician—with wounded and sick creatures. In those days my ambition was to be a veterinarian."

"I'm sure you'd have been a fine veterinarian."

"Perhaps." She studied him a moment. "Did you ever harbor such ambitions? I mean, haven't you wondered what you might do if you were born Independent Fesh, for instance?"

"I'm afraid the training for my future occupation began too early for me to consider even in imagination any other alternative." He gave a short, uneasy laugh. "But perhaps it won't be a total waste. I might be able to accomplish something worthwhile somewhere along the line."

"What is it you want to accomplish, Alex?"

He considered the question, searching for words, for true words, but none seemed apt. Finally, he sighed.

"I want to accomplish everything, of course. Find all the answers, solve all the problems, right all the wrongs, stop all the . . . senseless suffering."

"An ambitious program," she said softly.

"Yes. Well, I've learned to temper my ambitions out of necessity, or recognition of some of the basic facts of life and human nature."

"But you haven't given them up."

"I was fortunate enough—or damned, depending on your point of view—to be born into a position of some power. Perhaps I can put that power to good use. Otherwise I'll simply find it difficult to justify my existence."

She nodded, as if he'd answered all her questions, but her reaction seemed equivocal, both satisfaction and regret.

"You are, indeed, an ambitious young man, Alex, and you aren't damned by your birth; you're damned with open eyes and a conscience. Perhaps it's fortunate you were born to power. They call you a replicate of your father, you know; the Black Eagle. Perhaps you'll be called that too, one day."

He looked at her, trying to understand the sadness shadowing her eyes.

"That comes with the House Crest. It's an ambiguous term; it evokes both admiration and fear." He paused, then asked, "What does it evoke in you?"

"Admiration," she replied without hesitation, "but I don't happen to find myself at odds with the Lord Woolf." She looked down, eyes fixed on the rose in her hand. "You aren't like your father. You'll be a greater man than he or a total failure as First Lord. If you fail, it will be because you're too much a human being."

He was silenced, and in that moment she seemed a seeress reading the future in the velvet petals of the rose. Then he looked away, toward the terrace.

"My apprenticeship isn't finished yet, Adrien. I may not be a greater man than my father, but I won't fail."

"And the price of success?"

"It's the price of failure I must consider."

She looked up at him now, and he was thinking of choices and turning points.

He *could* love this Selaneen, and knew her capable of loving him. And it *was* an error. It was also all but inevitable, once they met.

And he met her as a potential bride.

There was an element of cruelty in that. Alexand knew his father would do everything in his power to see his son as happy—"blessed," as he put it with total sincerity in spite of his agnosticism—in his bride as he had been with Elise Galinin. But the decision, the choice, would be Phillip Woolf's, not Alexand's or Adrien's.

Her thoughts were turning on the same choices. That was evident when she finally spoke; evident in the quick glance toward the terrace before she turned to look out over the city.

"You know why we're here, don't you, Alex?"

He nodded silently, waiting for her to go on.

"We're here because the possibility of a marriage, or, rather, an alliance—between our Houses exists. Lord Woolf is astute enough to realize my father is now the most powerful of the three Lords of Centauri, and that the Corcord has only begun to tap Centauri's resources, and certainly astute enough to realize Orin Selasis may steal a march on him if he isn't careful. So you and I are very casually introduced. The idea seems to be to put the potential nuptial couple together, and if we don't end up hissing and clawing at each other, then it's assumed we're compatible, and negotiations on political and economic planes can proceed." She paused, eyes half closed. "And later, Mother will say to me, 'I'm so glad you had a chance to talk to Ser Alexand. Such a well bred young man. Don't you think so, dear?'"

He asked quietly, "And how will you answer that?"

She laughed, tilting her head to one side. "Why, I'll tell her I found you boorish and uncivil, and I can't imagine what any girl would ever see in you."

"Ah. Do you treat all your suitors so badly?"

"No, of course not. It's all part of the game. I suppose if

one finds the game intolerable, there's always the cloisters. A second cousin of mine chose that alternative: the Sisters of Faith." Then she looked around at him, her laughter warm and for the first time almost childlike. "Oh, Alex, I should have warned you—I talk too much."

"I haven't found myself bored." He rose and turned toward the city, watching the aircars flashing along the Trafficon webs. On Torbrek's flanks sheet lightning glowed, too distant for thunder. "How old are you, Adrien?"

"Very nearly fifteen. Why?"

"I don't know." His eyes strayed to the terrace. "Walk with me down to the east corner. Mother keeps a flock of black swans in the pond on the level below. She'd be hurt if I didn't show them off for her."

Adrien smiled fleetingly at that, then rose and fell into step with him, letting another silence grow that had no emptiness about it. They were nearly at the end of the garden terrace before he broke it.

"Adrien, I know all about the courtship game. Most of the Serras delight in it; it's their whole purpose in life. But for you, it seems a waste."

She laughed. "And what other purpose have I? No, Alex, if you pity me, you must also pity yourself. You're as much on the auction stand as I. You won't find it necessary to work so hard at pleasing your potential mates—by custom that's their function—but you're still on the stand. You were born to that as you were born to power. The Lords of the Concord are no more free than their Bonds."

They reached the end of the terrace, but Alexand was hardly aware of the pond below or the graceful black birds with their scarlet beaks, whose passages sent Vs of ripples across the glassy surface.

"Is there no answer to that—our serfdom or that of the Bonds?"

He was thinking of Theron Rovere. *A tree must bend with the winds of change....*

She looked up at him. "An answer? I doubt it, and certainly I can't complain about this particular get-acquainted encounter."

"Nor can I. It's probably the only way I'd have learned your name."

"You'd probably have learned it sooner or later."

"I'd have tried." He recognized that as truth now; he would never have been satisfied until he knew.

"Would you? Why?"

He shrugged. "To assuage my curiosity, I suppose; to answer some questions."

"What kind of questions?"

He turned and leaned back against the balustrade, watching her and being watched, and not caring.

"It's hard to put into words. Questions like why you remind me so much of Rich. I call him my linked-twin soul. Sometimes we can all but read each other's minds. I wonder why I feel that same rapport with you."

She didn't speak for some time, and when at length she did reply, her voice was nearly a whisper.

"If you find the answer to that, Alex, tell me. Perhaps it would explain why I feel the same way about you."

Her eyes were so black they were paradoxical; like fathomless waters, the surface reflecting lights and almost opaque, but beneath it, revealed in passing shadows, were unexpected, vertiginous deeps.

He looked away; alarms were shrieking in his head.

Your best defense is doubt. . . .

I am a human being. By the God, I am a human being and choice is my birthright, or I cease to be human.

But he had another birthright, and so did Adrien. There would be no choice for either of them.

Only hope.

Hope for what? He didn't know Adrien Eliseer. There could be untold factors within her mind and being that would shatter illusions and turn hope to gall. Yet he'd already made himself vulnerable to her; vulnerable to shattering along with the illusions.

"Alex, there's no joy in safety; it's only comfortable."

His head came up, he stared at her, and he felt stripped. Only Rich was capable of that, of responding to words he hadn't spoken.

"There's something to be said for comfort."

She nodded soberly. "And a great deal to be said for responsibility, but I'll still make room for hope. I'm strong enough to withstand pain, and willing to accept the risk, and I can't live without hope."

Alexand felt the tension draining from him. Adrien Eliseer. Tuck, his Bond valet, would say she had the witching way; the Beyond power. Some things were by their very nature irrational: they could not be comprehended on a rational level.

The wind drew a strand of her hair across her forehead. He started to push it back, but stopped, remembering the watching eyes on the terrace. She smiled at that and pushed it back herself.

"Yes, I'd almost forgotten our purpose here, but that's the source of my hope. I'll tell you this, and I know it isn't...ladylike, but if you're the kind of human being I think you are, you'll understand. We're here because your father and mine are considering a House alliance; a marriage. Whether it will ever come about remains to be seen, and the decision will be predicated almost entirely on such impersonal factors as economics and politics. Whatever my father decides, I'll accept for the sake of the House. But I'll still hold this hope: on a very personal level, Ser Alexand, I'll hold the hope that one day I'll be your Lady."

He searched vainly for words, gripping the balustrade against the urge to reach out and take her hand.

"Adrien, you have more courage than I." He paused, then, "Serra Adrien, I share your hope."

Her eyes closed briefly, and even when she opened them again, they were still shadowed by her downcast lashes. Then she looked up at him with a whisper of a smile.

"Alex, we don't really know each other. I've only expressed a hope. Nothing more."

"In other words, you ask no commitments of me." He laughed softly. "You don't have to *ask*, Adrien."

He looked down at the pond, watching the intersecting patterns of ripples in the wakes of two swans. Long after they passed each other, the wavelets meshed and crossed, the pattern expanding endlessly across the water.

7.

Alexand had learned the art of escape at an early age, but as he grew older he found it increasingly difficult. Size, for one thing, was against him; it wasn't so easy now to slip unnoticed out of a crowd. But if the crowd was large enough and clamorous enough, he could still manage it, and now he was alone on the first storage level, looking down through one of the many openings giving visual access to the assembly lines on the level below, where thousands of scarlet-and-black-clad Bonds, under the close eye of Fesh techs and overseers, manned the rows of moving belts carrying to completion the complex mechanisms that would transmit voices, images, and impulses across micromillimeters or light years.

A humming sound caught his attention. He turned and saw a dekaton loader moving along the aisles between the storage shelves, the Bond driver riding high above the plasifoam cartons. These were all yellow; they were keyed by color to the shelves where they were to be deposited.

Except for an occasional passing loader, this level was deserted, and Alexand was enjoying the privacy and the opportunity to study the assembly processes without benefit of a pressing mob of nervous executechs, managers, foremen, and overseers all vying to convince their Lord of their worth.

The Montril factory was DeKoven Woolf's third largest; only the Concordia and Bonaires plants rivaled it in size and output. The House owned outright all but four of its fifty manufacturing sites, and Montril was one of those four, which made it—or, rather, Lord Charles Desmon Fallor—a constant thorn in his father's side.

Alexand thought of Adrien Eliseer's cool assessment of the situation. The lease was a lever on Woolf, but a lever tilts both ways. Unfortunately, there were factors in this case that qualified that theoretical truth. Phillip Woolf might hint at abandoning the Montril site in negotiating with Fallor, but he'd do a great deal of compromising before he carried out that threat. DeKoven Woolf couldn't afford the disastrous capital loss. Not in light of the mushrooming annual increases in Concord tax levies. The House had last year surrendered half a billion 'cords, twenty thousand conscript Fesh, and fifty thousand tax Bonds to the Concord; nearly twice the previous year's levy.

But no House was free of that ever increasing burden. Some Lords, Alexand knew, and suspected Fallor was one, reduced the strain on their capital reserves—or their opulent life styles— by shifting the burden to their Fesh in House tax levies, or by cutting maintenance expenditures for their Bonds. Short-sighted, Phillip Woolf pronounced, and Alexand found the truth in that self-evident, but apparently few members of the Court of Lords did.

A tree must bend with the winds of change. Theron Rovere. You'll haunt me till I die.

He leaned forward to rest his arms on the railing, feeling the ache of tension in his shoulders.

Perhaps that was one reason this tour of inspection seemed such an enervating experience. He kept seeing everything through Lector Theron's eyes, seeing the signs of stubborn calcification that wouldn't let this tree bend.

Signs like VisLord Kelmet Woolf, Phillip Woolf's cousin, resident Lord in charge of the Montril plant; its production and profit figures attested to his efficiency. Yet Alexand's initial reaction to Kelmet was mistrust. Perhaps it was because he was so arrogantly obsequious, or because he had organized Woolf's itinerary so minutely, scheduling exactly what he would see exactly when.

Something else set Alexand's teeth on edge. The first subject Kelmet broached, once the amenities were concluded, was enlarging the compound guard here. That, Woolf argued, would mean a new guard conscript, which wouldn't set well with House Fesh after last year's large Concord conscript.

Kelmet had only shrugged and said, "The price of order, my lord."

That wasn't original to him. It had become a catchphrase, a glib rationale passed down from the Directorate to the Court of Lords to the Fesh with every new tax levy demanded to finance every new expansion of Conpol and Confleet. Alexand distrusted the rationale, although he had heard it on his father's lips. He particularly distrusted it coming from Kelmet Woolf.

But perhaps he was doing the man an injustice, simply

projecting his resentment at being here. And he was tired. It was afternoon here, but his inner clock half a year behind. It was autumn in Montril, and the city was gray with snow, which everyone insisted was unusually early. It had been a long day and the worst was yet to come: the dinner reception at the Fallor Estate. Not an inviting prospect with the Fallor and their assorted kith and kin. And Julia.

Julia Fallor was a living cliché, and, perversely, every time he thought of her, he was reminded of Adrien Eliseer.

He wondered how Julia would have responded to Rich's cruel baiting at the Galinin Estate, and knew she'd have been among those laughing on cue with Karlis Selasis.

He frowned, concentrating on the assembly lines, trying to put out of his thoughts the memories of Adrien and the sharp sense of solitude created by Rich's absence.

Rich might have come along on this trip, but he had a choice, and Alexand knew, although neither of them had spoken of it, that Concord Day marked the last time Rich would ever appear in public except at his parents' insistence. That insistence, Alexand had no doubt, would not be forthcoming.

Rich had a choice. So, let him make a recluse of himself; let him close himself behind the walls of the Estate. He had his studies, which consumed him and always would, even without Lector Theron. And he was loved there.

Alexand didn't have a choice; this was his apprenticeship, and it would entail numberless separations from Rich in the future. And when he reached Age of Rights—

Four years. His hands contracted into fists. Those would be Rich's last years.

But custom commands.

Every Elite male upon reaching Age of Rights by time-hoared custom paid his due to the Concord in the coin of four years service in Confleet, and not even Phillip Woolf could spare his son those four years. Directorate seats, although in practice hereditary, were by law elective by the Directors or the Court of Lords. Such a breach in traditional custom might precipitate the unseating of a House, while ineptitude or corruption would be blithely tolerated.

For the same reason, Mathis Galinin, Chairman of the Directorate, was equally helpless, although he had lost his younger son to the custom. Confleet protected its Elite conscripts as best it could, but a few didn't survive, and that risk was constantly increasing. For years after the Fall of the Peladeen Republic, Confleet's only real function had been controlling the pirate fleets of the Brotherhood and other Outsider clans, or the enigmatic Society of the Phoenix, but neither the Brotherhood nor the Phoenix accounted for the frequent Confleet expansions in recent years. Confleet was becoming an adjunct of Conpol, policing not the remote reaches of space, but the Concord.

Rather, the Bonds.

Uprisings, they were called, apparently causeless and aimless, but always incredibly costly in lives and damage. DeKoven Woolf had suffered only three minor uprisings in the last year. *Minor.* Catastrophes thus qualified only in relation to those suffered by other Houses, which were too violent on too large a scale to be controlled by House guards, necessitating Conpol and Confleet intervention.

Yet by hallowed tradition, when he was twenty, when he became a Lord, he would enter the Confleet Academy in Sidny to learn the lordly arts of war. Against Bonds. He would practice those lordly arts while his brother—

The hum of a loader distracted him. He glanced over his shoulder and saw it moving toward him—a small, mobile mountain of plasifoam cartons, these all blue. But the aisle was six meters wide; there was ample room for it to pass.

At any rate, he reminded himself, he still had five years' grace before he reached Age of Rights, but only a few more minutes' grace here before he must rejoin the entourage surrounding his father. Kelmet, he noted, had joined the group, but at the moment Woolf was occupied with Master Camden, the plant manager, who was speaking earnestly, hands constantly in motion. Alexand smiled at his father's intent, probing expression. Camden would get no easy pats on the back from his Lord.

The hum of the loader was louder now, and he heard a shift in tone that signaled an increase in speed.

He looked around. The loader was twenty meters away.

Again, he turned his attention to his father's progress. Undoubtedly the Bonds, like the Fesh, had been warned of their Lord's impending visit. They kept at their work assiduously, but Alexand saw the furtive glances cast toward Woolf, and there was much in them that disturbed him. Sometimes there was awe, as if they were witnessing the passing of a lesser god, but too often there was fear and resentment.

The hum of the loader impinged on his consciousness again, but this time it sounded the inner alarm of instinct, the adrenalin surge that hit at the solar plexus.

He spun around, his back to the railing.

And it was only now, with the machine closing the space between them by milliseconds, that he recognized the threat underlying that shift in speed, this unswerving approach.

Blue. Blue plasifoam. That was all he could see. He still couldn't make sense of the fact that the loader with its dekaton of cartons was on a collision course with the railing at exactly the spot where he stood. It was only when his eyes met those of the man at the controls of the loader that he understood.

The Bond meant to kill him.

The wall of blue loomed, the hum became a shrieking whine. He saw that face in minute detail, every sweating pore magnified, and he saw glaring from the pale eyes something desperately brutal, agonized, insensate, insane, and terrifying.

From somewhere within him the question echoed.

"Why?"

He wasn't conscious of his cry. He vaulted to one side in a vain effort to remove himself from the point of impact.

And in the last split-second he saw a sudden change in that face: bestial hatred turning to horror and disbelief.

The loader skewed about, brakes screaming, the Bond twisted out of his seat in his violent effort to stop the juggernaut he had himself set in motion.

He turned the loader.

That fact existed in Alexand's mind like a bolt of lightning, as brief and as awesome.

But the turn, even though it averted the collision with the railing, threw the load, tossing cartons like feathers in a whirlwind, and Alexand hit the floor at the same instant the first cartons came smashing down.

Footsteps, voices; jangling, shuffling around him.

"Sirra, it—it was an accident! I swear by the holy saints! I—I never *saw* him! He run out in *front* of me!"

"'Zion, it's Ser Alexand—"

"What happened here? What *happened?*"

Damn, would they be quiet? The Bond—where was he?

"An accident! Sirra, I swear it!" The man was sobbing.

Alexand pulled himself up into a sitting position head pounding, trying to order his muddled senses in the welter of movements and voices surrounding him.

He must see that man.

"Holy God, what's going on here?"

"—the Lord Woolf's first born!"

"An accident, sirra! An *accident!*"

". . . get this mess cleared before—"

"He's coming! The Lord Woolf is coming!"

Alexand forced his eyes into focus on the wreckage of smashed cartons and shards of delicate machinery littering the floor; the silent hulk of the loader loomed over the disjointed activities of Fesh overseers and House guards.

"Ser Alexand?"

A hand on his right arm; one of the guards. Alexand pulled away. That grip was agonizing.

Yet he wouldn't let the guard see the pain.

"Ser, let me help you."

"No! I'm . . . all right." He turned, reached for the railing with his left hand, and levered himself to his feet.

"The Lord *Woolf . . .*"

The approaching entourage sounded like a marching Confleet squad.

Fenn Lacroy called it stress-pain training, and Alexand put it to the test now. The breathing first, slow and deep, one breath for every five heartbeats; the ordered shift in concentration outward to the imminent threat. Alexand couldn't let his father, or anyone, know he'd been injured. He wasn't sure why. Only that it was necessary.

And he *had* been hurt. His right shoulder. It might be nothing more than a bad bruise or sprain; he was only sure that it was painful. He crossed his arms under his cloak so he could support his right arm with his left without making it obvious.

His father was moving toward him in the van of a wide-eyed cluster of officials and guards, with Kelmet Woolf only a pace behind him, but Alexand was intent now on the Bond. He was on his knees in the debris on the floor, flanked by two guards and an overseer with the meter-long, double-tongued rod of a charged lash ready in his fisted hand. The Bond observed his Lord's approach with slack jaw, his face bloodless. He looked as close to death as any man Alexand had ever seen. And he was.

An accident. The whole thing was so badly thought out, there couldn't have been any conscious planning behind it. Yet neither could Alexand doubt that this man had intended to kill him.

Why? That question must be answered.

And another question. At the last moment, the Bond had turned the loader. That must be answered, too. But not here; not now.

"Alexand! Are you all right?"

He turned to find his father close to him, the eagle visage a closed mask.

"Yes, Father." He spoke carefully to avoid slurring the words. The pain was getting worse.

Woolf's eyes narrowed, then moved in a comprehensive arc, taking in the wreckage, the loader, finally fixing on the Bond; his voice was ominously subdued.

"What are you called?"

The Bond cringed, then answered in a stumbling rush, "Quin, my lord. "Q-quin Selm. Oh, my lord, it—it was an accident! I swear—I swear by all...I never...meant..."

Woolf didn't speak; he only looked at the man, eyes unyielding as stone, and that chill scrutiny silenced him, reducing him second by second to dumb paralysis; his head sank forward by degrees as if the muscles were giving way under the weight of his unspoken sentence. Alexand watched him numbly, and the irrational conviction grew in him that if his father spoke the word, "Die," as a command, the Bond *would* die on the moment.

Finally, Woolf turned to his son. "Alex, what happened?"

He didn't look at his father as he replied, but at the Bond. "It *was* an accident, Father, and I must admit it was my fault. If he hadn't turned the loader in time, I'd be dead."

Quin Selm. He must remember that name.

The Bond's head jerked up, eyes glazed, uncomprehending.

"You're...quite sure?" Woolf asked softly.

Alexand nodded. "Yes. Quite sure."

Woolf frowned briefly. Alexand's pallor hadn't escaped

him, nor the careful rhythm of his breathing, nor the tense set of his shoulders.

"Well, I'm relieved to hear that." His hand went out to rest on his son's shoulder in an apparently casual gesture, went unerringly to the *right* shoulder.

Alexand flinched; only a momentary flicker in his firmly controlled features, a jerking intake of breath.

Woolf turned away. "Fer Jenson, have you had any trouble with this man before?"

The warehouse foreman hesitated, frowning at Selm. "No, my lord, not to my knowledge."

"Again, I'm relieved. Kelmet—" He looked around and found Kelmet Woolf eyeing Jenson doubtfully. "Alexand and I have had a long day. We'll continue the tour tomorrow. Master Camden? Have my 'car brought to the landing roof."

Camden relayed the order to a lesser official, then, hands clasped anxiously, "My Lord, I deeply regret this terrible incident. I'm only grateful Ser Alexand wasn't hurt."

"Yes. Now, tomorrow morning I want to discuss the assembly system for the new SynchCom transmitter. Have your techs available at 09:00." He went to Alexand's left side, every movement artfully casual, even when he leaned close, speaking in a low tone only he could hear.

"Can you walk?"

Alexand controlled his surprise, managing a quick nod, and Woolf turned to Camden and the waiting officials.

"I've noted some problems today which I'll discuss with the various department heads later, but on the whole I'm pleased with what I've seen. You may all take pride in your work as the House takes pride in you."

That called up a murmur of grateful comment and a flutter of bows, and Woolf started to move away, but Master Camden stopped him.

"My lord? Uh . . . the Bond. What shall we do with him?"

Quin Selm found himself the focal point of two pairs of DeKoven Woolf eyes and began trembling anew.

Woolf said tersely, "Nothing. It was an accident, and my son accepted full responsibility."

The Bond stared blankly, and it was only after two attempts that he managed to get any coherent words out.

"M-my lord, the Holy Mezion bless you! And—and you, Ser . . ." He gazed at Alexand with even less comprehension, and there met only a cool stare.

Quin Selm hadn't seen the last of him, but now Alexand turned to face the seemingly hopeless task of reaching the landing roof without giving way to the pain that sapped his strength and spread an icy chill over his skin.

Nulgrav lifts, corridors, pedways—an endless distance. He refused to surrender. And all the while, his father was at his side, a ready presence. More farewells at the landing roof; interminable pleasantries, and somehow Woolf got rid of Kelmet. Finally, Hilding at the open door of the 'car, and once inside, Alexand heard his father's voice, blurred against the ringing in his ears.

"Hilding, get us to the estate as quickly as possible! And 'com ahead to Dr. Dall. I want her waiting in Alexand's suite when we arrive."

Generators whined, sudden acceleration pressed him back into the cushioned seat, and finally he could give in, could take his father's hand and hold on, squeezing hard against the pain.

8.

The sun had long ago set; the windowall to his left was dark, spangled with distant lights hazed in snow.

The door slid open and Alexand turned his head on the pillow to watch the soft-treaded approach of Dr. Hariet Dall, gray-haired, wearing an antiseptically white tunic with the red Conmed caduceus on her allegiance badge. She came around to the left side of the bed, eyes moving in a quick visual assessment.

"What time is it?" he asked.

"It's 19:10, Ser. Have you been awake long?"

"A while. I don't know how long." His watch, along with the rest of his clothing, had been removed. He lay quiet, enjoying the warmth of the thermblanket. His right shoulder was bandaged, his arm immobilized in a sling; there was some pain, but it was bearable.

"Well, let's see how you're progressing." She strapped a biomonitor cuff on his left wrist, paused to study the readings, then removed it with a brief nod of satisfaction. "Your physical readings are good. How do you feel?"

"All right. What's your diagnosis?"

"Oh, aside from assorted bumps and bruises, you broke your collarbone. Rather a bad break, too, but I doubt there'll be any permanent impairment to the use of your arm."

That possibility hadn't occurred to him, and he felt a momentary alarm even as she assuaged it.

"Ser, your lord father is waiting anxiously for news of you. Do you feel well enough to see him now?"

"What? Oh—yes, 'com him, please. He'll be worried."

And, he added to himself, angry. Alexand had broken one of his father's cardinal rules: *Never go among Bonds, or into a Bond area alone.*

Dr. Dall politely retreated into the adjoining salon when Phillip Woolf arrived. He was dressed in formal regalia, shades of blue with silver brocade, dress boots of a blue so dark as to seem black. He sat on the bed beside Alexand, his frown of disapproval leavened with concern.

"Alexand, I won't lecture you on wandering into Bond areas without a guard. That shoulder should provide enough of a lesson. Are you comfortable?"

"Yes. I'm sorry I caused so much trouble, and the lesson is quite clear." Then he frowned, noting his father's formal attire. "'Zion, I forgot—the dinner at the Fallor Estate."

"Yes. I've prepared myself for it, but I'm not sure I should leave you tonight."

"Father, you know I'm in good hands with Dr. Dall, and I feel very well, really. Besides, you have the lease negotiations to consider."

"Unfortunately. At any rate, *you'll* be delivered from the evening's festivities. No doubt Serra Julia will be quite disappointed." His expression was carefully noncommittal, but there was nothing gratuitous about that casual reference to Julia.

"Well, that might be one way to solve the lease problem in the future," Alexand said flatly, as much aware of the coolness of his own tone as he was of his father's probing gaze. "And Fallor is a habitual fence rider on the Directorate. An alliance by marriage should put him more consistently in the Galinin-Woolf camp."

After a moment, Woolf said, "You've never told me what you really think of Julia."

"I don't really know her. Anyway, she's only thirteen—and don't laugh because I'm only fifteen." Woolf managed to restrain his amusement while Alexand added, "At any rate, my feelings for Julia at the moment have no bearing on the future."

"At the moment, no. But remember this, Alex—as I do— an Elite marriage is an irrevocable covenant, and no House can withstand the stresses of a bad marriage without suffering from it."

Alexand only nodded, and his father's next question caught him entirely off guard.

"Tell me, what did you think of Serra Adrien Eliseer?"

Alexand felt his cheeks go hot, but that he couldn't control.

"I . . . I enjoyed talking with her very much."

Woolf studied him, smiling almost imperceptibly, then, "She's a very bright girl, so Elise tells me."

Alexand said tightly, "Yes, she is."

"And blessed with the Shang features. In fact, your mother assures me she'll be a swan one day."

A swan. A black swan. The currents of passage fan out in intermeshing waves endlessly. . . .

He cleared his throat and looked for his watch, forgetting it wasn't on his wrist.

"Father, it's getting late. I mustn't keep you."

Woolf hesitated, then with a nod came to his feet. "I won't stay long, but I suppose I must put in an appearance." He switched on the intercom by the bed. "Dr. Dall, come in, please." Then he turned to Alexand with a black, arched brow raised. "I'll convey your regrets to the Fallor as convincingly as possible."

Alexand smiled. "Well, there had to be some recompense for this shoulder."

"No doubt." Then, as the door opened, "Dr. Dall, my son tells me he's feeling very well. At least he assures me he's in good hands with you. I'll go on to the Fallor Estate. You can reach me there."

"I'm sure there's nothing for you to worry about, my lord." She reached into a pocket and took out a small pill case, then filled a plasex cup with water from the dispenser on the bedside table. "Ser, I'm going to give you a sedative. It's very important now that you get plenty of rest."

Alexand tensed at that. He had an abiding distrust of sedatives and, beyond that, personal and compelling reasons not to let himself be sedated now. He watched helplessly as Dr. Dall uncapped the case and extended it toward him, ready to tap a capsule into his hand.

She said firmly, "Come, Ser, get this down. Your lord father won't be so worried if he knows you're resting."

Alexand glanced at his father, then held out his hand for the capsule and quickly brought it to his mouth. Dr. Dall had the water ready, but after the first swallow, he began to cough, grimacing—with no pretense—at the cutting pain in his shoulder.

"Lean back, Ser. A deep breath . . . slowly now . . . there, that's better."

The spasm disappeared, and with it the capsule—under the covers. He took a long, careful breath, searching for any awareness of his deceit in the doctor's eyes. There was none, nor any in his father's anxious gaze.

"Alex, you're sure you'll be all right?"

"Yes, of course, Father. Don't worry about me."

"I'll try not to. Dr. Dall, you have an open 'com line to me. Don't hesitate to use it." Then he pressed his son's hand briefly. "Rest well, Alex."

"I will. Good night."

He closed his eyes, listening to his father's fading footsteps, the snap of the closing door. Dr. Dall didn't leave. She would when she thought him well asleep. He'd simply have to wait.

9.

Alexand had anticipated some of the problems he would encounter on entering the compound and forearmed himself. His suite was as a matter of course furnished with a comconsole equipped with House memfile inputs, which were open to him with the computer's identification of his voice print. Thus he knew there were six compounds, each housing ten thousand Bonds, and that a Bond named Quin Selm was registered to Compound A, Block SE-15-FU322, and that the work shift to which Selm was assigned ended at 20:00. From that he guessed the airshuttles would arrive at the four compound gates at about 20:30.

The memfiles, however, could not tell him exactly where in Compound A Quin Selm might be at this particular time, and he was well aware that finding one Bond in this small city would be difficult, if not impossible, since he couldn't ask any of the guards or overseers for information. If they recognized him, which was likely, they'd feel obliged to inform Lord Woolf that his son was wandering about a Bond compound unescorted. But he had in mind a solution to the problem of locating that one Bond.

He was also aware that he was breaking his father's rule again, going alone among Bonds, but there was no alternative to that. He *would* have some answers.

There were other problems, however, that he hadn't foreseen. The cold, for one. The cold that seemed to numb every part of his body except his injured shoulder, and there the frigid, snow-bearing wind served to intensify the ache.

The other unforeseen factor was fear.

Alexand had little experience with fear, and it didn't occur to him to expect it. He'd never ventured into a Bond compound like this, incognito and without guards, and he found himself in alien territory. A paradox, that. He would one day be Lord of these Bonds, the compounds would belong to him. Yet he didn't belong in the compounds.

He had also forearmed himself—literally—with a light X[1]

laser in a spring sleeve sheath, but now as he rode an elevated pedway, anonymous in an equally anonymous crowd, the gun offered no assurance. The Bonds riding the 'way with him gave him a little space along with wary stares, yet he felt short of breath, hemmed in by voices, accents, odors, unfamiliar to him, and the sedate movement of the 'way seemed maddeningly slow.

But what he had anticipated as the worst hurdle was behind him. The gate. That had been surprisingly easy.

He had waited in the estate 'car near the north gate until the 'shuttles disgorged their loads of off-shift workers. His cloak was blue-gray, unadorned, typical Fesh attire, and he was tall enough not to seem obviously under age. A Fesh clerk or Grade 1 tech entering the compound on some minor errand. His face-screen was off, but the hood of his cloak was up, shadowing his face. Not unusual in view of the weather; most of the Bonds were similarly hooded.

He didn't offer to show an ident card; he couldn't, of course, but he wasn't sure whether it was expected of a Fesh. Apparently not, or perhaps the guards were too distracted by the influx of Bonds, who *were* expected to present their cards for the register comp. The guards let him pass without a second glance.

But here inside the compound his face-screen was on. He wasn't so concerned about being recognized by the Bonds, who had no access to vidicom newscasts and only occasional access to the House comsystem, but there were a few Fesh in the compound, mostly the ubiquitous guards, and they weren't conveniently distracted like the gate guards.

He looked ahead and saw a junction of 'ways, and felt the double thuds of his heartbeat against his ribs. Here was another unforeseen problem: the possibility of getting lost. He didn't have time to wander aimlessly around the compound. His father wouldn't be gone more than two hours, and Alexand intended to be back in his bed at the estate well before he returned.

A moment's consideration put the panic down. He must stay on this 'way. It was one of the main radials leading to the center of the compound, and that was his destination.

And in fact, getting lost was the least of his concerns. He had only to stay with the crowds. The central plaza was also their destination; the dining hall was there. Beyond that, all

DeKoven Woolf compounds built in the last three generations were constructed on the same circular, wedge-sectioned plan, including those in Concordia; a simple, efficient design adopted by nearly every House.

But not all of them.

Alexand looked out at the dormitories as he passed, solid blocks of buildings rising from the ground two levels below, looming another two levels above him, with veins of smaller 'ways connecting them with this moving artery. He was remembering a conversation between his father and Lord Lazar Hamid of Pollux overheard at a dinner at the Home Estate.

"Really, Phillip, you're begging trouble. Those huge dining halls, and *parks*, for the God's sake. You give them too many places to *gather*."

Woolf had politely refrained from pointing out that D'Ord Hamid had suffered ten times as many Bond uprisings as DeKoven Woolf, but had noted that the cost of maintaining the centralized compounds was appreciably lower, and that, if necessary, the plaza areas could be isolated with shock screens at a moment's notice.

The pedway sloped gradually downward, and Alexand felt an anticipatory tension in the people around him. Still, their voices were oddly subdued. Perhaps it was his presence. Ahead, the buildings gave way to a wide clearing, the plaza park; he could barely see it for veils of snow, and the trees were only smudges of gray. His destination would be on the far side. The chapel.

There were nine more chapels in the compound, he knew—Bond religion apparently resisted centralization—but the plaza chapel was always the domain of the *Elder* Shepherd. That adjective implied veneration won by wisdom and long years of service, and every Bond in the compound was considered part of the Elder Shepherd's flock.

And the Elder Shepherd was the one person in this compound who would be likely to know where to find a Bond named Quin Selm at this particular time; not only to find him, but to bring him to Alexand without arousing his suspicions.

He pulled in a deep breath, letting it out in a brief white cloud. Shivering; he couldn't seem to stop it. The 'way moved him inexorably past lighted windows casting glowing shafts at monotonously regular intervals. The plasment walls were tinted different colors, but they melded into a bleak gray. The artificial lights, perhaps, or the snow.

The snow.

His breath caught as shock tightened every muscle and sent spasms of pain down his arm and back. He'd been so preoccupied with himself, his purpose, his fears, that he hadn't given the incredible fact of snow inside this compound a thought even while he shivered with the cold that fostered it.

The atmobubbles should be activated.

A mechanical failure. That must be it.

He looked down over the railing. The 'way was only one level above ground now. The snow was piled nearly a meter deep against the walls. No mechanical failure would take as long to repair as it took that snow to accumulate to that depth.

He closed his eyes. Dizzy. He waited until he was sure of his equilibrium, wishing desperately he could get off the pedway, could stop moving. Finally, he looked at his watch. Half an hour. He'd left the estate half an hour ago, yet it seemed half a day—half a night.

The 'way angled down between single-level buildings built in long arcs to conform with the circular shape of the plaza. He could see the bottom of the 'way, the Bonds moving left to the dining hall. None of them chose to cross the paved lane circumscribing the park; their evening meals awaited them in the hall.

He didn't pause at the end of the 'way, but crossed the paving, finding it treacherously slick where the snow was packed by footsteps. When he reached the park, he stopped under a frost-rimed elm and looked back. Against the glow of the hall windowalls the Bonds were dark silhouettes, spacing themselves under the prodding of the guards into slow-moving lines at the entrance.

He found anger as much a part of his awareness as cold now; it was a product of the cold. Why weren't the 'bubbles on?

The snow was unseasonable, so he and his father had been told, but, even if it were true, there was no conceivable excuse for letting these people suffer from this cold.

Kelmet Woolf. Only he could be responsible for this.

Fesh peculation was so common it had to be accepted as a fact of business. The rule of thumb was that for every 'cord of profit to the House, ten 'cords were lost along the way and channeled into various Fesh pockets. But subverting the 'bubble system was too large an undertaking to be carried out successfully by Fesh. It could only be done with the approval—or, rather, at the behest—of the highest ranking authority, in this case the resident VisLord. Did Kelmet think Phillip Woolf would fail to notice such blatant fraud?

But the compounds weren't included on the scheduled tour of inspection. Alexand had questioned his father about that. His time was short, the Fallor lease negotiations were his primary concern, and, although he had never liked Kelmet personally, he trusted him; he was a good manager.

A better manager than Woolf realized, apparently.

Alexand turned and set off down the path that bisected the park. His boots made a soft crunching in the white-and-gray solitude, his cloak flapped in the keening wind, and only the angry clenching of his teeth kept them from chattering. And with every step the light was dimmer. He thought at first it was because of the trees over the path until he passed a helion stanchion and saw that the light wasn't on. Before he reached the center of the park, he determined that three-quarters of the helions were dark. More good management.

He walked on in numb anger, wondering what other forms of good management Kelmet was indulging in to his own profit. He had hoped to keep this foray secret from his father, but he must be told; he must know how his trusted steward repaid his faith.

Alexand was near the hub of the park now, an open expanse of white sparkling in the light of a single helion mounted above a frozen pond that should have sported a tumbling fountain. The wind had a longer sweep here, and he pulled his hood around his face, his pace quickening. But when he reached the pond, he stopped short.

Something was lying in the snow near the path. Small and dark. He might have overlooked it if the light hadn't caught in a brief reflection in its eye.

He stood paralyzed not by cold, but by horror that was irrational in view of the size of the creature. Not as big as a cat. It was some time before he realized it wasn't even alive. Frozen; the snow was slowly burying it in white.

Alexand had never seen a rat, but he recognized this beast

and understood his horror at it. A product and carrier of filth and disease, its presence here, so close to where people ate and slept, in this park meant for their pleasure, was incomprehensible.

His stomach cramped with nausea; he began running, past the frozen pond, across the white waste beyond. It was only when he reached the trees that pain finally stopped him. He leaned against a black trunk, panting, every breath tangible in a puff of vapor, until finally he had the pain and himself under control.

The chapel. He must find the Elder Shepherd.

He'd come here for answers and no doubt he'd already found some of them, but he wanted Quin Selm's answers.

The chapel would accommodate five hundred people, but there were no more than thirty here now, scattered among the pews, kneeling with arms crossed, hands resting on opposite shoulders in the attitude of prayer peculiar to the Bonds. Alexand paused inside the door, his shivering muscles relaxing in the welcome warmth that made his hands and face tingle with the rush of blood.

The only light was that of candles, a soft, amber light that didn't reach the curved vault of the ceiling. Along the side walls between narrow, arched windows in deep niches, were small altars, each banked with votive candles and surmounted by a crudely painted ikon of a saint. The main altar was set into an arched recess six meters in height and consisted of a raised dais with a long, high table against the wall; on the table was a row of tall tapers arranged in three groups of three. Enclosed in the arch above the altar, painted in the same primitive style as the saints on the side walls, was the image of Yesu Kristus, Avatar of the All-God, the Holy Mezion.

Alexand stared transfixed at it. The Orthodox Church of the Fesh and Elite never employed visual images so realistic, instead relegating the Mezion to an abstract plane. There was power in this grim, unblinking figure, drawn within a radiant *mandorla*, zigzags of drapery folds delineating the form, large, black-outlined eyes staring out of an implacable face, both hands raised in blessing. This immutable image was paradoxically comforting; stern, demanding, omniscient, but still, and above all, just. This was, Alexand thought, the Mezion that Bishop Colona would have seen in his desert visions seven centuries ago.

A Bond wearing the gold-colored skullcap of a chapel acolyte was finishing the lighting of the altar candles. Alexand walked down the center aisle, treading lightly in the intimidating quiet. When he reached the altar dais, the acolyte turned, then bowed, eyeing him a little warily.

"Sirra? May I be of service?"

Alexand kept his voice low, as the acolyte had. "Where will I find the Elder Shepherd?"

He hesitated only briefly. "Father Hezaki is in his visitation room, sirra. This way."

He bowed to the image of the Mezion, then led Alexand to a door opening to the right of the altar. His knock was answered by an unquestioning invitation to enter, and the door slid open to reveal a small, candle-smoked room. One wall was solid with shelves of jars and bottles filled with leaves, seeds, roots, and powders. The Shepherd was, apparently, like so many of his fellows, a practitioner of herbal medicine. On the far wall under a painted ikon was a miniature altar decked with candles, and in the center of the room, a narrow table empty except for a battered relic of a tea brew. In front of the table were two straight-backed chairs, and behind it another.

That chair was occupied.

The Elder Shepherd Hezaki, tall, lean to the verge of emaciation, attired in a long black-and-scarlet robe and white skullcap; a shock of white hair and a long white beard; dark eyes looking out of age-creased sockets with penetrating directness.

"Father, there's someone to see you," the acolyte said.

Hezaki's eyes shifted to Alexand, still standing outside the door in the shadows.

"Show him in, Micah." Then, when the acolyte stepped aside for Alexand to pass, Hezaki, realizing his visitor wasn't Bond, rose and bowed respectfully.

The Shepherd asked, "Sirra, may I be of service?"

"I'd like to speak with you privately, Hezaki."

"Of course. Micah . . ." A single glance was sufficient. The acolyte bowed, to Alexand first, then to Hezaki, and slipped out the door, closing it behind him.

Alexand said, "I hope Micah hasn't a tendency to curiosity."

The Shepherd smiled. "He wouldn't listen at the door, sirra, if that's what you mean. I'm Elder Shepherd to these people, and they hold me in some respect."

Alexand accepted that as an undeniable and understandable truth. He pushed back the hood of his cloak and reached under the collar for the thin, metallic ring circling his neck. When the face-screen went off, he asked, "Hezaki, do you know me?"

He didn't—not at first. Then his eyes narrowed, and what Alexand thought to be fear, he recognized after a moment as concern. There was no hint of surprise or shock. He folded his hands and bowed from the waist.

"You are Ser Alexand, the Lord Woolf's first born."

Alexand went to one of the chairs in front of the table and sank into it. He kept his cloak fastened, the sling hidden.

"Be seated, Hezaki." He waited until the Shepherd resumed his chair. "I've come here to ask your help. Do you know a Bond named Quin Selm?"

"Yes, I know Quin."

"Do you know where he might be now?"

"Well, perhaps . . ." He paused. "Ser, may I ask what you want of Quin?"

"I want to talk to him alone, to ask him some questions. I could have had him brought to me rather than attempt to come to him, but that would mean involving other people, and this is a personal matter."

The Shepherd was bewildered at that. "A personal matter between you and—and *Quin*, Ser?"

Alexand gave him a purposely direct scrutiny. "You're an inquisitive man, Hezaki."

He stiffened slightly at that pointed reminder, but still met Alexand's gaze resolutely.

"Perhaps, Ser, but Quin is one of my flock."

"He'll come to no harm through me unless it's in the form of just punishment. You have my word."

Hezaki nodded, apparently satisfied. "I think Quin is in the chapel now, Ser. At least, I saw him there a few minutes ago, and that surprised me. He must've come straight from his work shift without stopping for his supper, and Quin isn't a man to miss a meal. Excuse me a moment." He went to the door and called softly into the chapel, "Micah, is Quin Selm still here?"

A short pause, then, "Yes, Father, there he is in the corner at the altar of Saint Kahma."

"Tell him I want to talk to him."

Alexand wondered what significance Saint Kahma had for a man who had almost committed murder, a man who gave up his evening meal to come to this chapel.

The Shepherd returned to his chair and closed his eyes for a few seconds, his lips moving silently. He found solace in his prayer and new resolve; that was evident in his face when he looked up at Alexand.

"Ser, may I ask a boon of you?"

"You may ask, certainly."

"You said you want to talk to Quin alone, but perhaps you'd . . . let me stay. I swear by the Holy Word nothing I hear will go further."

Alexand hesitated. He hadn't wanted a witness, yet he found the idea attractive. Selm might feel more free to talk in the Shepherd's presence. He might also feel *less* free to make another attempt on Ser Alexand's life.

"Yes, Hezaki, I'd be grateful if you'd stay." He paused, then, "Tell me, what kind of man is Quin Selm?"

Hezaki considered the question, then shrugged. "Why, Ser, he's a good man. His word is always proof, and it's said he's a hard worker and kind to his wife and children. Yes, Micah?" That was in response to a knock on the door; then, as the door opened, "Ah, Quin—come in, please. Thank you. Micah."

Alexand switched on his face-screen, turning as the door closed behind the acolyte, and at first he thought Micah had made a mistake; this was the wrong man. But there was no mistake. This face Alexand would never forget, but now, although his presence put some anxiety in it, neither hatred nor fear altered its contours.

Alexand indicated the vacant chair. "Sit down, Selm."

The Bond glanced uncertainly at Hezaki, then went to the chair and sat gingerly at the edge.

"It isn't Hezaki who wishes to speak to you." Alexand switched off his face-screen. "He called you at my command."

Selm went white, then slid out of the chair to his knees,

rough hands raised in supplication.

"Oh—oh, Ser...*please!* Mercy! Before the God, I never meant—I didn't—"

"Quin, get off your knees!"

Selm flinched at his sharp tone, then obediently pulled himself up and backed into his chair, nearly knocking it over in the process, and Alexand sighed. It was hard to remember that this frightened man—a good man, if Hezaki judged him well—had only hours ago been so clearly intent on his murder.

"Quin, I've come here for some answers. If I'm satisfied, I promise you, no harm will come to you, but I must understand what happened today. I must know, Quin—why did you try to kill me?"

He heard Hezaki's quick intake of breath at that. Selm only moaned wretchedly, hands locked together, mouth working, but emitting no sounds recognizable as words.

Alexand leaned forward, carefully restraining any impatience in his voice as he said, "Please, Quin, I have very little time. Don't you understand? If someone you'd never even seen before tried to kill *you*, wouldn't you want to know why?"

Still no coherent response. Alexand tried again. "I backed you up this afternoon when you said it was an accident. Did you think I was so befuddled I actually believed that? I know you intended to kill me, but I let your lie stand. I let you live."

Rather than taking hope from that, Selm loosed a thin, despairing wail, his head sagged forward exactly as it had this afternoon under Phillip Woolf's cold scrutiny, and it came to Alexand that he had the same power over this man.

But he didn't want that; there were no answers in that.

"Quin, I let you live because at the last second you turned the loader. If you hadn't, I'd be dead. I couldn't believe you were an entirely evil man in the face of that, so I let your lie stand, and I came here to find out what kind of man you are, what made you decide to kill me in the first place, and why you didn't after all."

He waited in hope of an answer, but Selm only stared at the floor, whimpering like a wounded animal, and Alexand recognized defeat. So many barriers overcome to get this close to the truth, but this, the barrier of fear, baffled him.

"Ser Alexand, perhaps if I could...well, it might be easier for him to answer your questions, if...if *I* asked them."

Alexand looked at the Shepherd and nodded. "I hope so. Go ahead, Hezaki. Please."

Hezaki leaned toward Selm, brows drawn. "If you've done wrong, you must answer the Ser's questions for your *soul's* sake. Now, tell me, Quin—for your soul—what happened this afternoon?"

For what seemed a long time, Selm gazed at Hezaki with a childlike mixture of faith and guilty reluctance, then he burst out, "Oh, Father, I *did* do wrong! The holy saints forgive me, I did *wrong!* It—it come over me like a dark spirit. It was . . . maybe it *was* a . . . dark spirit."

"Perhaps it was," Hezaki assured him. "Go on. Tell me what happened."

Selm kept his eyes fixed on Hezaki, avoiding Alexand except for one flashing, fearful glance.

"I was driving a load to the blue shelves. Nobody was around, except . . . well, then I seen the Ser there all alone looking down at the assembly lines. He—he was standing in the aisle I had to go down to get to the blue shelves."

"Did you recognize him?"

"Not . . . right at first. I . . ." He hesitated, his features inexplicably wrenched. "Ah, Father, I thought it was Jeron! I thought it was a Beyond Soul, standing all alone, waiting for me. I thought it was *Jeron.* . . ." He began to weep, coughing sobs that racked his body.

Alexand stared at him, bewildered, and in some indefinable sense frightened. He turned to the Shepherd.

"Who is Jeron?"

Hezaki's lined face was drawn, reflecting Selm's agony.

"Jeron was Quin's younger brother, Ser. He . . . died."

Selm was trying to get himself under control, but Alexand didn't press him. He was thinking of Rich, and he understood that agony now; he recognized it.

"When did Jeron die, Hezaki?"

"It was a week ago today, Ser."

Alexand closed his eyes. Only a week. A short span of days.

After a moment, he asked, "Did Jeron resemble me?"

"Why, yes, in some ways. He was older, but dark like you, and a handsome boy."

Selm was wiping his eyes with his big hands, the sobbing

stopped now. "Pardon, Ser, I—I never used to cry like . . . like a little childer."

"Grief is nothing to be ashamed of, Quin. I'm sorry about your brother."

The Bond gazed at him in unabashed amazement, and Alexand hesitated. Selm had at least reached the point where he was capable of addressing him directly; he was reluctant to jeopardize that tenuous rapport, but there was one question that more than any other must be answered now. He wasn't sure why; only a sensed conviction that it was a key.

"I don't want to open old wounds, Quin, but I must know. How did your brother die?"

Briefly, there was a hint of that brute hatred in the man's eyes again. Then he turned away abruptly.

"I—I can't tell you, Ser."

"You . . . *can't* tell me?"

"I can't! *Please*, Ser, I can't! He'd kill me, too, if—" He stopped, horrified at his own words, his eyes, filled with dread, moving slowly to Alexand's face.

"*Who* would kill you?"

He turned away again. "No! I can't—"

"Who, Quin?" He put an authoritative edge in that.

"I . . . the—the workgang . . . foreman. . . ."

Alexand was jarred again with rage. Another trusted steward. But he masked the anger, keeping his tone level. "Did this foreman kill your brother?"

The only answer was a choked groan. Selm's hands curled into fists on his knees; he stared blindly at the floor, candlelight caught in the beaded sweat on his forehead, and Alexand realized he was again met with the barrier of fear.

But he had an ally against it now. Hezaki needed only a look and a nod; he resumed his gentle interrogation.

"Tell me, Quin; tell your Shepherd. How did Jeron die?"

At first Selm seemed physically incapable of answering that, even for Hezaki, and when at length he did speak, it was as if he were in a drugged trance.

"The . . . foreman gets black spells. Sometimes he—the dark spirits come over him, and he lets out with the charged lash. That day, Jeron . . . he was *sick*. He never should've made his shift that day, but he—he was saving up his free days. Remember, Father? He was . . . going to get married."

He paused to control another threatened onslaught of weeping, and Alexand wouldn't have interrupted the narrative, except that part of it didn't seem to make sense.

"Quin, if he was sick...time taken out for illness isn't counted against a Bond's free days."

Selm glanced up at him and immediately dissolved into confusion. Alexand turned to Hezaki.

"Why didn't Jeron get a sick pass from the infirmary?"

But Hezaki seemed as confused as Selm. "I—I don't think they give...anything like that."

Alexand felt the anger surfacing again; more good management, no doubt.

"Did Jeron go to the infirmary, Quin, when he realized he was ill?"

Selm nodded, his gaze again fixed on the floor. "Yes, Ser. He come to Father Hezaki first, and he said he'd best go to the 'firmary. He saw Ferra Sang. She's always kindly. But she said there wasn't nothing she could do. She told him to stay off his shift, but he was...saving up his...free days."

"What was wrong with him? Do you know?"

"I—I think it was . . . the lung fever."

"What's that?"

Again, Selm was reduced to confusion. Hezaki said, "Ser, I think you'd call it . . . new . . . newman? I'm sorry, I'm not sure of the word."

"Pneumonia?" Even as he said it, he expected Hezaki to shake his head. That couldn't be it.

"Yes, Ser, that's what I've heard it called."

"But that's impossible!"

Hezaki seemed embarrassed, hands fluttering in a palms-up gesture. "I . . . probably didn't . . . hear it right, Ser."

"No—no, that's not what I meant. Forgive me." Alexand took a deep breath; his shoulder was aching miserably. "You heard very clearly, Hezaki."

Pneumonia. An anachronism; a disease so easily controlled, it had nearly ceased to exist except in association with acute degenerative conditions.

Why was there nothing the kindly Ferra Sang could do for Jeron Selm when he went to the infirmary? Was it because the medicine to treat his illness wasn't available? Because the money allotted to the purchase of medical supplies had been diverted to someone's pocket?

Selm had again sunk into that trance-like state, and Alexand felt an overwhelming reluctance at the necessity of forcing him to continue his bitter narrative.

"Hezaki, I must have the whole story of Jeron's death."

The Shepherd nodded and turned to Selm. "Quin? You were telling me about the day Jeron died. You said he took his work shift even though he was sick. What happened then?"

Selm managed, finally, to respond, the words coming in painful spates.

"We was on the same—the same workgang, Jeron and me. It was . . . before the noon stop. He was driving a full loader to the red shelves. There's a bad turn before . . . anyway, he—he run into a shelf, and the loader turned over and everything come crashing down, and . . . and then the . . . foreman, he—the black spell come over him, and he started in on Jeron with his lash, and then with—with his fists. Oh, 'Zion, he wouldn't *stop!* He kept on hitting him and hitting him, and—and finally Jeron went down. The loader—he hit his head on . . . he hit his head . . ." Selm doubled over, burying his face in his hands, his body shuddering with renewed sobs.

Alexand left him to his grief, too numbed, too filled with impotent rage to ask or hear more. When at length he looked at Hezaki, he found him watching him intently. Something in his eyes made Alexand uncomfortable. He didn't understand it.

"Hezaki, is this true, what he says of Jeron's death?"

"I can only say that I heard the same story from others of my flock who were there."

"There were witnesses, then?"

"Only Bonds, Ser."

There wasn't a hint of bitterness in his tone, and Alexand wanted to weep. There *should* have been.

"If you can, question him further about this afternoon."

"I'll try, Ser. Quin?" It was some time before Selm was capable of responding. Hezaki rose and went to him, resting his hands on his shoulders. "Quin, you said that today when you saw the Ser, you thought it was a Beyond Soul, that it was Jeron."

Selm nodded, swollen eyes downcast. "Yes, Father, I . . . thought it was . . . Jeron."

"What did you do then?"

"I . . . seen it *wasn't* Jeron. It was . . . the Ser." He didn't even glance at Alexand, turning his look of abject appeal on Hezaki. "All at once, I knew who he was, and there he was— and . . . and Jeron was dead, and . . . the black spell come over me. I felt the breath of the spirits of Nether Dark, and— oh, Father, the Mezion have mercy on my soul, I—I lifted my hand against—to . . . to . . ." He covered his face again, rocking back and forth.

Hezaki said gently, "The Holy Mezion tests his faithful to know the worth of their souls. Perhaps you had your Testing today." There was a chant-like cadence in that, and Selm seemed to take comfort from it; his hands fell away from his face, although his gaze remained fixed on the floor.

"Quin, Ser Alexand said that at the last moment you turned the loader. Is that true?"

"I—I guess . . . yes. The Ser spoke to me. He shouted . . . something. Oh, Father, I never wanted to kill him. I never wanted to . . . to kill *anybody*. I only . . . I don't know what I wanted. I don't know . . . I don't know. . . ." The words died with a whimpering sigh.

The Shepherd looked at Alexand questioningly, and he nodded.

"That's enough, Hezaki. Thank you." For a time the small room was a place of silence encompassed in the Bond's desolation. "Quin?"

Selm finally managed to meet his gaze, but only briefly. "Yes, Ser?"

"Are many of the foremen prone to 'black spells'?"

"Not . . . like this one."

"What is his name?"

"Oh, Ser! If he knew I told—"

"He won't know, and I can find out, but it would be better for you if I didn't have to go through House channels."

Hezaki returned to his chair and sank into it. "Quin, you'd best tell him. He won't betray you."

That assuaged Selm's doubts. He swallowed hard, frowning down at his clasped hands.

"He's called . . . Fer Naylor, Ser. I—I don't know his forename."

"The surname is enough. Now, I want you to take a vow."

Selm stared at him. "A vow, Ser?"

"A vow of silence. I want your word that you'll never speak of what happened today, nor our meeting tonight, to anyone at any time. Will you swear to that?"

Selm nodded solemnly, then turned to Hezaki in mute appeal, and after a moment, Alexand understood why.

Hezaki shaped the vow into words for him.

"Quin, swear this on the Holy Words and on the holy saints, who never sleep, and on your immortal soul. You will never speak of these things as long as you live to another soul living or dead on pain of eternal damnation."

Selm repeated the oath after him, word for word, and the last phrase put a cast of dread in his eyes that was still there when Alexand said, "Thank you, Quin. That's all I ask. You may go now." Then, at the Bond's incredulous stare, "Yes, I know you tried to kill me, but I can understand grief. The important thing is that you *didn't* kill me. I only hope such a . . . black spell never overcomes you again."

"Oh, Ser, I . . . may the Mezion smile on you in this world and the Beyond." He rose and with a hasty bow stumbled to the door. But there he paused and said softly, "Ser, you are of the Blessed."

Before Alexand could even wonder at that term, he was gone, the door snapped shut.

And now the toll of pain and exhaustion came home to him. He pulled himself to his feet, resting his hand on the table until the dizziness passed. At least he had his answers.

"Ser, are you well?"

Alexand only nodded absently to that. "I must hurry, Hezaki, and I haven't the time—even if I had the words—to thank you adequately for your help and for all I've learned from you. You're a man of true wisdom."

Hezaki bowed. "Ser, you do me honor." Then he added, , "Perhaps you'll do me another honor—or grant me another boon. Let me go with you to the compound gate."

Alexand smiled. "I'd be grateful for your company." And his protection. That was the real reason for this "boon," but he didn't force Hezaki to put that into words.

10.

Phillip Woolf stared out at the snow-shrouded lights, feeling in the silence of this incomprehensibly empty room the chill grip of fear. In his right hand he held the golden disk of his pocketcom, open, but for the moment forgotten.

He turned, his eyes moving to the empty bed. He should have known. Something rang false about that accident. He should never have left Alexand alone.

The soft buzz of the 'com brought his head around. "Yes, Ensing?"

The image framed in the 'com was helmeted, a captain's chevron on the scarlet cloak.

"My lord, we've found Ser Alexand."

Woolf's muscles sagged with relief, then tensed again in anger—at Alexand, for making his father suffer like a damned soul this last half hour.

He asked levelly, "Where is he?"

"He just left the plaza chapel in Compound A, my lord."

"Is he alone?"

"He's with the Shepherd. They're on one of the radials headed for the north gate. He seems to be talking with the old man. I can't see his face; he's got his 'screen on."

Woolf nodded. "Keep your men out of sight, but someone must be close to Alexand until he's out of the compound."

"Yes, my lord. Should we hold the Shepherd?"

"Hold him? Why?"

"Well, I just thought . . ."

"Captain, didn't it occur to you that he might be with my son at his behest? Unless the Shepherd makes a clearly threatening move against Alexand, he's to be left alone. 'Com me when Alexand leaves the compound." He snapped his 'com shut impatiently. His hands were shaking, but that didn't surprise him.

One son dying, and now for Alexand to take such risks—
And there would be no more sons.

Perhaps Elise was right in keeping it secret even from Al-

exand. Woolf closed his eyes. It had been such a heartbreaking
blow to her. Even now he knew it was sometimes hard for her
to believe he loved her too much for it to matter.

Thank the God she wasn't here now.

The last report had been from a guard on the estate landing
roof. Woolf sat in a chair near the empty bed, containing the
anxiety and irrational anger that still threatened to erupt within
him. It seemed an interminable length of time before he finally
heard the whisper of the door opening.

He came to his feet, but for a moment stood silent, staring
across the room at his son, who looked back at him with a
level gaze in which there was no hint of guilt or surprise; only
a shadow of regret.

Woolf's anger dissolved. He crossed the room, stopping
a pace from Alexand. The anger was gone, he realized, because
he was suddenly aware that his son had crossed the line between
childhood and adulthood tonight. The decision to embark on
this solitary and dangerous sojourn was an adult decision. The
aftermath of fear was in his face; he had recognized the risks
and found them worth taking.

"Alex . . ." Woolf reached out to him, drawing him into his
arms as if with that embrace he could hold on to that vanishing
childhood.

"Father, I didn't want to worry you. Believe me, I didn't
want—"

"I know, Alex, I know." He felt the chill of his cloak; he
was shivering, swaying on his feet, and Woolf's concern
shifted to the immediate problems of the broken bone, the
sedative not taken, the exposure to cold.

"Come, Alex. First, I'm getting you into bed, then I'm
going to call Dr. Dall. Holy God, you're half frozen."

"I—I know. That's . . . one of the things . . . I must talk
to you about."

Woolf turned the thermblanket to high, too distracted to
make sense of that, concerned only with his son's pallor, and
the tension around his mouth that was an index of pain. But
when Woolf reached for the intercom, Alexand stopped him.

"No. Not yet." He took a shaky breath and added, "Give
me a few minutes first. Then you can call Dr. Dall."

Woolf didn't argue further, but occupied himself with getting Alexand undressed and under the thermblanket. When this was done, he sat down on the bed beside Alexand. It was some time before the chill left him.

Finally, Woolf said, "Well, Alex, I hope your venture was successful, whatever its purpose."

There was a shadow of grim memory in his eyes. "Yes, it was successful, but I'd hoped you wouldn't have to be . . . concerned by it."

Woolf laughed. "So you thought you'd take a little stroll in Compound A, and by the time I returned, you'd be back in bed, sound asleep, and I'd never be the wiser. Well, you underestimated Dr. Dall's conscientiousness. She came in to check on you about an hour after I left."

"It doesn't matter. I'd have had to tell you anyway. I . . . made an inadvertent tour of inspection tonight, and you must know about some of the things I saw and learned."

Woolf hesitated, on the verge of suggesting that those things might wait until morning, but said instead, "All right, Alex. Tell me about them."

"First, I gave my word that no harm would come to the people I talked to."

"Then I'll back it up, unless you were entirely outside the bounds of reason."

Alexand shook his head, frowning. "I can't betray these people, but I will if you won't honor my word. And I'll betray them in another sense if I can't tell you what happened—what *is* happening out there."

Again, Woolf didn't argue. "Very well. I'll honor your word even if you *were* outside the bounds of reason. But you must make me a promise in exchange—that you'll never again break the rule and go into a Bond area alone."

"I can't promise I'll *never* go into a Bond area alone."

"Until you reach Age of Rights," Woolf amended with a short laugh. "By then you should know better, anyway."

"All right. I . . . can promise that."

"Good. Now, tell me about your inspection tour."

He nodded, looking past Woolf to the windowall, eyes as cold as that night vista.

"Some of it's simply subjective impressions. The feeling that the Bonds were too quiet; too subdued. And the guards too arrogant. Some of it's secondhand information." He turned his head to look at Woolf. "For instance, in the Montril compounds it's customary to count workdays lost to illness against a Bond's free days."

Woolf raised an eyebrow. "That's certainly not House policy. You said this was secondhand information?"

"Yes, but I trust my source. The Elder Shepherd Hezaki. A remarkable man. I doubt he's capable of falsehood."

"That *would* make him remarkable."

Alexand studied his father, then turned away with a nod.

"You'd have to spend some time with him to understand or believe that. I also learned that the compound infirmary is apparently so short of medical supplies that it couldn't—or wouldn't—treat a Bond suffering from pneumonia."

"Pneumonia? That's impossible."

Alexand laughed caustically. "My words exactly. Impossible both that no help was available to the man, and that he should be suffering from pneumonia. I wouldn't believe it either, except for certain facts I observed—personally—that make pneumonia reasonable in Compound A." He paused, looking out past the windowall. "Father, the atmobubbles weren't on in Compound A, nor I'm sure in any of the compounds. I doubt that A would be singled out for any purpose."

Woolf stared at him, groping for an explanation. "A malfunction. Something must have gone wrong..."

"How long would it take to repair a malfunction? Long enough for snow to accumulate to a depth of a meter? And in the park the fountain was off and the pond frozen. That's more than a malfunction, and so was the fact that only a quarter of the helions were on in the park."

Woolf felt the pounding of his pulse in his temples, the chill tension of anger that drove him to his feet and to the windowall. The snow was a silvery mist beyond the estate's 'bubbles, and it had never occurred to him that the miniature cities beyond weren't shelled with similar invisible protective barriers.

This morning he'd checked the general accounts for the Montril plant, and now one figure was starkly clear in his memory: 1,680,000 'cords; the cost of maintaining the 'bubble systems for 210 days last year.

It could only be Kelmet.

"Damn him! *Damn* him!"

He turned and found Alexand watching him and realized he had already reached the same conclusion about the perpetrator of this insupportable fraud. Woolf took a deep breath; it came out in a weary sigh.

"Elise was right, Alex. She never trusted Kelmet simply because she didn't like him. I've never liked him, either, but I didn't accept that as reason enough not to trust him."

Alexand nodded. "It isn't enough; not in itself."

"I wonder. But corruption can't be tolerated on any level, and the higher the level, the more dangerous it is."

"Father, there's more going on in the compounds, but uncovering all of it will mean a thorough investigation."

"Yes. What else did *you* uncover?"

"Only one other piece of . . . concrete evidence." His mouth tensed. "I . . . I saw a rat in the compound."

"A rat!" Woolf stared at him and found himself again objecting, "That's impossible!"

"No, it's only intolerable, and there's no chance I'm in error. The creature was dead. I had a very good look at it at close range. I don't know a great deal about rats, but I do know that if there's one, there are many. And considering the other evidence of negligence, deprivation, and cruelty, this isn't surprising."

The word "cruelty" stopped Woolf for a moment; it seemed too intensely subjective. He returned to the bed and sat down.

"Well, I'll have to change my schedule for tomorrow," he said briskly. "The first thing on my agenda will be a personal inspection of Compound A."

Alexand's eyes flashed up to his, reflecting both hope and gratitude, but that quickly turned to calculating doubt.

"You'll probably find everything in good order there if Kelmet happens to overhear this conversation."

Woolf laughed and reached for his hand. "I've never trusted Kelmet enough not to expect him to slip monitors into my private rooms. However, I *do* trust Master Dansig; he checked both our suites a few minutes before we arrived this morning." As he spoke, he turned Alexand's palm up and with his index finger drew the letter C.

Alexand's quick smile said he understood that silent message and knew Woolf intended to inspect compound C, not A.

"Thank you, Father." He lay silent for a moment, eyes

narrowed. "I was thinking, if this kind of thing can happen here, in a DeKoven Woolf compound, what must it be like in compounds where indifference and neglect are House policy? Like Selasid or Cameroodo compounds, or Hamid and Fallor, Tesmier, Orongo—the list is endless."

"Well, not quite endless, but I suppose it must include a majority of the Houses in the Court of Lords. Mathis and Trevor Robek and I are rewriting our resolution for a standard of Bond treatment, you know, but I haven't much hope for it."

"But don't the Directors realize—" Alexand subsided with a sigh. "No. If they did, the resolution wouldn't be necessary. Well, I admire your tenacity, you and Trevor and Grandser. I'm... proud of you."

Woolf smiled. "At least you know my intentions are good. Now, perhaps you should tell me why you went into that compound. It began this afternoon, didn't it? With that so-called accident."

Alexand nodded, letting his head fall back into the pillow. "That Bond *did* try to kill me, but it was so badly thought out, it couldn't have been premeditated, and the important thing was that he *didn't* kill me. He was ready to crush me with that loader, but at the last moment he changed his mind. I saw his face, and he was suddenly... horrified, and he turned the loader. The turn was so fast it threw the load, and that's the only reason I was injured."

"But, Alex, whether he changed his mind or not—"

"I know. For perhaps ten seconds he *was* intent on killing me. Should a man die for a few seconds? If his case came before a court, the plea would be lapse of sanity."

"But his case won't come before a court, and you—"

"No, of course it won't. He's a Bond. But isn't he also a citizen of the Concord? Why should Bonds be excluded from the Concord judicial system?"

Woolf frowned slightly. "It's up to the Houses to deal with Bond discipline, punishment, or grievances. That's why we have Litigation Boards in every compound."

"But not every House has them, and what good are they to a Bond with a grievance if it happens to be against his Fesh overseers? The boards are manned by Fesh."

"Who would you *have* man them? Bonds?"

Alexand leaned forward intently. "No, that's not—a *Con-*

cord tribunal, not a House board. We must give them some
meaningful legal recourse for their grievances; some recourse
other than . . ." He stopped and, as if suddenly aware of pain,
sank back into the pillow, breath catching. Finally, he said,
"I'm sorry, Father, I seem to have lost track of my story. That
Bond, Quin Selm—that's why I went to Compound A tonight.
I wanted to know the reason for that lapse of sanity. I had to
talk to him on his own ground or I'd get nothing from him
except more hysterical vows in the name of his saints that it
was an accident. Even then I doubt I'd have had any answers
if it weren't for Hezaki. Quin would talk to him, even in my
presence, but not to me. He was . . . afraid of me."

"Under the circumstances, he should've been. So the Shepherd acted as your liaison?"

"He asked that *boon* of me. He also asked the boon of
accompanying me to the compound gate, and I'm sure I could
have walked through a crowd of rioting Bonds without a face-
screen and been perfectly safe with Hezaki at my side. He has
power over them we don't; power over their souls."

"All the Shepherds do, and that worries me sometimes."
Woolf put that in as a reminder; Alexand spoke of that power
with such naïveté. "Alex, we must always be concerned when
power over the behavior of so many falls into the hands of so
few. Now, what did you find out about Selm?"

Alexand hesitated, for a moment distracted, then, "I found
out why he tried to kill me. Quin had a younger brother, Jeron.
They were on the same workgang. One day Jeron was ill—
yes, he was the one who was told nothing could be done for
him at the infirmary—but he decided to work his shift anyway.
He didn't want to lose a free day because he was saving them
for . . . he was going to be married soon. He probably wasn't
functioning too well, or perhaps it was only carelessness; I
don't know. Anyway, he ran a full loader into a storage shelf
and turned the loader over. I assume the damage was consid-
erable, but should a man die for that?"

"What do you mean?"

Alexand's tone turned remote and cool. "It seems the gang
foreman—a man named Naylor—occasionally suffers what
Quin calls 'black spells.' In other words, he gets heavy-handed
with the charged lash and his fists."

"Fists? That isn't allowed."

"You mean you don't condone it, nor use of the lash except as a threat. At any rate, when Fer Naylor saw the results of Jeron's collision, he was overcome by one of his black spells and proceeded to beat Jeron both with the lash and his fists. From Quin's account, it . . . went on for some time. Until Jeron fell against the loader and hit his head. Apparently that was the immediate cause of death."

"Of death!" Woolf rose abruptly and began pacing, feeling caged with anger. Alexand was right; because he didn't condone something didn't mean it didn't happen. But a man couldn't be everywhere at once. It was Kelmet's responsibility to maintain discipline among his Fesh, but what could one expect of a man who would profit by depriving the Bonds entrusted to him of warmth, medication, or basic sanitation?

Then he frowned. Alexand was so thoroughly convinced about all this, it was hard to maintain any objectivity.

"Alex, I'll have to check this story. It may simply be a fabrication to excuse that Bond's behavior today."

He turned when there was no immediate response. Alexand seemed to be resting, his eyes half-closed, and Woolf felt an unexpected sense of vulnerability in him. Still, there was a calm containment in his voice when he spoke, and a hint of acid irony.

"How will you check the story? The records will undoubtedly show that Jeron Selm, Bond, died in an accident when his loader overturned. Anyway, it would never occur to Quin that his behavior today could be excused by *any* fabrication, and Hezaki said he heard the same story from other Bonds who witnessed Jeron's death."

"That doesn't necessarily make it true."

"The Bonds wouldn't lie to their Shepherd, and Hezaki wouldn't lie to me."

"You can't be sure of that."

"*Yes, I can be sure.*"

His left hand closed into a fist, and Woolf was at a loss to understand the taut charge in those words. He returned to the bed and took Alexand's fisted hand in his; it was a moment before it relaxed.

"All right, Alex. Assuming the story is true, then, how does it justify Selm's attempt to kill you?"

"It doesn't justify it; it only explains it. Quin saw his brother brutally beaten, watched him die, too frightened to lift a hand for him, and that happened only a week ago. A *week*. How would we feel if Rich . . . how *will* we feel . . ."

"Alex . . . please." Woolf couldn't tolerate that; not now.

Alexand nodded. "I'm sorry, but understanding Quin's grief is the key to understanding his behavior. At least, his mental state. Today he was driving along the aisles where he and his brother worked together, where Jeron died."

"And decided to avenge his brother's death on you?"

"No, Father. At least, not consciously. At first he thought I was Jeron."

"You were . . . but—"

"I know, Jeron is dead, but for Quin that doesn't preclude the possibility of seeing him. A Beyond Soul, standing there waiting for him. Then he recognized me and somewhere in his mind he made the connection between that foreman, who wears the crest of DeKoven Woolf, and me, the First Lord's first born. That's when those few seconds of insanity occurred. He didn't think; he only reacted—to his grief and bitterness. But the important thing is that he stopped himself, and that's why I don't think he deserves to die. He isn't a violent man. He was only acting under emotional stresses beyond his control, and that could happen to anyone."

Woolf looked down at his son's hand and sighed. "Alex, I . . . I suppose it *was* remarkable that the man could control his irrational impulses under those circumstances, but you must understand that I find it difficult to be forgiving when I think how close he came to killing you."

Alexand smiled fleetingly. "Yes, I guess it's easier for me, since it was my life. I wouldn't be so forgiving if I thought there was a chance he might put his hand to murder again, or if my forgiveness might inspire others to try it. But no one saw what happened today, and Quin took a vow of silence witnessed by his Elder Shepherd. I doubt even the SSB could get it out of him now. He believes he's possessed of an immortal soul and liable to eternal damnation."

Woolf nodded absently. "Well, I'm glad you found the answers you sought, and especially glad you survived the quest."

Alexand's eyes were heavy with his body's need for sleep, and now he seemed nearer to surrendering to it.

"I didn't want to worry you, but I had to make the quest. And Quin answered some larger questions. I'm sure his case isn't unique."

"The circumstances of his attack on you were certainly unique, and I should hope there aren't too many more Quin Selms running about loose."

Woolf felt a tension in Alexand's hand, and although his eyes were still half-closed, there was no longer any hint of somnolence in them.

"But there *are* others. That's the point; that's the only meaningful result of my quest. These compounds are nurturing grounds for Quin Selms, and it's a continuing miracle we've had so few uprisings."

"*These* compounds are exceptions in the House, and you know how they became 'nurturing grounds.'"

"Yes, I know, and I know most Woolf compounds are notable for their humanity, but the basic problems are present in our compounds just as surely as they are in Selasid or Cameroodo compounds." He was leaning forward again, and Woolf found the hectic light in his eyes intimidating.

"Alex, our House policy is to treat our Bonds fairly, but I can't prevent or even be aware of every injustice suffered by any of the four million Bonds allieged to the House, and certainly I can't do anything about the Bonds in other Houses. Oh, Alex . . ." He was dimly aware that Alexand had withdrawn his hand. "The Bond problem is simply a fact of life, and nothing can be done about it."

For a long time Alexand didn't move, didn't even seem to breathe or blink, and there was something so achingly hopeless in his eyes that Woolf wanted to turn away.

"No . . . that's not . . ." He shook his head, his gaze fixed on Woolf's face. "It's a fact that something *must* be done about. A tree must bend . . ."

"*Alex!*" He sagged into his father's arms, breath hissing between his teeth. Woolf eased him back, frightened at his pallor; his forehead was sheened with perspiration even while he shivered with a new chill.

Woolf reached for the intercom. He got an immediate response from Dr. Dall. She was on duty in the estate infirmary, but asked for only five minutes to reach the family wing. With a long sigh, Woolf switched off the intercom and studied his son. His eyes were closed now, but not in sleep; the new chill had quieted.

Finally, he said, "Alex, I'll do what I can about the facts you've brought to my attention."

Alexand opened his eyes and after a moment nodded. "I know you will, Father." A pause, then, "What about the foreman?"

Woolf frowned. "He'll be something of a problem. I can't call him to account for Jeron Selm's death on the testimony of a Bond." Then, before Alexand could protest, "You know it would never stand, and it would only rally the Foremans Guild to him, and I'd prefer to avoid another guild imbroglio. The Broadcasters Guild nearly shut down the PubliCom System last year."

"Calling Naylor to account for Jeron wouldn't help Quin, either. It would probably get him killed."

Woolf looked at his son sharply, but couldn't deny that possibility.

"Have you any thoughts on dealing with Naylor, Alex?"

"My first thought is to send Fer Naylor to the Concord, with our compliments, in the next tax conscript, but we can't wait three months to deal with him, so I guess there's only one thing to do: transfer him to another position where he has no personal contact with Bonds."

"Remove him from temptation, so to speak?" Woolf nodded with satisfaction. "I'll check his AQ file. Surely there's some other type of work he's qualified for. I'll take care of it tomorrow morning."

"Thank you, Father. What will you do about Kelmet?"

At that, Woolf rose and crossed again to the windowall, hands clasped tensely behind his back.

"I'll remind him that a VisLord can also be removed, in a manner of speaking, from temptation." He smiled coldly. "The Isidis plant. Bryn Woolf is a very astute man, you know; perhaps too astute to be wasted in the deserts of Mars. Of course, if I assign Bryn another estate, that would leave a vacancy to be filled."

Alexand gave a brief laugh. "Kelmet in Isidis? Father, he'd never survive it."

"Which will give him something to think about. I'll not tolerate his—" The door chime startled him. Dr. Dall. He said sharply, "Come in!"

She spared Woolf a nod for a bow and a short, "My lord," and went straight to her patient, and it was a measure of Alexand's physical state that he accepted her ministrations, including an enkephaline injection, without protest or even a single question.

At length she arranged the covers around his shoulders, then reminded him, "My 'com sequence is set on the intercom, Ser. Just touch the emergency call button, and I'll be here in a matter of minutes."

He only nodded, not even opening his eyes. She smiled at that, then turned down the light level and crossed to the windowall where Woolf stood waiting.

"He'll sleep now, my lord. Don't worry about him. I hope you sleep well, too."

"Yes, I'm . . . sure I will. Good night, doctor."

When she had gone, he went to the bed and sat down beside Alexand; he didn't wake. Strange, Woolf thought, in sleep the child was still so evident in his face.

A tree must bend . . .

What did he mean by that?

Still so young. So much to learn, and so many of those lessons would be painful. Growing up is always painful. Or perhaps it isn't growing up, but the necessary process of hardening. Perhaps they're one and the same. He laid his hand gently over his son's, his thoughts turning to the future. To Alexand's future.

Adrien Camine Eliseer.

Elise was undoubtedly right about the daughter of the Eliseer. *The only bride for Alexand. You know he won't be satisfied with the usual simpering Ladyling. He'll need someone like Adrien. . . . I diagnosed it as love on sight, Phillip, and I believe in such phenomena. After all, I fell in love with you the moment we met.*

It was too early for definite commitments, although in this case the political situation might make informal commitment at an early date advantageous.

Love on sight. He smiled at that. Elise was too pragmatic to accept that in a literal sense, but she recognized the strong initial attraction existing between some people that, if disillusionment doesn't set in, grows into love.

And hadn't he, in that sense, loved Elise on sight, too? He sighed, remembering her as his bride before the Altar of Lights in the Cathedron of Concordia. She was only seventeen, and political necessity impelled her into matrimony at that tender age. The marriage had already been arranged, but that premature finalization was precipitated by his father's sudden demise; it was the House of Galinin's statement of support to DeKoven Woolf's new First Lord, only twenty-three and marked by most of the Concord's Lords for inevitable failure.

Yet he hadn't failed, and he owed that to a great degree to his young bride, who found herself a First Lord's Lady when she was little more than a girl, and whose predecessor, Woolf's mother, Lady Matilde, abdicated in her grief and retreated to a Sisters of Solace convent, where she survived her husband by only five years. Yet Elise had met the challenge as Woolf had, and her faith in him had never flagged, nor his in her, nor their love for each other.

And if Elise was right about Adrien Eliseer, if she might prove to be even half the wife to Alexand that Elise had been to him . . .

Well, he could do this much for his son.

Woolf rose and crossed to the door, pausing there to look back at Alexand. He felt an inexplicable chill, a premonitory sensation too vague to take concrete form.

He turned away and slipped out into the salon.

Nerves. Nothing more. It had been a long day.

11.

Alexand at long last felt truly at home. It was past midnight, and he was tired after the hectic flurry of homecoming and an evening of what his mother airily lumped under the heading of "socializing," but here in the quiet of Rich's room, he experienced a mental second wind.

The separation had lasted only five days, yet it seemed much longer, and all through the evening, Alexand had impatiently awaited its end and this time with Rich. Dinner was served in the blue banquet hall in the residential wing, an "informal" affair with only six courses and sixteen guests. Phillip Woolf and his family seldom dined alone, and Alexand accepted the dinner and guests coming on the heels of their homecoming as a matter of course. His parents, he noted, accepted Rich's absence as if it were also a matter of course, Elise lightly parrying the guests' inquiries with the lie that Rich had caught a mild viral infection at the beach. The truth, Alexand knew, as she did, was that Rich was exercising his choice of seeking seclusion, and his parents could allow Rich that.

Alexand didn't have that privilege. Thus, two hours after his arrival at the Estate, he had donned dress attire and joined his parents at an oval table under the sparkling canopy of a Manela chandelier for an evening that met his resigned expectations for length and boredom. Even when the guests at last took their leaves, the comfortable rituals of retirement seemed protracted, especially with the Bond attendants—particularly Tuck, who had been Alexand's valet since he was eight—so curious and solicitous about his injured shoulder. Even after they were sent away, there was Dr. Stel's visit; he usually came to check on Rich before bedtime, but tonight he also gave Alexand's shoulder a critical scrutiny. And upon his departure, Phillip and Elise Woolf came in for their last good nights.

But finally they also departed, and Alexand, as was his custom, left his room, passing through the door into Rich's room—the door that had never in his memory been closed—and here, with Rich ensconced in his bed, Alexand sitting cross-legged at the foot, the aureole of the canopy light making the bed an island of light in the warm silence of the room, they had spent the last two hours in wide-awake conversation.

This, Alexand realized, was what he missed more than anything else in Montril. Only when Rich was too ill was this informal custom neglected. It began so far back in their childhood, he couldn't remember when they hadn't ended each day with this kind of dialogue.

Tonight's conversation was centered almost entirely on Alexand's "accident" and his venture into the Bond compound. Rich seized hungrily on every detail, while Alexand patiently probed his memory for answers.

"Alex, did Hezaki use the term 'Nether Dark'?"

"No, but Quin did. He said something about—'feeling the breath of the spirits of Nether Dark.' Where did you hear the expression?"

"Harlequin. Apparently it's the Bond version of hell. These dark spirits must come from Nether Dark, and Beyond Souls from—what did Harlequin call it? The Realm Beyond the Farthest Star. More poetic than the Orthodox Church's Heavenly Realm, you'll admit. Hezaki said people are *infested* with dark spirits?"

"Actually, it was Quin who used the expression most, Rich, but that was the implication."

"An infestation results in 'black spells'—insanity. Remember what Lector Theron said about insanity?"

Alexand hesitated, surprised and relieved that Rich could talk about Theron Rovere so easily—or at least make it seem easy.

"What in particular about insanity?"

"That primitive people invariably regarded it as a form of possession or infestation." He smiled wistfully. "And he said the science of psychology notwithstanding, that's a very pragmatic way of dealing with insanity."

Alexand nodded. "Yes, I remember."

"That foreman—Naylor—he *must* be insane. What else would make a man treat people that way?"

"People? Rich, you're talking about Bonds, and not everyone recognizes them as human beings."

Rich started to protest, then caught the teasing glint in Alexand's eye. Still, his laugh was short.

"Well, you and I can agree on that. What about Father?"

"What do you mean?"

"I . . . I've had the feeling you're holding something back; something to do with Father."

Alexand frowned, then after a moment rose and went to the windowall. A clear night; the sea of Concordia's lights shone under a full moon whose wan light seemed a reflection of the city's luminescence.

"Rich, I'm not . . . holding anything back unless it's something I don't understand myself. Father was not only remarkably tolerant with me, but he took care of Naylor's transfer the next morning as he promised, made an inspection tour of Compound C, and ordered an Internal Procedures investigation of the Montril plant." He paused, smiling mirthlessly. "He also had it out with Kelmet. I wasn't invited to sit in on that meeting, but Kelmet was a changed man afterward."

Rich laughed, but didn't comment. He waited silently, and Alexand, still looking out at the city, finally said, "The Bond problem is a fact of life and nothing can be done about it. Maybe that's it."

"Father said that?"

"Yes. I had the feeling not only that he was wrong, but that there was . . . fear in it." He walked back to the bed and sat down again; Rich's eyes never left him. "But perhaps *I* was the one who was afraid."

"Afraid of what?"

"That he's right Rich; that nothing can be done."

"I don't believe that."

"Well, I don't *like* to believe it."

"You don't, really, do you?" Rich didn't seem to expect an answer to that, but went on, "Actually, this is a case where the problem hasn't been sufficiently identified. The Bond problem. And if you were wondering why I asked so many questions about your sojourn into that compound, I'm using you as a source."

Alexand raised an eyebrow. "A source? Of what?"

"Information." He hesitated self-consciously. "You see, I . . . I'm going to do a thesis."

Alexand looked at him, surprised at first; thirteen-year-olds didn't aspire to theses. Then he smiled. At least, *most* thirteen-year-olds didn't.

"Rich, that's . . . well, an ambitious undertaking, to say the least."

"I'm not really sure I can do it, but I want to try, and Lector Theron could—I mean, if I sent him the rough drafts maybe he'd offer comments or criticism."

Alexand nodded. "I'm sure you can count on the criticism, and you'd better have everything tidy and proper to the last word. So your subject will be the Bond problem?"

"Nothing *that* ambitious. I thought I'd start with Bond religion. Remember, the last—on Concord Day, Lector Theron said something about how little research had been done on Bond religion? Well, he was right. I scanned most of the material in the University and Archives memfiles in a day. And the other sources—well, there's only one, actually: the Shepherds. There aren't any written sources. Apparently the Shepherds carry it all around it their heads and pass it down from one generation to the next purely by rote memory. Think of that, Alex. It's incredible."

"If Hezaki is a fair sample, they're incredible men. But how will you get at your sources? I hope you don't intend to go into the compounds to talk to the Shepherds personally. Father will think I'm a bad influence on you."

Rich tilted his head to one side. "Aren't you? But don't worry. I thought I might bring the mountain to the Mezion, so to speak. I know Father won't let me go to the compound chapels unescorted, and you can imagine how much cooperation I'd get from the Shepherds with a brace of guards standing over them. Anyway, I believe in the Galinin Rule: Leave them their religion. At least show proper respect for it, and I don't consider bringing armed guards into a chapel at all respectful."

Alexand smiled and lay back on the bed, folding his left arm under his head. He was beginning to feel the drag of sleepiness at his eyelids.

"So you're going to have the Shepherds brought to you?"

"Yes. The school room. The recording equipment can be kept out of sight, and if Father insists on guarding me, it can be done discreetly with monitors. It's a comfortable and private place; I don't think it would be intimidating to the Shepherds, and certainly *I* shouldn't be intimidating. I'll start with Father

Adamis; Harlequin is in his flock, and he can make the first
overtures for me."

"He'll be a good liaison, and I wish you luck." Then he
added with a studied sigh, "'Zion, you make life difficult for
me, you know. I mean, it's hard to keep up with a little brother
who insists on acting like a genius."

Rich smiled at that, but it faded at Alexand's next question.

"Has anything been said about . . . a new tutor?"

Rich nodded, eyes flicking down. "Mother and I had a long
talk about our future education, and she's come up with a
marvelous idea. First of all, she said there's no use trying
to . . . to replace Lector Theron with one tutor, so we'll have
specialists in various subjects, but she also thought we might
augment our private studies with classes at the University here
in Concordia."

That dispelled any trace of sleepiness; Alexand sat up, smiling in anticipation.

"That would be great, Rich, and I doubt we'd have any
trouble passing entrance tests for the basic courses. Unless
there's an age limit."

Rich was smiling, too, containing an excitement that seemed
to make his eyes a deeper blue.

"There isn't. Mother checked that. And the spring session
begins in two weeks. We may be too late to get some of the
courses we want, but I think—"

"*Some* of the courses? How many do you plan to take?"

Rich shrugged. "Oh, only two or three to begin with, but
there's a sociotheology class that's Pri-One for me. Simon
Kimodo. Lector Theron talked about him, you know."

"Yes. Rich, will it . . ." He hesitated uncertainly.

"Will it bother me to appear in public so much?" He took
a deep breath, letting it out in a long sigh as he leaned back
against the pillows. "Well, it would, Alex, and that almost
stopped me until Mother pointed out that my crutches wouldn't
attract nearly so much attention if I weren't Phillip Woolf's
son."

"If you weren't . . . you mean, she's suggesting you enter
the University incognito?"

Rich nodded, the light in his eyes rekindled.

"Yes. Simply as a Fesh. The crutches would still attract
attention, but—well, it would be different somehow. At least

I think I could tolerate it that way."

"But don't you think people will recognize you? How are you going to pass yourself off as a Fesh?"

"Mother also pointed out that most people depend almost entirely on costuming for identification, and on expectation. And it's true, you know. To begin with, most of the students and all the teachers at the University are Fesh, and where would they have seen me except on an occasional vidicom newscast? And always with the family, and always surrounded by guards, etc., and trussed up in full regalia with boots and brocade. But if I were to dress as a Fesh, perhaps wear my hair a little shorter, and just go about my business as if I were a Fesh— well, maybe a few might think I look a lot like Richard DeKoven Woolf, but I doubt it would occur to any of them that I really *was* Richard DeKoven Woolf. A First Lord's son playing a Fesh—who'd believe it?"

Alexand considered that with an eyebrow raised. "Well, you have a point there, but you *will* encounter a few Elite at the University, and some of them you've met face to face and at close range."

That didn't daunt Rich. "Yes, but there are very few Elite I'd know attending the University now, and I'll just have to be careful to avoid them. Besides, most Elite don't really look at Fesh or Bonds. I'll bet even you could put on a Bond tabard and slip into Uncle Ives's suite and give him his evening bath, and he'd never know the difference. Anyway, I think I can manage to play the Fesh at the University. I'm going to give it a hard run, at least."

"Has Mother talked to Father about this?"

"Not yet, but as she said, all he'll be worried about is my safety, and that almost stopped me, too. I mean, what kind of Fesh goes about with Woolf guards in tow?"

"But the two of you arrived at a solution to that?"

"Mother did. I could be guarded from a distance. She said we have agents in Security who can all but fade into the plasment."

"Well, she seems to have the matter well in hand—as usual. Now if she can just get Father in hand."

"You think that isn't 'as usual,' too? But I won't do it unless it's on my own terms, Alex. I . . . just won't. And there's another stipulation. No one in the house will know my Fesh pseudonym. Not even the family."

Alexand knew Rich was watching his reaction to that closely, and gave him not even a flicker of an eye.

"Well, I can understand that. Your real identity could slip out and you'd be right back where you started—the Lord Woolf's son. Besides, if no one can connect you with DeKoven Woolf, you won't have to worry about any future theses expressing ideas that might be embarrassing to the House."

His cheeks went red. "That . . . occurred to me."

Alexand smiled at that, then sobered as he asked, "But what about your invisible guards from Security? Won't they have to know your pseudonym?"

"Why would they? All they have to do is keep me in sight and make sure I'm not attacked by a berserk history lector— or whatever it is that Father will be worried about. They don't have to know what name I'm using, and they won't know." Then he clasped his hands together, closing his eyes briefly. "Oh, Alex, I have to do it this way. I want whatever I do, anything I achieve, to be mine. I want to . . . to be *me*."

Alexand nodded, his gaze drawn to the windowall. "I can understand that too, Rich."

"I know. I wish you could . . ."

"That kind of me-ness is one thing that doesn't come with the Crest Ring." Then Alexand smiled. "But thank the God that doesn't apply to the second born."

"I hope Father doesn't think it does." He paused, eyeing Alexand intently, then, "Alex, don't you want to know what my Fesh name will be?"

"Come on, Rich, you *know* I want to know."

Rich reached for a scriber and lightpen from his bedside table, and his seriousness in protecting his new identity was brought home to Alexand by the fact that he chose to write the name, not speak it aloud. The chance of their rooms being monitored was remote, but it was always a possibility. He wrote two words, then turned the screen for Alexand to see.

Richard Lamb.

Alexand studied it, smiling at the ironic overtones, and at one aspect of it that Rich wouldn't have considered: what animal except the lamb was so generally regarded as a symbol of gentleness?

Or of sacrifice?

He put that thought aside, smiling at Rich as he hurriedly cleared the screen.

"Thank yóu, Rich."

He shrugged. "Don't thank me for something it's not in my power to withhold from you."

"Then I'm grateful for that." Alexand looked at his watch. "But did you know it's 01:00?" He rose, stretched his free arm, and yawned. "I don't know about you, but I'm tired."

Rich nodded, then, as if he'd just thought of it, "By the way, did you check your comconsole? There's a lettape for you. It came in today; a SynchCom transmission from Castor."

"Castor?" Alexand felt a disconcerting warmth in his cheeks. "From Adrien? Oh, Rich, why didn't you tell me sooner?"

"Selfishness. I knew I'd lose you immediately, and I wanted to hear about your adventures in Montril."

Alexand attempted an indifferent shrug. "Why would you have lost me? A 'tape won't dissolve if it isn't read on the moment." He had turned to face the windowall, but the nocturnal vista only reminded him of pearls like stars in night-black hair.

Rich said, "Alex, I can't believe you're trying to delude me, so don't delude yourself."

"Delude myself about what? I . . . don't even know her."

"You keep saying that. All right, I suppose it's true, but I think you'll get to know Serra Adrien Eliseer a great deal better in the future. Her name came up when Mother and I were at the beach. Mother was probing."

"For what?"

"How you really feel about Adrien."

He asked numbly, "What difference does it make?"

"Possibly a great difference, considering the political situation with Eliseer and Selasis. Certainly a great difference to Mother. She liked Adrien very much; enough to call her the only possible bride for you, and she said Father agrees with her. I know it can't be counted done until the contracts are signed, and that's a long time in the future, but the odds are very high that they *will* be signed."

Alexand was incapable of responding to that, closing his eyes against an unexpected vertigo.

I'll still make room for joy. I'm strong enough to withstand pain and willing to accept the risk, and I can't live without . . .

"Rich, I hope you're right."

"So do I. And I'll make a prediction: next year at the Concord Day balls, you'll be Serra Adrien Camine Eliseer's escort." Then he added with a wry smile, "And further, the society reporters will describe you as a 'striking' couple."

Alexand could only laugh at that, and he still felt the warmth of it within him even when it faded.

"Rich, I'm very lucky to have . . ." He stopped before voicing the thought: to have two linked-twin souls.

Rich nodded, smiling gently. "I'll make another prediction, Alex. The Contracts of Marriage *will* be signed by the time you reach Age of Rights."

Age of Rights. Five years. It seemed a long time. So much could happen in five years.

But, Adrien, *I* can't live without hope, either.

PHOENIX MEMFILES: DEPT HUMAN SCIENCES:
                                SOCIOTHEOLOGY (HS/STh)
SUBFILE: LAMB, RICHARD: PERSONAL NOTES
                        27 DECEM 3251
DOC LOC #819/19208–1812–1614–27123251

Lectors Fensly and Cordeli have published a new translation of the *Disasters Diary*, and although their annotations leave a great deal to be desired, it was a pleasure—at least a moving experience—to reacquaint myself with the *Diary*.

It wasn't, of course, actually a diary of the Disasters, but simply a personal journal kept by a woman of the period, and her accounts throw more light on the everyday life of the independent agrarian family—a way of life that has no modern parallel—than on the history of the disintegration of her civilization. Mary Hobson and her husband, whom she calls "Bob" (which is probably a nickname rather than a forename, and might have referred to short stature), lived on a farming-grazing complex in eastern Conta Austrail near the ancient city of Brisbane, where they bred sheep on land they held in sole ownership. The Hobsons were also members of a religious sect that disapproved of abortion or contraception—this at a time when the population had soared over eight billion, according to some estimates, ten billion in others. And that vast population was entirely confined to Terra. (Or "Earth," as it was called before the Confederation Lords became so enamored of ancient nomenclature during the extraterrestrial colonization phase. I've always liked the old term; it had such rich meanings in the language of the day.)

Mary Hobson's antagonism to population control is commented on at length by Fensly and Cordeli as a phenomenon of the time, and they present evidence that her religious sect numbered its adherents in the billions. The lectors find that incomprehensible, yet I wonder if they balk at the equally incomprehensible fact that today our religious and social doctrines sanction the enslavement of seventy percent of our population. One thing the study of history has taught me is that no one has a right to laugh at the fallacies of the past, and something Fensly and Cordeli have overlooked is that their attitudes toward birth control are not shared by the majority of Fesh, and Bonds are generally encouraged by their Lords to be fruitful and multiply. Their Lords do practice birth control, but not out of any concern for overpopulation; their concern is for divisive House successional battles and the dilution of power. Fensly and Cordeli can be smug about the matter because overpopulation is not really a problem today with the total population at about four and a half billion spread over nine planets and five satellites. That doesn't mean it won't be in the future, nor does it mean we've learned the bitter lesson taught by the twentieth century and the Disasters, any more than Mary Hobson recognized the lessons of informed prognostication, or even of common sense available to her.

In 2030, when her civilization was on the verge of crumbling under the weight of that glut of human beings, and when this surviving volume of Mary's diary begins, she reports that a neighbor chided her on the birth of her fifth child (she bore seven altogether), which suggests that some of her contemporaries were concerned about overpopulation, but Mary blithely informed her neighbor, so she tells us, that "God will provide."

What the God provided beginning in that fateful year was the Great Drought. However, Conta Austrail—at least the eastern and southern sections—was spared the worst of the Drought, so Mary's personal experience of it is limited. She describes four unusually dry years and is constantly outraged at the rocketing prices of food at nearby markets. She also quotes lettapes—rather, the handwritten "letters" of the period—from a cousin in Noramerika, who pleads for financial aid so he and his family can move to Conta Austrail. He was also a small landholder and reports his land parched and blowing away in black dust storms, his family reduced to beggary. We don't know his fate; her subsequent attempts to contact him proved futile.

A friend in Brittan—or "England," as Mary calls it— tells her of government food rationing, and if the translations of measurements are correct, they were at a starvation level. Mary corresponds with that friend, whom she identifies simply as "Cora," for another five years, and is increasingly dismayed at Cora's accounts of mass starvation, large-scale civil disorder, and the death of her husband in an encounter between army police and factory workers. The letters become sporadic, and finally, after an interval of a year, Cora mentions in what proved to be her last letter that her two children are ill with "that new kind of flu."

That was the beginning of the Pandemic, and "that new kind of flu" was only one of many mutating virus forms that along with more conventional diseases—like typhoid, typhus, bubonic and pneumonic plague, yellow fever, scarlet fever, diphtheria, malaria, smallpox, and cholera—in a period of twenty years killed an estimated four billion people.

Mary Hobson, in Conta Austrail, was isolated to a great degree from these disasters, although not unaffected by them. She reports that Bob has butchered most of their sheep; it has become too expensive to maintain the herds, and there is no market for the wool—no factories to convert it into cloth. But for Mary, the God still provides. "We have the land and we can live off it until all this settles down."

But it didn't settle down. She reports, almost casually, in 2040 that Bob is building an electrified fence around their house and nearby fields "to keep those gangs of hoodlums out." A year later, Bob is pleased at acquiring a store of ammunition for the weapons the family depends on to defend its holdings. "Can't look to the police any more," Mary tells us. "They're as bad as the gangs." She also tells us that these gangs, or "rovers," have all but taken over the city of Brisbane. "It's worth your life to go there now."

And a few months later, it apparently *was* worth her eldest son's life. He didn't return from a trip to that ill-fated city. Mary mourns, "The worst part is not knowing, but I told Bob, none of us is going after Sid. None of us is ever setting foot outside the gates again."

Her only news from beyond her gates in the following years comes from a radio communication system. In 2045 she enters in her diary vague reports of wars between "Russians," "Americans," "Chinese," and other peoples or "nations." Her information on these events indicates the deteriorated state of communications. She knows less of the Nuclear Wars than we do today, and her reports show a time lag of up to four years. For instance, she notes the death of the king (of "England," it is assumed) in 2048, but by then the island of Brittan, like most of Noreurope, was a radioactive ruin.

But the Hobson family survives in its isolated bastion. There are even poignant descriptions of such commonplace events as the celebration of various holidays, and in 2049 the marriage of her daughter Livia to Ben Lewis, who lived on a nearby landholding. Mary is especially pleased that a traveling minister of her religion was present to sanctify the vows. We are also told of seasonal farm life, crops planted, tended, harvested. The crops, however, were seldom bountiful, too often deformed and stunted, or devoured by insects. One summer she describes swarms of grasshoppers "bigger than your hand," and the following autumn, the invasion of their fields by armies of hairless rabbits.

No more does she assure us that the God will provide. Her God has become an avenging God. "This is what comes to a world full of sin. God's will be done."

Mary Hobson couldn't know the magnitude of the wages of sin in the rest of the world, of the estimated seven billion deaths that resulted from famine, pollution and chemical poisoning, disease, war, the mutant plagues, and, finally, anarchy. She was isolated in her farm bastion as to a great degree Conta Austrail was isolated from the worst of the Disasters. That, and the fact that its resources weren't as gutted by the excesses of the twentieth century as were those of the rest of the planet, and that it wasn't so extensively urbanized, explains why Conta Austrail became the site of the new renaissance after the Second Dark Age. But isolation didn't save the Hobsons.

The Pandemic finally, in 2052, reached their farm keep. We don't know from Mary's description of the symptoms which of the diseases rampant at the time struck her family down. She refers to it simply as "the fever." Her youngest child succumbed first, then, within a week, her husband and the remaining four children still at home or surviving. Mary tells us she buried them all herself and prayed for their souls, "but it didn't seem right, there being no priest to say last rites." But she hopes her God will understand.

In the last entry in the diary she says she will have to leave the farm. "They'll come to burn it down as soon as they find out the fever was in it." We don't know who "they" are; perhaps her rural neighbors. And Mary realizes she will be a pariah, since she's been exposed to the disease.

"I didn't catch it, though," she notes. "Maybe somewhere I can find another farm where they won't know about the fever. I've still got a strong back and a lot of years' work in me. I can pay my way. Nothing else to do but go out and look for a place to take me in. God's will be done."

The diary was found nine hundred years later in the excavation of the medieval enclave of Renhold near Sidny. How it got there we'll never know, but we do know the enclave was established in the early twenty-first century during the Disasters. Perhaps Mary Hobson did find a place that would take her in.

CHAPTER II: Septem 3246

●Ⅱ●

1.

The Lord Evin Daro Galinin, first born of Lord Mathis, heir to Daro Galinin and the Chairmanship, was dead. And with him, his only son, Marc, and the Lord Alexis Arment Ivanoi.

Alexand stared at his father, hearing the words echoing and reechoing. He felt himself caught in a sort of sensory warp. That fact, those terse words, made a mockery of the reality around him.

12 Septem. Today was his birthday: his seventeenth birthday.

He wondered why that irrelevant fact came to mind, why something so meaningless in the face of this disaster assumed the proportions of portent; why the only physical sensation he was aware of was the weight of the gold medallion at his throat—Rich's birthday gift to him—and the ruby and black jade ring on his right hand—a gift from Adrien Eliseer.

Adrien...

Even she seemed unreal, infinitely distant; more than time or light years.

Morning sunlight slanted through the wide door into the gymnasium and fell onto the ruffled waters of the thermal pool, casting shivering reflections, gossamer veils of light, impalpable, yet somehow more tangible than the reality of walls and water and tiled floor and heavy-scented, tropical foliage. More tangible even than the four persons who shared this light-spun silence with him.

Dr. Kairn Bettis, Rich's physiotherapist, moving like a sleepwalker to help Rich out of the pool and into a sitting position on the rim. And Rich, frail and weightless as a bird, suddenly drained of all substance, pulling close the towel she draped around his shoulders.

139

Fenn Lacroy, sinewy hands curling reflexively at his sides; he had dropped his fencing foil, yet Alexand couldn't remember hearing the sound. Nor could he remember what had happened to the foil that had been in his own hand.

And the quivering reflections moved across Phillip Woolf's taut, saturnine features, catching in the pale irises of his eyes.

The reality was in the words, not in this segment of space/time.

Evin and Marc Galinin and Alexis Ivanoi are dead.

The reality was in the wellsprings of grief those deaths would tap. Lord Mathis and Lady Camma Galinin, herself dying, in one blow robbed of their only son and *his* only son. Elise Woolf bereaved of a brother. Lady Marcessa Galinin, who must mourn a husband and a child at once.

And Honoria Corelis Ivanoi, who had loved her husband, and must grieve his loss and comfort two sons, one little more than an infant, the other a child of five.

Wellsprings that would be inexhaustible.

And finally a voice in the eternal silence that had lived no more than seconds. Alexand saw Kairn sagging, her hands tightening on Rich's shoulders, saw her lips moving, but her voice seemed strangely disembodied, as if it came from within his own mind.

"The God help us . . . Evin Galinin . . ."

The next voice was his own, and it seemed as disembodied as Kairn's.

"When, Father?"

"About two hours ago."

Alexand knew he would have to face the political implications of these deaths, knew they spelled a disaster that might destroy Daro Galinin and Ivanoi. And DeKoven Woolf. Orin Selasis would be waiting, ready to pounce at this unprecedented opportunity. But Alexand couldn't make the mental shift into that plane yet. In the eye of memory was the patriarchal face of Mathis Galinin. How would he tolerate this? How would he hold on to his sanity? He had already had to grieve the loss of one son, and now both Evin and Marc—

"My lord, shall we leave you?" Fenn Lacroy, glancing at Dr. Bettis, who rose and turned to Woolf.

He shook his head. "The news will be on the PubliCom 'casts soon. You needn't leave."

"How did it happen, Father?" Again, the voice was his own, but Alexand hardly recognized it.

Woolf's gaze moved to him, and the only light in his eyes came from the straying reflections.

"Evin was conferring with Alexis on some new power receptors. That's why he was in Tycho; he and Marc. There was a Bond uprising: a serious one. Confleet was called in."

Rich spoke for the first time; he seemed perplexed. "An uprising among the *Ivanoi* Bonds?"

Alexand noted the question, particularly the emphasis, but he was too numbed to consider its meaning. He turned to Lacroy and said quietly, "Bring my clothes, Fenn." Lacroy moved away silently.

Woolf was saying, "Yes, Rich, it was among the Ivanoi Bonds. Fortunately, it didn't spread to any of the other House compounds in Tycho." He was preoccupied, already geared mentally to deal with the political aspects of this tragedy.

"But, how did—did Uncle Evin and . . ."

"They were killed by the Bonds during the uprising."

"What? That's impossible!"

Alexand moved now as Fenn returned with his shirt and street boots and cloak, and it was like coming out of a drugged sleep. His equilibrium was dysfunctioning. He was only vaguely aware of Fenn helping him as he pulled off his fencing boots.

What did Rich mean? That the deaths were impossible, or that they couldn't have been caused by the Bonds?

Woolf seemed to assume the former interpretation.

"I know it's painful, Rich, but it's true. Alexand—" He turned and saw that he was already dressing. "Good. Hurry, please."

Rich clutched at the towel, shivering in spite of the humid warmth of the room.

"How did it happen, Father? Where were they?"

"They were in the Ivanoi Estate, asleep."

"In the *Estate*?"

"Yes."

"What about the Lady Honoria and their sons?"

"They weren't harmed, thank the God. The Confleet flagship is bringing them here to Concordia. They'll be staying at the Galinin Estate."

Rich closed his eyes. "Grandser—oh, Father, how will he bear it?"

Woolf knelt beside him, taking his hand. "Mathis is a strong man. He'll bear it, Rich; he must."

He nodded absently. "They were *inside* the Estate? Where did the uprising begin?"

"In one of the compounds; a guard station was blown up."

"Was that what started the uprising? There was no violence before that?"

Woolf's eyes flickered with annoyance as he rose. "I don't think so. The reports are still incomplete. Alex, are you almost ready?"

He nodded, fumbling at the sleeve fastenings of his shirt, and even with his mind staggering under the implications of the deaths, Rich's questions commanded his attention. The insistence itself was enough to make him wonder—and enough to test Woolf's patience in his distracted, tense mood. But Rich persisted.

"The compound where it began, was it near the Estate?"

"It was across Tycho at one of the smelters. No, it wasn't near. I don't understand—" He stopped; his hands flexed into fists, then relaxed. "We'll discuss it later."

"All right, Father, but you'd better give one possibility very serious consideration."

"Rich, I said we'll discuss it later."

But Rich seemed oblivious to his reined impatience. "Father, please—there may be more to this than a Bond uprising. You must consider the possibility that someone was simply *using* the Bonds."

Woolf stared at him, and Alexand froze. He had never seen his father unleash that cold, disdainful gaze on Rich.

"You may be sure," Woolf said tightly, "that we'll consider all possibilities, but at this point there's no doubt that these assassinations are solely the work of your damned Bonds."

Rich paled and turned away. "Of course. I . . . didn't mean—"

"Oh, Rich . . ." Woolf knelt beside him again, strong hands gentle on his shoulders, and now there was only regret in his eyes. "Forgive me. I'm . . . not myself today."

Alexand gave Lacroy a brief nod of thanks as he helped him into his cloak, relieved to see Rich muster a smile.

"I know, Father. Don't be concerned."

Woolf sighed. "We *will* talk about it later, I promise you, but right now Alex and I must go to the Galinin Estate. As soon as you can, go to your mother. She was very close to Evin."

Rich nodded. "I'll stay with her. Father . . . good luck."

Woolf's mouth was a grim line as he rose.

"We'll need it. Come, Alexand."

2.

It was only a few minutes past noon when Alexand returned, and he was vaguely surprised at that. The council of war at the Galinin Estate had occupied less than three hours' time.

He had his chauffeur leave him on the private landing roof off the family wing. By now the other Estate entrances would be mobbed with reporters. Even here his arrival was recorded from a mobile vidicam 'car, but from the respectful distance imposed by the House guard aerial patrols. He spared the guard at the entrance a quick nod and strode down the corridor, ignoring the pedway as too slow, although his only objective at the moment was his own suite and a hot shower to loosen the aching tension in his muscles. His father wouldn't have a moment's rest until after the Directorate meeting tomorrow morning; he was at the Hall of the Directorate now occupied with preparations for the battle that would take place at that meeting.

It would be a battle for survival.

Three deaths out of all the hundreds of thousands that occurred this day in the Two Systems, three deaths might change the course of history, might strip Arment Ivanoi of its Directorate seat, might pull Mathis Galinin down from the Chairmanship because he had been robbed of a clear line of succession; pull him down from that chair he called so damnably uncomfortable, the chair he held so tenaciously because he knew the alternative if he surrendered it.

The alternative was Orin Badir Selasis, a man who cast the shadow of a third dark age across the Concord without even recognizing it simply because he was so much a product of the Second Dark Age.

And a man who fattened on disasters, Alexand thought bitterly. Selasis was ready for this one; ready to present his own candidate for the Ivanoi chair: Theo Reeswyck, one of his multitudinous sons-in-law. And ready to present a candidate for the Chairmanship: himself.

That would mark the downfall of Ivanoi and Galinin; Selasis as Chairman could—and would—see to that. And without their support, DeKoven Woolf was also doomed.

Above all, Selasis would make sure of that.

Alexand had been privileged to witness the Lords of the beleaguered Houses laying their strategy because his father considered it part of his training, and it had been a highly educational experience, observing the objective assessment of weaknesses and strengths, existing and potential power alignments, and means of shifting or maintaining them.

But there was more to it as an educational experience, and perhaps his father had also been aware of that. The image was imprinted in his memory. Until he died, it would always be mordantly clear. . . .

Entering Galinin's private office a pace behind his father, the click of the closing doors startled him.

The Lord Mathis Daro Galinin, seated in the carved chair behind his desk in monumental silence, his eyes clear, not the slightest indication that he'd yet shed a tear. And Alexand knew he hadn't.

In a chair near the desk, the Lady Honoria Corelis Ivanoi, regally at ease, her head with its mass of golden hair balanced gracefully on the slender column of her neck, her brown eyes as clear as Galinin's and as untouched by tears. But there was something in her eyes that was lacking in Galinin's: a fierce determination lurking like a shadow behind the calm; a peculiarly female determination—the selfless fury of a mother defending her offspring.

Her hands rested motionless in her lap. Hours from a holocaust, from the terrors of an uprising that in itself should have set those quiet hands quivering. Hours from the death of her husband.

A marriage that had been more than a political and economic union; a union of love.

Alexis Ivanoi, a man Alexand remembered well because he was always remembered; a vibrant, able man, famous for his wit and charm, fired with seemingly limitless energy—the Lord Alexis was dead, and his widow, who had loved him, sat in dry-eyed calm, coolly contemplating the strategy of survival, and her white, graceful hands lay quiet like sleeping birds, bearing the only jewelry she wore: the rings of betrothal and marriage.

An education, indeed, there. In one shattering moment comprehension that all the years of instruction under his father's aegis hadn't brought home to him.

He would be capable of that one day.

"Ser Alex . . ."

He looked up, frowning. He had stepped into the anteroom with its twin doors opening into his and Rich's suites to find Fenn Lacroy standing at Rich's door. He seemed ill at ease, and well he might; his presence in the family wing was unusual.

"Fenn?"

"I—are you all right, Ser?"

"Yes. Quite all right, thank you."

"I came to see if Ser Rich . . ." He paused uncertainly. "He seemed so upset this morning. I was worried."

Alexand smiled now. Lacroy's almost fatherly attitude toward Rich was always a source of reassurance. He touched the 'com button beside the doorcon. "Rich?"

A brief silence, then, instead of a verbal response, Rich opened the door. He looked blankly at Lacroy before his surprise gave way to a warm smile.

"Fenn—come in. Hello, Alex."

Lacroy followed Alexand into the bedroom, his uneasiness still apparent, but alleviated by Rich's welcome.

"Ser Rich, I know I shouldn't bother you, but I—I was concerned."

"I appreciate that, and you're always welcome here."

Lacroy's broad, freckled face colored. "Thank you, Ser."

"And I'm entirely recovered from the initial shock." Rich looked over at his brother, who was unfastening his cloak, his expression brooding and preoccupied. "Alex, what about Grandser?"

Alexand hesitated, wondering how that question could be answered.

"Grandser is the Lord Galinin. He's not a man to be shaken even by a tragedy of this magnitude."

Lacroy nodded, then, "Ser Rich—your lady mother?"

"She went to the Galinin Estate to be with Lady Camma.

Alex, you probably just missed her. She's well, Fenn, considering the circumstances."

"I'm glad. Uh...may I help you with your cloak, Ser Alex?"

Alexand shook his head, then frowned, distracted by a dull clink; something dropping on the marblex floor. He looked down, but Rich was already bending, his hand moving swiftly, then, as he straightened, going to his vest pocket.

"What was that?" Alexand asked.

"What? Oh, I just dropped my lightpen."

Alexand draped his cloak over his arm. It hadn't sounded as heavy as a lightpen.

Lacroy cleared his throat; he was suddenly pale. "Well, I...I'd better get back to the gym." His eyes moved to Rich, oddly questioning and anxious. "If I can help in any way, please let me know."

Rich smiled. "Thank you, Fenn. And don't worry."

Lacroy looked at him, but made no response except a mumbled, "Goodbye, Sers," as he withdrew.

When the door closed behind him, Rich turned to Alexand. "Have the pieces of the disaster been put together?"

"That remains to be seen. Come, Rich, I need a shower and change of clothes. How is Mother—I mean, in truth?"

Rich followed him into his bedroom. "She's bearing up very well, but then she's not under immediate pressure like Father or Grandser; that gives her the privilege of weeping."

Alexand looked around at him. The image of Lady Honoria's calm face and quiet hands was bitterly clear. He sat down in a chair near the mirrored dressing room doors to pull off his boots, studying Rich as he eased himself into another chair.

"Rich, what about you?"

He shrugged. "I'm bearing up well, too. I haven't really had time to accept it in personal terms. I guess that comes later—after the crisis. Alex, is it...hopeless?"

"Almost, but neither Grandser, nor Father, nor Honoria Ivanoi are easily put down."

"Selasis won't pass up an opportunity like this, and he'll be using lethal charges. What are they going to do?"

Alexand rose. "Rich, give me a few minutes to shower,

then perhaps we'll take a walk."

Rich only nodded. Neither of them had to spell out the reason for that walk, that it would take them out of range of potential monitors.

"Alex, Adrien called while you were at Grandser's."

He didn't respond to that. He hadn't allowed himself to think consciously about Adrien during the last three hours. He couldn't and maintain the mental set for calculation demanded by this crisis.

Alexand turned, stopping as he caught an image in the mirrored doors: his own half-naked image. The ring gleamed on his mirrored hand. Two square stones set side by side; a ruby whose deep, liquid red rivaled the Mogok ruby of his father's Crest Ring in color, and a polished square of black jade incised with the letters: *ADeKW*. Only hours ago he'd taken this ring from its case and put it on his finger, reduced to silence because he couldn't adequately frame his feelings in words.

"What did she say, Rich?"

"She'd heard the news. She wanted to express her sympathy, of course, and . . . well, wish us all luck. I taped the call; it's on your comconsole."

His eyes shifted across the room to the console. "Did she want me to call her back?"

Rich seemed stunned, and Alexand regretted his choice of words. He'd made it sound as if returning her call would be an obligation, a duty. But he didn't try to explain.

Rich said, "No. She knew you'd be occupied with more pressing matters."

"I'll . . . call her tomorrow. After it's all over." He made an excuse for not looking at Rich by busying himself with undressing, giving him no time to comment. "Rich, you said something this morning, that Father should consider the possibility that there was more to these assassinations than a Bond uprising. What did you mean by that?"

Rich hesitated, his features tense with an uneasy frown.

"Oh, I don't know, Alex. I shouldn't have said anything. It's just that I've been studying these uprisings lately, trying to find a pattern in them. This didn't seem to fit the pattern I thought I'd found. First of all, I was surprised that the Ivanoi were hit with a major uprising. Alexis was always exceptionally kind to his Bonds, and most of the uprisings have been in Houses where the Bonds weren't treated so well. And there's never been an attempt on the lives of the Lords. These are never true revolts; they aren't organized or premeditated. They're just eruptions."

Alexand frowned at that. "Grandser said there were rumors that the Society of the Phoenix was behind this one."

"No. I don't believe that."

The reply was too quick; Alexand's eyes narrowed.

"Why not?"

"I just don't think it's that simple. Anyway, from what I've heard about the Phoenix, it's a small organization without much punch behind it. Sometimes I wonder if it exists at all. Maybe Conpol or the SSB invented it as a scapegoat for anything they can't explain."

"I find it difficult to credit them with that much imagination."

Rich smiled. "You have a point, but I still don't think the Phoenix is the culprit here. And, Alex, I've been watching the newscasts. There was a sequence at the InterPlan port in Tycho; the evacuation of the casualties. I saw a face I thought I recognized. It was a quick glimpse, and I can't be sure, but the name flashed into my mind; a sort of intuitive reaction."

"What name?"

"Bruno Hawkwood."

"*Hawkwood*?" Alexand felt a whispering chill.

The Master of Shadows—so he was called in Elite, Fesh, and Bond circles alike, a man known, and feared, on all levels. Bruno Hawkwood was Orin Selasis's Chief of Security, his master henchman, commander of a corps of well-trained shadow men like himself, spies and expert executioners. And Hawkwood was a member of the Order of Gamaliel, which added to his sinister reputation because it made him invulnerable to the tools of fear and greed he used so well.

Alexand's jaw tightened. "It would be futile to check the passenger lists, of course, but perhaps Father could have his agents in Badir Selasis check Hawkwood's movements in the last few days."

"Which would be equally futile. Hawkwood never leaves tracks." Rich sighed as he lifted his crutches and activated them. "And I'm probably imagining things. Or just looking for something to take the onus off... my Bonds."

"Oh, Rich..." Alexand felt the pain in those last words. "Father was distracted and anxious this morning. Afraid, if he's capable of that, for the House."

Rich nodded. "No human being is exempt from fear. But creating scapegoats is dangerous. Conpol is making a scapegoat of the Phoenix, which means that in many cases the true criminals—the pirates and smugglers, for instance—escape undetected. And now the Lords are making scapegoats of the Bonds, and that's a far more serious error." He pulled himself to his feet. "The pond, Alex; the terrace below the rose garden. I'll wait for you there."

3.

The air, made sweet with narcissus and rock daphne, had the crystal clarity peculiar to early spring. A gossamer wind tempered the afternoon sun and carried delicate scents up from the rock gardens bordering the pond to the sloping lawn where Rich sat watching the reflections of cumulus clouds wavering in the wakes of the swans. This year Elise Woolf's prized flock had been graced with six cygnets.

He had suggested the pond because of the open lawn above it. His back was to the Estate, and beyond the pond was the edge of the terrace. No one could approach within a hundred meters without being seen. But now he wished he had chosen another place; the black swans would only remind Alexand of Adrien. Rich wasn't sure why he was concerned about that, but he knew something was wrong and the reminder wouldn't be welcome.

Alexand was walking across the lawn toward him. Rich watched him, thinking how much he'd changed in the last year. He'd grown taller, of course; he stood eye to eye with Phillip Woolf now, and the resemblance between father and son was almost uncanny and, to Rich, paradoxical.

The apprenticeship was still in progress, and daily Alexand became more the first born, more the Lord, even if he were still addressed as "Ser." At least half his waking hours were spent with House business, either in learning processes, or in actual decision-making capacities. Only last week he'd been sent to the Martian PubliCom System center in Toramil to resolve a Guild dispute. With Alexand there were never any covert complaints from the Fesh because he was only a boy; most of them overestimated his age by two or three years. And Phillip Woolf was always notably pleased with his son's decisions.

Except when it came to the Bonds.

That was their only area of disagreement, but it went deep, to basic policy and attitudes. Rich had been aware of that for some time, but a month ago he had witnessed one of those disagreements, one occasioned by a minor matter on the surface: the expansion of the compound guard at the Bonaires plant. Alexand had been flatly opposed on the grounds that more guards would only create more problems. His father was equally determined that they had no choice; the compounds had already sustained two minor uprisings in the last year.

It had been like a fencing match with the charges set low. Still, like any fencing match, there was a tacit understanding that the encounter was less than deadly only by mutual consent. And the Bonaires guard *was* enlarged by a thousand men.

Alexand stretched out on the grass beside Rich, bracing himself with one arm, his hand moving unconsciously to the medallion at his throat. Rich smiled to himself; he had overseen its design and casting to the last detail, and Alexand's pleasure in its beauty and ironic symbolism had been ample recompense. On one side was a baying wolf, on the other a lamb. "The wolf shall dwell with the lamb," said the ancient prophet, and Richard DeKoven Woolf became Richard Lamb. It had seemed even more ironic when the Bond Shepherds began calling him Richard the Lamb.

Only one of them had ever known his real identity: Father Adamis. The secret was safe now; safe in death. Adamis died six months ago, and Richard Lamb had never appeared in a DeKoven Woolf compound.

Then Rich frowned, his pulse quickening.

The ring. Adrien's birthday gift to Alexand—he wasn't wearing it.

Something *was* wrong. But what? The change in attitude was all on Alexand's part, and it had occurred within the last few hours. Since the meeting at the Galinin Estate.

Elise Woolf had more than once called Adrien Eliseer the only possible bride for Alexand, and they had, indeed, made a handsome couple at the Concord Day balls last year. The society reporters, as Rich predicted, called them "striking," among more enthusiastic adjectives; they were already talking about a "marriage of destiny."

Rich regarded it as that, and as Alexand's only hope for happiness. He might look the part of a Lord and play it well, but there was too much about the role he found hard to stomach, and it would only get harder.

Rich turned his gaze toward the pond as he asked, "Who called the Directorate meeting, Alex?"

"Grandser—to save Selasis the trouble of mustering a Directorate majority."

"Naturally Orin wouldn't hesitate out of any decent consideration for grief."

Alexand laughed caustically. "This is his golden opportunity. Galinin without a male heir, Ivanoi's heirs only children. He won't hesitate for the bereaved. It seems almost too fortuitous. That's why I find the possibility that Bruno Hawkwood was in Tycho so interesting, but even if Orin is involved, you can be sure there'll be no way to prove it."

"He's going for the Chairmanship, I suppose."

"Of course, on the grounds that Grandser can't offer a clear line of succession now."

"And Ivanoi? I suppose his grounds there are that Alexis has no heirs past Age of Rights."

"And no surviving brothers. He'll try to unseat the House. Grandser's already granted Lady Honoria a full regency, and there's no one in the House to contest that. The question is whether the other Directors will agree that the regency includes the Ivanoi seat on the Directorate."

Rich gave a short laugh. "Having a woman—especially one like Honoria Ivanoi—on the Directorate will shatter a few precedents."

"I know. That will make it more difficult, and of course Selasis has a candidate to offer for the chair—Theo Reeswyck."

"*Reeswyck*." Rich sighed with disgust. "A logical choice—Orin's eldest daughter's husband. Alex, even if Grandser holds the Chairmanship, the balance of power will shift if Reeswyck takes the Ivanoi chair."

"Yes. It could give Selasis the Chairmanship eventually, if not now. And I'm not a sociologist, but it takes no expertise to imagine what would happen to the Concord with Selasis at the helm." He laughed bitterly. "Not to mention what would happen to Galinin and Woolf."

"Can Grandser hold him off?"

"Possibly." Alexand sat up, resting an elbow on his upraised knee. "Grandser's chosen his successor to the Chairmanship. He'll make the announcement at the beginning of the meeting

tomorrow and pull Orin's fangs on that issue at the outset. If
the Directors accept that, he'll have a better chance at holding
the Ivanoi chair."

"A successor? His brother Emil?"

"No, Emil's not well, and that means his son Rodrik would
fall heir to the Chairmanship within a few years. Orin's probably hoping for that. Rodrik would never support him, but as
Grandser says, he just hasn't what it takes for the Chairmanship."

"Then who will he name?"

Alexand laughed again, but there was no humor in it.

"Father."

"Father? But—"

"The Lords," Alexand said coolly, "tend to be dynastic
thinkers. Genes are of inestimable value to them; a source of
security. Incredible, isn't it, Rich? If they accept Father as
successor to the Chairmanship, it won't be because of his
qualifications for the position, but because it will mean the
eventual succession of Mathis Galinin's eldest grandson by his
eldest daughter." He looked at Rich with a sardonic smile that
was chilling. "*I'm* the rationale for the gambit simply because
I happen to be Elise Galinin's first born. *I'm* the real successor.
In theory, Father will be acting as a sort of regent until his
death, at which time I, and my Galinin genes, will ascend to
glory—and that damnably uncomfortable chair. And please
don't offer congratulations. I'm not up to that now."

It hadn't occurred to Rich to offer congratulations; he was
too stunned. But after the first shock, he recognized it as an
intelligent gambit. The genetic rationale would be convincing,
and Phillip Woolf was Galinin's only real choice not only in
terms of ability, but because his succession would maintain the
present balance of power. Galinin would probably make Emil
heir to the First Lordship of the House, which would put Rodrik
in the Galinin chair eventually, and there he might even be an
asset to Woolf as Chairman; Rodrik wasn't a strong man, but
he would offer Woolf no opposition and Selasis no support.

Rich managed a tight smile. "Grandser's fortunate he had
the foresight to wed his daughter to Phillip Woolf."

Alexand nodded. "The blood link will be hard to argue
down, especially for Sato Shang; he's a particularly dynastic
thinker, and his is one of the votes we must have."

"Let's see, Grandser has his own vote, Father's, and I assume Robek's?"

"Yes, Trevor can always be counted on."

"Ivanoi will be out of it, I suppose, until Honoria's right to hold the chair is voted. So Galinin has three votes and so does Selasis—his own, plus Cameroodo's and Hamid's. That leaves Shang, Omer, and Fallor on the fence."

"As usual."

"Any hint of how they'll vote?"

"No, but Grandser has some idea what Selasis will be offering—or threatening. The problem was to come up with counteroffers and counterthreats. That's what the meeting this morning was about. It was . . . quite educational."

Something slipped past the controlled facade then; amazement or awe, and despair. But it was immediately masked.

Rich asked, "What's the strategy, then?"

"Lao Shang we can probably hold. Orin will inevitably offer a cut in freight rates, but Shang's a proud man; if he's to be bought it must be on more subtle terms. Besides—" He glanced obliquely at Rich, "—Cameroodo's techs have come up with a polyboron steel that would have a rather detrimental effect on Shang's basic metals markets, but it hasn't passed the Board of Franchises yet, and Grandser and Father have more influence with the present Board than Selasis. Sandro Omer could go either way. He's trying to sell Selasis a new computer navigation system, which would be quite a lucrative contract if Orin accepts it. But, of course, Lord Sandro depends on Woolf commutronics equipment, as well as Ivanoi's rare metals, and Galinin's power sources."

"What about Charles Fallor?"

Alexand stared at the swans in their silent passages across the water, and Rich waited tensely.

"Fallor. Well, he's something of a problem since neither commutronics, rare metals, nor power are among his major costs in grain and cattle production. Unfortunately freight *is* one of his major costs, so Orin has a great deal of leverage with him. And then there's Julia."

Rich hesitated, feeling a premonitory chill. "Julia?"

"Yes, of course." The words were clipped, charged with acid amusement. "Fallor needs a strong House alliance now, and Julia's his hope for making one. Selasis is offering a marriage with Karlis. A perfectly matched couple, you'll admit. Actually, Orin is rather free with the promise of Karlis's favors. He's also offering marriage contracts with Shang's grand-daughter, Janeel, and Omer's daughter, Olivet."

"What does Grandser intend to offer Fallor to offset Karlis's favors?" Rich waited for the answer, dreading it. Alexand was too still, to all outward appearances entirely indifferent.

"Grandser had nothing more attractive to offer, nor does Ivanoi. But DeKoven Woolf does." A brief, introspective smile put a hint of light in his eyes. "Rich, Father wouldn't even suggest the offer until *I* brought it up. I know it occurred to him; it's so obvious. But even with so much at stake, he couldn't bring himself to voice it until I—" He closed his eyes, but only for a moment, and the light was gone. He looked at Rich and laughed. "At any rate, I consider my favors at least as attractive as Karlis's."

Rich stared at him, finding that sardonic smile beyond com-prehension and the iron self-mastery nearly tragic.

"Alex, not—not a marriage. Not . . . Julia Fallor."

"The *possibility* of a marriage. Father would go no further."

Rich turned away, feeling a sick weight within him. He understood now, understood why Alexand had seemed reluc-tant to return Adrien's call, why he'd removed her ring. And *he* had made the suggestion, offered himself, and tossed away—

Rich reached out and touched his brother's arm, and wasn't surprised that there was no response.

"Alex, if Father offered only a possibility, there's still hope."

"Hope." He nodded mechanically. "Yes, and if Selasis wins both his battles tomorrow, it won't make any difference. DeKoven Woolf won't be in a position to make my favors attractive to anyone."

Rich made no reply, and Alexand was silent, his eyes fixed on the swans; still, his expression didn't change.

The face is a mask, Phillip Woolf had said, or a window. If you hope to succeed or survive, you'll make it a mask.

But Alexand had never found it necessary to mask himself with Rich. This wasn't a mask, it was self-induced emotional paralysis. A mask might be put aside, but not this.

Rich turned away, eyes closed, and on this day of grief his tears were for the living. Perhaps some candles should be lighted in the Bond chapels. Candles for Saint Elpha, guardian of those who walked under the Shadow.

4.

Admittance to the small gallery overlooking the Directorate Chamber was granted by personal invitation from a Directorate Lord, and only relatives or close friends were likely to be tendered such invitations. In consideration of the rank of its occupants, the gallery was luxuriously appointed, the ten chairs lining the curved railing richly upholstered. Alexand sat at one end of the row looking down into the Chamber, ignoring the only other tenants of the gallery, the Lord Theo Albin Reeswyck and his brother, Gamil.

When they arrived, there had been a brief exchange of amenities before they took seats at the opposite end of the row. Theo's manner had been condescending, bordering on open contempt, but Alexand allowed himself no reaction to that except amusement. Reeswyck was here to witness his own triumph—his nomination to a seat on the Directorate—and the humiliation of Galinin, Ivanoi, and—obviously—Woolf.

Alexand looked down into the spacious, austere oval of the Chamber. The gallery was at one end, hidden behind the fine-meshed golden screen that lined the top half of the Chamber wall. Most of the right-hand curve was delineated by an expanse of windowall offering a spectacular view of the Plaza. Centered in the left-hand wall were double doors, three meters tall, of carved teak, and on the white marlite walls hung tapestries woven three centuries ago, transforming history into epics. To the left of the door, Lord Even Pilgram, with Bishop Colona apparently blessing the event, died dramatically at the Battle of Darwin. On the right, Lord Patric Eyre Ballarat accepted the surrender of the Minister-Keffe Tsane Valstaad with a crowd of Confederation Lords in attendance, which was taking artistic liberty with history.

The floor of the Chamber was carpeted in a rich gold hue, and woven in contrasting black was the circled cross of the Concord crest. The emblem was five meters in diameter, and spaced around its periphery were ten massive, karri-wood chairs. The one on the far side of the circle was larger than the others, with a small platform before it serving as a step and footrest.

The Chairman's seat.

Alexand stared down at it, that solemnly carved, venerable hulk that had been the object of ultimate desire for ambitious men for generations. It seemed too heavy to be supported by anything other than stone; heavy with tragedy and blood, portent and power.

He glanced at his watch. Ten minutes before the appointed hour; only two of the Director's chairs were occupied now. His eyes moved around the circle to the one nearest him, the Ivanoi chair, and to the smaller chair that had been installed to its right for this meeting.

Lady Honoria Corelis Ivanoi sat in that smaller chair. He had only an angled view of her back now, but he'd studied her closely when she entered the Chamber. She wore black, a high-necked, long-sleeved gown; her golden hair was hidden under an unadorned koyf from which a black veil trailed like an ominous cloud. The regal, immutable calm was intact.

Lady Honoria had been purposely relegated to the chair squeezed into the circle, but the Ivanoi chair wasn't empty. From the gallery, Alexand could see the top of the small, tawny-haired head of its occupant. Derek Arment Ivanoi, first born of the Lord Alexis, was learning early the lessons of power.

Like his mother, he was dressed in black. He sat the big chair with his black-shod feet projecting in front of him because the seat was too deep for his five-year-old legs, and he didn't move except to gaze around the Chamber and occasionally look up at Honoria for reassurance.

This child would sit patiently through the meeting, comprehending nothing of the verbal battles raging around him. He would sit quietly; no fidgeting; no laughing—or crying. Derek Arment Ivanoi was the first born. His obligations had undoubtedly been made clear to him.

Alexand might have pitied the boy if he allowed himself to dwell on his plight. He didn't. He understood his own obligations as well as Derek Ivanoi did.

And he understood now Honoria Ivanoi's unbreachable calm, her quiet hands. A name, a presence, existed like a shadow in his thoughts, something so loved, so vital to his being, he couldn't encompass the grief of loss. And today it might be lost to him. Yet he waited in calculating calm, shutting out the potential of grief; for him at this time and place it did not exist. He could not let it exist. His obligations were clear.

The only other occupant of the circle now was Trevor Hild Robek, whose House was built firmly on the Planetary Transystem franchises. He was both a friend and an ally to Woolf and Galinin, and it was he who had escorted Honoria and Derek into the Chamber. He sat in the chair to Derek's left, solid and compact, dark hair laced with gray; like an old soldier, wily and wary.

Alexand's attention shifted to the double doors as they slid open.

Cameroodo and Fallor.

They parted when they reached the circle, Fallor stooped and gray, although he wasn't yet sixty, his pinched features revealing his confusion when he saw Derek Ivanoi and his mother. But he recovered his usual smug aplomb by the time he settled himself in his chair.

It seemed perversely appropriate that Fallor would be the last to vote, since his was one of the votes both antagonists in the impending encounter were vying for. His turn at voting was determined by the position of the Fallor chair in the circle, and the sequence of voting was determined by entrenched tradition whose genesis was lost in the shadows of history. It began with the Chairman and moved to his left around the circle. Fallor, on Galinin's right, always voted last.

Julia Fallor's father would have the last word today.

Alexand turned his attention to the man who had entered with Fallor. James Neeth Cameroodo, Lord of Mars, tall, stringently lean, the hint of negroid structure in his dark face revealing his racial origins as the leopard of the House crest revealed its geographic origins in Terra's Sudafrika. Unlike Fallor, Cameroodo could never be called a fence rider. His position on any issue was always clear. He stood with Selasis not out of friendship, but because Selasis's reactionary tendencies were in agreement with his.

Cameroodo showed no hint of surprise at seeing Honoria and Derek Ivanoi, and even offered her a courtly bow before he seated himself. Still, he didn't speak to her, even though they were separated only by the still-vacant Hamid chair.

The doors opened again and the man who entered was a marked contrast to Cameroodo. Sato Lao Shang's racial heritage was oriental; he was slight of body with wizened features and a balding head, yet he carried himself with profound dignity. He crossed the circle at a circumspect pace, then on reaching the chair to Cameroodo's right, turned and bowed to Honoria Ivanoi and spoke a few words to her, apparently condolences, then formally greeted the Lords present, and finally seated himself to wait silently beside the equally silent Cameroodo.

Sato Shang's show of courtesy to Lady Honoria didn't surprise Alexand, but neither did it offer any hint of his intentions. He could be fully prepared to destroy Ivanoi with a word, yet he would still extend Honoria that courtesy because it was her due; her birthright. A dynastic thinker.

Again the doors opened, and Alexand's eyes narrowed. Interesting that two of the habitual fence riders entered accompanied by a Selasid faithful. Shang had been alone, but Fallor had Cameroodo, and now Sandro Delai Omer was enjoying— or at least tolerating—the company of Lazar D'Ord Hamid.

Hamid was carrying the conversation, but Omer apparently concluded it for him when they reached the circle, stopping at his chair to Robek's left, while Hamid crossed to the chair next to Honoria Ivanoi. His surprise at seeing her and Derek literally stopped him in his tracks. He made an awkward bow to her, his round face hotly pink, then he went hastily to his chair, and from that time on, although no more than a meter's space stood between them, he spared her not even a glance.

A man of myopic subterfuges, so Phillip Woolf characterized Hamid. And a vain man, prone to decking himself with an abundance of ornament and given to extremes of fashion that only emphasized his paunchiness and short stature. A fool, and generally recognized as such, who held a Directorate chair only by virtue of heredity, and headed a financially successful House by the same accident of birth. Even a fool given the resources of a virgin planet could be successful. The House held a series of foodstuff franchises as well as Concord grants on most of the developed land on Pollux. Failure was all but impossible.

Alexand looked across the circle to the man whom Hamid had escorted into the Chamber. Sandro Delai Omer, a fence rider who seemed to take sardonic delight in the role and who was generally clever enough to profit by it. Like Hamid, Sandro Omer was vain, but with some justification. A handsome man whose refined features fell just short of delicacy, he wore his dark hair long, curling around his face, yet in spite of his tendency to affectation in manner and dress, there was nothing effete about him. Alexand knew his father's grudging respect for him. And he knew there was no way to guess how Omer would cast his vote. He wondered if Omer himself had yet decided.

The circle was almost filled, but the principals in the impending drama hadn't yet appeared. Alexand watched the doors, and at length they opened for the Lord Orin Badir Selasis.

He had presence; Alexand gave him his due. Orin Selasis moved into the Chamber like a mountain; a man of massive proportions, yet he walked with a light-footedness that with the long robes gave a paradoxical impression of floating. His steel-gray hair was combed back from a high, sloping forehead that made an unbroken line with a prominent, subtly hooked nose; his mouth might at one time have borne the stamp of sensuality, but it was only unyielding now, and hinting of cruelty.

But his face was dominated by the eyepatch, a black ellipse that seemed to give prominence to the other eye, a chameleon green with a reptilian aspect engendered by the pouched socket and the very singleness of it.

Selasis moved, floated, to his chair without so much as a nod to anyone present, betraying no awareness of Honoria or Derek Ivanoi. He took his seat between Omer and Fallor, and the huge chair was dwarfed by his bulk.

Alexand was so intent on him that he didn't hear the gallery door open. He was only alerted to the new arrival when he heard the Reeswyck exchanging greetings with him. Alexand listened to the voices. He recognized the newcomer, but chose not to acknowledge him.

But this latest arrival wouldn't be put off. "Well, Alex, come to take a lesson from the proceedings?"

Alexand didn't turn. "Isn't that why you're here, Karlis?"

Karlis Selasis laughed, a sound unrelated to humor. "I think I just might enjoy *this* lesson."

Alexand swiveled his chair a scant quarter turn and looked up at Karlis with a dispassionate eye that finally made him turn away. The Lady Idris Svynhel Selasis had been one of the Concord's reigning beauties, and Karlis was very much her son. It was rumored that he had been the model for the two Leador Neogreco sculptures Selasis donated for the entry court at the Concordia Sports Arena last year, and the resemblance was too obvious to be denied. Leador had no doubt enjoyed his model, and the two figures were among his best works. The faces were particularly telling, and Alexand had been amazed that the sculptor had not only carved excellent like-nesses of that nearly perfect face, but had imparted so mani-festly the ruthless sensuality in it. Perhaps it was too subtle for the Selasids, or perhaps they didn't take exception to it.

Alexand turned back to the Chamber while Karlis seated himself, leaving one empty chair between them, then leaned forward, staring blankly.

"Holy God, now we've got women and children sitting on the Directorate."

Alexand said levelly, "We have the first born of Alexis Ivanoi and his regent." A pause, then, "You know about the regency, of course."

Karlis's fair skin reddened. He was clearly not aware of the regency, but he said airily, "Of course I know about it. Who doesn't?"

Alexand didn't comment. The doors were opening again. It would be his father.

The Lord Phillip DeKoven Woolf was today every centi-meter the Black Eagle, even to the somber hue of his attire, the formal surcoat embellished with gold brocade, the cloak, bordered in black fur, set back on his shoulders, emphasizing their breadth. On entering the circle, Woolf paused, then crossed to Lady Honoria, bowed, and exchanged a few words with her. He didn't bow to Derek—that would be inappro-priate—but offered him a nod of recognition and a brief smile before he went to the chair between Shang and the Chairman's seat.

"Well, it's beginning to look like a family reunion." Karlis gave a caustic laugh, then turned his attention to the opening doors. "Finally. Here comes the old man."

Alexand wouldn't allow himself the indulgence of anger

now, but neither would he let that pass unchallenged. His voice was low, the words spaced.

"Karlis, don't ever let me hear you refer to the Lord Galinin as 'the old man' again."

Karlis turned, lips curling, on the verge of asking what he intended to do about it, but the answer was obvious, and it became equally obvious that Karlis wasn't willing to take him on in a point of honor.

But Alexand wasted no more thought on Karlis. The Chairman had arrived.

The Lord Mathis Daro Galinin, robed in black, a stark contrast to his white hair and beard, seemed an ancient patriarch reincarnated, and in his grave face and imperious bearing was a grim promise: Mathis Galinin would not surrender to man or fate. And these proud and cynical Lords responded, however reluctantly or subtly; he was the focal point of every eye, and his entrance created a hushed tension, the rustle of his robes was audible as he approached the Chairman's seat, stepped onto the footrest, and turned to survey the circle.

Alexand counted them off around the circle as the votes would be heard: Galinin, Woolf, Shang, Cameroodo, Hamid, Ivanoi, Robek, Omer, Selasis, and Fallor.

That sequence of names hadn't changed for four generations. He wondered if it would be the same at the Directorate's next meeting.

Mathis Galinin, he had no doubt, was asking himself the same question.

5.

Adrien left the clavalier, Master Duboi, and the Isawa *Sonatina* in mid-measure at the news that a SynchCom lettape was being transmitted from Concordia for her. She ran down the corridor 'ways, too impatient to bear with their sedate movement, still running even when she reached her salon and crossed to the comconsole. She had awaited this through the endless hours of a sleepless night: a call, a lettape—anything to break the silence she knew was more than preoccupation with the crisis in Concordia.

Now she touched the repeat switch for the third time and watched the words take form on the screen again, moving inexorably from the bottom to the top.

She wondered if she would ever be capable of moving again, and found it a matter of indifference. She was equally indifferent to the fact that her heart still beat, her lungs still drew air into her body, her mind could still translate letters into words, words into meanings. She was even capable of recognizing the pain behind the terse sentences.

. . . my father offered no more than a possibility of a marriage alliance, and he did so only when I suggested the gambit myself. I was thinking of the House, of Galinin, Ivanoi, and the Chairmanship. It is for such decisions that I've been trained. The efficacy of that training is obvious.

Charles Fallor turned the vote and saved Galinin and Ivanoi—for now, at least. He also turned the possibility my father offered into a probability, or rather, an inevitability. Fallor turned the vote once, and he can turn it again, and Orin Selasis is waiting to offer Karlis in my stead should Father try to renege. The balance of power is still too precarious to risk a Fallor-Selasis alliance.

You will understand what was—and still is—at stake. I needn't explain my decision further, but neither can I ask you to forgive it. And I know you will also understand that there's nothing more I can say, nothing we can ever say to each other. Not in words.

Perhaps we saw a Rightness in a Testing.

But this I will put into words: Adrien, never doubt I love you, and I always will. . . .

The lines slid past and off the screen. The final word remained imprinted on her retina: *Alexand.*

A sound; somewhere an insistent sound. The door chime. She heard it and recognized it, but she was incapable of responding to it.

A Testing. It *would* be a Testing. She wondered if she had the courage for this.

Alexand . . .

Her hands convulsed into fists.

The chime again. The door opened. Still, she couldn't move, couldn't tear her gaze from the blank screen. Absence was in that square of emptiness.

"Serra Adrien?"

The voice was gentle and familiar, and somehow it gave her strength to turn her head toward the door. Dr. Lile Perralt, reflected sunlight striking his grizzled white hair, emphasizing the anxious lines in his face. He started toward her, then stopped a few paces away.

"Adrien, what's wrong?"

She methodically removed the lettape spool from its slot, staring at it. She must answer Perralt. She wasn't sure she could tolerate it, but it must be done. He deserved no pain in doubt.

She tossed the spool into the syntegrator.

"I had a lettape from Alex." She looked up, briefly frightened at his pallor; there was that hint of illness in it she'd noted with increasing frequency in the last year. "It was about the . . . Directorate meeting." She turned from the screen and walked toward the couch near the windowall, vaguely aware that Perralt was following her. "Fortunately, Selasis was stymied both in his bid for the Chairmanship and in his attempt to unseat the Ivanoi."

"I'm relieved at that. Can you tell me about it?"

He meant was it something for his ears, but perhaps he also realized that she might find the telling difficult.

"You understand politics, Dr. Lile; you know every victory has its price. Its casualties."

"Yes, and I'm sure Galinin paid a high price for this victory."

"It wasn't only Galinin's victory. It was also Ivanoi's and Woolf's."

Perralt hesitated. "And what was Woolf's price?"

The Castorian sky was so dark, even at noonday; indigo blue, verging on black. Black was still the color of grief.

"Charles Fallor cast the deciding vote; the vote that stymied Selasis and saved Ivanoi and Galinin, that made Phillip Woolf heir apparent to the Chairmanship." Why couldn't she say that it was Alexand who was actually the heir? "That vote was bought with the promise of a marriage."

"Oh, Holy God . . . Alexand and Julia Fallor?"

"Yes."

The room seemed to be getting dark. It made her dizzy.

Alexand, I loved you from the first; I saw a Rightness in it, and it was there. And how can I ever call anyone else my Promised, my husband, my Lord?

"Adrien!"

Perralt caught her as she fell, eased her onto the couch, and held her when the sobbing began. He offered no words, knowing she was past hearing them. He was relieved that she was capable of tears, relieved that it was he who was here now so she would feel free to weep. Those agonized sobs racked him, but she must have them out.

On some level he was thinking that he must contact Phoenix HQ. Ben probably knew of the outcome of the Directorate meeting through the Concordia chapter, but he might not know the price of the Fallor vote. The Woolf succession to the Chairmanship was welcome news, but the Fallor-Woolf alliance would be a weak one and a blow to the Society's hopes for Eliseer. It must be stopped if at all possible.

Later. He'd make the call later.

Now all he could think of was Adrien, sobbing in his arms, this lovely young woman who was so exceptional among her peers as to be capable of loving with all her being, who was paying the price for that rare gift because she was the daughter of a First Lord.

And Ser Alexand—he was equally cursed or gifted. What of that young man born into a crucial position at a crucial time? A young man marked CP-One by the Phoenix, the highest

Critical Potential rating for an individual.

Phillip Woolf had made a bargain with Fallor for survival. Perralt wondered what the long-range results would be, and if it would seem a bargain in the end.

6.

It was still cool at night, a scent of frost in the air. Rich made his way along the balcony fronting the gymnasium, hearing the hum of his crutches under the rasping swish of his footsteps in the night quiet; the lights from the gymnasium threw multiple, ghostly shadows of his cloaked figure across the marblex. Finally, he stopped and leaned against a pillar to catch his breath; it was a long walk from the family wing. He might have saved some effort by taking the main corridors with their pedways, but his chances of being seen were reduced this way, especially so late at night.

Concordia was a glittering galaxy of lights sharp and clear in the cold air. He searched the moonless sky for the constellations of the Southern Cross and the Centaur, found them, then after a moment turned to look into the gym. This was another reason he'd chosen this route: he could be sure Fenn Lacroy was here and that he was alone.

The SportsMaster was seated on a bench against the far wall by the foil cases, cleaning the foils and testing the charges. Rich wasn't concerned that Lacroy would see him; he was too intent on his task, and the interior lights were too bright. Nor was he surprised that he was in the gym at this hour; it was more home to him than his apartment.

Rich took a bracing breath. His pulse rate was up, and that, he knew, couldn't be attributed solely to physical exertion. Fear. But fear in one form or another wasn't a stranger. He resumed his slow, halting pace and at the end of the balcony turned into a corridor that took him to the gym door. The S/V and shock screens were on. He shifted his weight to one crutch and reached for the doorcon. Like most of the locks in the Estate, this one was keyed to his thumbprint or voice as it was for every member of the First Lord's family.

Lacroy looked up from his work, his blunt features reflecting

169

first annoyance, then surprise.

"Ser Rich!" He put the foil and cleaning tissue aside and started to rise.

"That's all right, Fenn. Don't get up."

He relaxed, at least partially, watching Rich curiously as he crossed the expanse of floor and finally sank down on the bench beside him.

"I'm always glad for your company, Ser Rich, but I'll admit I hadn't expected it. It's after midnight."

Rich propped his crutches against the bench. "Yes. Well, I had to wait until Alex was asleep."

Lacroy frowned dubiously. "Ser Alex doesn't know you're here?"

"No one does. Ease your mind on that."

"I . . . don't understand."

Rich reached into an inner pocket of his cloak. "I won't fence with you, Fenn. I think you're afraid you *do* understand." He opened his hand, and on the palm was a thin, nearly transparent disk no larger than his thumbnail. "Is this what you were looking for yesterday when you came to my suite with Alex?"

Lacroy stared at the disk, and the color drained from his face, his eyes flashing up to meet Rich's. Then he turned away.

"What makes you think I was looking for something?"

Rich sighed and returned the disk to his pocket. "I can't expect you to answer my questions. I was hoping you would. And you needn't be concerned for yourself at the moment. I haven't told anyone about this. I assume we're free of monitors here?"

Lacroy replied noncommittally, "Why wouldn't we be?"

Rich nodded, ignoring the question. "I'd suggest a stronger adhesive be used on these devices. This might've fallen from Alex's cloak at a far more inopportune time." He paused, but Lacroy didn't respond. "Fenn, I checked the House memfiles. DeKoven Woolf has never manufactured a minicorder like this, and if it isn't a Woolf product, it isn't Concord. Fortunately, it does function in Woolf headsets. It's quite a clear recording. The entire strategy for the Galinin-Woolf-Ivanoi counteroffensive against Selasis is on this tape."

Lacroy sagged forward, his elbows on his knees, big hands

hanging limp. Rich had never seen anything like defeat in his face, but it was in every line now.

"What are you going to do, Rich?"

"I don't know."

"There's only one thing you can do. You know that."

"Perhaps there's only one thing I *should* do, but there are many things I *can* do. I should tell my father, and I might. That isn't a threat; I'm only being honest with you."

Lacroy's hands tightened into fists, his features contracted, then both went lax as he asked, "What are you asking of me? What do you want?"

"I want some answers. That's all. As for the tape, I'll return it to you if you can assure me it won't be used against Woolf or Galinin. Of course, the information on it would be of little use to anyone now." He smiled faintly. "Although I'm sure Lord Orin would've paid a high price to have it yesterday— before this morning's Directorate meeting."

Lacroy straightened, staring at him reproachfully.

"Rich, not *Selasis*. Whatever you think of me—"

"I wasn't suggesting it was intended for Selasis. That assumption would be absurd. You've been allieged to DeKoven Woolf for what? Twenty years?"

"Nearly eighteen."

"An allegiance shift from Hamid, wasn't it? At any rate, your relationship with Father is very close; a man in your position could wreak havoc. If you were a Selasid agent, Woolf would be in a far weaker position by now, and Selasis in a stronger one. Besides, I doubt a Selasid agent would survive Father's security system for eighteen years."

"No," Lacroy said dully, "the tenure of most House agents is rather short."

"I have other reasons for assuming you aren't a Selasid agent. The origin of the device, for instance. Lord Orin wouldn't manufacture his own monitoring equipment. The manufacturing process couldn't be kept secret, and he doesn't think in technical terms, nor does Bruno Hawkwood. They'd use Woolf products because they're easily available, and the refinements of this device wouldn't be worth the risk." Rich paused, then, "And there's another reason: it isn't your style, Fenn. You aren't Orin's—or Hawkwood's—type."

Lacroy stared miserably at the floor. "But obviously I'm an agent of some sort. In the face of that, can you be so sure what... type I am?"

Rich smiled. "Yes, I can. As to what sort of agent you are—well, I have a great deal of time on my hands and access to high-priority Concord 'files. For the last year I've been doing some private research. The information available on this particular subject is scant, once you eliminate rumors and hearsay evidence, but I've sifted out a few nuggets of fact."

Rich could feel Lacroy's tension as he looked around at him.

"And what's the subject of your research, Rich?"

"The semimythical Society of the Phoenix."

Lacroy commented warily, "An interesting subject."

"Very. Fenn, what did you intend to do with the tape?"

He blinked, looking peculiarly blank for a moment.

"I... I can't tell you."

"I only want to know in general terms."

Again, he blinked with that same vacant expression. He frowned and shook his head.

"I *can't* tell you."

"Oh. The 'conditioning.' You literally can't tell me. Who can?" Again, that curious, fleeting confusion. Rich went on before Lacroy attempted to reply, "All right, you can't answer that, either."

"No, I can't, even if I would."

Rich looked up at the high ceiling. The room seemed very large now and somehow lonely. Loneliness is like pain; one never grows accustomed to it.

"Fenn, please—I *must* have some answers."

"Answers to what, Rich?"

"To my questions. At least a few of them before I—" He stopped, surprised to find his hands tensely clenched. He let them relax. "Certainly I must have some answers about the tape, and I came here hoping for... for hope, perhaps; for answers to the questions behind this tape. I won't use them against you or the Phoenix. At least... no, I shouldn't say that. If I'm not satisfied with your motives, I can't promise my silence. I suppose that makes it impossible for you to give me any answers."

When Lacroy replied, it was with some hesitancy. "I don't

know whether it's possible or not. I can find out if an exception can be made for you."

Rich focused intently on his face. "Will you? Will you at least ask if—whoever must make that decision? Fenn, *please*, if you care for me." Then he felt the heat in his cheeks and turned away; he hadn't intended to beg.

"I'll find out, Rich." His tone was unexpectedly gentle. "But it'll take a few days."

Rich sighed; that was all he could ask now. He reached for his crutches and levered himself to his feet.

"Thank you. I'll keep the tape." He studied Lacroy's re-action, but there was only a faint frown. "If you can satisfy me that it won't harm the House, you can have it. Of course, at this point it will be of interest only from a historical or sociological point of view."

Lacroy said absently, "That's our main line of work."

"Then we have that in common." Rich pressed the controls on the handgrips of his crutches and turned. "I must get back to my suite. Alex will worry if he wakes and finds me gone."

Lacroy came to his feet, gazing at him in frank bewilder-ment.

"Rich, you...I don't understand you. I mean, you came here tonight alone, without telling Ser Alex or anyone else, and even though it goes against all reason, I believe you. You came here with that tape, and you—you act as if it never occurred to you that..." He faltered, staring at Rich hope-lessly.

"That you might recover the tape and remove any evidence of your guilt by the simple expedient of killing me?"

He flinched as if Rich had struck him.

"That's...what I mean."

"Of course it occurred to me. You'd have no trouble ov-ercoming me, and I'm sure you could arrange an 'accident.' if you felt any qualms of conscience, you could salve that with the knowledge that you'd only be hurrying the inevitable by a few years."

Lacroy went white. "Rich, don't say that!"

"Why not? You know my illness is terminal, don't you?" The brief response seemed an overwhelming effort.

"Yes."

"I thought so."

"I've known about it for several years."

"And the Phoenix knows?"

"Yes."

"Yet the secret hasn't leaked out. Remarkable."

Lacroy averted his eyes, and when at length he looked up at Rich again, he was met with a gentle, ironic smile.

"Rich, you came here to test me—with your *life*."

"Yes, Fenn, I did."

"But, I might've, I . . ."

"You *might* have done a number of things, but I couldn't believe you'd kill me, and if I misjudged you to that extent, I don't think I'd have cared much whether I lived or not."

"Oh, Rich, please—you cut to my heart."

"I don't mean to cause you pain, but I was counting on your susceptibility to it. If you—and the Phoenix—are not such that you'd find it expedient to kill me, then I doubt I'll find it necessary to betray you. We may even be allies of sorts. Now, I must go." He began moving with his halting, sliding steps toward the door.

"Ser Rich . . ."

He paused and turned. "Yes?"

"I'll get those answers for you somehow."

"Thank you, Fenn. Thank you."

Lacroy wasn't aware of the tears on his cheeks until after the doorscreens went on behind that frail, wistful figure.

PHOENIX MEMFILES: DEPT HUMAN SCIENCES: BASIC SCHOOL
                                  (HS/BS)
SUBFILE: LECTURE, BASIC SCHOOL   2 JANUAR 3252
                                  GUEST LECTURER: RICHARD LAMB
                                  SUBJECT: POST-DISASTERS HISTORY:
                                  THE HOLY CONFEDERATION (2585–2903)
DOC LOC #819/219–1253/1812–1648–213252

At the beginning of his career of conquest and consolidation, Even Pilgram did not call himself a Lord, nor his domain a House, but he is credited with being the first to employ those terms—at least, in their modern usage. Originally, he called himself HoldMaster and his domain a Station, a term whose use in this context isn't clear. His Station was an area of indefinite boundaries covering at least ten thousand square kilometers in central western Conta Austrail, and an estimated twenty thousand people were Bonded to him. He is also credited—probably erroneously—with originating that term, but it should be noted that his "Bonds" included not only slave/serfs, but the middle class as it existed at the time, and even some elements of the upper class, such as the knight-warrior class.

Pilgram's village-fortress of Pilgramhold has been beautifully restored by the House of Kalister with the assistance of the University's department of archeology, and is considered a classic of late Second Dark Age parabolic-vault masonry. Bishop Colona's monastery and cathedron in Pilgramhold have also been restored, but they aren't the buildings in which Colona lived and worshiped before *The Revelations*; those were both razed before the end of his life to make way for the more grandiose structures we see now. The original Order of Renunciation monastery was a cluster of wood and stone buildings that could house no more than twenty monks, and its cathedron could honestly be called only a chapel.

The alliance between Colona and Pilgram was perhaps inevitable; they were both men of monumental ambition and served each other's purposes well. We might wonder what would have happened if Colona hadn't been sent by his Order to the remote monastery in Pilgramhold immediately after his novitiate in Perthhold, but it's probable that this political-religious alliance would have occurred eventually somewhere in Conta Austrail during the late medieval period. Historically, the time was right for the isolated feudal holds that dotted the continent to be united in a larger political entity to provide the stable basis for further social and cultural evolution. That consolidation needed both the impetus of a politically ambitious man like Pilgram and the unifying philosophic impetus of the new religion Colona offered.

There was, of course, little in Colona's *Revelations* that was really new; Mezionism is a peculiarly eclectic amalgam of existing faiths and dogmas. What was new was its unity.

During the preceding five hundred years, religion in Conta Austrail had devolved into hundreds of splintered sects as a result of the isolation of individual centers of population, and although most of these sects, like the Order of Renunciation, which dominated the holds of southwestern Conta Austrail at that time, were still recognizable as variations on Pre-Disasters Christianity, there was great divergence between them, and that in itself contributed to the continuing isolation of the enclaves.

Colona offered the True Way under the sanctifying cloak of divine revelation. There is little doubt that he did consider the doctrines codified in *The Revelations* divinely inspired, and if contemporary accounts are true, he suffered great tribulation in pursuit of that inspiration. A fellow monk (in *The Pilgramhold Codex*, ca. 2560) describes Colona in one of his ecstatic trances sitting naked in the desert under the sparse shade of a coolabah tree for "three and seven days, his each bone to be counted under his flesh, his eyes burned blind by the sun so that he might see inward to the true vision of the All-God."

That vision won him no favor in the Order of Renunciation hierarchy, and he was promptly ejected from the monastery as a heretic. He had, however, made something of a name for himself locally and aroused the interest of the HoldMaster, Even Pilgram, who took him into his hold and asked his instruction in his new religion. Pilgram was apparently subjected to some tribulation, too, during this process, but he came out of the experience a convert and with a powerful tool that insured the success of his subsequent campaign to unite the scattered holds of Conta Austrail into one political entity.

It was a holy war, of course, to which Pilgram, with Colona ever at his side, devoted the remaining fifteen years of his life. When he died at the Battle of Darwin, the Charter of the Holy Confederation of Conta Austrail had already been signed (literally in blood) by all but a handful of the nearly four hundred Lords or HoldMasters in Conta Austrial, and the white-and-gold circled-cross banner of the Church of the Holy Mezion was firmly planted in every inhabited area across the wide breadth of the continent.

Pilgram was a master of the difficult art of consolidation, and he produced three sons with the wisdom and vision to finish his campaign and make of the Holy Confederation a viable social and political organization. In this it has been suggested that they had good advice from Colona, who demonstrated a high degree of pragmatism in the consolidation of his spiritual empire. He survived Pilgram by thirty years, spending most of the last twenty in the cathedron built for him in Pilgramhold. We don't know the cause of his death, but descriptions of his funeral have come down to us, and we know that the ascetic who endured naked the blistering sun of the western deserts was buried in silk and brocade in a jewel-encrusted casket, attended by an estimated fifty thousand devout followers.

CHAPTER III: Avril 3250

1.

Alexand touched the control and the cabinet door slid back silently. And he almost laughed. Ser Alton Robek was a considerate host indeed. He provided his young guests—all 150 of them—with attentive servants, well appointed and very private quarters, food and drink in lush variety, and entertainment equally lush and various, including psychomaxic capsules or masks for those who wished to indulge in that illegal, but acceptable, form of self-entertainment.

And Ser Alton also provided for the morning after.

The spacious bath was walled in amber-tinted mirrors, softly lighted and pleasantly warm; there were stacks of heated towels, racks of cosmetic aids, and a 'com for calling the servants, the panel prominently placed by the marble basin and emphasized by a yellow light so that blurred eyes could find it.

And this last touch: a small cabinet offering remedies for headache, dizziness, nausea, and any other aftereffects of the night's festivities, each bottle marked in large, glowing letters as to contents and purpose.

The headache remedy was all Alexand needed. He downed one of the tablets and returned to the bedroom, wondering what Ser Alton could offer to remedy—what was it? Not depression. Ennui, perhaps.

He should have stayed home. His week's leave had been crowded enough with social and House obligations, and there was more remedy for ennui in an hour with Rich than a night of Alton Robek's revelries.

He walked to the open window, his passage silent, bare feet sinking into the thermcarpet. The room was still dark, but the eastern sky was coloring with fragile pinks that reflected on the calm sea and tinged the breakers at the foot of the sheer cliffs below him with lavender. The clean scent of the sea was borne on a light breeze cool on his naked skin. There was no evidence of the season visible from this window; still, the chill of the wind hinted of autumn and of winter to come. He looked down at the whispering surf and in this dawn solitude felt a curious sense of nonexistence, as if he displaced no space. It was not an uncomfortable sensation.

He turned and let his gaze rest on the fancifully canopied and curtained bed, an irony-weighted smile pulling at his lips. A remedy for ennui...

Ser Alton did his best.

Not that Alton had ever actually "provided" his cousin Elianne. The Lady Elianne Robek provided herself to whom she pleased, and Alexand pleased her.

He went to the bed and pushed back the filmy curtain. A remedy. At least a transitory one; that was something.

The Lady Elianne also pleased Alexand, but in the sense that he was pleased by an exquisite piece of sculpture, a work of art given the dimension of life. She lay on her side, blithely asleep, one arm crossing her breasts at an oblique angle, golden hair fanning across the pillow, her skin as silky as the sheet that crumpled in soft folds at her waist, clinging to the long, complex curve of hip melding into thigh. The night's revelry hadn't diminished her beauty in the least. The time would come when it would begin to tell, but she still held the bloom of youth in her fine, childlike features.

But Elianne was no longer a child. She was twenty-six, and six years his senior, yet he'd have guessed her to be no more than sixteen by her face and body, and by her behavior. If she would consider that a compliment, she didn't know him.

And that was true. She didn't know him and never would; she didn't really know herself. Elianne was a captive of her senses and found reason enough for her being in the exploitation of sensory stimuli. She didn't ask for more.

He recognized his ambiguity toward her, that he could enjoy her, indulge her and himself in those pleasures that delighted her, and still, if he never saw her again he would feel no sense of loss. Nor would she.

He sank down onto the bed and propped the pillows behind his back. He wouldn't try to sleep again; it would be futile. He watched Elianne stirring, turning languidly, but she didn't wake. He would leave her soon, and if his shoulders sagged at the thought, it had nothing to do with her.

Today was the Estre holiday, a celebration of resurrection whose roots were in another hemisphere where it marked the birth of spring. Yet tradition placed it in Avril, and it was celebrated then regardless of seasons, or even the lack of them, throughout the Two Systems.

Tradition also bound him to appear with his parents for the High Cantas at the Cathedron in Concordia this evening. And tradition bound him to return to the Confleet Academy in Sidny tomorrow. The week-long holiday leave ended then.

Five more months in Sidny; seven were behind him. And after the Academy certified him as qualified to wear the insignia of a Confleet officer, to go out into the worlds and engage the enemies of the Concord in mortal combat—

He didn't think past 15 Septem. Graduation.

Elianne stirred again, then turned and smiled up at him, coming awake with a child's instant alertness.

"Well. Good morning."

He laughed, watching her as she stretched herself, every movement as fluid as a cat's.

"Good morning, Elianne. I think you slept well."

"Beautifully." She sat up and looked out at the roseate sky. "But I'm not sure I'm ready to give it up yet. Tell me, Alex, do you *always* rise to greet the dawn?"

"Always."

"Mm. I know better." She leaned close to him, and, even though she didn't touch him, he could feel the warmth of her tawny-silk skin. "Can't you sleep, love?"

"I've slept. I was simply availing myself of your cousin's headache remedy."

"Oh." She smiled wryly. "Is it bad?"

"No. I don't indulge myself to that point."

"Well, that's very wise of you, my Lord Alexand." Then she laughed, her green eyes glinting. "We'll probably be the only ones mobile this morning."

"And how do you explain *your* mobility, my lady?"

"I'm just careful about *what* I indulge myself in."

Alexand laughed. "I see. How very wise of *you*."

He was aware that she'd drawn closer to him, and that her gaze kept straying from his eyes to his mouth, and it was curious that this creature of senses had the capacity to project her sensual orientation to anyone near her. He found himself acutely aware of the murmur of the sea, the cool salt scent of the dawn wind, the perfume lingering in her hair. There seemed to be a magnetic essence in the supple lines of her body that drew the eye.

She was silent for a while, and he felt himself being studied with the same detached pleasure he'd felt in watching her asleep. Her lips parted a moment before she spoke.

"Surely you don't have to leave so early."

"No."

"But soon, I suppose." She sighed. "Do you really have to go to that dull ceremony? Old Simonidis is so dreary."

Alexand smiled at that. "Yes, I have to go. Duty, Elianne; one must keep up the facade."

She laughed, still watching him, eyes half closed. "Well, that's one advantage of being second-class Elite. I don't have to worry so much about facades."

He frowned and turned away. "I don't like that term."

"Second-class Elite?" She gave that an insouciant shrug. "Well, if you think I object to being second-class Elite, you're wrong. I wouldn't trade places with the daughters of the First Lords for anything. Or with you, for that matter, my handsome young first born. A little condescension is a small price to pay for freedom."

He looked at her, surprised at that, and he wondered what she understood of the word *freedom*. But she was laughing again, a purring sound as tangible as a caress, and she moved closer, her thigh touching his.

"And I suppose," she said wistfully, "you *must* go back to Sidny tomorrow. Oh, Alex—what a bore."

He studied the contours of her parted lips; an extraordinary union of subtle planes and curves.

"Sidny is also part of the facade, and I've even less choice there."

"No. Oh, well . . ." Then she smiled, tilting her head to one side, the movement bringing her hair down over one shoulder in a silent cascade. "Alton said he'd heard that you volunteered for Confleet's next Altair expedition. Did you really?"

He smiled with her. She thought it nothing more than a joke, and perhaps it was. It was highly unlikely that the Directorate would approve the funds for that expedition.

He shrugged and said, "Yes, I volunteered for it."

"Oh, Alex, how marvelous! But why?"

As a statement of position, of personal conviction; it was a stand taken without hope, and in that it seemed typical of so much in his life.

He laughed and countered with, "Why not, Elianne?"

"Why not? Because you might fall into a hole in space or something like the *Felicity*, and then what would I do?" The soft laughter brimmed in every word. Her hand moved to the medallion at his throat, but it was only of fleeting interest. Her fingers traced a warm line along his collarbone outward to his shoulder and back again.

He regarded her silently, aware of the quickening of his heartbeat, the faster tempo of his breathing, and the less definable sensations evoked by her touch, her languidly alert gaze, her very presence, and aware that she knew exactly what she was doing and what she wanted.

Ennui. . . .

A smile curved his lips, but there was a coolness in his eyes. Elianne seemed unaware of it, watching him, never blinking, as he sat up and leaned close to her, brushing her hair back from her cheek.

"Well, Elianne . . . perhaps you'll have to volunteer, too, and we can fall into that hole in space together. . . ."

Her laughter again, and the whispering touch of her fingers along the long muscles of his back. His hands caught in her hair, pulling her mouth against his, but lightly; his lips were still closed, and he allowed himself a mental pause, poised on the brink of a choice. He looked into her eyes, cloudy green, and she smiled; a slow, sentient smile. He could read her pulse in her throat, and knew she read his, and he heard in the inner ear of his mind his own silent, dark laughter.

A remedy.

He closed his eyes and pressed his lips again to hers, one hand sliding under her arm around the sweep of soft-fleshed bone, the other pausing at the curve of her breast. His mouth was open now, the black laughter fading as he sank down into the bed, feeling the sinuous shifting of her body against his, the reactive tightening at the groin, the contraction of awareness that sought only sensation in the polished texture of her skin, the taut strain of bone and muscle under it, the momentum of pulse and breath. He was aware always, yet in a vague, nonspecific manner, of an exquisite skill in her every movement, in every part of her.

He reached out for that consummatory limbo, past conscious reaction, past thought, *in extremis*, where the center of motivation dissipated into every cell of his body, and he no longer had to think—only feel and act and react and act and feel; a complex of instantaneous perception and response, his consciousness so narrowed there was no awareness of Elianne except as an inseverable adjunct of his own body. And his body exalted in its vitality, spent its energies like a profligate, as if the wellsprings of power were infinite.

At length, when he reached the ebb of impetus, the nerveless reawakening, he heard again the dark laughter.

A remedy. . . .

He had a fleeting vision, a brief, waking fantasy, of Elianne and himself lost in the nonconscious limbo of lovemaking while the walls around them collapsed into the sea.

And that brought the dark laughter to his lips, but it lost its sardonic edge. He made no move to draw away from her, feeling the faint unconscious tremors, muscular aftershocks, lax flesh against lax now. He looked down into her face, lightly flushed, her eyes dilated. She was smiling in response to his laughter, even if she didn't understand it.

It didn't matter. He didn't understand it himself.

2.

Master Webster snapped his fingers, and Tuck obediently brought the shirt, eyeing the tailor with bemused tolerance, but still moving quickly to do his bidding.

Alexand gazed coolly at his own image as the Bond held the shirt for him. In the mirrored walls of the dressing room, the three of them and their multiple reflections made a stifling crowd. He shrugged on the shirt, and Webster fussed at the draping of the full, fine-pleated sleeves. Alexand ignored him, concentrating on the lacing at the neck, but when Tuck reached out to help him, a flashing glance made him draw back. The Bond was more familiar with his Lord's moods than Webster.

The tailor was intent on the blue-gray trousers, seamed with silver at the sides, a narrow decorative border of silver at the hem. He pursed his lips, nodding to himself. The fit was perfect, low on the hips, close to show off the young Lord's long legs. Webster considered himself a fortunate man: the Lord Woolf and his first born were ideal subjects on which to display his talents.

"Ah, Lord Alexand—excellent!" He gave a short, smug laugh. "And a formal suit without boots; you'll have all the young gentlemen tossing off their footwear!"

Alexand pulled at one sleeve impatiently. "The boots are far too martial, Webster; they aren't appropriate for a religious celebration." And he had enough of boots and military accouterments at Sidny; enough for a lifetime and more to come. "Next time, drop the seams on the shoulders a little more."

"Oh, yes, of course, my lord."

"The doublet—Tuck?"

The Bond held the doublet, with its elaborate silver brocade on pale blue, while Alexand pulled it on, frowning as Webster began making more fussing adjustments.

"Webster, I'm not a mannequin." His tone was sharp, and the tailor retreated a pace. "Who designed the brocade?"

"Why, that's Mano Damik's work. If it doesn't please you—"

185

"It pleases me very much. Tell Fer Damik for me, and authorize a fifty 'cord bonus for him."

"Ah, yes, my lord, I will."

Alexand turned to let Tuck help him into the surcoat, a clear blue with slashed sleeves, open in front to expose the brocaded doublet. There was no sash; the surcoat was so subtly fitted, it needed only a silver catch at the waist. Otherwise, it was unadorned, and Webster had balked at that; he had a penchant for decoration that neither Alexand nor Phillip Woolf had yet managed to subdue entirely. But now he tilted his head to one side, beaming with complacent pride.

"Ah, my lord, marvelous! If I do say so myself, my finest creation!"

Alexand studied his image with deliberate skepticism. "Possibly, Webster." Then he tensed, seeing a reflected movement in the mirrored walls: Rich at the open door, floating in the nulgrav chair. Alexand pulled at the surcoat's lapels, swallowing at the constriction in his throat. Rich still used his crutches at the University, but at home he depended more and more on the chair. The crutches asked too much of his failing arms and hands.

"Hello, Rich. Come to see the draping?" He called up a smile, watching his brother in the mirror as he maneuvered the chair into a corner out of the way.

"I wouldn't miss it." Rich grinned slyly. "The tailors will be indebted to you."

"Will they?"

"You're breaking precedent again. The cut of that surcoat and no boots. Thousands of new wardrobes will have to be made."

Alexand laughed. "Then I've made some contribution to the general welfare of humankind—or at least *tailor*-kind. Master Webster, you may go now."

Webster's expectant smile faltered; then he bowed.

"Yes, my lord. Oh—the cloak?" he asked hopefully; he so much preferred to see the entire ensemble together.

Alexand only glanced at the cloak on the clothes rack. "I'm sure it will be quite satisfactory; I don't need to try it."

"Oh. Yes, my lord." But he still hesitated.

Alexand studied him coolly, then finally gave him a brief smile. "I'm pleased, Webster. Thank you."

He sighed gustily and bowed again. "Thank *you*, my lord."
He turned and bowed to Rich. "Good night, Ser Richard."

"Good night, Master Webster."

Alexand caught Rich's eye in the mirror, but neither of
them spoke until Webster had made his exit and they heard
the bedroom door snap shut behind him. Then they both
laughed aloud, and Rich said, "I suppose this was his finest
creation again."

"Of course. Tuck, the jewelry case, please." Then to Rich,
"You look damnably comfortable. Anticipating a quiet evening
with your tapes, I suppose—and stop gloating." He chose three
rings and a sapphire medallion on a long chain. "Thank you,
Tuck, and that will be all; you're free for the rest of the night."

"Thank you, my lord." He put the case away, then paused
to bow to Rich on his way out. Rich waved him on with a
smile.

"Good night, Tuck. Blessings of the holy day to you."

"And to you, Ser. Peace be."

The Bond would also commemorate the Estre holiday this
evening, but in a crude chapel rather than the magnificent
Cathedron of Concordia, and Alexand wondered if Tuck would
understand that his Lord envied him that. He fastened the
medallion at his neck, then surveyed his image once more.

The Lord Alexand. It had been seven months since that
fateful birthday: Age of Rights.

What rights, he wondered; what rights accrued to him at
that magical age? The right to sign House documents without
the bother of having a proxy drawn up. The right to sit in
meetings of the Court of Lords should he wish to waste the
time. The right to surrender four years of his life to Confleet,
learning and practicing the lordly arts of war.

That was all; nothing else had changed. Except that he was
now addressed as *Lord* Alexand.

His gaze shifted from his own image to Rich's, and he
became aware of his brother's intent appraisal.

"Very handsome," Rich said quietly.

"Webster knows his craft. I'll give him credit for that, even
if it comes a little reluctantly."

"I don't mean just the suit."

Alexand shrugged uncomfortably as he turned to leave the
room with its mirrors and multiplied images.

"Some brandy to celebrate the holy occasion, Rich? I suppose it should be wine."

Rich followed him through the bedroom to the alcove where the view of Concordia was framed in the oval panes of oriel windows.

"I'll have brandy. Wine is only a surrogate for blood."

Alexand went to a sidetable on which a decanter and a set of crystal goblets waited. He filled two glasses and, after handing Rich his, turned to the windows.

"Perhaps blood would be more appropriate for the times."

Rich made no comment on that, looking out at the city, refracted in the multiple panes, its lights, like the stars, coming to life in the waning glow of sunset.

"How was Alton Robek's beach party, Alex?"

"Boring." Alexand turned, laughing, and slumped into a chair near Rich. "Holy God, the 'cords wasted, and the end result monumental boredom. But perhaps Alton's guests aren't capable of anything else."

"That's ironic since Alton seems to have made relieving boredom his goal in life."

"At least he doesn't seem to take his role as future First Lord of Hild Robek too seriously. But even if I count myself among the congenitally bored, Alton's gathering had one advantage." He took time to taste his brandy, his smile turning icy. "It wasn't the kind of party any daughter of a First Lord could properly attend."

Rich nodded absently. The Fallor were in Concordia for the holiday, and Alexand had been forced to endure Julia's company as her escort to three levays already during his week's leave, and tonight after the High Cantas would again be her escort at a banquet at the Galinin Estate.

Estre didn't compare as a social holiday to Kristus Eve or Concord Day, but it still generated a flurry of banquets and balls, and drew many of the Lords to Concordia. Among them, Rich knew, was Loren Camine Eliseer, with his family. Rich knew this because he still corresponded with Adrien. That had begun long before the Galinin-Ivanoi assassinations and continued sporadically since, given impetus by Adrien's studies in sociology at the University in Helen. Rich had even sent her copies of Richard Lamb's theses—under another name—

and he'd never made a secret of their correspondence, but Alexand had shown no interest in it.

Or rather, Rich thought bleakly, he allowed himself no interest. For the last three years he hadn't so much as spoken her name in Rich's hearing.

Rich wondered if the Eliseer had been invited to the Galinin banquet tonight. For Alexand's sake, he hoped not.

And for Adrien's.

It was curious how a negative shape reveals the positive form it encloses. After that fateful Directorate meeting, Adrien seemed to suffer a memory lapse similar to Alexand's. In her lettapes to Rich she hadn't once mentioned him, not even a polite inquiry after his health.

Rich sipped at his brandy; it seemed bitter on his tongue.

"Alex, it hasn't been much of a leave for you, between House affairs and social obligations. I'm sorry."

"Don't be, Rich. It's enough to be away from that damned Academy and to have a little time with you. You restore my soul, you know, and it needs it."

Rich met his brother's eyes, for once unmasked, if only briefly. "You know any soul restoration I offer is only a matter of reciprocation. But speaking of House affairs, what about your conference with Father and Grandser this afternoon?"

Alexand laughed, the mask of cynicism falling into place again as he raised his glass, swallowing the brandy without savoring it.

"*My* conference? Rich, I was only there as an observer—as usual. Trevor Robek was there, too, by the way. Grandser intends to present the G-W-R resolution to the Directorate again. They were discussing some compromises he's written into it since its last defeat."

Rich leaned forward attentively. G-W-R was a shorthand designation popular with newscasters for the Galinin-Woolf-Robek resolution, a canon of rules for Bond treatment that would be enforced by an agency of the Concord rather than individual Houses. Its standards for living conditions and general treatment were only decently humane, yet, since its introduction seven years ago, it had been voted down four times by the Directors on the grounds that it invited interference with internal House affairs.

"Holy God, Alex, I hope it passes this time. Did you—I mean, was anything said about a system of appeals courts for the Bonds?"

Alexand put his glass down on the table by his chair, then rose, and moved restlessly to the window.

"Yes, something was said. *I* said it, to Father's chagrin. I keep forgetting I'm still supposed to be seen and not heard."

Rich was chilled by the bitterness in that, and wasn't deceived by the smile that accompanied it.

"What was the reaction to it?"

"Mixed. Grandser was interested. In fact, he'd already given some thought to expanding the existing judicial system to include Bonds. Trevor was . . . shocked, I think. His liberalism has its limits."

Rich waited, then asked, "And Father?"

"He was dubious. He was concerned that Bonds might abuse the privilege, that it would undermine discipline in the compounds, and, as he pointed out, a concept so . . . so radical would guarantee failure of the resolution."

Rich nodded numbly, staring at his brother's taut, aquiline profile. "Were you satisfied with that?"

"Do you mean, was I satisfied with Father?" Alexand turned, his gaze direct and intent. "It isn't my prerogative to demand satisfaction of him. He's First Lord of the House."

"And you?" Rich held his breath.

"I? I'm an abstraction of sorts, something existing only in potential. Perhaps my problem is simply that I had Theron Rovere as a teacher and have Richard—" He started to say Richard Lamb, but caught himself, "—and a sociologist for a brother. I see the problems—the crises—and I know *something* must be done about them, but nothing *is* being done. And Father . . . five years ago he spoke of the resolution in terms of basic humanity. Today he talked about giving the Concord a means of 'policing' Bond compounds. But this wasn't the right time to discuss it further, and there'll be no time in the near future. This is one aspect of this Confleet business I hadn't considered—its effect on my relationship with Father." He left the window and returned to his chair. "We can't talk freely about House or Directorate affairs via vidicom from Sidny; the risk of monitoring is too high. But there's no way around Confleet, so it's futile to complain about it."

Perhaps, Rich thought, but it was impossible not to resent it, as he knew Alexand did, as he himself did. He didn't pursue the subject, letting a silence grow, and at length Alexand turned and looked at him with a smile devoid of cynicism.

"Rich, we've had so little time together this week—I meant to ask if you had a copy of your last thesis for me."

He nodded. "I have it taped. You can take it back with you tomorrow for whatever leisure Confleet allows you."

"There's enough between the drills and strat exercises. Is this the one on master/slave group interactions?"

"Yes. Lector Canzor approved it, but he suggested I present it to the Board of Censors as a Pri-Two document."

"Another one? Your alter ego believes in living dangerously. And your methods of collecting data—"

"Please, Alex." Rich laughed, trying to dispel his brother's concern. "You know I'm in no danger from the Bonds. In fact, ironic as it may seem, they regard me as a sort of holy man; one of the Blessed."

"It isn't the Bonds that worry me."

"Then what? I have official sanction through the University to enter most of the compounds."

"*Most* of them." He eyed Rich doubtfully. "Does that include the Selasid compounds, for instance?"

"Well, no, but I have means of getting into them safely. Besides, safety isn't all important. You must understand that and accept it, and you must have enough faith in me to realize that I don't take unnecessary risks."

His acquiescence first took the form of a long, resigned sigh, as it usually did; this wasn't the first time the subject had been discussed.

"All right, Rich, but *you* must understand if I worry about you. What exactly are your 'means' of entering compounds unofficially?"

Rich felt a brief mental disequilibrium. He knew its cause, and it didn't bother him except that it would be evident to Alexand in a fleeting blankness of expression. Then he surrendered to a sigh of relief at the chime of the pager.

Alexand rose, his frown of annoyance hiding something close to dread. "Damn. That means Mother and Father are ready to leave." He went to the dressing room and emerged with his cloak, tossing it carelessly around his shoulders.

"Don't wait up for me. It will undoubtedly be a long night."

Rich activated the chair and accompanied him to the door. "It will only *seem* long to you. I'll probably be awake anyway when you return. Alex . . ." He paused, at a loss for words. So little time, and so much to be said; so much that couldn't be put into words.

Alexand reached out for his hand. "If you aren't awake, I'll roust you out. After all, tomorrow my incarceration resumes."

"I'll be awake."

3.

"Satya!"

But the Shepherd was gone, back into the compound; the grate over the storm drain barred an empty darkness. Rich sagged against the compound wall. It seemed to be shaking, and he stared across the pedway channel to the opposite wall, then above to the elevated 'ways, rattling with the pounding footfalls of squads of brown-and-green-clad Selasid guards rushing toward the compound gates at the head of the channel. The walls would fall, he'd be trapped, buried alive. . . .

Screaming—or was it only the sirens shrieking in mad disharmony? No, he *could* hear the screams of agony and terror from behind the walls. Or perhaps they were only echoes out of his memory.

"Oh, Holy God . . . help me. . . . Alex, where . . ."

He couldn't even hear his own words in the rending roar of sound—men and machines pounding toward the compound, making devastation of disaster. It was so dark, and yet it had been midafternoon when he sat in Satva's chapel only . . .

Only minutes ago?

Smoke. It was the smoke that eclipsed the light, welling out over the walls, pooling in this narrow channel. He was coughing, eyes burning, running with tears. The transit plaza at the open end of the channel—he must reach it somehow. His hands shook on the grips of the crutches. They were already on maximum lift, but his muscles were trembling uncontrollably. He lurched a few steps toward the plaza, staggered against the wall. Dark shapes were moving toward him; at first he couldn't make sense of them. A Conpol squad, an agglomeration of black shapes, white helmets bobbing in the haze. They passed him as if he didn't exist, and he himself wasn't sure of his own existence except for the pain that bound every shivering muscle.

He slid down against the wall, his legs wouldn't hold him; he crouched there, fumbling under his cloak for his pocketcom. He couldn't die here.

Alexand . . . help me. . . .

No. Fenn. It was Fenn Lacroy's voice he heard now faintly on the 'com. It took so long to explain, to get the words out and make them understandable.

But he would be here. Fenn would come, would help him.

Rich huddled against the wall, racked with pain and grief. Satva . . . the old man would never survive this.

But Richard Lamb would. Alexand was coming.

No—Fenn. Fenn was coming.

Alexand was in Sidny, hundreds of kilometers away.

4.

Outside the control booth the darkness was absolute except for the red and blue lights weaving their intricate patterns. The only sounds were the humming and ticking of instruments, and at irregular intervals voices emerging from the earpiece of his transceiver headset, and the sound of his own voice as he spoke into the disk connected to it by a fine, curved rod and poised a few centimeters from his lips. In the black void outside, the lights had definite forms: the bristling spheres of deep-space Troop Carrier Corsairs, the flagships; the elongated shark-shapes of Corvets, spiked along their flanks with X^7 gun-mounts; the sleek, darting arrows of Falcons. Alexand's voice was quiet, as mechanical as the instruments surrounding him.

"Rank 2 Falcons, deploy on tangent vectors. Rank 3, hold your positions relative flagship." His eyes flicked up from the stat screens as ten red lights moved under the impetus of his command. A voice buzzed in his ears even as he saw the flash of white light.

"Falcon R2-A on line to Red flagship. R2-C is hit."

A V-shaped wedge of lights was taking shape near the Blue Corsair flagship. Alexand glanced at the position screen and the navcomp board and spoke into the mike again.

"Red flagship to Corvets 2, 3, and 6. Move out at arc vectors 45°/30°/70° RF. Stand by for attack on Blue Falcon wedge. F-R2-A, close in on Corvets in guard formation at Blue flagship." The blue wedge was moving toward the red flagship, but the red Corvets were arcing behind and holding. "Rank 3 Falcons, move out to radial shield formation at fifty kilometers RF. F-R3-A, prepare to close with Blue attack wedge on my order. Flagship artillery, deploy mine screen at forty kilometer radius." He looked up and saw the tiny fireflies exploding from the Red flagship.

Then another voice, "F-R3-A on line to Red flagship. Blue Falcon attack wedge now within range."

"Stand by, R3-A. Flagship to Falcon Rank 1 and Corvets

1, 5, and 9. Close in on Blue flagship. Fire at will." A series of white flashes erupted in the darkness. "Hold strike reports until further notice."

The Blue flagship was under attack, but its protective complement of Falcons was almost entirely concentrated in the attack wedge aimed at the Red flagship. If the Blue commander ordered a retreat, Alexand knew his forces would be dangerously divided. He smiled faintly as the wedge drove steadily toward the Red flagship. No retreat would be ordered; his strategy was based on that assumption.

"Flagship to F-R3-A. Close in on Blue wedge. Corvets 2, 3, and 6, proceed with flanking attack. Falcon Rank 2, hold your positions." He paused, watching the lights. The Blue wedge was under heavy attack, but it didn't turn back. "R2-A, deploy three Falcons to support attack on Blue flagship. You will hold your position with the remaining two Falcons. Flagship open for strike reports."

He listened intently, his eyes shifting constantly from the monitors to the lights. The mine screen was taking its toll now, and the Blue wedge was crumbling. A moment later he saw a white flash at the Blue flagship and the strike reports were overridden by another voice.

"Red Corvet 5 to flagship. Blue flagship has been hit."

Alexand leaned back, taking a deep breath. The sound screen clicked off, and he heard a murmur of comment; the holojector chamber became only an open space as the lights came on, a circular area surrounded by a row of seats occupied by thirty black-uniformed cadets. He removed his headset and looked across the circle to the other control booth—to the "enemy."

From the beginning, Cornel Tomas Vincen had taken a sardonic delight in pitting his two high born students against each other at every opportunity. Again, Alexand found himself matching wits with Karlis Selasis.

Cornel Vincen rose from his monitoring console midway on the circle between Alexand and Karlis.

"Well, Corpral Woolf, that was rather well executed. Corpral Selasis, I hope you're aware of the error that gave Woolf his advantage?"

Karlis shot a venomous glance across to Alexand, then turned to Vincen attentively. "Of course, sir."

"And your error, Corpral?"

"Uh—well, I assume you mean the . . . attack wedge."

"Exactly. You left your flagship exposed. However—" He turned to Alexand. "You took a great risk, Corpral. Had Selasis elected to retreat, most of your ships would've been trapped between his flagship and the Falcon wedge."

Alexand only nodded respectfully. "Yes, sir."

Vincen addressed the class as a whole now. "This was a relatively simple exercise: two forces of equal armament in an open field. The problem was at the outset in that the Blue forces were lying in ambush for Red's emergence from SynchShift. Corpral Woolf's gambit in sending the Scout out of SS first was good, but I might add seldom effective in actual battle conditions."

Alexand took note of that last phrase, and it had a hollow ring. Confleet had no enemies to engage on this scale or on these terms. It was all a game, a dogmatized fallacy that served no purpose except its own perpetuation.

"But all factors considered," Vincen was saying, "both contenders in this exercise conducted themselves well. Now, our next exercise—" He stopped, frowning in annoyance at a soft buzz. He took out his pocketcom. "Cornel Vincen on line."

The cadets concentrated more attention on this interruption than on his previous remarks, and when Vincen looked across at Alexand, their eyes also shifted to him.

"Yes, of course. I'll send him down immediately."

Alexand felt a premonitory chill as Vincen put away his 'com, paused a moment, then said, "Corpral Woolf, there's an emergency message for you in the comcenter. Report immediately to Leftant Ames."

Alexand came to his feet and somehow managed to bring his right hand to his left shoulder in a salute and get out the expected, "Yes, sir."

It took more time to traverse the few kilometers from the Confleet IP port in Concordia to the Estate than it had to reach the city from Sidny. Hilding was waiting at the port with a House Faeton-limo and had an express grid priority clearance, but the tangle of traffic still kept them hovering with no forward movement for minutes at a time.

Hilding glanced back into the passenger compartment. "I'm

sorry, my lord. There's been an uprising, you know. The Selasid Estate compounds."

Alexand only stared resentfully out the window at the snarled confusion, noting the high concentration of black Conpol 'cars. The uprising was of no interest to him except that it was responsible for this delay.

His father's message had been terse and to the point. Rich had collapsed at the University this afternoon. Alexand had been granted an emergency leave, and Confleet was providing transportation to Concordia.

Collapsed. What did that mean?

But Alexand hadn't asked for an explanation. His only thought had been to get home to Rich as quickly as possible, but it was nearly dark when Hilding set the Faeton down on the private roof off the family wing. Alexand didn't expect anyone to be waiting for him there, and particularly not Fenn Lacroy. But it was Fenn who hurried toward him as he left the 'car. Alexand waited for him, finding a new source of anxiety in his tense posture and worried frown.

"Fenn, how is Rich?"

Lacroy glanced back at the guards at the entry, keeping his voice low. "He'll recover, my lord, but he wanted me to tell you what happened. Rich didn't tell your parents the whole story. He didn't want to—to worry them."

"*What* whole story? What happened?"

Lacroy hesitated; he seemed to have a hard time putting the words together. "Well, it's true he 'commed me to pick him up this afternoon when he . . . got sick, but he wasn't at the University. He was outside the Selasid compound where the riots broke out."

"Fenn, was he . . . inside the compound when the uprising began?"

He nodded bleakly. "Yes, my lord. The Bonds got him out safely before the compound was sealed off, but it was . . ." He averted his eyes, his ruddy features unnaturally pale. "He—he just seemed to break down once I got him into the 'car. He was . . . weeping."

Alexand had to fight the urge to double over, as if he'd taken a blow to the stomach. He turned blindly toward the entry, almost stumbling in his haste and with the dizziness that made the ground move under his feet. He hardly gave the doors time to open, and a hapless guard had to move quickly to avoid a collision, nor did his pace abate until he turned into the corridor on which the anteroom into his and Rich's suites opened.

The crowd gathered there making him pause, if only briefly. They were all Bonds, perhaps twenty of them, waiting silently, patiently. He recognized Tuck, and Gillis, Rich's valet. And Harlequin sitting cross-legged against the wall, the electroharp in his lap, his hands resting on the mute strings. None of them spoke, or seemed to move; they only watched Alexand pass with eyes full of silent questions.

In Rich's room he stopped short, wondering at the pressing quiet. His parents were standing near the bed, and Dr. Stel was at Rich's side, but at first Alexand was only aware of his brother, who lay motionless, eyes closed, his arms stretched out at his sides; his long, graceful hands seemed too frail to hold onto life.

Alexand looked over at his parents, standing arm in arm. Phillip Woolf seemed outwardly unmoved, but the pain lurked behind his disciplined features. It was in his mother's face, too, and not so well hidden. Alexand went to her and held her in his arms as she'd held him when he was a child.

"Mother, I'm sorry."

She nodded, looking up at him with clouded eyes. "Thank the God you're here. He was asking for you."

If Woolf's smile lacked warmth, it was only because of his distraction, an inward bewilderment.

"Alex, did you have any trouble getting here?"

"Some. Conpol declared an emergency state."

"What? Oh—yes, the Selasid uprising." He showed no hint of awareness that it had anything to do with Rich's collapse.

Alexand looked over at Rich and asked, "What is Dr. Stel's diagnosis?"

Woolf's shoulders moved in a half shrug. "Nervous strain and exhaustion. He's been pushing himself too hard with his work." He glanced at Alexand. "Don't mistake me, I'm glad for his interest in his studies, but sometimes I wish he wouldn't take it quite so seriously." He seemed about to add more, then looked at the door, frowning vaguely. "Are those Bonds still holding vigil in the hall?"

Vigil. An apt term, yet there was a caustic edge to it.

Alexand said, "Yes, they're still there."

"Phillip . . ." Elise reached out for his hand. "Don't send them away. You know how they feel about Rich."

After a moment he managed a smile for her. "Yes, of course, darling."

Alexand turned and crossed to the bed, and Rich stirred, a tenuous moan escaping him.

Dr. Stel said, "I've given him a light sedative. I can't give him too much; he's too close to shock."

Alexand eased down on the side of the bed, numbed at Rich's deathly pallor, the feverish brilliance of his eyes when they opened. His hand moved uncertainly, seeking Alexand's.

"Alex . . . you're here."

"I'm here."

Rich nodded, his head turning against the pillow as his eyes closed again.

"A Testing . . . the Holy Mezion tests the Blessed to . . ."

"Rich?"

There was no answer. He sank again into sleep.

5.

The clocks of humankind ticked over to a new day. Midnight. But the clocks of reality moved in slow shadings; there was nothing outside the windowall to tell of a new day. Concordia was all the stars, its light dimming the fainter lights in the sky. Harlequin sat on the floor near the windowall, knowing nothing of the new day. His hands moved ceaselessly, and the music spun out from those deft, misshapen fingers with the thoughtless grace of the turning of a world and the falling of rains and the curling of surf.

Rich still slept, only rarely moving or making a sound, and then only nearly inaudible sighs. The lumensa wall was set low, its shifting spectra providing the only light in the room except for the pervading glow of the city. Concordia at night was as beautiful as a phenomenon of nature, a visual feast that never palled, and yet across the city toward the east the rubble of disaster was even now being sorted, the dead and dying were being counted.

Alexand stood at the windowall watching the lights; he thought about Orin Badir Selasis and his compounds, medieval sinks of squalor and fear. It wasn't surprising that Selasis had been hit with yet another major uprising. And he was thinking that if he had any ambition to serve humankind, he would destroy Orin Selasis as one would excise a malignancy, even if it cost him his own life.

He nearly laughed aloud then, the bitter futility taking the shape of sardonic amusement, as it always did. What naïveté. It amused him that he was still capable of it. It wasn't enough to destroy Selasis. He was only a symptom; he owed his existence to the disease.

Alexand found his thoughts wandering to holojected, computerized battles in pseudospace. What would it be like to play such games with real ships, real guns, real lives? It wouldn't be so difficult to outmaneuver a Confleet mentality. A man of imagination could wreak havoc with their stylized choreography. And perhaps that was what Confleet needed, what the

Concord needed. Something to jolt its short-sighted, self-satisfied Lords into awareness that change was inevitable; their only choice was how it would be brought about.

A simple enough choice: compromise or catastrophe.

But how many of the Lords of the Concord were even aware that they were faced with such a choice? Galinin, perhaps.

And Phillip Woolf, heir to the Chairmanship?

Fear. No human being is exempt from fear.

Rich's words, yet they called up the memory of Theron Rovere.

He was dead now. He had died last year of a mercifully sudden and final heart attack at the age of eighty-seven in an SSB Detention Center. Rich knew about the DC. Alexand wasn't sure when or how he learned of it, but he knew and accepted it because Rovere did.

In his last lettape to Rich, Rovere had written lightly of the compensations of old age. One didn't have to see the end of some things; that was precluded by one's own end. And he'd spoken with pride of Rich's work. He didn't know Rich's pseudonym—only because that might mean inadvertently giving the SSB the name of Richard Lamb and his connection with DeKoven Woolf—but he'd read all his theses, and he was proud of his student, his intellectual heir. Rich wasn't yet at Age of Rights, yet he held a degree in sociotheology, a third-degree rank in the Academicians Guild, and ten theses by Richard Lamb were now listed in the Archives.

Phillip Woolf might also be proud of his son for these achievements, but he didn't know about them. He honored his pledge to Rich not to interfere with his life at the University; he even dispensed with the guards after the first year, and in time he became too preoccupied with House and Concord crises to be concerned with Rich's work, and Rich discouraged any interest in his studies on the part of both his parents.

Alexand had read all his theses, and he was as cognizantly proud of his brother as was Theron Rovere. But now he considered the price Rich paid for the insights put so dispassionately into those meticulous, elegantly delineated dissertations. He wondered if Rich would find the risks worthwhile now and knew he still would.

I must understand them, Alex; I must know why. Then perhaps I can help them, help all of us—

The scream caught him entirely unaware, paralyzing every response. The sound shivered along his nerves even after it had ceased.

Rich was sitting rigidly upright, staring ahead of him with eyes as blind as Harlequin's. The music had stopped.

"My—my lord?"

Alexand shuddered and started toward Rich even as he answered Harlequin's vague inquiry.

"It's just a nightmare. Keep playing—please."

By the time he reached him, Rich was fully awake, reeling from the aftershocks of whatever vision of terror it was that brought forth that scream. Alexand waved on the bedside light and sat down beside him, gripping his shoulders. Rich stared at him, then collapsed into his arms.

"Oh, God . . . Alex—" There were no more words; they were lost in uncontrolled weeping.

Harlequin had resumed playing, casting out a silken weave of sound as soothing as the sea, and the lumensa made blue and green shadows. Alexand held Rich, making no attempt to stop his weeping. He held him until the sobbing stopped, and he didn't know how long it was; the only time here was marked by Harlequin's 'harp, and his were infinite strands. But finally the tension left those spare limbs; Alexand reached for the control console and brought the head of the bed up at an angle, and Rich sank back against the pillows, his face drawn and white. His eyes had a fevered light that made the blue lambent. He looked at Alexand soberly, and when he spoke, it was as if he were continuing a conversation that had never been interrupted.

"The information is available, Alex. The problem is that no one in the Concord has bothered—or dared—to put it all together, to draw the inescapable conclusions from it."

Alexand smiled at that. Rich didn't consider it necessary to verbalize the transition between those aching sobs and this calm, objective statement.

"Can you blame them, Rich? It's always easier to ignore or deny the unpleasant."

"I can't condone cowardice; not when the cost will be counted in untold millions of innocent lives." Then Rich's gaze shifted to Harlequin, and a smile relaxed his features as he listened to a new melody taking form while the lumensa answered with new colors. "Alex, what time is it?"

"A few minutes past midnight."

"I've had a long rest. But you look tired."

He shrugged, then, "Rich, I . . . talked briefly to Fenn when I arrived this evening."

Rich took a slow breath, and his expression didn't change, but the hectic light in his eyes intensified.

"He told you where I was this afternoon."

Alexand was silent for a time, feeling the pain of the memories in Rich's mind.

"Rich, I'm sorry."

He nodded his understanding of those few words, then turned and looked out at the lights. "I had a baptism today, Alex; a baptism in horror. No one can go through something like that and come out of it unchanged." He paused, his eyes slipping out of focus. "It was an education, this baptism. I learned a lifetime in an hour. I learned . . . something new about death, and, above all, I learned about fear. Fear is the most powerful destructive force human beings are capable of unleashing or suffering. The mother of cruelty, the sister of death." He looked up at Alexand. "You understand that, don't you?"

"Yes."

"You of all people must understand it. Fear can eat away whole civilizations, and ours is rotten with it. But we're dealing with a social unit here, even if it's a large and complex one, and sociological principles apply. There are ways of tempering and even reversing mass trends—*if* the problems are recognized and dealt with soon enough. And you'll be in a position one day to do something about the problems. The God help us, I hope it isn't too late."

Alexand looked away from him. "Don't invest too much hope for our civilization in me."

"Why not?"

He frowned. He'd made that statement without thinking, and he didn't want to amplify it.

"Because 'one day' is a long time in the future, and it may never come. I'm not in a position to do a damn thing about anything right now."

"No, not yet, but there's power in being an heir. Father

holds the titles, but you're his son, his first born. He loves you, and he trusts you."

"Well, then, I can only hope he never ceases to love or trust me. Otherwise, your touching faith in me as the hope of civilization will never be realized." His tone was light, almost joking, but Rich didn't smile, nor did he respond for some time. His intent gaze didn't falter, but now it was curiously detached and analytical.

Finally, he asked, "Alex, is the rift so deep between you and Father?"

"There's no rift, Rich. Maybe it's just that seven months with Confleet have given me a rather pessimistic outlook."

"Confleet isn't the source of your pessimism." He shook his head slowly. "Holy God, what an error to teach *you* the mechanics of war."

Alexand raised an eyebrow; he felt an odd chill at that, but doggedly held on to his light tone.

"Why? Are you afraid I have the makings of a new Mankeen?"

"That's an interesting—and perhaps indicative—phrase: a new Mankeen."

"Is it?" He hesitated, then, with a short laugh, "Rich, I think you're taking me more seriously than I am."

"Well, I'm a sociologist, Alex. It seems to be endemic in the trade to take things seriously, and I know the climate is almost right. I can name at least twenty minor Houses and eight or nine major Houses that might align themselves with a new Mankeen now, and I know that potentially, by aptitude and training, you're capable of organizing and leading the dissident factions not only among the Elite, but among the Fesh. They'd flock to your banner in a moment if you could expand your present image of the Concord's crown prince into that of a *hero* prince. That wouldn't be difficult. You have a built-in foil: Selasis. You couldn't ask for a better focus of polarization. The potentials there—"

"Rich!" Alexand stared at him, baffled by those coolly spoken words. "Your imagination is slipping its scholarly moorings."

"I doubt it. At least it's crossed your mind that something concrete must be done if we're not to keep sliding down into a third dark age, and it's crossed your mind, however fleetingly, that *you* might be compelled to do that something."

Alexand turned away from Rich's probing gaze, but in his mind's eye were the red and blue patterns of holojected battles.

"Of course it's crossed my mind. What hasn't? But passing thoughts aren't conscious intentions. I'm no Mankeen, and I never will be. How did we get off on that morbid subject, anyway?"

Rich smiled. "Because I forced it."

"Why?"

"I suppose because I've come to a point of decision in my own life. I'm not sure of the full extent of it yet; I need a little more time. But I know I've wasted too much time already." He looked at Alexand, a fathomless melancholy in his eyes. "For instance, with you. There are things I've observed and conclusions I've drawn because I'm trained for them, but I haven't discussed them with you because I knew you didn't want to talk about them. But I haven't time now to be so cowardly, or even so kind."

Alexand felt himself closed in. "Rich, I don't understand."

"I know, and I hardly know how to explain." He paused, his eyes still on Alexand, then, "When you were at the University, I was interested in the reactions of the Fesh students toward you. They talked freely around me, of course, and I know their attitudes are reflected among the young Elite. You're regarded as the young man with everything, the golden princeling of the Concord, and it seems so bitterly ironic, because none of it—wealth, title, admiration—is enough to satisfy you."

"Am I so demanding? If I'm not happy with all that, something must be wrong with me."

"I said to *satisfy* you, not to make you happy. Happiness is an ephemeral state. I suppose on some level I'm foolish enough to think I can help you. On a more objective level, I know you to be a dangerous young man, considering your birth, your training, and your state of mind. You have three years of active duty in Confleet ahead of you, and today I had a taste of what you might encounter—what you undoubtedly *will* encounter. You won't come out of it unchanged any more than I did. And I . . . I'm afraid, Alex. I'm . . . afraid . . ."

He faltered, the words choked off, and it came unexpectedly, creating an aching silence.

"Oh, Rich. . . . Haven't you enough pain of your own without assuming mine?" Then he asked, "You're afraid I'll be driven to make a new Mankeen of myself?"

"In one sense or another, and I know what the end results would be, both for the Concord, and most of all, for you. I . . . I only hope you find something to satisfy you that won't destroy you."

"Perhaps I will, Rich."

"But you really don't believe you will."

Alexand looked at him, then away, shoulders rising in a quick shrug.

"One can—or perhaps *must*—hope. What do the Shepherds call it? Humankind's gift to itself. And they also say that every gift has a price."

Rich smiled fleetingly at that. "So they say. What is it you hope for? What would satisfy you, Alex?"

He turned to look out at the dazzling profusion of Concordia's lights; they began to waver and blur.

"I'm not really sure, Rich. What *can* I hope for? I'm a living fossil, like the ginkgo trees in the Plaza. I always thought it fitting that ginkgos were planted in the shadow of the Hall of the Directorate. In the end we'll all topple together—the ginkgos, the Concord, and I. My problem is that I have a high regard for music and poetry and art, for the refinements of mathematics and science. For civilization; for that accumulation of our unique capabilities as human beings gathered over the millennia. I resent anything that threatens that; I resent it to my soul. And I have a high regard for the unique capabilities of individuals. Harlequin." He stopped to listen, closing his eyes. "Harlequin is a genius. Yet he's a slave. I resent anything that deprives anyone—including myself—of his humanity. It's too rare a gift. Choice, Rich, that's the crux of it. I'm no more free to make my own choices than a Bond, not the important choices in life. And I know what would . . . satisfy me. A *real* hope; something solid enough to embrace with conviction, something to devote my energies, my *self* to. A cause. Perhaps that's what I mean. A cause that offered a hope for giving all human beings the right of choice, and by the God, giving *me* that right; the right to *choose* my *own* strictures. Freedom is only another figment of the human imagination, but choice—that's the source of our humanity, and that's what makes civilization possible. Give me a cause, Rich—that's what would *satisfy* me."

The words had spilled from him in a rush, and now they echoed in a silence even Harlequin's music couldn't penetrate. Rich was motionless, his eyes never leaving Alexand's face, and the old, nearly telephathic bridge of comprehension existed between them.

Finally, Rich took a long, trembling breath, and the silence dissolved.

"Perhaps I *will* give you a cause."

It hit like the shock of a foil striking home, that quiet statement, even to the reactive tightening of muscles. Those words, that hint of a promise, might mean nothing under other circumstances, but Alexand couldn't believe that now; the conviction wouldn't be shaken that they did mean something, and something tangible and specific.

"Rich, what . . . what do you mean?"

But Rich shook his head, his eyes closing wearily.

"I told you I'd reached a point of decision today; I was forced to it. But I can't explain it now. I can only ask you to be patient, and perhaps . . . to forgive me." He paused, frowning. "I suppose I'm trying to warn you, or rather prepare you for something."

"Then can't you tell me what it is?"

"A separation. That's all I can tell you now."

A separation. The word created a cold hollow around itself. As if Confleet weren't enough—what else could separate them?

Rich reached out for his hand, and that small movement seemed an immense effort.

"Alex, I'll never let myself be separated entirely from you. I need you too much, and I think you'll need me. Perhaps we'll just be walking different paths." There was an unspoken plea behind his eyes, a plea for patience. The hectic light was wavering.

Alexand nodded. "You and I will always walk the same path, Rich. We'll talk about it later. But you must do whatever you want to do—whatever you feel you must do."

"I promise you this much: my decision—you'll know about

it; you'll understand." He sighed, his breath coming out as if forced by the weight of his sagging muscles. "I've so little stamina. Alex, when—how long can you stay? I mean, before you must go back to Sidny?"

"I'm not returning to Sidny until I'm sure you're fully recovered, and if anyone wants to bring me before a court-martial for that—well, so be it."

Rich managed a brief laugh at that. "Well, I don't intend to take that long at recovering." After a moment he looked across the room at Harlequin. "How long has he been here?"

"Nearly five hours."

"He'd play until he starved to death if someone didn't stop him."

"I'll stop him. Now, go to sleep. Please."

Rich nodded; his eyes were already closed.

Alexand had every intention of going directly to bed once Rich was asleep and he'd sent Harlequin away. But he found it difficult and finally impossible to leave Rich. He felt himself in a kind of vacuum, and the solitude of his own room, even as a thought was intolerable.

Loneliness.

A simple thing, and there were no answers for it.

But he could draw up a chair by the bed and look out over Rich's motionless figure to the lights of Concordia. He could tell himself that Rich might wake with another nightmare, that he might need him.

But there would be no more nightmares this night; Rich wouldn't need anyone.

Alexand knew that he needed Rich, even his silent, sleeping presence. There was so little time left.

6.

Rich watched Fenn Lacroy attach a small disk to the read-out console. No doubt it served the same purpose as the flat, black instrument he always had at hand during these private dialogues. Jamblers; insurance against monitors.

The school room was silent except for a Bachanti *Chorale* playing softly on the speakers. There would be no interruptions. Rich had made the school his personal domain, and his privacy was respected by everyone, including his parents. They might come here, but generally they gave him warning. Alexand wouldn't feel that necessary, but he was safely in conference with his father and Galinin.

"How are you feeling, Rich?" Lacroy asked, inserting a tape spool that seemed to come magically into his hand into the console.

"Very well, Fenn, and three days bound to that bed was quite enough for me."

"I'm sure it was, but it served its purpose. You look well. These are the extrapolation sequences you asked about; the latest series."

Rich guided his nulgrav chair to the console. "I appreciate being allowed to see them."

"HQ *wanted* you to see them."

Rich looked up at him speculatively, then turned to the screen and studied the abstracted patterns and graphs one by one. There were alternative and cognate series covering time periods ranging from ten to fifty years. From a scholarly point of view, he found himself again amazed; the ex seqs were beautifully drawn.

And their common factor—the catalytic factor—was Alexand.

Rich studied them for a full half hour, with Lacroy looking over his shoulder. When he came to the end of them, he leaned back and said dully, "No doubt the last series would result in what would be called the 'Woolf Wars.'"

Lacroy perched on the console counter, frowning. "You

mean the possibility that Alex and his father would be in opposite camps in a political-military confrontation. As I understand it, that seq means an alliance between Lord Phillip and
Selasis against Alexand. I find that hard to swallow."

Rich nodded, staring at the screen and the cold, objective
symbols. Translated, they spelled horror and grief.

"So would Alex and Father—now. But Selasis will always
be a contender, and a three-way battle is untenable. Two of
the contenders inevitably join against the third. Fenn, there's
nothing here on the Eliseer line."

"Only because it had no bearing on these seqs. We haven't
given up on it, but the odds get worse every year. You know
about the rumors of a Robek-Eliseer match?"

He frowned at that. "Adrien and Alton Robek?"

"Yes. It's still in the rumor stage, but we caught another
rumor that's more encouraging. Selasis may be looking to
Shang for a bride for Karlis. Janeel Shang, Lord Sato's grand-
daughter by his first born."

Rich considered the possibility, trying not to take too much
hope from it.

"If Selasis commits himself to Shang, that would take the
pressure off Father on the Fallor match. And he's getting a
great deal of pressure from Lord Charles lately. Perhaps he's
heard the rumors, too, and wants the contracts signed while
he still has some leverage. Does Father know about the Shang-
Selasis rumors?"

"Yes."

No doubt Fenn had made sure of that. Rich looked at the
screen once more, then turned away and guided his chair across
to the windowall. Beyond the protective, verdant grove was
a world, and worlds, with numberless potential time bombs
ticking toward their individual zero hours, and his brother was
one of them. But the eucalypts whispered in the wind, heedless
of the season, wearing their eternal green even on the verge
of winter.

Fenn joined him at the windowall, but he seemed too preoccupied to notice the trees or the season.

"Rich, I know how you feel about Lady Adrien and Alex,
but the odds are still against them unless something unexpected
happens in the near future. Eliseer won't hesitate if Robek
offers a match."

Rich stared out into the grove. "I know. You said your HQ wanted me to see those ex seqs. Why?"

"Well, we've been watching Alex since the day he was born, of course, and since the Galinin-Ivanoi assassinations we've been especially concerned about him."

Rich sighed. "So have I, and I recognized most of the potentials in those ex seqs long ago. A great deal depends on Father, of course."

"Of course."

"By your carefully noncommittal tone," Rich said, with an oblique smile, "I assume you're wondering if I'm also aware of Father's increasingly reactionary attitudes."

"He's still my Lord, and I respect him, but—"

"I know. He's still my father, and I not only respect him, but love him." Rich paused, pulling in a long breath. "But I'm not blind. Nor am I blind to Alex's potential. I'm especially worried about this damnable Confleet business. Three years of active duty, Fenn; three years to risk involvement in Bond uprisings, to risk—" he stopped, overwhelmed by memories, still so fresh, and by an encompassing fear. "—to risk death for a tired old custom."

He forced his thoughts into focus again. "So the Phoenix recognizes Alex's potential as a disruptive factor. Why tell *me* about it?"

"Because we're also aware of your influence with him."

Rich shook his head decisively. "You can't look to me to avert any catastrophe Alex might precipitate. The chances are I won't be here when a crisis arises. I can't ignore my fate. I hope the Phoenix isn't making that error."

Lacroy looked down at the floor. "No."

"I'll do what I can, but if the Phoenix regards Alex as a threat, it must be prepared to offer him an alternative course of action—something other than making a new Mankeen of himself."

"But . . . what alternative can we offer?"

"I don't know. As I said, I'll do what I can, but now I must consider an alternative for myself or, rather, draw my plans." He seemed to feel a chill as the leaves turned concurrently, tugging at the branches, in the fitful wind.

Lacroy asked warily, "Your plans, Rich?"

"You know what I mean. We've discussed it before, and I've made my decision. I can no longer satisfy myself with half measures."

Lacroy nodded, turning to look out the windowall, but his expression displayed less affirmation than that nod.

"Did the Selasid uprising have anything to do with your decision?"

"Of course it did, Fenn."

"Maybe you should give yourself a little more time." His tone was casual, but he couldn't meet Rich's eyes.

And Rich smiled at that. "No, I don't need more time; I've wasted enough as it is. The decision is made."

"But it will mean leaving—" he sighed, still looking beyond the windowall. "—leaving your parents and . . . and Alexand."

The wind gusted, freeing a shower of leaves.

"I've given that due consideration, particularly leaving Alex. But it won't be a total separation. In fact, little more than Confleet has already imposed on us. However, I still insist that my one stipulation be met. No—there was a second: only those who *must* know who I am will be told; I *will* protect the House."

Lacroy finally looked around at him, and it was obvious that he was still uncomfortable with the decision.

"I've discussed your stipulations with HQ. Only three people there will be involved. You can trust them, and they'll take contingency conditioning."

"And my first stipulation?"

"That . . . didn't go down so easy, but you're an exception to almost all our rules. It was accepted. You've had security conditioning, but you'll still have to watch what you say."

"Of course, and it isn't as much of a risk as it might seem. I'm sure your contacts at HQ know it's worth taking. Alex may be Chairman one day."

"It was considered worth taking." Fenn paused, his big hands flexing unconsciously. "Rich, are you sure—"

"Yes. I'm sure." His flat tone cut off further argument, and finally Lacroy's doubt gave way to acceptance.

"I guess I should be whooping for joy, but maybe I'm too much a part of . . ."

"The family?" Rich nodded. "It won't be easy for anyone."

"Least of all you."

Rich didn't respond to that, instead turning his chair and crossing to his desk.

"The research professorship is the best cover alternative, Fenn. How long will it take to set it up?"

"I don't know exactly. Probably about a month."

"Good. Let me know as soon as possible." He began sorting through a stack of tape spools. "A month. That should give me time to finish this thesis."

Lacroy followed him to the desk, frowning absently. "When does Alex return to Sidny?"

"Day after tomorrow." Rich paused, staring down at the spools. "At dawn."

7.

Tuck vainly attempted to stifle a yawn as he closed the suitcase. "Will you be taking anything else with you, my lord?"

Alexand turned from the windowall, where a glow of pink in the east augured the approaching dawn.

"No, Tuck, that's all."

The vidicom was still on; he'd been watching an early newscast. He started for the comconsole to turn it off, but paused as he passed the foil case on the wall. The matched pair of foils gleamed: Toramil tensteel with his initials woven into the design on the damascened guards; beautiful blades, perfectly balanced for his hand. They had been Fenn Lacroy's gift to him at Age of Rights.

The gift had been overwhelming, not only because he knew the cost of foils of this quality, but because Fenn had been so proud. Alexand had left for Sidny a week later.

That was his first departure for the Academy. In the long months he'd owned these foils, they'd seldom been used.

"My lord, shall I call Fer Hilding to bring your 'car to the roof?"

Alexand roused himself and went to the comconsole. "No, I'll call him." He glanced at the door into Rich's room, open as it always was, but in a sense closed with sound and vision screens. "I won't need you for anything else, Tuck. Thank you, and I'm sorry to get you up so early."

"Don't worry yourself about that, my lord." He bowed and added, "The Holy Mezion be with you on your journey. Peace be."

Alexand hesitated, then nodded. "Thank you."

Peace.

He heard the door close behind Tuck and the word echoed hollowly in his mind. Tuck knew where he was going, and must have been at least vaguely aware of the meaning of the images glowing on the vidicom screen, three square meters of three-dimensional, full-color disaster—scenes from the Handyne uprising that erupted yesterday in Edbor. Yet Tuck left

215

him with that blessing, and meant it, as hope or prayer, to his soul.

Peace be.

He stared at the screen. The Gorimbo compounds in Sahrafrika now. The uprisings seemed to come in clusters, as if the savage violence of one sent out sparks even across the deeps of space to ignite others. The Concord had enjoyed a month-long hiatus before the Selasid uprising, then, within less than a week, there had been five more major uprisings. The first of these had been in Toramil in the Cameroodo Estate compounds, and in that there was a certain irony, since Cameroodo was Selasis's staunchest Directorate ally.

Earlier in the newscast, another item had been mentioned, almost casually: the Directorate at its meeting tomorrow would be considering another proposed Confleet expansion. Conpol was also asking for more funds, and the commander of the SSB would make a personal appeal for more men and money. After this week of revolts, the requests would undoubtedly be granted. It would mean higher taxes to sharpen the bite of economic recession, more tax Bonds and Fesh alliged to the Concord, more minor Houses on the brink of bankruptcy. Yet it would be done; the Directors would see no alternative.

And another item the 'caster had passed off even more casually: yesterday the Directors had voted against funding the proposed Confleet-University exploratory expedition to Altair, as Alexand had anticipated they would. The fate of the *Felicity* apparently hadn't entered into the decision; it wasn't even mentioned, and, paradoxically, it was Orin Selasis—who stood to profit most, at least initially, from the expedition, since his House would build the ships for it—who spoke out most strongly against it. But it was Charles Fallor's comment that the 'caster quoted in reporting the Directorate's refusal to fund the expedition. "We've got trouble enough in the Two Systems. Why go to Altair looking for more?"

Alexand turned off the vidicom and sat down at the comconsole. He inserted a blank lettape spool absently, wondering why the rejection of the Altair expedition weighed so heavily in his thoughts. Not because he had volunteered for it; that had only been a gesture, and he had never expected anything tangible to come of it, never anticipated traveling to that mystery-veiled star. At least . . .

No. He had expected nothing of it. He was wondering, too, how his father voted on that issue, and thinking of his meeting with his father and Mathis Galinin two days ago. \

Alexand had again been only an observer, and the subject of discussion had again been the Galinin-Woolf-Robek resolution. They had decided against presenting it to the Directorate this week as planned. Later, perhaps, when the political climate was more amenable. Alexand had wondered—silently—if they believed that was likely to occur in the near, or even distant, future.

He frowned, the clock on the console providing a reminder. His farewells to his parents had been said last night, and he insisted neither of them hold dawn vigil for his departure. He'd also asked that of Rich, but he couldn't bring himself to leave without some final message. He touched the "record" switch, watching the light go on, listening to the faint hum, but after a silent minute he turned it off again; his mind seemed suddenly blank. The quiet voice behind him startled him.

"If you're trying to compose something for me, save yourself the trouble."

He turned. Rich was coming through the door joining their rooms, floating in the nulgrav chair. He was still in his night clothes, but he wore a cloak over them as if he were prepared to brave the morning chill outside.

Alexand said, "I'll gladly save myself the trouble. Did I wake you?"

"With the S/V screens on the door?" He laughed at that. "Of course not. But if you hoped to avoid me this morning, that's unfortunate. I didn't intend to allow you that." His tone was light, yet there was a purpose hidden behind the nonchalance; a sober and deep purpose.

And it came to Alexand that this wasn't unexpected. Unconsciously, he'd been waiting for it, waiting for Rich to choose his time. He rose and went to the bed where his black Confleet cloak lay.

"I haven't called Hilding yet. The landing roof will be deserted and a good vantage point for the sunrise."

The eastern sky was banded with pink and orange and only a few stars were visible in the north, away from the encompassing glow of the city. Alexand fastened his cloak against the chill as they emerged onto the landing roof and crossed in silence to the far edge, his footfalls a solitary cadence against the hum of Rich's chair. The metalite railing was still glowing, delineating safe landings. He gripped it with both hands as he looked out over the Estate. The rambling palace still slept, but at the foot of the wooded ridge the factory was awake and working at full capacity; it never slept. Nor did Concordia. The city might doze a little through the night, but its distance-dimmed, rumbling hum never entirely ceased.

He looked around at Rich, who had stopped his chair beside him at the railing, and saw the longing in his eyes as he gazed out at the lights veiled in dawn mist.

A turning point.

Alexand recognized this dawn as a turning point. At least it would be that for him. Rich had passed his turning point five days ago in the squalid terror of the Selasid compound. Toward what would he turn now?

"Alex, I have something I must tell you."

"I know."

Rich smiled faintly at that. "I told you I'd made a decision and that it might mean a separation."

Alexand held himself in tight rein, recognizing the quickening of his pulse as a product of fear.

"Is this to be a permanent separation?"

"No. At least not a complete one."

"I'm grateful for that, then."

Rich paused, his eyes fixed on his brother's still, taut face, feeling the aching question behind it.

"Alex, I won't leave you without explaining why. I couldn't stand that barrier between us. It would be more deadly than the barriers that *will* have to exist. At least I'll explain as much as I'm free to. This was one of the terms I made, and it was accepted with great misgivings."

Alexand hesitated, frowning. "Accepted by whom?"

"I'll explain that. But first I must warn you, you'll be given information no one else has ever possessed without the protective mechanism of conditioning."

"Rich, what—"

"All in good time," he said, raising a quieting hand. "The word 'conditioning' should give you a clue to my intent. I've been a sort of part-time member for some time, but now I'm going to become a full member. I've investigated it thoroughly, and I'm convinced that my peculiar talents will bear fruit through this organization as they never could otherwise. I've found a tool that will serve my purposes—my hopes—by letting me become *its* tool." A pause, then, "I'm speaking of the Society of the Phoenix."

Alexand at first could only stare at him, stunned. The Phoenix. The quicksilver phantom as apocryphal as its namesake; Conpol's elusive scapegoat.

It occurred to him that he should feel some sense of outrage. Rich's declared intention amounted to treason. Yet it was a contradiction in terms to equate Rich with treason. Still—and the thought was numbing—membership in the Phoenix was legally an act of treason and punished as such. By death. Yet Rich was willing to risk that, even the precious scrap of life left to him.

"Ah, Rich, what a pair of sons Phillip Woolf has sired. You think me a potential Mankeen, and you're joining the Phoenix. I wonder what he did to deserve us."

"His error was in insisting that we be taught to think." Then he sighed, and there was a mordant regret in his voice as he added, "I hope he won't ever have to know about this."

Alexand was silent for a moment, then, "Rich, what can you tell me about the Phoenix? I'd at least like some assurance of your safety and your..."

"My health? Don't be concerned about that. I'll have the best of care; in some ways better than I can get anywhere in the Concord."

"From a revolutionary organization?"

"It isn't a revolutionary organization, and it has many aspects, one of which is intensive research programs in all fields, including medicine." He hesitated, perhaps reading the hope in Alexand's eyes. "But they can't work miracles. They can give me a little more time, possibly, and make me more comfortable."

Alexand nodded bleakly. "I'm relieved at that." He leaned back against the railing, hands tight on the luminous metal. *A little more time*. Rich's calm acceptance always seemed beyond comprehension. "Exactly what kind of separation are you talking about? How does one join the Phoenix?"

"Well, it varies with individuals. Some members enter the

Society by the expedient of 'dying.' As for me, within the next month, I'll be offered a research professorship at the University in Leda."

"Leda?" Pollux; the Twin Planets. It seemed immensely distant.

Rich said, "With SynchShift ships, Leda is only about four hours from Concordia." Then he frowned down at his folded hands. "And don't ask me why Leda. I can't answer that. Nor should you draw any conclusions about the Society from *my* future location. The Phoenix is ubiquitous in the Concord. I'll simply be working where I'm most useful."

"This offer of a research professorship—I assume it's valid on the surface?"

"Yes, and I did have a similar offer from the University in Toramil a few months ago. It isn't at all unreasonable. A high honor. High enough, I hope, that Mother and Father won't be surprised when I accept the Leda offer."

Alexand saw the shadow of remorse in Rich's eyes when he spoke of his parents. It would be hard for them, especially for Elise, and Rich was keenly aware of it.

"Will you be going alone?"

"No, Dr. Bettis will be with me."

"Kairn?" It would seem natural enough; she was his physiotherapist and a qualified physician. "Rich, is she—"

"Yes." He sent him an oblique smile. "Kairn is a Phoenix agent. I can tell you that because she won't be coming back to DeKoven Woolf—ever."

Kairn Bettis. She'd been born to the House, and after her allegiance shift to Conmed, returned to serve it, and Rich, with skill and devotion. Alexand felt a fleeting sense of betrayal. A Phoenix agent. Then he laughed inwardly. Rich was also a Phoenix agent.

"Rich, has the Phoenix other agents in the House?" He turned in time to see a curious expression of confusion on Rich's face, and wondered at it; he'd seen it before.

"I told you, Alex, the Phoenix is ubiquitous. We have agents in every House and every level of the Concord. I can't be more specific."

"No. Forgive me. Will I be able to communicate with you or see you?"

"Yes. I'll return to Concordia for holidays. It would arouse suspicion if I didn't. But I can't risk talking so openly again, and when I return I'll be under stronger conditioning. The professorship will be in the name of Richard Walden, by the way. I'll have to give Father a name."

"You're still not admitting to Richard Lamb?"

"No. Richard Lamb is associated with certain doctrines Father would find . . . embarrassing. Walden will be given an academic history and even a few noncontroversial published works. He'll be on record to the last detail, in case anyone checks. I'll correspond with Mother and Father—and you—by regular vidicom and lettapes. The 'com and 'tape seqs will go through a special exchange the Phoenix has for what it calls its double idents. Everything will be retransmitted to me."

"You won't actually be living at the University?"

Again, Rich displayed that odd, fleeting confusion. "I . . . can't say where I'll be."

"It doesn't matter, as long as I can stay in contact with you."

"We can't talk freely. The dangers of monitoring at your end are obvious, but there may also be some danger at my end. I'm entering the Phoenix as Richard Lamb, and only a few members will know my real identity, and they'll be conditioned. I've been assured that my personal communications can't be monitored by other members, but I still don't want to increase the risk of revealing Richard Lamb's connection with Richard Woolf. I intend to protect the House."

Alexand nodded, looking up at the sky, a deep, cold blue at zenith; all the stars had faded.

"Rich, how . . . how will you be 'most useful' to the Phoenix?"

"Doing what I do best," he replied with a brief smile. "Studying the Bonds. I'm something of a rarity—a qualified sociologist with an interest in the Bonds and an established rapport with their leaders. That is, the Shepherds. I have expertise in an area vital to the Phoenix, and it can offer me means of gathering and interpreting data the Concord can't match."

Alexand's eyes narrowed. "Why are the Bonds vital to the Phoenix?"

Rich looked up at him sharply. "Are you afraid we might *use* the Bonds in a destructive way? You know I'd never accept that. Remember that in the last thirty years, the most obvious symptom of the Concord's instability is Bond uprisings. They're not only a symptom, but a contributing factor, an exacerbating factor. That's why the Bonds are vital to the Phoenix."

Alexand felt chastened and vaguely confused. He hunched his shoulders against a chill gust of wind.

"What else can you tell me about the Phoenix? It must offer more than unusual research facilities to induce you to take the risks and make the sacrifices it involves."

Rich leaned forward, a light in his eyes that stirred equivocal responses in Alexand, both curiosity and fear, and, underlying that, an uncomprehended hope.

"Alex, it offers a great deal more. We've shared everything important in our lives, and I don't think it would be possible for me not to share this with you. And it's important from a political standpoint that you understand the Phoenix, both for its sake, and the Concord's. The Concord will have to deal with it eventually as something other than a band of pirates and/or radicals. The first thing you must understand about the Phoenix is that it is *not* a revolutionary organization. Our ultimate aim is admittedly to change the existing power structure, but not by revolution. By a process of evolution."

Alexand commented, "Evolutionary processes are notably slow."

"True, but not nearly so destructive."

"Still, evolution implies long-range planning and immense patience. It would be a rare group of people capable of that kind of sustained effort."

"The Phoenix is such a rare group. I'm realistic enough to assume the Society isn't made up of paragons, and to realize that it constitutes a concentration of power, which is always dangerous. Power vacuums inevitably attract ambitious men, and that could destroy it, or at least subvert it. That's my main concern, not its capacity for long-range planning or intelligent use of its power. But if I'm wrong, if I'm disappointed in any way, you'll know. I'll make sure of that somehow."

Alexand felt a dry tightness in his throat that continually threatened a break in his voice.

"All right, Rich, but if this is such a benign organization, how do you explain the raids and sabotage?"

He only shrugged at that. "A great deal of that must be laid at the feet of the Outsider pirates and smugglers; Amik the Thief and his Brotherhood, or the petty independent clans. But the Phoenix does indulge in small-scale military operations. It also uses sabotage occasionally to maintain certain power alignments, and even stoops to piracy to procure supplies otherwise unobtainable, or to increase its military capabilities, or simply to make the Concord aware of its existence in terms it can understand. That's part of the General Plan, but a small part, and a recent development."

"Recent? It seems to have been going on for a number of years."

"Recent in terms of the Society's history." Rich gave him a crooked smile. "This isn't a go-by-night organization, Alex. There's already a second generation born into its ranks. The Phoenix predates the Fall of the Peladeen Republic. It celebrated its fiftieth anniversary this year."

Alexand's jaw went slack, then he repeated distractedly, "Its fiftieth anniversary . . . but why is it no one knew about it all that time?"

"That was also part of the General Plan."

"But how did it come into existence? How many people are involved in it?"

Rich blinked and hesitated. "I can't tell you how many members there are."

Alexand took note again of that momentary confusion; it was as if Rich had briefly lost track of the conversation.

"Is that the conditioning?"

"Yes. One form of it; sec-con. Security conditioning. The form the SSB usually encounters is the Total Amnesia Block."

"The SSB claims Phoenix conditioning can't be broken."

"Not the TAB. At least they haven't succeeded yet. But they haven't given up; they still keep trying when they think they have a likely candidate."

Alexand knew something of the SSB's methods, and the thought chilled him. Rich was vulnerable to that now.

"So the Phoenix has been in existence for fifty years, but who founded it, and why?"

Again, that momentary blankness. "I can't tell you who founded it. Only why."

"Can you tell me if the rumors that Andreas Riis was the

founder are true? I mean the Polluxian physicist."

Rich shook his head. "I can't give you any names. No—I can give you one. The Society was originally funded and as a fledgling nurtured in strictest secrecy by the Lord Elor Ussher Peladeen. It was his hope that the spirit, at least, of the Republic might one day be resurrected through the Phoenix." He smiled faintly as Alexand's eyebrows came up.

"Perhaps I've underestimated the last Lord of Peladeen all these years."

"He has been too often underestimated in our histories. The other founders of the Phoenix were nearly all Republicans, and most of them scientists and scholars. They recognized the inevitability of the Republic's defeat and formed the Society and, with Lord Elor's help, set up the facilities to carry out their work and maintain themselves in secrecy. The Phoenix has many purposes, and one is the preservation and expansion of knowledge, with particular emphasis on various aspects of sociology. Their work is phenomenal, Alex. They have data gathering systems the Concord can't begin to equal, and everything is grist for their computer mills from the cost of a kilo of wheat to House alliances to the armament status of Confleet. They have experts in everything from technosociology to psychohistory to correlate the information and pinpoint trends and patterns. It's like a giant biomonitor; they measure the vital signs of the whole complex of the Concord."

Alexand found himself smiling at Rich's enthusiasm, yet it gave him a profound sense of solitude.

"Why the concern for the Concord's vital signs?"

"Well, to continue the medical analogy, one must understand a patient's disease before attempting to cure it. And that's our ultimate purpose, Alex, to cure the Concord's illnesses, to save its life."

"And that might involve radical surgery?"

"In one form or another. I'd prefer to say radical *treatment*. Certainly the patient will have to undergo serious changes, and here the analogy begins to fail. What I'm talking about are major alterations in a societal power structure."

Alexand leaned back against the railing; its light was fading slowly with the brightening light of the sky.

"Rich, the other night you talked about my potential as a new Mankeen."

"You're wondering if the Society was the source of that idea? They didn't introduce me to it, but they ran some extrapolation sequences that put it in a more objective framework."

Alexand's mouth tightened. "Why is the Phoenix interested in me as a new Mankeen?"

"Not to encourage you in that direction. Alex, you're rated CP-One. That's our top 'Critical Potential' rating, and it means you're considered very dangerous as a disruptive factor; dangerous to the Concord and the goals of the Phoenix. If you think you might make another Mankeen of yourself, I warn you the Phoenix will do everything it can to stop you." He paused, then, "You doubt that?"

"If their purpose is to change the existing power structure, I'd think they'd welcome a new Mankeen."

Rich shook his head. "No. Those ex seqs lead to war and total anarchy on almost every variant. That's what we're trying to avoid—not foster. If it were necessary, the Phoenix would destroy you before letting you become a new Mankeen. I don't mean destroy you literally; we don't employ methods of that sort, and we'd be reluctant to weaken DeKoven Woolf. But we'd stop you."

Alexand felt that as an almost personal threat, and from Rich it was deeply disturbing. But the pronoun "we," he realized, was only a measure of Rich's identification with the Phoenix.

"What do you mean by saying the Phoenix would be reluctant to weaken DeKoven Woolf?"

"One of our functions is to bolster the more liberal Houses; Woolf falls into that category. Usually it's a matter of getting the right information to the right people at the right time. Sometimes overt action is necessary—and I can't explain that further."

"Then let's get back to general terms. The Phoenix intends to bring about change in the existing power structure. How can it hope to accomplish that *without* revolution?"

Rich took a deep breath and looked out at the city. "We *must* accomplish it without revolution. This patient won't survive that kind of cure. The Society has worked out what it calls the General Plan. It has three major phases. We're still working toward Phase I, and the immediate goal is to establish a foothold within the Concord hierarchy, necessarily at the level of the Court of Lords to be effective." He paused, and Alexand didn't understand his abstracted frown until he went on. "Unfortunately, Phase I can't be accomplished without bloodshed, and in a way it will be a revolution, but a limited and controlled one that will *not* involve the general populace and, above all, not the Bonds. In the General Plan ex seqs it's referred to as a military offensive or engagement."

Alexand folded his arms under his cloak, tensing with the inner alarm of suspicion, yet it was quieted by the regret he read in Rich's eyes; he waited silently for him to explain.

"The military phase will be brief, ideally consisting of one massive attack in a limited area, and our primary objectives will be Concord military and police facilities. It will be a small war, but that won't make it less a war, nor less tragic to those affected by it. Nor less distasteful to us. But we must have Phase I, the foothold in the Concord hierarchy, because we'll have to work through the existing power structure to bring about the reforms we consider vital to the Concord's survival. Ultimately, we'll get that foothold by bargaining for it, and that's the real purpose of the military phase. That's the only way we can force the Concord to the bargaining table."

Alexand nodded. "In other words, you must—again—make the Concord aware of your existence in terms it can understand."

Rich smiled at that, but only briefly.

"Yes. We have to force them to take us seriously. And believe me, Alex—you *must* believe this—the Society's leaders are reluctant to accept the necessity of even a limited war, but it's the only alternative, and that's not just opinion; that's based on ex seqs drawn by experts over decades. We've had to accept the necessity, because if we fail, the only other alternative for the Concord is a third dark age. We've had to compare the casualties that will result from our war with those that will result from the collapse of our civilization."

That created a silence, and Alexand knew Rich was considering those casualties, looking back with the cognizant perception of a historian on the last civilizational collapse.

"What happens after Phase I?"

"A lot happens after Phase I—we hope. First, we'll use that

foothold to bring about a gradual process of reform, working through established channels. Our objectives will be to break down the feudalistic system and spread the power base into the middle class, as well as developing a literate lower class and relaxing the barriers between all classes. The dynastic House system will be maintained, but the concentration of power within them reduced. In this phase there will be a very real danger of revolt—*true* revolt—of two kinds: reactionary revolt among conservative Lords, or a liberal revolt fostered by an impatient middle class. Maintaining a balance between stability and reform will be difficult, but if that can be managed, we'll be ready for Phase II. That begins with the establishment of electoral processes. That is, when individuals are given a voice in their government by vote. These elections will be limited at first and will probably evolve from the Guilds; they already use majority vote to some degree within their membership. The right to vote will be progressively extended to all adult citizens, and at the same time the issues decided by election will be enlarged until finally we reach our ultimate goal—Phase III, the establishment of a true democratic republic. It might be a form of monarchal republic; there are advantages in maintaining vestiges of the hereditary system. But it must be—in the words of our Charter—'a form of government that will provide a maximum of individual choice, opportunity, and judicial equality within the limits of a stable system.'"

Alexand listened attentively through this, and Rich's calm tone made it all sound imminently reasonable, almost inevitable. But a mental backwash soured the hope when he stopped.

"We used to dream of such things, Rich, talking into the small hours of the nights, solving humanity's problems with all our adolescent erudition. But the ideal is a long way from the real."

"Yes, it is," Rich said softly. "The ideal envisioned by the Phoenix is at least five and possibly seven generations from the real."

Alexand's head came up, and it took him a moment to focus on Rich's transcendentally composed features.

"Five to seven . . . *generations?*"

"Yes. Phase I *must* be accomplished in the near future, or there'll be no power structure to work through or save, but

Phase II and III . . ." He smiled. "As you said, evolution is a slow process."

Alexand needed a moment to digest that. He found it difficult to sort his thoughts from his emotions, from a hope he kept trying to put down.

"Rich, the plans might be practicable, but to see that they aren't lost or betrayed over that many generations—"

"The chances of failure have been calculated. Assuming Phase I is accomplished within the next ten years, there's approximately a fifty percent chance of achieving Phase III."

"And the chances of achieving Phase I—have they been calculated?"

Rich nodded. "They're calculated almost daily as changing events affect the data. The last figures I saw put the chances at between thirty and forty percent." He leaned forward, meeting and holding Alexand's eyes. "We've also calculated the Concord's odds for survival. The chances that the Concord will survive more than thirty years under present conditions run between ten and twelve percent. They drop to five percent over a fifty-year period."

The ring of truth was in those figures. Alexand listened to the vibrant, vital hum of Concordia, yet he wondered if the Phoenix might even be showing an unwarranted optimism.

"Rich, do you really . . ." He couldn't go on.

"Yes," Rich said quietly, "I *do* believe. I believe the Phoenix offers at least a slim hope of averting a third dark age, the only hope available to the Concord."

"And the Concord brands the Phoenix traitor."

Rich laughed tolerantly. "Of course, but the Lords know nothing of our real aims at this point. Not that they'd consider us any less traitors if they did." For a moment he was silent, studying his brother's face, the lean planes lighted by the glow in the eastern sky. He said with a sigh, "You were right, Alex. Father has sired a strange pair of sons. I suppose I shouldn't have told you all this. I've made you an accessory to treason."

Alexand shrugged at that. "Treason is relative; it usually depends on who wins. I envy you, Rich. You've found . . . a cause. If you're right about the Phoenix, if it does offer a hope for averting another dark age, then you have no choice but to pursue it."

Rich nodded, turning his gaze again to Concordia, rose-hued, its lights, even in the burgeoning dawn, a scintillant sea vanishing into distance.

"Look at it, Alex. Have you ever tired of seeing it? The city of lights. Was ever an appellation so appropriate?" He paused, then added almost in a whisper, "The lights must never go out."

Alexand could find no words. After a long silence, Rich turned his luminous eyes on him.

"I've detained you long enough. You must go now."

Alexand looked at his watch and nodded. "Rich, when will I see you again?"

"Concord Day. Octov. I'll miss your graduation leave in Septem, but I'll be home for the Concord Day holiday."

Six months. Half a year. An interminable time, yet only a month more than the separation Confleet imposed on them.

Alexand turned to look out at the city.

The lights must never go out.

"I'll miss you, Rich, and I'll never be free of fear for you from this hour on, but I can only offer my respect and admiration. And my love." He looked down at his brother. "You're my linked-twin soul, and you carry a part of me with you, as I hold a part of you—always."

Rich didn't speak for some time; he gripped the arms of his chair until his knuckles were white, then finally he said, "Alexand, you've loved me with all your heart, and in a few years you'll be repaid with grief, and that seems a bitter recompense. I can't spare you the grief, and it might seem that in leaving you now I'm only adding more, but I believe beyond a doubt that the seeds I'm planting will bear fruit one day, and perhaps you'll taste some of the fruits of the harvest; you and your children. That's the only way I can make restitution for the grief, and the only form of immortality I can believe in." Then he smiled and reached for his brother's hand. "Besides, I expect your first born to be named for me. I'd hate to think of my namesake growing up to a heritage of rubble. I'll leave you now. No landing-roof farewells."

Alexand held that frail hand and found in it the strength he always did; the strength now to hold back the waiting pain.

"Rich . . . good fortune."

Rich released his hand. "Peace be, Alex. Goodbye."
Alexand couldn't bring himself to speak that word.

PHOENIX MEMFILES: DEPT HUMAN SCIENCES: BASIC SCHOOL
                          (HS/BS)
SUBFILE: LECTURE, BASIC SCHOOL   9 JANUAR 3252
                          GUEST LECTURER: RICHARD LAMB
                          SUBJECT: POST-DISASTERS HISTORY:
                          THE HOLY CONFEDERATION (2585–2903)
DOC LOC #819/219–1253/1812–1648–913252

Lord Patric Eyre Ballarat is often called the true heir of
Even Pilgram (whose last genetic heir died childless in
2514), and there are obvious similarities. There is also a
bias on the part of many historians to see the PanTerran
Confederation as a natural culmination of Pilgram's Holy
Confederation. The former was, however, in no way inevitable, and was in fact a first in human history, and might
just as "naturally" have grown out of the Sangpor League,
the Sudamerikan Allienza Salvador, or, even more likely,
the powerful Sudafrikan Union.

What Pilgram and Ballarat had in common was that they
were both successful at conquest and consolidation, and
both made of their campaigns holy wars, but even in these
affinities there are more points of divergence than conver-
gence. Time tends to foreshorten the sequence of events as
they become more distant. We lose sight of the fact that
nearly as much time separated Ballarat from Pilgram as
separates us from Ballarat. Whatever they might have had
in common as personalities is irrelevant in the face of the
vast differences in their historical contexts. Pilgram lived
in a strictly feudal world in which the primary source of
energy was animal (including human) power, sovereignty
was still rooted ultimately in the exchange of fealty for
protection, and trade was conducted primarily on a barter
level.

Ballarat's world was quite different, although it might

be argued that it couldn't have existed without Pilgram's consolidation of the feudal holds. In that sense perhaps he *is* Pilgram's heir, but so are we all. The Holy Confederation hastened the advent of Conta Austrail's renaissance, which was, unlike the renaissance following the First Dark Age, also an industrial revolution. Some knowledge always survives a dark age, and humankind entered the Second Dark Age at a more technologically advanced level in the twenty-first century than pertained in the fifth century when it entered the First Dark Age. Even in Pilgram's time a few crude radio communication systems were still in operation. His strategic use of this "word-winger" contributed to his military success, in fact. I doubt that he or anyone who employed radio devices at the time understood how or why they worked; their construction, maintenance, and use was a matter of tradition hoared with dogma, but with the advent of the Holy Confederation, pooling and expansion of knowledge by interchange became possible. The first organized educational institutions—the forerunners of the University System—were established during this period under the aegis of the Church, and when some of the great libraries were later discovered in the ruins of Canber, Brisbane, and even in Melborn before it became the site of Concordia, the intellectual soil had been prepared for the seeding of that precious knowledge from the past.

That seeding precipitated a technological renaissance that evolved far faster than the social structures supporting it, and that's one problem our era shares with Ballarat's: our social structures still haven't caught up, and various factors have combined since then to further retard them.

But in the twenty-ninth century, the technological resurgence was more obvious than the social lag, and, as is so often the case, the resurgence hinged on one key invention. That was the energy amplification/storage cell, whose invention in 2761 was credited to Lord Cilas Darwin, although it was probably developed by scientists allieged to him, and was undoubtedly based on twenty-first-century prototypes. Hydroelectric power and fossil fuels were the primary sources of power before the development of the Darwin cell, but neither were abundant enough to adequately power an industrial renaissance. The Darwin cell, however, made possible full exploitation of solar power, even without the advantage of beamed solar power systems, and the Holy Confederation took the first step into a new age.

In the century between that crucial invention and Ballarat's emergence into the light of history, much that is familiar in our world came into existence. The term "Fesh," for instance, derived from "professional." More important, the first industrial—as opposed to landed—Houses appeared, which led to the establishment of the franchise system. The term "House" came into general use during this period, too. Prior to the development of exclusively industrial Houses, terms such as "domain," "dominion," "province," or the archaic "station" were used to describe the primarily geographical boundaries of sovereignty.

The Holy Confederation flourished, expanded, and differentiated at an astounding rate so that one generation's world was all but unrecognizable to the next. Industrialization begat trade, and trade begat the need for expanded markets and the means to reach them. The Holy Confederation moved out into the world via waterborne and airborne craft that seem slow and even dangerous to us, but were wings to the Confederation. This was a period of reaching out, of the rediscovery of Terra and of the receding boundaries of knowledge, and there is evident in its extant writings on almost any subject a blithe optimism we can only look back on with envy.

Among other things, the traders and explorers of the mercantile and industrial Houses of the Holy Confederation discovered that although many parts of the planet were still blighted by the poisoning of pollution and exploitation, and the scars of nuclear war left by the Disasters, people and cultures were thriving in other areas. None of the cultures had advanced beyond feudalism, but that didn't make them less attractive as markets for the products of Conta Austrail's industrial Houses, or as producers of raw material for further industrialization.

This was a crucial period not only because of the many changes that did occur in a relatively short time, but because of one change that might have occurred, which would have drastically altered the future course of history, but did not occur. The Fesh, the middle class that burgeoned inevitably during this period, did not escape the dominion of the Elite. (That term, of course, didn't come into general use until after the Wars of Confederation.) The Fesh did not break the allegiance system to their Lords, perhaps because House specialization blunted the effects of individual specialization, or perhaps it was simply attributable to the lag between social and technological development. As a corollary, the Bond class also remained bonded to their Lords. It might be noted that there was some potential for upward movement from one class to another during this period, which may have made the class restrictions more acceptable. Another factor is that the Orthodox Church was a dominant social force—far more so than today—and one of the Church's doctrines was the sanctity of allegiance. The Church also offered individuals the option of what was essentially another class, that is, becoming part of the Church hierarchy. "Tithe" conscriptions were not yet practiced, and entry into Church service was entirely voluntary. At any rate, the Holy Confederation moved into the industrial renaissance with its feudal foundations intact.

An important factor initially overlooked by contemporaries in this pre-Wars period was that the Holy Confederation's interactions with other cultures inevitably changed them. It hastened their emergence out of feudalism so that the primitive cultures that had once docilely provided markets and raw materials finally became manufacturers themselves, or developed their own marine fleets and began to threaten, by competition or piracy, the Holy Confederation's mercantile Lords.

It was at this pregnant point in history that Lord Patric Eyre Ballarat appeared, and it was Ballarat who made enemies and heathens of the "outlanders," and convinced the other Lords of the Holy Confederation that it was their duty and destiny to conquer the enemy and make enlightened Mezionists of the heathen.

CHAPTER IV: Octov 3250

●∥

1.

The screens and the comconsole occupied only a part of Alexand's mind; enough to stave off boredom. The rest could be devoted to anticipation. Only a few more hours stood between him and a week's leave: the Concord Day holiday.

It would entail more long evenings with Julia Fallor, but even that seemed a small price for a few days at home, out of the black uniform; a few days with Rich. He would be home for the holiday, too. Home from Leda, from the—

A stir of sound in his ear alerted him. He adjusted his headset as one of the 'com screens flashed to life.

Leftant Commander Evret.

"Flagship *Stanton* to Corvet *Ariad*..."

Alexand touched a lighted button on the console.

"*Ariad* to flagship. Leftant Woolf on line."

"Commander Evret for Major Goring."

"Yes, sir. Just a moment." Alexand swiveled his chair toward Goring, who occupied the command seat in the center of the Corvet's crowded control deck. "Major Goring?"

The major was talking to the navcomp officer; he looked up, obviously annoyed at the interruption.

"What is it, Leftant?"

"Commander Evret for you, sir. Intership FR310."

"Oh." His annoyance vanished as he switched on his headset, turning his attention to the small screen mounted on the arm of his chair. "Major Goring on line, Commander."

Alexand's hand went to the console, and his screen went blank, but he neglected to turn off the audio circuit. He was expected to do so, and apparently it didn't occur to Goring that he wouldn't. He never checked, and Alexand eavesdropped regularly without a qualm. As he listened, he looked up at the vis-screens lining the curved walls above the arc of consoles.

". . . on stand-by status, Major. A serious Bond uprising is in progress in the Alber compounds in Canadia. Lord Fallor has requested Confleet forces to stand in reserve."

Alexand's eyes narrowed, but there was no other indication of his sick dread. Fallor. That carping fool, Charles Fallor. His future father-in-law, no less.

"Of course, Commander. Is the status critical?"

"The reports are confused, as usual. At least they have some idea what started this one. Some damned Shepherd was executed, and the Bonds went berserk when Fallor's guards wouldn't let them have the body."

Terra's flat curve bisected the screens; Alexand stared at the image fixedly, the dread turning to anger. *Ariad* was passing over the Eastern Coastal Wastes of Noramerika, and those millennium-old scars seemed a fitting symbol.

If the Bonds had revolted because they were denied the body of one of their religious leaders, they were justified. The Rites of Passing, the ceremonies surrounding the cremation of the dead, were of profound significance to them; a soul denied these rites might be excluded from the Beyond Realm. And the Galinin Rule stated unequivocally that Bond religious ceremonies were not to be interfered with or curtailed unless they constituted an immediate threat. It was highly unlikely that a threat existed in letting the Bonds carry out the circumspect ceremonies of the Rites.

He knew what had happened. Some officious House guard had taken matters into his own hands and capriciously—or fearfully, out of ignorance—denied the Bonds what they had every right to expect. And by that one mindless act, another holocaust had been unleashed.

He stared up at the cloud-shimmered images on the screens, a lapis lazuli world turning under them, turning toward Alber, while Evret's voice rasped in his ear.

". . . five hundred Fallor guards and a hundred Conpol officers, but reinforcements are on the way from Montril. I'll have orders from FleetComm within ten minutes."

Alexand turned to the console, apparently reading a status communication, but his finger rested casually on the Intership button. He would have to switch off when Goring did, or the lighted button would betray him.

". . . only on stand-by, Major, but order your Falcon complement into closed-V formation. We may be making a fast change of course."

"Very well, sir."

"That's all, Major."

Alexand pressed the button. He expected Goring's voice next, and he was startled that it wasn't his.

"Hey, Alex . . ."

The voice was close, low-pitched, carrying a sibilant smirk. It belonged to the man seated next to him, the *Ariad*'s gunnery officer.

"What the hell's wrong with you, Alex? Just think—a few more hours and you'll be making it with sweet Julia."

Any reply he might have made was cut off by Goring's starchy, "Leftant Selasis!"

Karlis Selasis stiffened and looked back at Goring. "Yes, sir?"

"I will tolerate no idle conversation on this condeck. Leftant Woolf . . ."

Alexand turned. "Yes, Major?"

"Put me on shipboard and complement frequency—and switch in the sig-mod circuit."

"Yes, sir."

He moved about the task automatically, his bitter rage in no way evident. The uprising in Alber was foremost in his thoughts. He had no doubt their unit would be called in; he knew Charles Fallor. But, on another level, he was thinking that one day he'd find out who had arranged his assignment to the same unit, to the same ship as Karlis Selasis. There was malicious intent behind that. It couldn't conceivably be accidental.

2.

Alber was called a compound city, and it was more a compound than a city, housing the twenty thousand Bond laborers who tilled this portion of the earth claimed by Lord Charles Desmon Fallor. And in the waning afternoon light, Alber was a beleaguered island in an endless sea of grain fields golden in the autumn of the northern hemisphere. The final crop of the year was ready for harvest, and it was going up in flames. The Bonds had fired the fields around it.

That had been Alber from the air. From the ground, it was a Stygian world in which masses of men and machines moved in incomprehensible patterns, submerged in a pall of black smoke that confined visibility to a few meters. Alexand felt himself a blind pawn on a trimensional chessboard, his only awareness of the game the movements of the pawns around him and the voices buzzing in the receiver in his ear. He knew they were outside the south gate of Alber, he knew the immediate objective of the 1,600 'Fleeters of Evret's unit was to stop the outward flood of Bonds and drive them back to their compounds, but that was all he knew, all that bore any semblance of purpose or rationality.

The sound was staggering: the devouring roar of the fires; the rumble of emergency 'cars overhead, swimming through the smoke, sirens shrilling; the hissing shrieks of compressor nozzles spewing chemicals to contain the ravenous flames; the pounding beat of thousands of booted feet; the ampspeakers erupting with commands and demands; the sound of his own breathing amplified by the filter mask.

And as they moved deeper into the blackness, a sound that seemed born of the stifling smoke, that seemed only an accident of nature, like the whining of wind.

A chorus.

It was only a vague moaning at first, but as they marched inexorably closer—a long black line echoing the advancing lines of the fires across the fields—it resolved itself into a wordless threnody of abject terror.

Alexand's own terror at that sound was irrational and atavistic. It was a primeval sound, all the more awesome because it seemed to have no tangible source.

He marched into the darkness, muscles registering the cadenced impacts of his footfalls, but his body seemed no longer his own. He was only part of a larger entity, that long black line. Orders crackled in his ear, and if they were for him, he obeyed; if they were for others, he ignored them. The stubble crumbled under his boots like fine bones, the heat from the fires came in searing waves, and, even with the goggled filter mask, the smoke burned his eyes and throat.

The wailing chorale was louder, and still he could see nothing beyond the black line except black smoke. His body moved, part of the line, his footfalls part of the rhythmic thudding. He wondered how many kilometers they had crossed, or how many meters; how many hours they had marched, or how many minutes. Through the narrow field of his goggles, he saw shapes materializing ahead as if newly created out of the bitter black clouds, and he heard the disembodied voices from the ampspeakers: *"Attention! All Bonds return to your compounds. All Bonds return to your compounds. Attention! All Bonds return to your compounds. . . ."*

It went on and on, a meaningless litany serving as a counterpoint to the pounding fugues of equally meaningless sounds. The shapes resolved as the black line advanced: X^4 gun crews; two men to each gun. Miniature cannons, floating lightly on their nulgrav mounts, directed into the smoke.

X^4s against unarmed Bonds?

It didn't make sense. He expected the guns to vanish if he looked closely; they could only be nightmare illusions. But they became more real with every step, and rage assumed solidity in his mind in direct ratio, an intensely personal sensation that severed him from the long black line.

Yet he still reacted when the voice in his ear commanded a halt behind the gun crews. He still responded with every other man in the line when he was ordered to unholster his X^2 and attach the shoulder brace. He obeyed when he was told to bring the gun into firing position, and felt the brace against his shoulder like an iron hand.

The spectral chorus howled behind the smoke, and he wondered if those wails, waxing and waning like tide-drawn waves, weren't born in his own mind.

Until the wind changed.

It shifted with the caprice of natural forces that only the human mind could interpret as purposeful; the darkness faded to a dull, reddish glow, and finally he saw the source of the wailing chorus, and his breath stopped with nausea.

Thousands. He could only think thousands. Thousands of nebulous figures coalescing out of the carmine haze; thousands of milling, scrambling, trampling, reeling Bonds, like leaves tossed and tumbling in the wind. White and blue, their tabards, tinted blood brown and ash gray in the murky light. Men and women, young and old. And children, some clinging to a mother's hand or clasped in her arms, more running aimlessly, lost, abandoned. He could hear the gasping and coughing now. They had no filter masks; they were running blind, choking for breath. The stubble was strewn with dead and dying, victims of the smoke or the panic of the mass.

"... *return to your compounds immediately. Attention! All Bonds return to your compounds* ..."

The ampspeakers boomed their mechanical, unheeded commands; Alexand stood transfixed, hearing the chorus suddenly mount, seeing a change in the random movements, the beginning of a concerted movement in a single direction.

The turning of the wind ...

That wayward shift had opened what must seem to the Bonds a corridor of light out of darkness, out of the lethal smoke. They were beyond realizing that the light led them away from the compounds in defiance of those monotonously repeated commands, that it led them straight toward the long black line and the X^4s.

"*Turn back! Attention Bonds! To your compounds!*"

Even the voice of the ampspeakers changed pitch. Alexand felt the tension shivering through the black line and the wrenching acceleration of his pulse. Out of that disordered mass another multicelled entity with a collective will was emerging, an entity driven by savage desperation.

For the first time he felt fear in more than an atavistic, generalized sense. He was afraid for his life. That despairing, mindless mass was rolling toward the black line with a rumbling roar and the implacable momentum of an avalanche, and for an endless moment it seemed inconceivable that any human power could stop or withstand it.

But only for a moment.

He heard an order, but his mind was still automatically sorting the buzzings in his ear; it wasn't for him. It was for the X⁴ gun crews.

"Fire!"

He was encompassed in whining lightnings, and his mind sorted a new buzzing in his ear.

"Ariad crews, prepare to open fire."

The answer to the lightning wasn't thunder, but an explosion of shrieks born of something more than terror; born of agony. And he wondered why his vision was suddenly so clear, why no protective mechanism switched on to numb his senses.

"Guns at ready . . ." He obeyed, gloved hands locked on cold metal.

Why he could watch an X⁴ beam slice through a man's body and hear that one, individual scream so clearly; see a woman tumble to the ground, her legs cleanly severed, watch her insensate thrashings, and pity her that she still lived.

"Gun safeties off . . ." And again he obeyed.

Why he could watch the first rank falling into the black stubble, shuddering, maimed bodies smeared with soot and earth, and see every face in sharp detail. Why he could watch the next rank falling over their bodies, living and dead, and every gaping mouth had its own timber, each voice as distinct, as tangible as a knife blade.

"Aim . . ."

Why his sense of smell was so heightened; why he could distinguish the odor of burning stubble from that of burning flesh, and both from the pervading stench of fear. And still they kept coming out of the smoke, rank on doomed rank.

"Fire!"

He heard the hot whines of laser beams around him, but his gun was at his side. He stood motionless, silence moving through his veins.

How many had already died here on the fields of Alber for the body of a Shepherd? He would not add to the toll.

"Leftant Woolf! Didn't you hear my order?"

This voice wasn't in his ear 'ceiver; it was behind him and less than a meter away. He turned slowly, the images lingering

on his retina, and looked through that tumbled, bloody montage
to Major Goring. He had stripped off his mask, as if his outrage
wouldn't tolerate that barrier to expression; he was shouting
against the roaring and shrieking, but his anger had nothing
to do with the carnage.

"Leftant—I gave the order to fire!"

Alexand methodically removed his own mask. The capri-
cious wind was still blowing; the veils of smoke eddying around
him had the clean bite of a cauterizing agent.

"I chose to disregard it."

"You—you *chose!*" Goring seemed to swell with the rush
of blood to his face as he became aware of the curious glances
from the other men. "By the God, when I give an order,
Leftant, you'd damned well . . . better . . ."

Goring would always wonder how he did it, how, with the
slightest lift of his chin, a subtle change of expression, *Leftant*
Woolf silently reminded him that he wasn't giving orders to
a raw cadet fresh out of the Academy; he was giving orders
to the Lord Alexand DeKoven Woolf. The reminder came as
a shock. Leftant Woolf had played the game up to this point,
had been a model officer.

But it was the Lord Alexand who said tersely, "You'll find
me in my cabin, Major," then turned on his heel and walked
away into the fog of smoke toward the ships. Goring's hands
knotted into fists. He pivoted to face the staring 'Fleeters,
insect-like behind their masks.

"Back to your positions—all of you!"

They obeyed, but with a hint of reluctance. He strapped on
his mask and activated the mike, concentrating on the pressing
mob beyond the Confleet line.

"Guns at ready!"

The response was quicker, a concerted snapping motion.

"Aim . . ."

Again, a unison response. He watched it with grim satisfaction. But one man was slower than the others, and Goring
swore inwardly, reading the open contempt in the goggled
eyes.

Karlis Selasis.

As if *one* Lord's son wasn't enough.

"Fire!"

The lightning sprang from the muzzles and the air shivered with a new onslaught of shrieks.

Two sons of Lords, And not just *any* Lords' sons—the first born of Woolf and Selasis.

"Guns at ready . . ."

3.

"My lord..."

The guard at the entrance to the family wing hesitantly raised a hand. Alexand paused, watching his gaze falter. He knew. No doubt all Concordia knew by now, and to a Fesh House guard, that fruitless revolt on the fields of Alber must seem an incomprehensible act of treason or cowardice.

"What is it, Ket?"

"Uh—your lord father asked me to tell you he wishes to speak with you at your earliest convenience."

Which meant immediately. The Plaza ceremonies would begin in an hour.

Alexand nodded and walked away down the empty corridor, listening to the regular thuds of his booted feet, a tangible reminder of his own existence here, in this hall—home. He still carried the smell of smoke and burned flesh in his cloak.

The Lord Woolf would, no doubt, be impatient. But Alexand went to his own suite first. His bedroom was lighted and furnished with fresh flowers; that would be at his mother's behest. Tuck was waiting for him, and so was the dress uniform.

"Welcome home, my lord."

Tuck was standing by the open dressing room door. The black, gold-embellished uniform hung on the rack inside, multiplied by the mirrored walls. Tuck's usually cheerful features were drawn with uncertainty.

He knows, too, Alexand thought, and almost laughed. It didn't surprise him that the news was already out. He'd returned to Concordia aboard the flagship, enduring a long monologue from Commander Evret. The flagship was the last of the fleet to touch down, and Karlis Selasis, aboard *Ariad*, had arrived well ahead of him.

"Thank you, Tuck. It's...good to be home." Alexand took off his cloak and handed it to him, glancing toward Rich's room, seeing the welcoming light within it. Thank the God Rich was home.

"Will you be dressing for the evening now, my lord?"

"No, not yet. I'll page you later." He stripped off the jacket, tossing it on the bed as he crossed to Rich's door.

The long months of absence seemed to dissolve. It was as if Rich had always been here, waiting for him. They'd both been through experiences in the last half year that had inevitably changed them, but some things were immutable.

Rich was at his desk console. When Alexand came in, he waved off the reading screen and turned the nulgrav chair to face him. An empty chair was placed nearby, and on the desk was a decanter and two crystal glasses. Rich reached for the decanter as Alexand went to the empty chair, feeling the quivering of his taut muscles as he sank into it. He took the glass Rich offered and tasted the brandy, holding it on his tongue to mask the clinging taste of smoke, and studied his brother's almost translucent face, the eyes that were warm as a summer sky, but too large, too intensely alive for that thin face. Yet he looked well. He'd lost a little weight, but his color was good.

"Rich, how are you?"

"I'm well, Alex. Very well."

"And . . . are you still enjoying your work in Leda?"

Rich's response was guarded, as all their communications had been, but there was no hesitancy in it, no doubt or equivocation, and it told Alexand everything he needed to know.

"Yes, I'm enjoying it, Alex. It's all I expected and hoped it would be."

"Thank the God." And tonight that prayer of thanks wasn't only for Rich's sake.

"We'll talk about it later." He paused, his luminous eyes shadowed. "Alex, I'm sorry about Alber."

"I know." And he did know. Now. He had thought he understood what Rich suffered in the Selasid uprising, but now he knew he hadn't grasped more than a fraction of it. Now he understood.

"I'll have to face up to Father soon, Rich. Have you any idea what he's been told?"

"The gossip has it that you panicked under fire—"

"Under *fire*?" He laughed bitterly. "Karlis has been busy."

Rich nodded, taking a moment to taste his brandy. "Of course, but he isn't generally considered a credible witness.

Certainly not by father. He got his information directly from Commander Evret."

"Then he was probably given a fairly accurate account. Evret is honest, if nothing else. He said he wasn't any happier about having me in Confleet than I was in being there; he only hoped both of us survived the experience."

Rich laughed. "An honest man, indeed."

"Yes. Well, I wasn't looking forward to this evening to begin with, but this should make it doubly unbearable. I suppose Julia is mortified."

"We've had no communication from the Fallor."

"I see. That means she's definitely mortified, which almost makes it worthwhile."

Rich made no response, but there was a question implicit in his silence. Alexand looked across to the windowall, listening to the music on the room speakers: a Simonetta *Chanson*; a slow minor melody against a shimmering fugue, graced by an unexpected dolchetta solo in the coda.

Art demands form; the elusive light of creative impulse captured, confined in universally comprehensible order. Yet order is a fragile thing, far more fragile than the unquenchable impulses of creativity.

His eyes moved to his brother, who waited with fathomless patience.

"It wasn't worth it," Alexand said finally. "I had time enough on the flight home to think it out." The smell of smoke was still with him; he took a swallow of brandy. "At the time my gesture seemed right; morally right. But I failed to recognize something, and there was also an element of cowardice in it because I made my great protest from a position of safety, flanked by thousands of 'Fleeters with a line of X⁴s in front of me." He paused to bring his trembling under control. "Rich, that mob—there was a moment when I was mortally afraid; afraid I might die. But when the guns opened fire, my life was no longer in danger."

"You weren't protesting the necessity of self-defense."

"No, but my point is, I failed to recognize it. Or the necessity of the defense of order; social order. What I was protesting—other than the sheer magnitude of the carnage—was that the uprising should never have happened, and *that* protest is valid."

Rich sagged back into his chair. "Yes, it is."

"You know what caused the uprising?"

"Yes."

He knew through the Phoenix. Alexand nodded absently. Under other circumstances, he'd have been impressed by the efficiency of their communication system, but it didn't seem important now.

"It was a futile and feckless protest, Rich. Still, I learned something from it—that when violence reaches that point, justice becomes meaningless. It doesn't matter then what triggered the violence. The protest, if it's to be valid or effective, must come *before* the triggering act. Afterward, you're dealing with an entirely different set of factors."

Rich shook his head through a long sigh. "Alex, I find you incomprehensible sometimes."

"You don't agree?"

"I agree entirely. That's not what I mean. I'm not deceived by your calm or your objectivity. I'm only amazed that you're capable of either right now."

Alexand closed his eyes. "Don't . . . burden me too much with your amazement." Then he pulled himself to his feet, thinking that a drenaline tablet might be advisable to see him through the evening. "At least I can honestly assure Father that I won't repeat my one-man revolt. . . ." His eye was drawn to the leather-bound tape-spool case lying on the desk. He wondered why he hadn't noticed it before, noticed the initials on it.

Another world. Wherever he was on this endless day, that world seemed unreal and spiked with reminders of yet other worlds.

The initials were embossed in gold script: A.C.E.

Adrien Camine Eliseer.

Rich said, "Adrien sent me some tapes today. She's studying with Layn Powers at the University in Helen, and she taped some of his lectures for me."

Alexand only asked absently, "The Eliseer are in Concordia now?"

"Yes. They're guests of the Robek for the holiday. Alton is her escort tonight."

Alexand made no response; he couldn't deal with that now. "Rich, I must go talk to Father."

"I know. Alex, I'll be awake tonight when you return."

He looked at Rich and finally nodded. "Thank you."

He found his parents sitting in one of the window alcoves in Woolf's private salon, a room that was typical of the man himself in its spare, elegantly restrained décor. They were both dressed for the Plaza ceremonies, Elise in pale blue satinet, Woolf in rich brown velveen, and whatever the subject of their conversation, they were deeply engrossed in it when Alexand entered the salon. Elise was the first to look up, and it seemed to take a moment for her to recognize him. Then she rose and hurried across the room to embrace him.

"Alex, you're home—thank the God."

He smiled and said lightly, "You look lovely, Mother. How are you?"

She smiled, too, but a little unsteadily. She wouldn't be unaware of the repercussions of his choice today at Alber, but the concern in her eyes was for him.

"I'm fine, Alex, but you must be exhausted. I wish you could just rest tonight."

"I'll rest tomorrow." He looked past her. Phillip Woolf hadn't left his chair. "Hello, Father."

Woolf called up a smile, but it was remote and cool, and Alexand felt an irrational urge to laugh. The Lord Woolf was displeased. But then he had every right to be.

"I'm glad your leave was only slightly delayed, Alex."

"Did you expect it to be canceled? It only takes a few hours to put down an uprising." He walked with his mother to the alcove, then pulled up a chair and sat down facing his father. Woolf made no reply to his comment; instead, after a brief pause, he looked at his wife.

"Darling, we'll have to leave for the Plaza soon."

It was a cue, and she took it unhesitatingly, but there was a cast of anxiety behind her smile.

"Yes, of course. I must put on the finishing touches." She paused to kiss Alexand's cheek. "I'll see you later, dear."

He pressed her hand to his lips, smiling because she was smiling, and watched her go, wondering at the straightness of her back, the quickness of her step. The door closed on a silence. Woolf rose and turned to stare out the window, and

Alexand leaned back, stretching his legs out in front of him, studying the tense lines of his father's shoulders.

"I gather Karlis has already spread the news about my insubordination."

Woolf turned, his aquiline features closed. "Of course. It's all over Concordia by now."

"And you're embarrassed by it."

"'Embarrassed' is hardly the word."

"What is the word, then—'shamed'?"

Woolf met his gaze directly, his eyes cold, but behind the coldness, Alexand recognized the pain of betrayal, and that disturbed him more than the coldness.

"Yes," Woolf said, "*shamed* would be more apt."

"I'm sorry for that."

"Sorry for what? The act itself, or its effect on me?"

Alexand felt a numbness growing within him, as if the protective mechanisms of his mind were finally, too late beginning to function.

"I'm particularly sorry for the effect on you. I regret the act itself only in that it was ill advised. It wasn't the proper context in which to take a stand."

Woolf went white. "A *stand!* Alex, you're remarkably cool about this. Ill advised... proper context—Holy God, you're talking about an act of insubordination. *Mutiny.* Commander Evret would have every right to bring charges against you, and that would be a historic first: the first time a Lord of DeKoven Woolf has ever been brought before a martial court."

"He won't bring charges against me."

Woolf turned away abruptly. "If Evret knew me better, you might not feel so damned self-confident about that. I'm not sure I'd object if he did bring charges."

"I'm not sure I'd object, either, but no charges will be brought. It will stir up some gossip, but that will settle in time. And I'll be a good little soldier from now on; a good, unthinking, unquestioning soldier."

Woolf turned and took a step toward him, his anger fading into uncertainty.

"Alex, I... I suppose you've spoiled me. You've never done anything I couldn't take pride in. Sometimes I forget you're still so young. Perhaps I expect too much."

Alexand knew that if he let himself think about this conversation, he couldn't control the urge to weep. He held on to his blanket of numbness.

"Perhaps you do expect too much, Father."

Woolf looked down at his son, and his frown reflected bewilderment and a vague, nameless regret.

"Well," he said finally, glancing at his watch, "we're due at the Plaza in a short while."

Alexand nodded, then rose and started for the door.

"Alex . . ."

He turned when he reached the door and looked back at his father, aware of the span of space between them.

"Yes, Father?"

"Alex, we'll talk about this again. Later, when there's more time."

"Will we?" The protective blanket was slipping. "*What* will we talk about? Will we talk about the cause of that uprising? Will you bother to ask me why I chose not to fire into a panic-stricken, unarmed mob, half of them women and children? Will you ask me *why?*" He touched the doorcon and the panels slid open. "No, Father, we won't talk about it again."

He stepped out into the anteroom, and the doors snapped shut behind him.

4.

He had shown inexcusably poor judgment.

Alexand raised the plasex goblet to his lips and closed his eyes. He had turned up the volume on his earspeaker, as if the compelling beat and grating dissonances of the music could drown out the raucous voices, the peals of drunken, drugged laughter. At times, he had the irrational conviction that if he could find the right switch, he could turn off those sounds, too.

Poor judgment and a childish desire to wipe that expression of haughty superiority from Julia Fallor's face.

Julia, with her flaxen hair glittering metallically; a thin face, but with strong bone structure, a face that might have been beautiful, and he supposed she *was* considered beautiful. But he always had the feeling that a flame wouldn't burn her, it would melt her. Like wax.

And tonight Julia's usual hauteur, the pride she took in being the accepted Promised of the Lord Alexand, was mixed with embarrassment. She was embarrassed about Alber. She had even gone so far as to suggest to him, at the Galinin ball, that he shouldn't have worn the Confleet uniform. His response to that had silenced her on the subject for the rest of the evening, but his disgust for her, for the stultifying ceremonies and niceties, the cloying atmosphere of avaricious curiosity sugared with mannered courtesies, had overwhelmed his judgment.

Elianne Robek. The eternal child.

Elianne had approached him at the Delai Omer ball, greeting him with a familiar exuberance that made Julia redden and lift her chin in contempt that said silently, *second*-class Elite. Elianne cut her down with a few swift verbal thrusts, smiling sweetly all the while, but Alexand had had enough of Julia's arrogance, and when Elianne suggested the float, he acquiesced without a second thought.

Alton's found this swervy float, love. About six levels down in the Outside, I guess....

Elianne reveled in anything with a flavor of danger as long as it wasn't truly dangerous. She delighted in forays into the Outsiders district as she did in the milder psychomaxic drugs. Even at the ball it was obvious she'd already indulged in maricaine.

Anyway, Jamie and I—Jamis·Cadmon, you know; the lucky boy's my escort—we're exing this high-collar fest. Alton knows how to find the float. Come along, love. . . .

Perhaps if Julia hadn't objected then that it would be unseemly for her to be seen in a float, and in the Outside at that . . .

Poor judgment.

Elianne had mentioned her cousin Alton Robek more than once, but it hadn't registered. And Rich had told him.

Tonight Alton Robek was escorting the Lady Adrien Eliseer.

It hadn't registered until after he landed the sleek Cariol twin-seater on the roof of the float in the heart of Concordia's trade district on Phillip Bay where the city's "Outside" flourished.

Elianne and Jamis Cadmon were waiting, Elianne's laughter bubbling over the music blaring from the surrounding casinos, stimutheaters, psygame houses, and maxobooths. Elianne, elated, cheeks flushed; Cadmon, blearily grinning. The attendant who took the 'car wore an ornately sheathed knife at his waist, and that unnerved Julia, but Alexand knew it to be simply a badge of manhood here. On this level of the Outside, at least, its denizens lived by providing forbidden fruits to the Elite and even Fesh who could afford them, and no one was likely to jeopardize their high profits by threatening the clientele with bodily harm.

Even then the significance of Alton Robek's name hadn't registered; not until they were hurrying across the roof to the entrance, until Alexand saw the Bond standing by a 'car marked with the Robek crest. A giant of a man, waiting with practiced patience; he wore the blue-and-silver tabard of the House of Eliseer.

Lectris. Adrien's personal guard.

Alexand knew he should have turned back then, but the time for the decision passed in his confusion and self-disgust. They were given earspeakers at the entrance, and he moved mechanically through the process of handing cloaks to the attendants and paying the exorbitant door charges. He was only vaguely aware that Julia was still making self-righteous noises as they moved down the nulgrav shaft into the cavernous heart of the float.

The dimensions of the place were impossible to determine; the darkness was total and seemed infinite. Varicolored shimmeras drifted among the glowing strands crossing the void, a trimensional spider web, jeweled with lights like droplets of dew. Shadowy figures moved along the strands, literally floating in the .1 g weightlessness, and far below, a shimmering, multihued disk was dotted with figures moving in frenetic rhythms incomprehensible until the earspeakers were activated. But Alexand hadn't turned on his 'speaker then; not until later when the distraction seemed imperative.

Elianne launched herself into the void, golden hair floating around her head; she spun languidly, laughing with the abandon of an infant, or of the insane, caught a passing shimmera and tossed the glowing globe to Cadmon before her hand closed on a lighted strand to stop her descent.

Transparent spheres floated in the darkness, some only large enough to seat two people, others ranging in size to a capacity of ten or twelve. A shout, loud enough to carry over the music Alexand wasn't hearing: Alton Robek standing at the opening in one of the pods.

"Elianne! Over here!"

And the airborne passage through the emptiness, one hand guiding him along the strands, the other clasping Julia's. And if he'd cared, he might have seen that the smugness was gone and a nervous giggling had set in.

The gravity level within the pod was still slightly lower than normal, and he put his empty glass down carefully. He stared at it fixedly for some time, then finally looked up and across the table.

Adrien Eliseer was watching him, and as their eyes met she smiled, a faint, wistful smile that said she knew his thoughts. No doubt she did.

The waiter appeared with more drinks, and Alexand welcomed the diversion. But even when he wasn't looking at her, Adrien's image was in the eye of his mind.

A swan . . .

The patterns of passage fanned out across still waters, an endless interweaving.

The fair cygnet had become a swan.

She wore a gown of simple lines threaded with pearls; pearls woven in intricate designs on the bodice and sleeves, falling in dense strands from the waist to the floor; pearls starring her raven-silk hair. And in the dim light, she seemed luminescent.

Alexand felt the two of them locked in a void of silence. The voices, the laughter, even the existence of four other people in this confined space, were only peripheral awarenesses and totally unreal. He wasn't even sure of his own reality. The images of Alber hovered at the edges of consciousness, but even they seemed unreal, like the memory of a vivid nightmare.

If there was reality within his grasp, it rested in the quiet, watching eyes of the young woman across the table from him, wrapped in soft light and calm; in the soul bond that existed between them, impervious to time or separation, the bond that he could not in her presence deny.

But now he forced himself to look at Julia Fallor, and the sick disgust was renewed. He'd succeeded in shaking her smug hauteur; he'd succeeded all too well. She leaned across the table toward Alton, coming between Alexand and Adrien, listened avidly as Alton passed on a vulgar bit of gossip, then threw her head back with a high pitched laugh.

Alexand downed half the contents of his glass in one swallow, more concerned with the anesthetic qualities of the brandy than its taste. Out of the corner of his eye, he saw Alton take a small, jeweled cylinder from the sleeve of his surcoat, but it didn't make an impression on him at first. Not until he heard Elianne's squeal of anticipation.

"Oh, Alton, you darling!"

Alton laughed, aquiline features drawn into a cold, mask-like grimace of amusement, his pale eyes, despite the dilation of the pupils, alert and rapaciously alive. He opened the cylinder and spilled the contents in the center of the table with a mocking flourish, and it was only then that Alexand's attention came into full focus on this byplay, and his hand moved unconsciously to turn off his earspeaker; he didn't want distraction now. He stared at the triangular blue tablets scattered on the table.

Eladane. Instant euphoria. And for the careless, or those

sensitive to its chemical properties, instant insanity, or even death.

He was well aware that Alton, Elianne, and Cadmon had already indulged in maricaine; he even suspected that Julia had, probably unknowingly. Adrien had taken nothing; her first drink, a mild liqueur, was still almost untouched. The use of maricaine was so common, it had only disturbed him because it enhanced the atmosphere of manic hilarity. But eladane was a far more serious matter, psychologically, physically, and, above all, legally. Conpol might wink at maricaine, but not at eladane.

Elianne swayed against Alexand as she reached for the pills, her green eyes avid and intent. But Alton, grinning sardonically, clamped his hand on her wrist.

"Ah-ha! Me fine Lady—just what the hell d'you think you're doing?"

Again, the pealing, child's laugh. "Oh cousin mine, you wouldn't hold back on a sweet thing like *me*, would you?" Her tone was syrupy, and there was nothing cousinly about the sloe-eyed look she sent him.

Alton leaned across the table toward her with a grotesque leer. "What's it worth to you, Elianne, little Cuz?"

"That all depends, darling, on what you had in mind."

He raised her hand to his lips, eyes fixed on her face, and, still grinning, bared his teeth and bit at her finger, making a growling sound in his throat, and this gaucherie called up a chorus of laughter. Alexand stared at Julia, aware of the length of her fingernails resting on the table, the predacious curl of her hands.

Alton joined the raucous chorus, then, with great deliberation, dropped one of the tablets in Elianne's glass.

"Far be it from me, Cuz, to deprive you of *any*thing." Then he swept up the tablets and, suddenly magnanimous, extended his palm first to one then another. "Takeoffs on me, friends! Time to liven up this soddy party. Jamie boy, don't be shy! Here." He dropped a tablet into Cadmon's drink. "Enjoy yourself. Adrien?" His grin faded as he encountered her cool gaze. "Hey, love, you're supposed to be having a good time. Come on, try one of these." He leaned close to her, but she didn't move, not even to withdraw from him. "You'll love 'em, I guarantee you!"

"I'm forced by convention to accede to your whims, Alton, but not to this extreme." Her tone sent a livid flush into his cheeks.

"*I'll* try one, Alton."

Alexand tensed. Julia. He made no overt move, but his voice sliced through the brittle laughter.

"Julia, that's eladane. Leave it alone."

She drew herself up haughtily. "I don't recall asking *your* advice, Alexand."

"You're getting it anyway. Leave it alone."

She hesitated, then stiffened at Alton's jibing laugh.

"Julia, darling, you didn't tell me you were Alex's little automaton. Tell me, do you do *everything* he asks?"

The hectic, laughing chorus again, and Julia reddened.

"I do exactly as I please, Alton!" And she reached for one of the tablets.

"Julia!" Alexand lunged for her hand, but too late; she'd swallowed the pill. He watched helplessly as her eyes widened and she sank back into her chair, giggling softly.

He turned on Robek. "Alton, damn you, if—"

"'Zion, what's the matter with you, Alexo? Let her enjoy herself." Alton looked at Julia and laughed with sadistic relish. "It's *her* choice."

Alexand said coldly, "It *is* her choice, but the responsibility is entirely yours."

"So it's all mine. Why not?" He laughed again and extended the palmful of pills. "Hey, Alexo, how about you, m'lord? Huh? Little joy ride?" Again, the laugh, vicious and sibilant. "Come on, don't be such a damned stiff! You can't tell me you never take off now and then. Look—I'm offering free tickets to happy town!"

"And I'm offering a warning: Back off, Alton."

Alton's glittering eyes narrowed, lips drawing back.

"I'm all a-quiv. A thousand pardons. Wouldn't want to corrupt our noble and fearless *Leftant* Woolf."

Alexand felt the blood drain from his face. His first thought was to leave before his anger got out of control, and if he hesitated, it wasn't because of Julia Fallor, lolling in her chair, tittering inanely at Alton.

Adrien. She was pale, eyes averted in helpless repugnance. He couldn't leave her, desert her to Alton and his games.

Alton leaned back, his derisive laugh underscored with triumph; Alexand hadn't answered the challenge implicit in that reference to *Leftant* Woolf.

"All right, Alexo, have it your way. You want to miss all the fun—hey, Elianne, flying high, Cuz?"

Elianne was on her feet, arms raised, hands pressed against the curve of the pod. She laughed, tossing her head back and forth in a steady rhythm.

"Oh, glory! Oh, Alton, darling—look at the music!" She did a quick pirouette, crashing into the wall, and, still laughing, fell against Alexand. He caught her before she collapsed onto the table.

"Elianne! For the God's sake—"

Her arms twined around his neck, her mouth pressed to his, tongue moving against his closed lips. He pushed her away, fighting the impulse to bring the flat of his hand across that pretty, child's face, but she only laughed as he shoved her unceremoniously into her chair and a moment later blithely turned her amorous attentions on Cadmon.

Alexand closed his eyes, feeling himself immersed in a new nightmare, bludgeoned with that incessant laughter. He looked across at Adrien, but she was intent on Julia, who was slumped with her elbows on the table, eyes half closed, her mouth a grinning red smear. Adrien was frowning as if she were puzzled. He reached for his glass and tipped it up, finishing it off in one swallow.

And through the distorting lens of the plasex, he saw Adrien's eyes turn toward him, that puzzled look still there, then sudden realization and a warning that came too late.

A second later it hit.

He was spinning in emptiness, and yet he hadn't moved. His muscles and flesh told him he was still sitting steadily in his chair, but his mind sent conflicting signals: the terrifying reality of falling.

Eladane.

He lurched forward, his hands coming down hard on the table, the glass leaping out of his grasp, skipping across the surface. His field of vision was filled with explosions of color, every sound doubled itself, fading out first, then rushing in on him, a hideous cascade of cackling. He fought for control, some isolated bastion of reason in his mind deploying for a desperate, last-ditch battle. The pod shifted, upside down, whirling; the babbling-screaming-cackling beat at him, pulsing in agonizing bursts of orange and red, echoing with the moaning anguish from the fields of Alber.

And finally rage engulfed him, a white, molten rage burning through the smoke black fog of chaos. And with it came some measure of control. The dizziness was still there, his vision blurred, the sounds still distorted, but as he came to his feet, the babbling chorus was stopped at its source.

He steadied himself with one hand on the table, his eyes making a slow circuit of the suddenly fearful faces wavering grotesquely in the racked lens of his vision. Only Adrien's face was clear.

Finally, he focused on Alton Robek, slack-jawed, stuttering, "Now—now, Alex—Holy God, loosen up! Just—just ride with it, or you'll—"

Alexand moved suddenly, the timing and precision an agony of self-control. Left hand braced on the table, right hand lunging across to close on the crest medallion at Alton's neck, a turn of the wrist, tightening the chain, jerking him forward. His spastic reaction sent glasses tumbling and called up shouts of alarm.

"A-Alex, look, it—it was only—*Alex!*"

His hand tightened on the chain, wrenching out that final cry. He stared down into Alton's purpling face, and knew himself capable of tightening his hold until something broke, and knew it might be Alton's neck.

"Alton, you foul-minded, arrogant fool! One last warning—from now on, stay out of my path!"

Abruptly, he released the chain, watching Alton fall backward in jerking slow motion. He felt himself swaying with the shifting of his own equilibrium and held on to his rage doggedly; it was the only way he could keep the drug at bay. He looked once at Adrien, but he was incapable of explaining or apologizing for leaving her. He only knew if he didn't leave, he might lose control entirely.

"Julia!—" The rage burned hotter as he brought her startled, waxen face into focus. "I'm leaving. Are you coming with me?"

She hissed, "Leave me alone!" The words were slurred, as irrelevant as her attitude of pained indignation.

"Very well." He looked around the pod, a savage irony in his tone. "My lords and my ladies, good night."

"Alexand, wait! Don't—"

Adrien came to her feet, but he had stepped out of the pod; she saw him fall slowly until he caught a guide-strand, then began working his way unsteadily toward the lift. She whirled around, black eyes flashing.

"Alton!"

He was fastidiously wiping some spilled liquor off his doublet; he looked up at her with a twisted half smile.

"Let him go, Adrien. He'll get over it."

"You'd better *hope* he gets over it! Holy God, you *are* a fool! Even if he isn't sensitive to eladane, he's in no condition to fly a 'car. How do you expect him—"

"That's *his* problem." Alton's laugh was openly malicious. "Might be an interesting ride, though. Knowing ol' Alexo, he won't call for help."

Adrien took a step toward him, her open palm meeting his cheek with a resounding crack. "You're worse than a fool, Alton. *You* drugged him—you and this simpering bitch, Julia!"

"Why, you damned—" He surged to his feet, but stopped mid-sentence, silenced by the imperious, unflinching contempt in her eyes.

She said softly, "Alton, see Julia home. I'll find my own way."

She turned on her heel and stepped out of the pod.

5.

Phillip Woolf had left the sounds of revelry behind, left his wife to smile and beguile the remaining guests in the ballroom and wonder what he had heard on his 'com to precipitate his abrupt departure. Now he strode down the silent corridor toward Alexand's suite; he didn't recognize the chill within him as fear, or count the accelerated beat of his pulse. He passed through the anteroom, his hand struck at the doorcon, and when the door slid open, he was five paces into the bedroom before he came to a stop.

It was a soft sound that was both laughter and weeping; an irrational sound, gone in a moment.

Alexand.

He lay staring blindly upward from his bed, his body half covered, naked. A biomonitor was strapped to one wrist, and Dr. Stel was studying the readings. Rich was at the bed, too. He turned now, the chair humming toward Woolf.

"I thought you should know about this, Father."

"Rich, what happened?"

"He was drugged. Eladane."

"*Eladane!*" Woolf stumbled to the bed. "The God help us. Alexand?"

There was no response. His eyes were dilated, nearly black, staring up out of his pale, gaunt face, reflecting a bleak despair that was numbing.

"My lord, I don't think he can hear you." Dr. Stel was watching Woolf from across the bed, his manner sober, but reassuring, as it always was.

Woolf straightened. "How serious is it, Marton?"

"At this point, there's nothing to worry about." The doctor glanced down at Alexand. "I've given him an antidote and a sedative. He's reacting very well. He isn't sensitive to the drug, fortunately. That would've have been apparent by now."

It was typical, Woolf thought, that his parental anxiety turned to anger once it was assuaged. He tried to keep it in rein, tried not to think about Alber, but he'd had Alber thrown in his face with varying degrees of subtlety all evening.

The anger sagged out of him; it was so meaningless with his son's unguarded, haunted face before him.

Alexand, if I could only understand.

"How did this happen, Rich? Eladane, for the God's sake." He looked around at him. "Why?"

"Why *what?*" His steady, cognizant gaze made Woolf frown, and he didn't attempt to reply. "Father, what are you thinking? That Alex took eladane voluntarily?"

"No. I . . . can't believe that."

Rich smiled. "I'm glad to hear that. Come—there's someone waiting to talk to you. She has all the answers, and we shouldn't detain her too long." He turned the chair and moved toward the door into the salon off Alexand's room.

Woolf felt confused and despised the feeling. *She.* Who was he talking about?

The salon was lighted with a single stabile shimmera on a small table near the windowall. Woolf was startled by the towering Bond standing beside the door; the man was vaguely familiar. But he was distracted from that enigma.

Adrien Camine Eliseer had been seated by the small table, and now she rose and stood waiting, caught in the shimmera's light, ghostly and luminescent in a gown of white—no, a gown of pearls.

Woolf stopped, staring at her. At first, he thought it was only because her presence was so unexpected, but finally he realized it was because she called up a memory that was equally unexpected. He was remembering in the finest detail, as he hadn't for years, the first time he saw Elise. She had been younger and in appearance very different from Adrien Eliseer, yet there was some elusive quality they held in common.

The hum of Rich's chair roused him. Woolf followed him toward Adrien, smiling to put her at ease.

"My lady . . ."

She bowed her pearl-starred head, a restrained gesture that still conveyed the respect of a full curtsy.

"Good evening, my lord." But the restraint faltered when she looked at Rich. "Rich, how . . . is he?"

"Still in limbo at the moment, but Dr. Stel has it under

control. He'll be all right, Adrien. Don't worry."

Her dark eyes closed, and her only response was a nod.

Rich turned to his father. "I know all this seems puzzling and even improper, but keep one thing in mind: after he was drugged, Alex—being unreasonably proud and in fact incapable of *being* reasonable—intended to make his way home unaided from the Outside in central Concordia. You can guess his chances of survival in his condition. Adrien probably saved his life tonight." He paused, but Woolf stood in stunned silence. "Adrien will explain everything, Father. If you'll both excuse me, I'll go back to Alex."

Woolf listened to the hum of the chair, heard the door open and close, and the room seemed oppressively quiet. He absently waved Adrien to her chair while he drew up another, watching her, hardly aware that he was doing so.

"My lord, I hope I can explain everything to your satisfaction."

He nodded distractedly. "I hope so, too." Then he glanced back over his shoulder at the huge Bond.

"I can ask Lectris to leave, my lord, but he's already deeply involved in this out of necessity. He was at the float, or rather, waiting patiently outside. At home, they call Lectris my shadow; I seldom go anywhere without him, and I've found it . . . convenient to continue the practice when I'm with Alton. Lectris was on the landing roof, and I knew I could trust him, and so can you, my lord. He flew Alexand's car for us."

"He has a 'car permit?" That was unusual for a Bond; as unusual as the gun he carried.

She smiled obliquely. "I don't like being surrounded by strangers. I have only two personal servants, both of whom I've known since childhood, and both Bonds. I know them and trust them. But Lectris and Mariet have to do multiple duty. Lectris is both my bodyguard and chauffeur. At any rate, when we reached the private landing roof here, Lectris had to help Lord Alexand to his suite. I'd 'commed Rich, and he made sure there were no guards at the entrance or in the halls. No one saw us bring him in, but his condition was such that Lectris's assistance—and strong back—were absolutely necessary."

Woolf frowned slightly; he wasn't pleased at putting so much potentially damaging information in the hands of a Bond.

"My lady, perhaps you'd better tell me what happened at the float."

"Of course, my lord."

She calmly unfolded the story, a succinct account uncolored by emotion. That she despised Alton Robek and his friends couldn't be doubted, yet she allowed herself no overt expression of her feelings, and Woolf was as shaken by her self-possession as by what she told him. He was reminded of Alexand; she had the same capacity for detached containment. He recognized it as something Alexand had learned from him, an exigency of survival for a First Lord, but in this lovely young woman it seemed sadly incongruous.

When at length she concluded her story, he rose and paced the floor, taking time to consider it. Finally, he stopped, facing the windowall. It looked north, away from the city; only a few clusters of lights dotted the blackness.

He was profoundly grateful for Adrien's intervention; she probably *had* saved Alexand's life. She'd also shown commendable discretion and averted a possible scandal: the first born of DeKoven Woolf, indirect heir to the Chairmanship, indulging in an illicit drug. Or so it would be told. He turned, studying Adrien, who still waited silently, unmoving and apparently unmoved.

"Adrien, are you quite sure it was Julia who put the eladane in Alex's glass?"

She nodded, and for the first time a hint of emotion flashed in her eyes: a deep, chill contempt.

"Yes, my lord, I'm sure. Unfortunately I wasn't sure—or, rather, I didn't understand what I'd seen—until after the fact. There was a distraction, but I caught a movement out of the corner of my eye and an exchange—no words, only gestures—between Julia and Alton. It was his idea, of course, but she was closest to Lord Alexand."

Woolf sighed and returned to his chair. In one sense Adrien had shown a dangerous *lack* of discretion. She'd left Alton, her sanctioned escort, to accompany Alexand—alone. Lectris wouldn't be considered a suitable chaperon. The gossip-mongers could fabricate out of that a tale that would destroy her reputation, and no First Lord would consider her as a bride for his son; the Robek match would never take place, and that Directorate alliance was vital to Loren Eliseer.

"Adrien, don't you realize that if any of this gets out *you'll* suffer more than Alex. Most people will choose to believe he took the eladane voluntarily, and that will be damaging to him, especially coming on the the heels of—" He stopped, frowning. "But it will be far more damaging to you."

Her chin came up, and her black eyes fixed unflinchingly on him. "And far more damaging to my House, my lord. I'm well aware of that. But when I followed Lord Alexand to the roof, he was in his 'car determined to take off, alone. I knew he wouldn't call anyone to help him and that the risk of someone seeing and recognizing him, and recognizing his drugged state, would only increase if I tried to detain him there. I knew he was incapable of getting home safely by himself and, above all, I knew he needed a doctor. I *didn't* know if he was sensitive to eladane. I had to weigh the risks to my reputation against the risks to his life."

Woolf smiled ruefully at that calm declaration. "Please don't misunderstand me. I'm deeply grateful to you, but I can't understand why he wouldn't call someone to help him."

"Who would he call, my lord?"

Woolf shrugged uncomfortably. "I don't know. Hilding— *someone*. It doesn't matter who."

"But it did to Alexand. You must remember he wasn't thinking clearly; he couldn't."

"I suppose it's unreasonable to expect him to think the problem out logically in his state, but I—" He paused, then came to his feet again. "Why didn't he call *me?* Would that take so much logical consideration?"

She said quietly, "Perhaps he thought he'd already caused you embarrassment enough for one day."

Woolf turned abruptly, stung by that. "I assume you're referring to the Alber incident?"

"Yes." The response was flat, uninflected.

He said coolly, "My lady, Alexand has never done anything to cause me embarrassment, and I will not waste so much as a moment's thought on Karlis Selasis's crude allegations."

At that she smiled, an engaging smile that put him off balance.

"I've always known you to be an extraordinary man, my lord, and it's borne out in the fact that you *aren't* embarrassed.

Only an extraordinary man could overlook the misunderstandings and gossip this has caused."

Woolf replied tightly, "One can't be bonded to public opinion, my lady."

"But too many men in your position are. I'm pleased for Lord Alexand's sake that you're the exception. His behavior at Alber might seem foolish, and it was a hopelessly futile gesture, yet it showed great humanity and even courage. One might be proud of a son capable of that."

"Proud?" The incredulous word slipped out, carrying a bitter emotional charge. He saw her ingenuous smile turn faintly ironic and realized he'd been deftly maneuvered into a revelation he hadn't intended to make.

Will you bother to ask me why, Father?

Woolf turned to the windowall, away from her probing gaze.

Of course, she couldn't be expected to understand all the political ramifications of Alexand's "futile gesture," still . . .

"Tell me, Adrien, are *you* proud of him?"

"I . . . would be proud of him, yes, even recognizing it as a foolish act, because it was a humane act, and . . . perhaps because I've always had an overactive imagination. So Mother tells me. Strange how people of little imagination fear it. I saw the newscasts this evening, my lord; the scenes from the Alber uprising. The 'casts show so little, but I could imagine what it was really like. Not the full scope of it—that would take more than imagination—but enough. Enough to understand why Alex . . ." Her dark eyes closed. "He's not a soldier, my lord."

Woolf moved toward her, covering the space between them so silently, she didn't seem aware of him. He asked softly, "Adrien, does he still love *you?*"

She looked up at him, the contained calm shattered, as vulnerable as a child learning grief, as stunned as if he'd struck her.

"Oh, please, my lord . . ." She turned away, trembling, one hand pressed to her mouth, and Woolf couldn't even ask her forgiveness; he didn't trust his voice. This was the price of a political victory. Alexand was still paying it, too; it was only now that he understood this. Adrien's grief revealed his.

The only bride for Alexand. It had been so right; everything about it had been right, until political expediency intervened, and now they would be bound for their lives in the chains of matrimony that were for the Elite unbreakable—part of the bitter price of power—bound to Alton Robek and Julia Fallor, who were arrogant and witless enough to play games with an illegal and potentially lethal drug like—

He stiffened. Holy God, what was wrong with him? Had he lost his capacity to *think?* Life-and-death games with an *illegal* drug, and he stood moaning and muddling. Selasis would never have wasted so much time, given this set of—

"My lord?" Adrien was looking up at him, her composure restored, but when he didn't respond, she frowned uneasily. "My lord, forgive me if I've distressed you."

"No, my lady." He took her hands and gently pulled her to her feet. It's for me to ask *your* forgiveness. Your parents will be worried about you. I'll take you to the Robek Estate." He pulled out his pocketcom as he started for the bedroom door. "I'll have my 'car brought to the roof. Have you a face-screen?"

"I—why, yes, but you needn't be concerned about me."

He paused at the door and looked back at her. "Adrien, you may have saved my son's life tonight, and I intend to do everything in my power to see that you don't suffer for it. The first thing I must do is see you to the Robek Estate safely and explain the situation to your father. And while I'm there, I have something to say to Trevor Robek. Now, excuse me a moment. I must leave a message with Rich."

She could only nod numbly, too drained to make sense of his intent, purposeful attitude. Lectris stared as the door snapped shut behind Woolf, then looked over at her anxiously.

"My lady?"

She managed a smile to reassure him. "It's all right, Lectris. Don't worry. Everything will be all right."

6.

Elise Galinin Woolf noted the time as she slipped into his bedroom. 11:45. It was unusual for Alexand to sleep so late. But Dr. Stel had given him a strong sedative last night, and yesterday had been a bitterly exhausting day. Alber was enough, but the incident at the float...

She stopped by the canopy post at the foot of the bed and looked down on her son, his features, in sleep, in a rare state of relaxation. Twenty-one, she thought, already a year past Age of Rights. And yet she wondered if a mother could ever really see her sons as men, if she could ever look at Alexand without seeing the child he'd been, the infant, and even the unborn being whose first stirrings she'd felt within her womb. For Phillip it was easier; a father sees the man in his son from the beginning, and his arrival at adulthood is a fulfillment of expectation.

She closed her eyes, thinking of Rich, of the expectations that would never be fulfilled. That inevitable failure made Alexand's arrival at adulthood infinitely important. But he must never know *how* important; that was too great a burden to cast on his shoulders.

She heard the change in the pace of his breathing, and a smile curved her lips. He stirred, pulling in a deep breath, then sat up abruptly. He didn't seem to recognize her at first, then he relaxed.

"Good morning, Mother."

"You're almost too late for that greeting." She went to the windowall and turned off the glass shading; the midday sun flooded the room. "That should be a shock for you. Shall I page Tuck?"

"No, I don't need Tuck underfoot." He rose, took his robe from a chair by the bed, and pulled it on as he joined her at the windowall. "What time is it?"

"Nearly noon."

"Holy God, why didn't someone call me?"

"Why should we have called you? You needed the sleep,

and there was no reason to disturb you. Alex, how do you feel? I'm so very sorry about last night."

He hesitated, then, "I seem to be entirely recovered. That gown is very becoming, Mother. Blue is always your best color. And the chaplet is new, isn't it?"

She touched the golden band, cast in the shape of delicate, intertwined vines, that confined her lambent hair.

"Yes. Phillip had it made for my birthday." She was well aware that he was putting her off, but she'd learned patience with both Alexand and Phillip. "Will you have some tea or caffay with me?"

"I'd enjoy that. Have something sent up while I prepare myself for what's left of the day." He turned and started for the bath.

"What would you like?"

"Oh, tea, I think. Perhaps some Black Shang. It's bracing, if nothing else."

"Very well."

Elise filled a cup from the platinade pot and offered it to him as he sat down beside her in the oriel window alcove. He tasted the tea and grimaced.

"Bracing; that's the only word for it."

She leaned back, watching him over the rim of her cup. He was fully dressed now, and outwardly relaxed, but his eyes were narrowed with a slight frown.

"Mother, I want to talk to you about . . . Alber."

"Alex, you don't have to explain yourself to me under any circumstances, and I talked to Rich last night; he told me what happened, and I understand entirely." She sighed and frowned into her cup. "I'm far more concerned about what's happening between you and Phillip than I am about the Alber incident."

He looked at her sharply. "Nothing's happening between us. I didn't expect him to be happy about this."

"But you expected something more of him than he offered. It was an error for Phillip to confront you last night, but he wasn't thinking too clearly." She paused, watching her son, seeing the shadow of regret haunting his eyes. "Phillip is a remarkable man, but he's only human. I don't know if he'll ever fully understand your decision at Alber, but I know he wants to see you happy. He may not understand what you really need of him, but he'll bend every effort to give you what he *thinks* you want."

"I know, Mother. I should talk to him now—or is he still busy playing the attentive host?"

"He leaves that to me. But he's been quite busy with something more important than hosting."

Alexand raised an eyebrow, then picked up his cup. "Busy with what?"

"The usual flurry of postholiday business." She sipped her tea, smiling privately. "But that doesn't come under the heading of something important. Actually, he started the wheels turning on this particular matter last night. First, he talked to Loren Eliseer, and later to Trevor Robek, Charles Fallor, and Lord Cadmon. He intends to protect Adrien. She took quite a risk in seeing you home safely, and Phillip is duly grateful."

A hint of color came into his cheeks at Adrien's name. "And I'm grateful for his concern for her."

"That was only one of his objectives. Oh—by the way, there's an important piece of news you were in no condition to comprehend last night, and Phillip didn't find out about it until after he'd taken Adrien to the Robek Estate. It seems that float was raided by a Conpol Narco squad half an hour after you left it, but before Alton and his friends made their exit."

Alexand's cup clattered into the saucer. "A raid on a float? For the God's sake, Conpol never wastes time with that sort of thing; not in the upper levels of the Outside."

She shrugged. "Phillip was surprised, too, so he called his man in—that is, Commander Bary of the SSB. There was an anonymous tip that eladane was involved. Conpol couldn't ignore that."

"Did this anonymous tip include the fact that the eladane was in the possession of Trevor Robek's son?"

"No, and I gather it was rather awkward for everyone concerned. Poor Trevor. He deserves better than Alton."

"Where did the tip come from?"

"No one knows. It was a taped audio call; a patched tape, and there was no VP ident on file for the voice."

"Larynx alteration, probably. But who ... Selasis?" He frowned. "No, he wouldn't take that tack to discredit Robek. Karlis makes him too vulnerable for a counterattack on those grounds."

"True, but don't scratch the gold on this gift for gilt, Alex."
She smiled, finding it difficult not to laugh aloud.

"Yes, I suppose I should be grateful Adrien and I were out
of the float before the raid. Father had enough . . . shame at my
hands for one day."

"You might have other reasons to be grateful. Considering
that eladane was involved, there could be all sorts of repercussions, especially for Alton. And another thing: Adrien is
sure it was Julia who put the eladane in your drink—at Alton's
suggestion, of course—in spite of your clearly expressed refusal to take it. A serious legal case could be built on that
alone."

He studied her a moment, then said flatly, "But no case *will*
be built on it."

"Probably not, but it gives Phillip a telling lever against
Charles Fallor. After all, Julia's pristine reputation is important
to him if he hopes to make an alliance with a major House."

Alexand looked at her intently, a stillness about him, as if
he were holding his breath."

"Fallor? But he already has—Mother, what do you mean?"

She took time to sip her tea, then put the cup aside. "Fallor
is in hard straits financially right now, and he needs a strong
House alliance. He's looking to Julia to make that alliance,
and up to this point he's had a choice: Woolf or Selasis. But
Selasis has apparently given up on Fallor and is concentrating
on Shang; Janeel Shang, Lord Sato's granddaughter. At any
rate, Julia's imprudent behavior has backed Charles into a
corner, and Phillip *may* get what he's asking for."

"And . . . what would that be?"

She laughed softly. "Oh, Alex, I think you know. He's
asking for your freedom. Freedom from the obligation to Fallor;
freedom to make the alliance with Eliseer. He's asking for
Adrien for you."

He rose and went to the window, putting his back to her,
and Elise sighed; she could have predicted that.

"Don't, Mother. Please."

"What, darling? Give you a hope that might be crushed?"

He made no response, and after a moment she rose and
went to him, feeling the unconscious tensing of muscles as she
rested her hand on his arm.

"Alex, I'm going to give you a bit of motherly advice. I thought you had courage, but now I wonder. It takes courage to embrace a hope, because it is by its very nature susceptible to destruction. If it weren't, it would be a fact, something inevitable or immutable. Hope is a great deal like love; to enjoy its bounty, you must make yourself vulnerable to the pain of disappointment, but it would be a sterile existence with neither love nor hope."

He closed his eyes, and she felt the relaxation of his body, saw at length the mask of self-containment slip away. Finally, he took her hand and looked down at it, at the betrothal ring Phillip had put on her finger so many years ago. Ruby for DeKoven Woolf; topaz for Daro Galinin.

"And I can't live without hope." He seemed to be speaking to himself with those words. Then he looked up at her. "Good advice, Mother. I'll remember it."

She laughed and threw her arms around him. "Oh, Alex, this hope won't be crushed—I know it!"

He laughed with her, lifting her off her feet with the exuberance of his embrace. She blinked against the tears, savoring the welcome sound of his laughter. How long had it been?

When he released her, he seemed a little self-conscious at his enthusiasm, but the light didn't leave his eyes.

"Well. Have you any idea when I might know if this hope is to be realized?"

"It will be decided in the next few days. Phillip must still make sure Fallor doesn't fall into Orin Selasis's hands. He might change his mind about Janeel Shang if Julia's loose, so to speak." Then, seeing his frown, she added, "But Phillip doesn't intend for her to *stay* loose."

"But how—" He stopped, eyes narrowing. "Robek."

"Yes. Alton's backed Trevor into a corner, too. Alton and Julia may find themselves married to each other in penance for their sins. Fallor was hoping for an alliance with Woolf or Selasis, but he'll take Robek now and be grateful. That still aligns him with Galinin and Woolf."

Alexand gave a short laugh. "It sounds like a *Volante*—everyone changing partners at the next chorus."

"So it does. Of course, there's still a chance it won't—"

"Mother, must I turn your sage advice back to you? In

matters of this sort, I'm well aware that nothing can be counted done until the contracts are signed." He paused, smiling. "But I'll hold the hope still."

"Good." She touched his cheek gently, then sighed and looked at her watch. "I must go check the cleanup crews; everyone falls into total disorganization after the holiday."

He nodded absently. "I thought I'd ask Rich if he'd like to spend a few days at the Barrier Reef estate."

"That would be a marvelous idea." He walked with her to the door, where she stopped, averting her eyes uneasily. "Alex, when you talk to Phillip—"

He laughed. "I'm not to let him know you've said a word about this *Volante* he's set in motion."

Her cheeks went hot, then finally she laughed, too. "He should know better than to tell me about it. It's asking too much of a mother to hold a secret like that." She touched the doorcon and stepped out into the anteroom, then paused to take his hand, studying the strong, muscular contours of it, remembering the hand that once lay in a tiny furled fist in her palm.

"Alex, it's good to have you home."

Alexand walked down the slate path, and the leaves of the eucalypts whispered happily among themselves in the spring breeze; as he crossed the footbridge, the white-foamed streamlet laughed aloud. A flock of lorikeets took flight at his approach in a joyful flourish.

Hope. Humankind's gift to itself, and every gift has its price. But perhaps he'd paid the price of this gift yesterday at Alber.

No. Not now. He refused to think of that now.

Rich was at his desk in the school room; he smiled as if he'd been expecting him.

"Alex, you look well."

He laughed. "I am well." He went to the desk, which was littered with tape spools and sheets of vellam covered with cryptic notes. "I'm sorry I gave you such a scare last night. It certainly wasn't intentional."

"I should hope not, but if nothing else, you got a good night's sleep out of it. How else would Dr. Stel get a sedative into you unless you were beyond balking?"

Alexand absently picked up a tape spool and turned it in

his fingers. "I may have more than a good night's sleep out of it. Can I talk to you about something? Something private?"

Rich understood that guarded query. "We're safe here. I've installed permanent jamblers and a warning system."

Alexand put the spool down and looked directly at Rich. "Mother just left me. She told me about certain plans Father is pursuing; plans for a Woolf-Eliseer marriage."

Rich regarded him with a bemused smile. "Yes, I know about that."

"What are the odds, Rich? In my favor?"

"I can only give you an educated guess. Yes, Alex, they're in your favor; yours and Adrien's."

Alexand's eyes closed briefly, then he laughed. "God, I can't get my balance. From . . . yesterday, to *this*. Did you talk to Adrien last night?"

"Not at any length. I wish I could have had more time with her. Father talked with her for quite a while, though."

"Did he?" Alexand nodded. "Mother says he wants to see me happy, and I believe that. Happiness may be an ephemeral state, but I'm grateful for it. Grateful to him."

"So am I," Rich said softly. "And grateful he finally has a chance to do what he's wanted so desperately to do all these years." He paused. "But something's bothering you."

Alexand's eyes flashed to his. "At least, something's aroused my curiosity."

"The raid on the float?"

"Yes." He turned and began aimlessly pacing the room. "Conpol wouldn't waste time on an Outside float normally, but they were told eladane was involved. An anonymous tip." He stopped to face Rich. "Where did that tip come from?"

"A Phoenix agent." The answer was flat, nearly devoid of expression. Then he smiled faintly and leaned forward. "You're always under surveillance; protective surveillance. An agent was on hand, and a monitor went into your pod at the float almost as soon as you arrived. And, by the way, if Adrien hadn't come to your rescue, someone would have brought you home safely, although your memory of the trip might've been a little vague. Our agent sent a Pri-One alert to HQ when he heard the word 'eladane.' He was in constant contact with his superiors, and they—at least, one of them—with me. The potentials inherent in the situation were recognized and the tip went to Conpol—*after* you and Adrien were safely out of the float. Alex, the Phoenix has been waiting for an opportunity to break Fallor's hold on Father since that hold came into existence. When the opportunity arose, they were ready. And so was Father."

Alexand shook his head, as if he could shake off the feeling of uncertainty. "But why, Rich?"

"Not because of any sympathy for star-crossed lovers. It's very simple. We protect and aid the liberal Houses whenever and however we can. That includes Woolf and Eliseer. Eliseer is of particular interest to us for the same reason it is to Father. Loren Eliseer is the strongest Lord in the Centauri System and the best hope for keeping Orin Selasis out of Centauri. Woolf and Galinin and the Phoenix have one thing in common, Alex: we all recognize Selasis as a threat to the stability and survival of the Concord. So, to protect Centauri and bolster Eliseer, the Phoenix encourages an alliance with DeKoven Woolf, with the future Chairman. Is that so unreasonable?"

Alexand took a long breath and let it out slowly. "The people responsible for this gambit—tell them for me, whatever their motives, I'm grateful. Perhaps the day will come when I can express it in more than words."

Rich smiled obliquely. "Perhaps it will."

"And Rich—" Alexand closed his eyes against the burning in them, wondering why he was trembling. "Rich, if this . . . this hope is realized, I know one thing: I'll never give her up again. Not for anything."

"A spirit weft," Rich said with a long sigh. "That's what the Shepherds would call it: a bond of souls. A spirit weft can't be broken. It's more than a life vow. It holds into the Beyond."

Alexand nodded. "Then I'm so bound."

7.

"Dr. Lile, my head is aching with all this effort." Adrien Eliseer waved off the reading screen and rose, noting the brief disequilibrium. Strange that it always seemed to take longer to *re*adjust to Castor's lighter gravity than to adjust to Terra's. "Come, let's go out on the terrace. I'll 'com Mariet for tea. I don't think I can bear to look at one more sporozoa or phytoplankton."

Lile Perralt's lined face crinkled with his smile. "It's mind-boggling, Adrien, I'll admit."

"That's not very encouraging. I'd never have enrolled in this microbio class if I didn't think I could depend on you to get me over the rough spots." She touched a button on the desk comconsole. "Mariet?"

After a moment, Mariet's face appeared on the screen. "Yes, my lady?"

"Tea for Dr. Perralt and me, please, in my suite."

"A few minutes, my lady."

"Thank you." She turned and took Perralt's arm as they walked out onto the terrace. "I only have two days before classes resume, and of course VonHart scheduled the test on the first day. You'd think he'd have more respect for the Concord Day holiday."

Perralt laughed. "Postholiday tests are an age-old tradition, Adrien, and it was your error to count on me to get you over these particular rough spots. It's been a long time since I've read a biology textape."

Adrien went to the terrace railing and looked up at the blue-black sky and the faint sprinkling of stars visible beyond the sheen of the atmobubbles. In spite of the 'bubbles, the morning light cast black shadows and narrowed her eyes into a reflexive squint. In the distance, seemingly impaled on Helen's towering, needle-slim buildings, hung the blue crescent of Pollux.

She turned, watching Perralt as he sat down in one of the chairs under the striped umbrella shading the table, noting the care with which he moved. He was perfectly all right, only a few years older than he liked to admit—so he answered all her anxious inquiries.

She smiled as he looked up at her. "Dr. Lile, you've been very patient with me, but I think I've learned my lesson. Science isn't my forte."

"Don't be so modest. You're doing very well, and I've heard of VonHart. He has a reputation for—" He stopped, looking toward the salon at the sound of footsteps. Then he rose.

Adrien's eyes widened questioningly as Lord Loren Eliseer walked out onto the terrace. It was unusual for him to take time in the midst of his workday for a casual visit, and she knew this would be a crowded day. He'd stayed in Concordia another day after the rest of the family departed and had just returned yesterday evening. She went to him, turning up her cheek for the expected paternal kiss.

"Well, this is a delightful surprise, Father. We're having some tea. Will you join us?"

"No tea for me, Adrien, but I will join you for a short while. Hello, Dr. Perralt."

"Good morning, my lord. Uh . . . perhaps you'd like to speak with Lady Adrien alone."

"No, Doctor. Please—sit down." He took a chair across from Perralt at the table, and Adrien approached slowly, studying her father, wondering at the light in his blue eyes, the slight flush that always colored his fair skin when he was pleased or angry. And she knew he wasn't angry.

"In fact, Doctor," he said, "I think it particularly fitting that you should be here, since Adrien calls you her second father."

Perralt glanced at Adrien. "I'm flattered, my lady."

"It's true, Dr. Lile, you know that." She sat down at the table, eyeing Eliseer. "What's this all about, Father?"

"Whatever do you mean? Is it so strange for me to pay a visit to my daughter?"

"It's strange in the middle of a busy day, and strange when you're grinning as if you'd just discovered the secret of turning sand into gold."

He laughed ruefully as he reached into the inner pocket of his doublet. "Such a suspicious nature she has, Doctor."

"I've learned deception is futile with her, my lord."

"Indeed, and I wouldn't attempt it." He had a flat, leather-bound case in his hand. Adrien felt a chill at the back of her neck; the case was scarlet, with the eagle crest of DeKoven Woolf embossed in gold on the top.

"Father, what . . . what is it?"

"Well, it seems this just arrived by special messenger from Concordia." When she made no move to take it from him, he put it on the table before her. "It's for you, Adrien."

She knew she was pale, and she couldn't control the trembling of her hands as she reached for the case and cautiously opened it. A folded slip of vellam fluttered to the floor, but she was too distracted to notice it.

A lining of black velvet; inscribed in the lid, initials shaped in a golden, intertwining scroll: A.C.E. and A.DeK.W. And, resting in a precise circle in the bottom of the case, glinting against the velvet, a necklace.

She gazed at it numbly. The delicate chain was beaded with pearls, and attached to it with a cluster of golden, pearl-dewed leaves, was a tear-drop stone a full three centimeters long, a magnificent, fiery stone with a blue cast, transmuting the sunlight into a shower of rainbow flashes. When it came to her that it was a diamond, she could only stare at it in bewilderment.

"Father . . . ?"

"It's an old custom, Adrien." He smiled as he handed her the vellam that had slipped from the case. "Here. I rather imagine this will make everything clear."

She unfolded the sheet, feeling the wrenching quickening of her pulse as she recognized the straight, spare handwriting.

Adrien—
Now I can say it, even put it down on vellam with no fear of consequences, and I find no words adequate. But you know my heart and mind, and can read past the words. The vows—the public vows—will be said and sanctioned later, but I've already taken my own life vow, a vow to love my lady until death. Thus this gift, asked by custom, offered in love. Pearls because they suit you, diamond for immutability. Never doubt I love you, Adrien, and I always will. . . .

"Alexand . . ." She wasn't aware of reading the name aloud, nor at first of her father's soft laughter. She looked up at him pleadingly.

"What does this mean?"

"It means you've just received the traditional betrothal gift, and in two weeks, you'll go to Concordia to take your vows and become the Promised of the Lord Alexand."

Tears slipped down her cheeks, falling onto the vellam; she closed her eyes to hold them back.

Alexand, all the vows are already made. . . .

8.

A marriage of destiny.

On the evening of 30 Octov 3250, the vidicom screens brimmed with the betrothal ball at the DeKoven Woolf Estate, and the society commentators agreed unanimously, and repetitiously, that it was a marriage of destiny. •

The newscasters and vidicam crews were excluded from the betrothal ceremony at the Cathedron, but the guests were inventoried in detail on their arrival. They represented all the Houses of the Directorate, and included the Chairman himself, and every Cognate House of DeKoven Woolf and Camine Eliseer. The vows were blessed by none other than the High Bishop, the Revered Archon Simonidis.

The ball following the ceremony attracted over a thousand guests, and was open to the ecstatic 'casters, all of whom gave glowing accounts of the *Cotilonna*, the stately circle dance that traditionally marked the betrothal of Elite couples, a dance in which the Promised pair and their parents formed a small circle within the concentrically larger ones of the assembled guests. It was reported that never had such a handsome trio of couples graced the inner circle of the *Cotilonna*: the betrothed pair themselves; the dark-haired Lady Galia and as a perfect foil, Lord Loren, fair and blond; the Lord Woolf, elegantly austere, and, of course, the recognized reigning beauty of the Concord, the Lady Elise.

The reporters catalogued the entertainments, the refreshments, the décor—the theme was gold, the huge ballroom was resplendent with it—and dwelt lovingly on the costumes, noting every nuance of detail. The betrothal ring and the fabulous blue diamond betrothal gift each rated a full five minutes in some accounts.

But if any of the 'casters noticed that soon after the *Cotilonna* the Promised couple was no longer in evidence in the ballroom, no mention of it was made. There were other couples to note and speculate about, especially Lord Karlis Selasis and Serra Janeel Shang, the Lady Adrien's cousin.

But there was general agreement that it was, beyond a doubt, as Frer Simonidis reiterated, a very auspicious occasion.

On my immortal soul, I take this vow for life and unto death . . .

Alexand listened to the sound of their footfalls on the slate walk and the soft whisper of the eucalypt leaves moved by a wind cool in the spring night. Adrien Eliseer would grace the House of DeKoven Woolf as Elise Galinin graced it, and she would grace his life; she would be a wellspring of strength, as Rich was, mentor and balance wheel, another linked-twin soul.

He looked down, watching the dappled moonlight moving across her quiet face as she walked beside him under the arc of his arm. This he would never forget: Adrien as she was now, as she was when she stood beside him before the Cathedron's magnificent Altar of Lights. She was all in gold, a gown of a gossamer material that shimmered in the currents of her slightest movement; a veil trailed behind her, a golden cloud caught in a brocaded koyf framing her face, edged in pearls that seemed to take warmth from her skin. At her throat the pearl-flowered diamond caught the muted light.

It would be nearly three years before this vow was finalized, but the legal covenant was already made in the Contracts of Marriage and given religious sanction tonight. The Church marriage ceremony would be only a formality to give the union the sanction of tradition.

But he didn't wish that final sanction done now, not while Confleet held him bonded. He would endure these next years so he could take his Promised to wife free of the invisible chains, the nightmares that haunted his sleep. First Alber, and now he could add to his mnemonic catalog of horrors the Delai Omer uprising in Coben only three days ago. And in Coben he had been a good soldier; a good, unthinking, unquestioning soldier. If only he could also be an unremembering soldier.

"What is it, Alex?"

Even the fleeting memories created a tension that transmitted itself to her.

"It's . . . not important; not now."

"It's something you don't want to talk about."

He shrugged. "Yes."

She was silent for a while, then with a long sigh she rested her head against his shoulder.

"So, it's finally done. I wonder when I'll believe it."

He smiled at that. "Frer Simonidis calls it done, and it would be nearly blasphemous to question his word."

That called up a short laugh. "I'd rather take old Malaki's word. He calls it a Rightness."

"Or a spirit weft?"

She looked up at him. "Yes, he used that term. Where did you learn it?"

"From Rich."

She nodded, smiling to herself. "I wonder what the Shepherds call him. A holy man, no doubt, and they'd be right. Thank the God he can be here now. I don't think I could call it properly done without him."

He drew her closer, savoring the calm of the night. "Nor could I."

"How long will he be staying?"

"A week. Until my leave ends; my special dispensation from Confleet."

That last word seemed to create a silence, a shadow.

"Alex, I . . ." She hesitated, then shook her head. "I can't find the words for what I want to say. It's Rich and you, and Confleet, and I know it's breaking your heart. I want to stop the pain somehow, but I . . . can't."

He stopped and looked down into her dark, somber eyes, his arm still resting on her shoulder.

"I know, nor can I stop all your pain. Sharing only doubles the pain, really, and yet it makes it easier to bear. A paradox, that."

Her eyes didn't leave his, nor did she smile, and the moon shadows moved softly across her face.

"Too much," she said after a long pause. "Too much is asked of you. Too much to accept; too much to tolerate. I wonder if you won't reach a breaking point."

He felt himself going pale, something chill in the wind. "I won't break."

"No. But you're damned with a conscience and open eyes. A dangerous combination."

He took her hand and looked down at the ring he'd put on her finger only hours ago. Ruby and sapphire; Woolf and

Eliseer. A life vow. And a hope; a desperate hope.

"Three more years, Adrien. I should be able to survive that."

"And will it all be over then?"

He hesitated. "I don't think past that."

"No." She pressed his hand to her cheek. "Forgive me, love. I've learned one lesson in life, but for the moment I forgot it. Joy must be taken in the present tense. We can remember the past and imagine the future, but we *live* here in the present. And Alex . . ." Tears brimmed in her eyes, and he couldn't at first resolve them with the laughter, warm as sun-drenched earth. "Alexand, my lord, this present is so full of joy for me, it spills over into both past and future."

He touched her cheek, wet with tears, and felt the tears in his own eyes. "And for me. Joy enough to see me through any future."

He made no conscious decision to kiss her; still, there was no surprise that it happened. He closed his eyes, hearing the soft wind in the trees, remembering and imagining, and holding this moment; holding the awareness of this linked-twin soul, of her whole being, mind and body.

"Never doubt I love you, Adrien."

"I never have, Alexand. I never will."

The words existed like lights in the leaf-scented darkness, fading slowly, one by one. Then she laughed and drew away from him, but still held on to his hand.

"Come. Rich is waiting for us."

Alexand found himself laughing as they started off down the path. "So, I must share you with my little brother."

"Well, I hope you don't think you're the only attraction in Concordia for me."

They emerged from the grove, still laughing, but at nothing more than an indefinable elation. He slowed as they moved across the grassy knoll toward the viewpoint pavilion, his attention caught by an unfamiliar pattern of lights.

Shimmeras.

A cluster of golden shimmeras floated inside the dome, and a small table had been brought in, replete with flowers and wine. And Rich was waiting, turning at the sound of their voices.

Alexand quickened his step. "Rich has prepared a private celebration for us, Adrien."

"Ah, how beautiful!" She broke away from him, running ahead to greet Rich with a laughing embrace.

There would be laughter for Rich, too, and nothing could mar or shadow this present. The lucent spring days would stretch themselves like cats in the sun, making a store of warm remembrances, and no grief, no pain, no dread could coexist with this laughter.

PHOENIX MEMFILES: DEPT HUMAN SCIENCES: BASIC SCHOOL
                    (HS/BS)
SUBFILE: BASIC SCHOOL   16 JANUAR 3252
                    GUEST LECTURER: RICHARD LAMB
                    SUBJECT: POST-DISASTERS HISTORY
                    WARS OF CONFEDERATION (2876–2903)
DOC LOC #819/219–1253/1812–1648–1613252

Motivation in itself never explains great historical figures—context and blind luck are inevitably major factors in "greatness"—but it's always interesting to consider. Lord Patric Eyre Ballarat in the period just before the Wars of Confederation (which began in 2876 and continued until 2903), had personal reasons for calling the "outlanders" enemies, particularly those who had turned to piracy. The House of Ballarat held franchises for the large marine vessels that carried most of the Holy Confederation's trade and suffered most directly from the depredations of pirates. It's possible that he also believed the "heathen" should be Mezionized. Certainly, if that weren't a sincere conviction, he was careful not to let it be known. Like Even Pilgram, Ballarat recognized the efficacy of a spiritual-political union, and he had his Colona in the person of Bishop Almbert, Eparch of the Cathedron in Sidny, which was then the largest city in Conta Austrail, in some ways equivalent to

Concordia today, although the comparison falls short in many areas. To be sure, the Holy Confederation's Council of Lords—which is analogous to our Court of Lords—met there, but the entire administration complex of the Council would fit into the Hall of the Directorate alone with ample room for Almbert's Cathedron. The Council was a very loosely organized body with little real power. Power in the Holy Confederation was vested in the Houses, and individual Lords maintained allegiance to the Confederation only to the degree that it served their needs.

Patric Ballarat is the first prominent historical figure about whom we have a great deal of personal knowledge. We know what he looked like from numerous two-dimensional, monochrome "photograms" that have been preserved for us: a sturdy, broad-shouldered man with thick, dark hair and an unusually—even for the period—full beard. After he became First Commander of the Armed Forces of the Holy Confederation, he is always shown in that uniform, even long after the Wars when he had retired to his Tasman estate. What is never fully evident in the photograms is that he was slightly below average height at no more than 165 centimeters. This obviously didn't prove to be a disadvantage to him. A few audio recordings have survived, too, most of them orations before the Council, as well as an especially stirring address to his officers on the eve of the Battle of Capeton, and, although the recordings are primitive by our standards, they still give us a measure of the forcefulness of the man and explain to a great degree his success in mobilizing the Holy Confederation to its extraordinary conquests.

Something of his forcefulness also comes through in his *Autobiography*. In the first volume he outlines—a little tediously—his House's history and his childhood, but the pace picks up as he goes on to describe his ascendancy to First Lordship of his House despite the fact that his father, although chronically ill, was still alive, and despite the opposition of his brothers, Hugh and Bryan. His marriage to Lady Noret Tadema, whose father was First Lord of the most powerful of the landed Houses, is recorded, as well as the births and histories of their two sons and two daughters, at least up to the time of his self-exile after the Wars. Ballarat was a remarkably good writer, and exceptionally well educated in comparison to most of his Lordly peers, and there we find a key factor in his motivation. His consuming interest was history, and he had what was often termed an obsession for the histories of the Roman and Brittish empires. The information available to him then was comparatively scant, but he devoured it all, and there is little doubt—in fact, in his *Autobiography* he spells it out very clearly—that his fundamental ambition was to make of the Holy Confederation an empire.

His imperial vision was not at the outset appealing to most of the Holy Confederation Lords. Here Ballarat found himself at odds with feudalism. The centralized government he proposed antagonized the more conservative Lords, who jealously guarded their power and prerogatives, and feared surrendering any part of them to a centralized power. But Ballarat was convinced that if the Confederation didn't move into an imperial phase, it would disintegrate into isolated feudal holds and revert to a pre-Pilgram state in spite of the technological advances made in the intervening three centuries, and it would then be at the mercy of the emerging powers and alliances outside Conta Austrail.

Undoubtedly, that consideration impelled him more than pique at the depredations of outlander pirates and competing merchant fleets, and more than concern for the souls of heathen. In fact, in his first efforts to interest the Lords of the Council in an imperial future, he said nothing about the unredeemed heathen, but spoke heatedly of the Sangpor League in Indonasia, which under the leadership of the King Madang Sambor was demonstrating its burgeoning power and confidence by wresting the established Sinasian and Indasian trade routes from the ships of the House of Ballarat. Other Houses whose fortunes were adversely affected by the loss of those routes—as well as the cargos sunk in armed disputes over them—joined Ballarat in demanding action from the Council, but the assembled Lords could only agree to make financial contributions to the House of Ballarat for the building and better arming of more ships.

But Lord Patric was only thirty then and not yet First Lord of the House. Five years later he had remedied that and undoubtedly learned more about politics. He had also found an ally in Bishop Almbert, for whom the idea of spreading the light of Mezionism to the rest of the planet— as well as spreading the power base of the Church—had great appeal. The formation of the Allienza Salvador in

Sudamerika and the growing power of the Sudafrikan Union under the leadership of Tsane Valstaad, as well as continually increasing losses of cargos, markets, and sources of raw materials, made Ballarat's later appeals to the Lords more convincing, especially with Almbert to bolster them with fiery sermons urging the faithful to join the sacred crusade to bring light to the unenlightened. And finally the King Madang Sambor made the fatal error of launching an assault on the city and Home Estate of the House of Darwin.

Under this spur, the Council was induced to accept the Articles of Union proposed by Ballarat, which among other things established the first Directorate, a body empowered to make decisions without the approval of the Council, to levy taxes on all Houses, and to create an armed force that, although it was funded and its manpower provided by the Houses, would be essentially independent of them. A few Lords rebelled at that wholesale surrender of their powers, but the weight of opinion was with Ballarat, and what had come to be called the Unionist movement held sway. With an empire to be gained—and a holy imperative to be served—to niggle at surrendering individual House prerogatives became tantamount to treason and heresy.

Patric Ballarat was, inevitably, voted Chairman of the newly formed Directorate and First Commander of the Armed Forces of the Holy Confederation. He mobilized in a remarkably short time an army augmented by naval and airborne forces that numbered half a million men. His troops swept through the Sangpor League holds, taking the cities of Timor, Jakarth, Tai, Bangkor, and Rangor. Almbert's priest-soldiers—and so they were actually called—followed in their wake, accompanied by the Lords chosen by Ballarat to hold and administer the conquered lands.

This victory spurred the Holy Confederation to even more extraordinary feats of production and mobilization. Ballarat struck into Sinasia, where he met little resistance in the independent domains of Kangcho, Sankeen, and Kashgar, and was delayed only for a period of two months while he laid siege to Paykeen. Meanwhile, a secondary force commanded by his brother Bryan met organized resistance from the Shogan Lords of Hokido, but occupied the city of Sappuro within twenty days, then advanced into eastern Ruskasia. There Bryan didn't meet resistance so much as huge, uninhabited stretches of land, but managed to find and subdue the holds of Okhotst and Yakutsk before Ballarat ordered him to seek more promising areas of conquest on the western coast of Noramerika.

Ballarat continued his westward thrust into Indasia, where the independent domain of Ceylonia after less than a year fell to his armies, and the loose alliance of the rulers of Calcut, Bangalor, and Poona laid down their swords and bows—their only weapons against the Holy Confederation's explosive-charged artillery and similarly armed airships—even before Ballarat's soldiers reached the cities, celebrating their entry with festivals. However, the nomadic tribes of Shek Mashet's Gulf of Persias alliance offered no such welcome, and Ballarat pursued those desert ghosts across dune and mountain for three years before Mashet came to terms. He did not in fact actually surrender, but simply agreed to let Ballarat occupy the city of Hamadan, which was the only established site that might have been called his headquarters, and in exchange the nomads were left alone in their desert fastnesses. The occupation of Hamadan was hailed as another victory in Conta Austrail, but it should be noted that this was the only occupied domain where Almbert's priest-soldiers didn't follow the real soldiers.

Even if the full terms of Mashet's "surrender" had been known in Conta Austrail, it's unlikely anyone would have been daunted. The Holy Confederation was enjoying an unprecedented economic boom, with the expenditures of war financed by its spoils, and the citizens of the Holy Confederation in every class benefiting from both. Even the loss of life was ameliorated by soldiers conscripted from domains subjected in the campaign, and those conscriptions were often voluntary. Ballarat chose the Lords who occupied the defeated territories carefully and laid stringent rules for fair treatment of their new subjects; he didn't want revolt biting at the heels of his imperial campaign, and it's a credit to him and his administrators that there were only three such revolts—and they were disorganized and short lived—in the whole of his twenty-seven-year campaign.

CHAPTER V: July 3253

●ıı●ıı●ıı●ıı●ıı●ıı●ıı●ıı●ıı●ıı●ıı●ıı●ıı●ıı●ıı●ıı●ıı●ıı●ıı●

1.

The city of lights. A smudge of white coalescing out of darkness, expanding in a slow, silent explosion until the window was filled with light.

Limbo, this voyage. Sometimes he had to remind himself to breathe, and sometimes he wondered if his heart would forget to beat. The pilot assumed he was asleep—Alexand huddled in the rear seat of the Scout, wrapped in a night-black cloak, whispering through a black night.

Strange, he'd traveled half a world away, and the smell was still with him; the odor of seared flesh and dust. He carried it in his very pores.

> *Will all great Neptune's ocean wash this blood*
> *Clean from my hands . . .*

Lector Theron . . . Theron Rovere. . . .

Alexand thought he was laughing until he felt the tears coursing through the dust on his cheeks; the dust from the labyrinths of the Kasai Orongo mines. Half a world away.

The words of the ancient poet/dramatist in their elegantly metered phrases—he had first heard them on the lips of Theron Rovere. In his childhood. When was that? And had it ever really been?

Lector Theron, will you never leave me in peace?

A million words he must have spoken in those apocryphal years; they kept floating up from the deeps of memory.

> *. . . No, this my hand will rather*
> *The multitudinous seas incarnadine. . . .*

"Captain Woolf? We're here, sir." Sargent Finley craned his head around, his voice hushed; a tone for waking the sleeping.

Alexand moved tentatively. "Thank you, Sargent." He

squinted out at the glare of light washing the landing field, listening to the dull slap of Finley's booted feet as he came around to open the hatch for him.

A sharp, biting wind; winter. Two hours ago, the tropic summer of Sahrafrika. Now, as he felt the pavement under his unsteady feet, cold cutting to the bone.

"Your 'car is over there, sir." Finley pointed toward the dark maw of a hangar. Waiting in front of it was the Faeton-limo with the DeKoven Woolf crest on the side. Hilding was approaching. Alexand watched him, finding the pattern of his scarlet cloak blowing in the bitter wind unutterably fascinating.

"Captain . . ." Finley still wore the grime of the dust, too, his face patterned with the clean areas that had been covered by goggles and filter mask.

"Yes, Finley."

"I—I hope it isn't bad news, sir."

Alexand looked at him dazedly. A Confleet officer wasn't called from the field of battle on an emergency leave for good news. *Battle.* The word jangled out of tune in his mind.

"Thank you, Sargent." He touched his right hand to his left shoulder in answer to Finley's salute, then moved away toward the dark, fluttering pattern of Hilding.

"My lord . . ."

Alexand didn't break step; now they were twin patterns of dark against light, scarlet and black.

"What time is it, Hilding?"

A pause. "Nearly midnight, my lord."

It had been 15:00 on a glaring hot afternoon when he left the Kasai Orongo mines, yet that had been only two hours ago. Not that it mattered.

Hilding maintained a polite silence as the 'car spun across the light-webbed sea of Concordia. But he was waiting.

Alexand stared at the back of his head, feeling the waiting. "Hilding, is it Rich?"

A sigh of hesitation, then he nodded. "Yes, my lord. Ser Rich . . . came home tonight."

Ser Rich.

The VisLord Richard DeKoven Woolf should be addressed as Lord Richard now, but that oversight was a token of affection, not disrespect.

Ser Rich came home.

There could be only one reason. No holiday prompted this unexpected return, and there had been no warning of it. Alexand closed his eyes, wondering why he felt no pain.

Three years. Three years playing henchman in the guise of duty; three years carrying Rich's secret with him.

Now Rich had come home.

"We heard there was some trouble in the Sudani area, my lord." The statement was a question.

"Yes, Hilding, there was . . . some trouble."

"We were afraid you were involved since your unit is stationed in Zandria."

"I was involved. The Lord Orongo called us in."

"Uprising in the mines, I understand. Terrible affair."

Alexand made no reply. No words were adequate, except perhaps Hilding's. Terrible affair.

At least—terrible.

"I heard it was that—that Society . . . the Phoenix, I guess they call it, that set off the uprising, my lord."

"Where did you hear that, Hilding?" No shade of expression in his voice.

"Oh . . . I don't know. I was just talking to some of the guards."

"In other words, gossip."

"I—well, yes." He laughed uneasily.

"Hilding, I don't know if there's any truth to the rumor. There'll be an investigation, I'm sure."

"Of course, my lord."

Hilding's noncommittal tone was eloquent. The investigation would be fruitless, and if the Phoenix was left to bear the burden of blame, it was only because Conpol didn't even know what questions to ask.

Alexand had asked questions of his own among the survivors at the mine, but none of them knew what had triggered the bloody, futile mutiny, and they had been too busy tending the injured and counting the dead to care.

Hilding was moving down into the exit grid; the mass of Concordia's lights were behind them, and ahead on the crest of the ridge Alexand saw the familiar pattern of lights.

Home. Rich had come home. To die.

2.

There were no guards at the family wing entrance, an anomaly to which Alexand gave scant attention. But Gate Steward Maxim Lews was waiting in the entry foyer.

"My lord, are you . . . are you all right?"

He looked at the old man, wondering at his shocked expression until he caught a glimpse of himself reflected in the glassed walls. It was a grim, begrimed image.

He smiled mechanically. "Yes, Maxim. Quite all right. Where's Rich?"

"In the upper terrace salon. Lord Woolf and my lady are with him, and the Lord Galinin."

Galinin. He frowned, then started down the corridor.

"Go to bed, Maxim. It's late."

"Thank you, my lord, but I have instructions."

Alexand paused. "You're expecting someone else?"

"Yes, my lord."

"Who?"

"I wasn't told."

Alexand left the pedway and turned down a side corridor, his pace quickening as he neared the salon, but when he reached it, he hesitated before touching the doorcon.

It had been four months since he'd last seen Rich. The ravages of the illness in that time . . .

A slither and click; then, as he stepped into the room, the sound repeated itself in a silence.

The salon was a favorite of Elise's, full of light at almost any hour of the day, its décor a comfortable mix of periods with individual pieces chosen solely for their beauty or personal meaning, the colors tending toward warm browns and golds. The ceiling was high and intricately coffered, with deep light wells, and the long windowall to his left as he entered offered a fine vista of Concordia. Tonight the light level was low, providing no distraction from the view, but the family was gathered at the other end of the room by the fireplace, his

mother seated with her back to the door, Mathis Galinin on
her right in a deep armchair by the hearth, Phillip Woolf standing on her left, gazing into the fire, the flames casting flickering
lights on his aquiline profile. And on the other side of the
fireplace in his nulgrav chair, facing the door—

Rich was dying.

Strange that it was one thing to know he'd come home to
die, but another to see that he was dying. His body seemed
weightless, as if it exerted no pressure against the cushions,
and so frail it seemed the smallest movement would shatter
him; his hands lay on the chair arms like exquisite abstractions
of glass.

Alexand had anticipated the accelerated deterioration, but
he encountered here something entirely unexpected: an inexplicable beauty, something refined to its essence. There was
an aura, as if this fragile being were in process of consumption
by some purifying white fire that burned from within. It was
in his face, the skin taut and translucent over the fine structure
of his skull, and it was most of all in his eyes. His eyes were
lenses concentrating the inner fire, the clear, depthless blue of
summer skies.

Behind those eyes, something unknowable. They saw past
the rim of life. Alexand had the startled sense of finding himself
in the presence of—what? He could find no words, except one
his mind objectively rejected: *holy.*

"Hello, Alex."

He crossed to Rich and took his hand, painfully aware of
its frailty, of the dry, chill feel of the skin.

"Rich—dear God, I've missed you."

It was perhaps some momentary shift in Rich's gaze that
reminded him that they weren't alone. Alexand looked to his
left, finding it an effort to call up a smile.

"Father . . ."

"You arrived in good time, Alex."

He only nodded, then went to his mother and kissed her
cheek. He frowned at the smear of grime left by that brief
contact. It sullied her clear skin.

"Mother, I'm not fit to touch anyone at the moment. How
are you?"

The smile was too forced, the handkerchief she raised to
wipe away the smear was twisted and crumpled. For the first

time, he realized she was showing incipient signs of age, and it came as a shock. Somehow it had never occurred to him that Elise Galinin Woolf was subject to the process of aging.

"How are *you*, Alex?" she asked, studying him anxiously. "You look so . . . tired."

He turned to Mathis Galinin, deeply ensconced in the armchair, sitting it like a throne.

"I *am* tired, Mother. Grandser, it's been a long time."

"So it has, and we're both the worse for wear. Alex, have you heard from Adrien lately? How is she?"

He tensed inwardly at that. Not that he didn't appreciate the affectionate concern in the query. Perhaps it was because Adrien seemed a last bastion of gentle rationality, something too precious to talk about only hours away from the Orongo mines, as if those horrors sullied her as the dust did his mother's cheek. He took off his cloak, noting the sheen of dust clouding the black cloth.

"She's well, Grandser. I called her . . . three days ago." It seemed much longer.

"A lovely young woman. She's entirely captivated me."

Elise smiled up at Alexand. "You aren't alone in that, Father. Alex, have you eaten? Would you—"

"Now, there's a typical mother." His smile faltered; the thought of food was intolerable. He turned and crossed to the refreshment 'spenser in the corner, tossing the cloak over a chair on his way. "I'm not hungry, Mother, but I could use a drink."

Galinin swiveled his chair around. "Alex, was that uprising under control when you left?"

He paused with his hand on the switch that set the revolving bottle rack in motion; the crystal decanters tinkled faintly among themselves. Then he jerked a towel from the dispenser and wiped his hands and face, staring at the dark smudges.

The question came from the Lord Galinin, the Chairman. It wasn't idle or gratuitous, and it couldn't be ignored.

"Yes, Grandser, it was under control, or nearly so."

"Have you any idea what started it?"

He took a decanter from the rack and read the imprint. "It began at the entrance of the main shaft. That's all anyone knows." He frowned at the bottle. "Canadia?"

Woolf responded absently, "I'm on speaking terms with

Charles Fallor again. He sent over a few cases."

Alexand pulled the stopper, feeling out his father's constrained attitude. It seemed more than grief. He poured the whiskey indifferently. Fallor's whiskey had never impressed him, but the bottle was in hand.

"Will anyone join me?"

There was no response to that. He capped the decanter.

"Alex, I've had reports from Conpol," Galinin said, "but they were garbled, as usual. You were there. I must know what happened."

Alexand stared at the quivering reflections in his glass. "I talked to some of the Fesh who were near the main shaft when it started, but they had no conclusive answers."

"Did you talk to any of the Bonds who were on the scene at the outset?"

He watched his own hand, resting on the counter, curl into a fist at his father's curt, impatient interjection.

"The *Bonds?* What good would it do to talk to them?"

And Alexand wondered if any of the Bonds who might have answered these questions had survived, if the answers weren't buried in the deepest shafts, strewn in mangled—

He squeezed his eyes shut, teeth cutting into his lip.

Adrien said he was damned with a conscience, but he was more damned with a clear memory, one that never ceased functioning, like heart and breath, outside conscious control, constantly gathering new images for new nightmares.

"Alex?"

Galinin. But Alexand was no longer capable of regarding him as the Chairman; it was all he could do not to shout.

"Grandser . . . please. Not now. The questions need answers. But I . . . need a little time." He took his glass and went to the empty chair between Rich and the hearth. He had to move slowly; he was assaulted by unexpected periods of dizziness. But they passed.

He turned to his brother and wondered why his direct, almost expressionless gaze made him suddenly aware of the ominous character of the silence around them. It was more than a response to Rich's agonizingly imminent death.

His mother's smile faltered when he looked at her; her hands tightened on the twisted handerkerchief. He turned to Galinin, surprised to see him avert his eyes. His father still stood staring into the fire, his face momentarily unguarded, the grief nakedly exposed. And something else.

Anger. And a pain that wasn't grief.

The answer to this silence came indirectly. When Rich began to speak, Alexand expected it, but his words at first seemed to lead away from it.

"Grandser, I'm concerned about Alex."

"We all are, Rich."

"In one sense or another, yes. I'm thinking of the effect of my demise on—"

"Rich, please—"

"No, Alex, don't put me off." He waited until Alexand silenced his own objections with a nod. "Grandser, the real nature of my illness has never been made public, but it will become self-evident in the near future, and that will make Alex extremely vulnerable."

Galinin pursed his lips, glancing up at Woolf, but he seemed out of touch, tuned out of this conversation.

Alexand laughed. "Ah. I see. You think someone might try to rid the House of its sole heir. Well, that wouldn't be so difficult. A Bond uprising would make such a convenient cover for an 'accident.'"

Rich nodded soberly. "Yes, Alex."

He couldn't muster a shred of concern for his vulnerability, and he laughed again, despite Galinin's stern look.

"Well, Rich, you have a point there, especially since I still have the extraordinary privilege of being assigned to the same unit as Karlis Selasis. Lord Orin's behind that somewhere; it has his malicious stamp."

Rich didn't respond to that. He turned instead to Galinin.

"Grandser, I know you've been stymied at pulling any strings for Alex; Selasis is watching for it, and he'll raise a howl. Fortunately, Alex only has two more months of active duty, but still, I think you should take the risk. His unit is being transferred to Leda in four days, and that will put a great deal of distance between him and any protection you and Father can provide."

Alexand's head came up at the matter-of-fact announcement of the transfer; he'd been told nothing of it. And Woolf was roused from his inward reverie, his response cold and bitterly sarcastic.

"We appreciate your keeping us informed of Confleet plans, especially since that transfer is classified Pri-One!"

Alexand didn't hear Rich's reply. He closed his eyes, stunned, the trembling going out of control. The answer to the weighted silence in this room was in his father's words.

Alexand knew the source of Rich's information: the Phoenix. He was only surprised about the transfer. And Woolf knew Rich's source, too. Otherwise, he'd have asked how Rich came to be in possession of Pri-One information. And that coldness, the icy contempt that had never been turned on Rich . . .

Alexand remained motionless, eyes closed, sorting the mixed threads of his own emotions, certain only of uncertainty. They were all at a nexus in their lives. There were factors here outside his ken, potentials only dimly sensed. A crossroad; a junction in timeliness.

He opened his eyes to find himself the focus of every other eye, yet when he spoke it seemed to startle them. Except Rich. He was waiting for the question.

"Rich, how did they find out?"

"I told them."

Woolf cut in. "Alex! You know about this? How long have you known?"

Alexand looked up at his father and understood the anger now; pain transmuted. He considered himself betrayed.

"Rich talked to me before he accepted the Leda post."

"Before he—Holy God, all this time you *knew*, and you didn't tell me? Didn't you think it might be of some interest to me that I was harboring a traitor in the House?"

"I don't consider Rich a traitor."

Woolf went white. "Then how do you account for the fact that he admits himself a member of the Phoenix?"

"Does that automatically make him a traitor?"

Woolf stared at him, his hands knotting. "Alex, I don't understand you!"

Elise's hand went out, resting on her husband's closed fist. "Phillip, please. Don't blame Alex for not telling you. Rich is his brother—"

"And Alex is my *son*, my first born! Has he no obligation to *me*—to the House?" Then he sagged under her penetrating, dry-eyed gaze. "I'm sorry, Elise, but this is all so incomprehensible."

The tension that had been close to a breaking point ebbed, and Galinin said levelly, "Alex's motives are beside the point now, Phillip, and neither of you are in a frame of mind to discuss them objectively." Then he turned to Alexand. "I'm sorry you've had to come home from that uprising to this, but obviously Rich has created problems here that must be dealt with."

Alexand nodded and took a swallow of the whiskey. It might have been water, but it helped wash away the smell. He caught the brief closing of Rich's eyes. Pain. Not something born of the mind; it was simpler and more tangible. Physical pain.

"Rich, how much have you told them?"

"Everything I could without endangering the Society." He took a pill vial from his tunic and held it hidden in his hand. "It would have been easier for all concerned if I'd kept the secret, and I wanted to."

"Yes. I know." He watched numbly as Rich opened the vial and slipped a pill into his mouth, and he wondered what kind of medication it was.

"But I couldn't take the easy way, Alex, and the reason will be familiar enough to you. An accident of birth. I'm the only member of the Phoenix who could gather in one room the Lord Mathis Galinin, Chairman of the Directorate, the Lord Phillip DeKoven Woolf, a Director and heir to the Chairmanship, *and* their mutual heir. I have two purposes in returning to Concordia. One is to act as an envoy, to give these prime movers of the Concord a true accounting of the Phoenix." He paused, his mouth shadowed with an ironic smile. "And to prepare them for the time when they come to the bargaining table with us in the age-old custom of merchants and princes to haggle over the fate of civilization."

"Never!" Woolf exploded. "The Concord doesn't bargain with thieves and traitors!"

Rich only nodded. "Thieves and traitors. Catchphrases are dangerous, Father. Those are your words. And scapegoating is even more dangerous; far more dangerous. It too often lets the real culprits escape unnoticed and unpunished." Then he sighed. "No, the Concord won't bargain with us. Not until it has no choice. The Phoenix is working toward that day, and it *will* come, or there may be no civilization left to haggle over."

"No doubt the Phoenix will see to that if we won't surrender to your demands."

Rich's head moved in a negative motion against the cushions of his chair.

"I think I made it clear that the very reason for our existence is to prevent a third dark age. When we haggle, it will be over the means of maintaining civilization. I know you think we'll never come to terms, and you may be right, but if you are, it will be because the Concord fails before the Phoenix is strong enough to force it to the bargaining. I expect no converts now. I only hope that later, and it may be years later, what I've said here will be remembered." He looked at Alexand, a mute sadness in his eyes. "The seeds I sow may never take root, but I was the only one who could sow them in this particular ground."

This particular ground. Alexand looked at his father, his uncomprehending anguish turned to implacable obduracy. This sterile ground. Perhaps Galinin offered more fertile ground, but he was an old man, and Phillip Woolf was heir to the Chairmanship.

"Rich, you said you had *two* purposes." Alexand's eyes were drawn to his mother. She was watching Rich, and perhaps he'd already explained part of his second purpose, but not all of it. The plea for understanding was too naked in her eyes.

Rich's gaze was drawn to her, too, but his reply was directed to Alexand.

"Yes, I have another purpose, and it's the more important of the two. Remember that. And remember that I've given it long and careful consideration. My purpose is the arrest and subsequent trial and execution—the martyrdom and apotheosis—of Richard Lamb."

"Arrest and—" Alexand put his glass down on the arm of his chair; it had almost slipped from his hand. And he held on; held his trembling muscles in check; held back the cry of pain until finally he could think again and even maintain a certain level of detachment.

"Your arrest. Then it's the SSB Maxim has been instructed to wait for. Who called them?" He didn't realize he was looking at his father when he asked that question.

Rich said, "I did, Alex. Not directly, and not 'them.' Specifically, Commander Quintin Bary."

Alexand felt the dizziness coming again.

"Please, Rich . . . why?"

"I'll explain, but first let me assure you—all of you—that everything possible has been done to protect the House."

Woolf folded his arms, as if that were necessary to contain his disgust. "We could use some assurances, but I doubt—"

"Phillip. . . ." Galinin was frowning slightly. Woolf raised an eyebrow, then subsided into grim silence.

Rich watched this exchange, then continued calmly, "First, understand that my apotheosis *must* take place in Concordia for maximum effectiveness. As the old saw has it, everything begins in Concordia. More people pass through this city in a day than in a month in any other city. They come from the farthest reaches of the Two Systems, and return there, carrying the news of Concordia with them. The importance of Concordia as a news distribution center will become apparent later. As for my arrest, an anonymous tip went to Commander Bary this afternoon stating that Richard Lamb, an agent of the Phoenix, is in Concordia. This was to give him a rationale for my arrest, since my association with the Society isn't known. A few hours ago, he received another tip on his personal 'com seq so that there's no record of it. He was told where he would find me and when." Then, noting their uneasy frowns, "Don't worry about Bary. First, you're all aware that he was born a Woolf Fesh and owes his present position to the House; he's still a loyal servant to Woolf, even if he wears the SSB face-screen. But the Phoenix doesn't depend on apparent good faith. Bary has been conditioned."

"Conditioned!" Woolf couldn't contain that expression of chagrin. "A commander in the SSB—"

"Yes, Father." Rich smiled faintly. "Military and police psychic types are generally highly susceptible to conditioning. At any rate, he'll say nothing to anyone about the tip. He'll come here, arrest me, and take me to the SSB Central DC. But once he leaves the Estate, he'll experience a sort of memory lapse. He won't remember where he found me, or the actual wording of the tip. But he won't be left empty-headed, so to speak; he's been provided substitute memories, and they'll be exact and clear."

Woolf was pale, too stunned to speak, but Galinin recovered after a moment and even managed a rueful laugh.

"I'm not sure whether I should be impressed or frightened by such efficiency and capability, Rich."

"Impressed, I hope. At least impressed that we're doing everything possible to protect the House. And I've had larynx alteration and fingerprint removal, which precludes standard identification. The only possibility is that someone might recognize my face, but recognition depends a great deal on expectation. As evidence of that, I was never once recognized in my six years at the University. And no one will expect Richard DeKoven Woolf in an SSB DC, especially not when—" he paused, glancing at his mother, "—when the records will show that he died tonight. And remember, I haven't made a public appearance—as Richard Woolf—since I was thirteen."

Woolf retorted, "But you admit there *is* a chance someone might recognize you. Do you realize what Orin Selasis could do with that?"

"He could ruin DeKoven Woolf and Daro Galinin, but with the precautions we've taken that risk is so minimal as to be nonexistent. My trial and execution will attract no attention—*unless* you interfere in any way. If you do, I warn you, you'll increase the risk to the point of real danger."

"But that risk won't exist if you *aren't* arrested."

Rich's eyes narrowed, turning cool and remote. "I must give you another warning, Father. Check with the SSB. You'll find Phoenix agents are adept at escape. There are even instances on record in which they seemed to literally disappear. You can't hold me or hide me. If you try to stop me, my arrest will simply take place elsewhere. Your only hope is to kill me outright now, and in that you'd probably be unsuccessful, even if you were capable of it. And I can't believe you are."

For a time the only sound was the crackling of the fire. Woolf seemed frozen, his face ashen, and Elise's voice impinged on the silence, soft as some lonely night wind.

"Oh, Rich, I still don't understand." Her eyes had the nacreous sheen of pearls, and as much life. And there was sorrow in Rich's eyes as he looked at her.

"Mother, forgive me the grief I inflict on you, but I must go through with this. I *must*."

"But it—it will mean a public execution."

"Yes, and as I intend to confess my so-called crimes freely, at least in general terms, my execution will occur within a few days. But Mother, don't let that prospect alarm you. I have very little time left. You know that. My doctors estimate a week, possibly a month, but no more. This is what I want; there's a reason for it. But your concern is personal, and perhaps it would be easier for you to accept if you knew I feel no dread. Only an anticipation of . . . relief."

Elise had turned away, but now her eyes, still bitterly dry, sought and found Rich's.

"Relief from . . . pain, Rich?"

"Yes. It has to do with the circulation, they tell me. It's been bearable until recently, but it's becoming uncontrollable. Nothing is so dehumanizing as pain. If I didn't have a purpose in seeking public execution as a means of final relief, I'd resort to soporifics; in fact, I'd have had it over by now. But remember, Mother, I've planned all this carefully and, I might add, it was accepted by my friends in the Phoenix with great reluctance. I believe in the Phoenix with all my heart and soul, and I want my death to serve my cause. It's all that's left me to give."

"Rich, I don't yet understand how your . . . death will serve your—"

"*I'll* tell you how!" Phillip Woolf's voice ripped into the quiet, exposing the ragged edges of his rage. "It's quite simple, Elise! Basic politics. Every revolution needs a martyr, and your son has set out to provide his *cause* with a suitable martyr! And what a perfect candidate he is!" Woolf laughed, and the sound was frightening. "A *crippled* martyr! Imagine it as he's *carried* to the execution stand. Now, there's an image to arouse pity—and wrath. And the wrath will be directed against the cruel and heartless Concord. That he was a *traitor* will be forgotten. All the mobs will remember is that pitiful—"

"Phillip!" Elise stared at her husband incredulously. "How could you—"

"How could *I*? Your son is the traitor here! Ask him how *he* could do what he's done. Don't you understand? When the Bonds come raging for our blood, it will be to *revenge* the death of Richard Lamb. That's his *purpose*—to give the Phoenix a catalyst. He could set off a bloodbath to make the Mankeen Revolt look tame by—"

"No! I won't believe that—not Rich!"

"Why not? You think he's still your loving child? He's a man, and he made his choice. He *chose* this damned Society. *That's* the cause he believes in with all his heart and soul. A band of thieves and traitors—and catchphrases be damned! The *enemy*, Elise!"

"He *told* you the Phoenix doesn't—"

"Elise, I know a hell of a lot more about the Phoenix than you do."

"But I know my son! Apparently you've forgotten, or you never knew him."

"For the God's sake, stop it!" Alexand rose abruptly, hands clenched at his sides. "'He'—'*your* son'—you talk about Rich as if he weren't even here. This is the VisLord Richard DeKoven Woolf; in any other context that alone would assure him the courtesy due a Lord's son. And this is a scholar and scientist, a recognized expert in his field. And this is an extraordinary human being capable of compassion and . . ." He stopped, his breath coming out in a long sigh, and turned away, toward the fire. The dizziness again.

He'd exchanged one nightmare for another, and neither made sense. And his father—

Alexand found himself met with a stranger in his father. Galinin had as much reason to feel betrayed, yet he displayed none of that acid antagonism. What had happened to Phillip Woolf?

No human being is exempt from fear . . .

That was at the heart of everything. Fear. That cancerous plague that robbed human beings of their humanity.

Behind Alexand's closed eyes a ghastly montage of images flickered with the red light of the fire, and his stomach convulsed with nausea.

Fourteen. He'd been directly involved in fourteen Bond uprisings in the last three years, and the Two Systems had been rocked with over two hundred serious enough to require Confleet intervention. He returned to his chair, sinking heavily into it, unaware that it was his own drawn, pale features that prompted the quiet around him.

He said, "Father, don't you understand what's happening? The Phoenix isn't our enemy. We have only one enemy: the fear that's swallowing up the Concord. It's a sickness, a contagious disease, and it's on the verge of pandemic."

Woolf stared at him and seemed to be grasping at the words, attempting to put them in a context of reason, and Alexand saw a crack in the stone wall of resistance.

Then he saw the crack sealed.

"You're talking nonsense, Alex. We haven't time to waste on philosophical bleatings."

Alexand flinched openly before he got himself under control. Time. His father didn't understand time. Perhaps because he didn't understand death. He hadn't seen enough of it.

Alexand turned to Rich, and found his luminous eyes fixed on him.

"Rich, what is it you hope to accomplish with your . . . martyrdom?"

Rich took a long, slow breath. The fires still burned, banked, behind his eyes, but his pupils were reduced to pinpoints. Morphinine. Yet he was still in pain.

"Alex, you know I don't intend to leave a legacy of violence, nor would the Phoenix tolerate that. My purpose is to create a legacy of peace."

Woolf stiffened. "*Peace!* Holy God, do you take us all for fools?"

Galinin's voice came rumbling from the recesses of his chair. "Phillip, I want to hear what Rich has to say. This isn't the time to give way to emotions."

Woolf's rigid posture didn't relax but, after a tense hesitation, he said curtly, "Very well, Mathis."

Galinin studied him, frowning, then with a sigh turned to Rich, and behind the ingrained skepticism lurked a shadow of his own grief.

"Peace, Rich? Surely you realize your execution might trigger violent reactions."

"I've been preparing for it for the last year, Grandser. A certain danger does exist, but I've done all I could to negate it, and I believe the risk is worth taking in light of the potential benefits that might result from it."

Alexand looked at Galinin, saw his furrowed brow as he considered that. But he *was* considering it; he was listening.

"'Peace' is a large word."

Rich nodded. "Indeed. To be realistic, all I hope to accomplish is to discourage the tendency to violent reactions among the Bonds. It might give the Concord a few more years before the internal pressures reach an explosive point. These uprisings—and the term is very apt—are in no way organized or purposeful; not yet. They're simply eruptions; intense pressures suddenly unleashed, comparable to geological phenomena. The Fesh generally instigate them, although they aren't aware of it. It might be an unjust punishment or a deprivation, a relatively minor incident, but in certain situations the Bonds' response to it may be quite violent. The Fesh in turn react with greater violence, initiating an uncontrollable reactive cycle. It can *only* be stopped at the beginning. I can't influence Fesh behavior, but I may be able to minimize the inevitable reactions of the Bonds, to stop the cycle at the outset—in some cases, at least."

Alexand was beginning to understand now, and perhaps he had recognized the true character of the light consuming this frail husk when the word *holy* came to mind.

Galinin asked, "How can you exert any influence over the Bonds by offering yourself up for execution?"

"Partly by providing an example of submission and acceptance, but it goes deeper. In order to understand it, you must know something of Bond religion."

"Well, then—" Galinin smiled faintly. "—inform me."

Rich smiled in response, and a subtle rapport seemed to exist between them: Galinin skeptical with the bitter wisdom of his years, but listening, still listening; Rich transcendently calm, in his voice the patience of raindrops against the armored flanks of mountains. Alexand gazed fixedly at his pallid face, almost disembodied in the shimmering light.

Rich began, "First, you must recognize the efficacy of direct verbal communication, not only from one person to another, but from one generation to another. In personal communication, the Bonds aren't at all inconvenienced by their technical disadvantages. Many of them are quite mobile in their assigned tasks, and they act as couriers. It's slower than vidicom, but any news of importance to them makes the rounds eventually. You must also understand that Bond religious and social structures cannot be separated. Religion is all they have; the source and means of enforcement of their social and moral codes. It was a wise decision to leave them that. The survival of the Concord to this point is probably chiefly attributable to the Galinin Rule and the wisdom of your forebear, Grandser. And I'm not deceived by your show of ignorance about Bond religion."

Galinin shrugged. "Still, you're the expert here."

"My one redeeming virtue. At any rate, the efficacy of direct verbal communication across *time* is what I'm leading up to. And the Holy Words. The Holy Words is far more than a verbal equivalent of our Holy Writ; it's an incredibly voluminous body of ritual, myth, magic, parable, poetry, and moral dogma, and it's transmitted entirely by verbal communication from one generation to the next through the Shepherds. They're phenomenal; walking memfiles. We depend so much on mechanical mnemonic devices, we have no concept of the quantity of information the human mind is capable of storing unaided. Some of their sources predate the Disasters, and generally very little is lost in transmission. I once went to some trouble to track down one passage quoted by a Shepherd. It was an exact quote from an ancient translation of the Pre-Disasters Judeo-Christian *Bible*. Parts of it are incorporated into our Holy Writ, but not this passage. There are five surviving copies of the old paper-page form of that book, and that's where I found the passage, locked in the vaults of the Archives where it hasn't been accessible to Bonds, even if they could read, for centuries."

Galinin raised an eyebrow. "Yet this Shepherd gave you a verbatim quote?"

"Yes." Rich glanced at Woolf, noting his growing restiveness. "I offer this example of the Shepherds' ability to retain and transmit information accurately over long periods because it's extremely important. The Shepherds are moral references. In case of doubt, a Bond has only to ask a Shepherd, and he'll dredge up a quote from the Words to dictate the proper mode of behavior under any given set of circumstances. The Bonds depend entirely on the Shepherds for moral guidance, and they in turn depend on the Holy Words. For instance, family disputes are discouraged because Saint Catarin of Lima laid the dictum, 'The ties of blood are sacred to the Holy Mezion; who raises his hand against his kindred, raises his hand against the

Mezion and shall be so doomed.' Saint Catarin is three centuries in her grave, but her words still set limits to behavior. The power in the dictum is implicit in the last part: '...shall be so *doomed*.' The Bonds have a very concrete vision of life after death; it's perhaps more real to them than this life, which is typical of a subject people. The dead go to the Realm Beyond the Farthest Star, where the Mezion and the myriad saints reside. The good live like Lords, of course. Evildoers are confined to Nether Dark, which is comparable to a compound detention center. Sometimes these 'Dark Souls' escape to infest the living." He paused, smiling. "That's how they explain Orin Selasis, the 'Dark Lord.'"

Galinin laughed. "That's as good an explanation as I've heard."

"It's a highly functional philosophy. But my point is that the threat of punishment in the afterlife is very tangible to them. They accept communication between this life and the next as casually as we accept SynchCom transmissions, and they think the saints are out there constantly *watching* them, and any moral deviation is duly noted and ultimately punished. This puts a great deal of leverage behind the words of long-dead seers and saints."

"I think, Rich," Galinin said slowly, "I'm beginning to understand your purpose."

Woolf, standing with his feet slightly apart, every line of his body bespeaking reined tension, said, "It's becoming quite clear, Mathis, and I find my fears not in the least allayed by this scholarly dissertation."

Fears. Alexand almost laughed. Always back to that. He stared into the fire, into the flickering images of disaster, of nightmare, while Rich replied levelly, "The possibilities *are* frightening, Father. I'm surprised no one has taken advantage of them before, and I'm deeply concerned that someone will."

"Why? You'd like to retain that privilege for the Phoenix?"

Alexand felt his muscles tighten. His father *was* listening, but he heard only what he wanted to hear.

Galinin's brows drew down; he sent Woolf a penetrating look, but addressed himself to Rich.

"You've convinced me that Bond religion offers a potentially powerful tool. How do you intend to use it?"

"I intend to become a saint." Rich glanced at Alexand and

smiled. "There's irony enough in that—a slightly cynical agnostic like me with ambitions for sainthood." Then he turned again to Galinin. "But sainthood *is* within my grasp. When I first began studying the Bonds, I used to memorize various philosophical passages before I went to the chapels and recite them to encourage the Shepherds to open their memfile memories. By the time I began the more intensive studies I carried out for the Phoenix, I'd acquired a name for erudition and wisdom comparable to the Shepherds themselves. They call me a holy man. Of course, my . . . affliction made it easier to gain their trust from the beginning. They regard it as a divine sign. A year ago, I began to realize I might be able to make use of this hard-earned reputation. For my purposes their religious tendencies are ideal: very conservative, with a rigid moral code reinforced by fear of punishment meted out by an omniscient pantheon of saints, and this I haven't touched on yet—extremely fatalistic. In spite of the increasing number of uprisings, Bonds are far more inclined to accept rather than react. How else would you keep seventy percent of the population in a state of virtual slavery?" He shook his head, sighing. "And how else would they explain their slavery, except by a deeply ingrained fatalism. 'What is, is a Rightness; the will of the Mezion is hidden to mortal eyes.'"

He paused, as if to gather his flagging strength, or perhaps to steel himself against the pain.

"So, I began my campaign. In the last year I've visited nearly three thousand Elder Shepherds throughout the Two Systems. No small task. I've been preparing them for my Testing. My martyrdom. I've warned them that it's coming, and I've laid my dictums. I scavenged the Holy Writ, the Word, the literature of all history, for sources. I even invented dictums of my own: 'Wrath mothers blood; submission mothers peace.' 'Dark Souls feed on anger; humility withers them.' 'The Mezion will Test you to know your soul; lift your hand against His tools and you are doomed, for they are the instruments of His will.' 'The way of the Blessed is peace. As all people are children of the All-God, they are all brothers. Who lifts his hand in wrath against any person, lifts his hand against his brother and reaps the harvest of doom.'" He hesitated, then, "Do you understand now, Grandser, what I hope to ac-

complish with my sainthood? They don't know I have a terminal illness. All I want them to know is that I went to my
death with absolute submission. Then these words and the years
I've spent with these people—studying them, guiding them,
even loving some of them—then all this will bear fruit. Nothing
I've said will be forgotten. It will be incorporated into the Holy
Words and locked in those memfile memories to be called up
when the occasion demands, and that will be at the beginning
of the reactive cycle, *before* the chain reaction of violence
starts. They'll think I'm out in the Beyond waiting to toss them
into Nether Dark if they defy my dictums, and the gist of all
the words I've poured into their memories is this: violence and
resistance are sins, submission and humility virtues; the Fesh,
Confleet, Conpol, etc., are instruments of the Mezion—or
brothers—and violence against them is a mortal sin." Rich was
leaning forward, his burning eyes fixed on Galinin. "Grandser,
do you understand?"

Galinin rested his white-bearded chin on his folded hands.
"Yes, I understand what you hope to accomplish."

Rich didn't move except for the whisper of a smile that
touched his lips.

"But you have reservations."

"Of course. Not about the feasibility of your plan. I don't
doubt that it would serve to inhibit the Bonds in future encounters with Fesh."

"Then you have reservations about me?"

"I haven't entirely dismissed the possibility that you may
be lying to me, but I find it highly unlikely." He paused. "No,
my reservations are for the Phoenix, of course. However, those
doubts can be resolved—on this particular issue, at least—with
a single question." His eyes narrowed, probing. "Rich, what
I must know is this: Have you ever told the Bonds that you're
a member of the Phoenix?"

The answer came without hesitation, firm and decisive.

"Definitely not. And for a very pragmatic reason: it would
destroy their faith in me. They regard me as a Beyond Soul
with no identity with any class, group, or organization in this
world. The few who have even heard of the Phoenix identify
it with the Outsiders, whom they distrust and fear. I've never
once mentioned the Phoenix or suggested that I was associated

with *any* kind of organization."

"But they'll find out if you're executed as an agent of the Phoenix."

Rich shrugged. "The charge will be meaningless. My execution will be a Testing, Grandser, and it will make no difference to them what brings me to it. You could charge me with anything, even murder, and they wouldn't believe it."

Galinin nodded acceptance. "And you're quite sure they have no inkling of your connection with the Phoenix?"

"Quite sure."

Woolf demanded incredulously, "Mathis, don't tell me you *believe* that? For the God's sake, it doesn't make *sense* that they wouldn't identify him with the Phoenix!"

Alexand asked, "Why not, Father?"

Woolf hesitated, as if seeking the source of a new attack. "*Why not?* What good will their damned martyr do them if the Bonds don't know his *cause*? *He* won't be available to sound the call to arms himself. The Bonds *must* know!"

Alexand stared at his father, at this man who had become a stranger to him, the man who had sired him in an act of love, and who had in love sired Rich, the son whose death, whose future nonexistence, he dismissed so callously with that impersonal phrase, *he won't be available*.

He asked, "Do they, Father? Do the Bonds have to know?" He expected the question to emerge as a shout, but it was quiet, almost toneless.

Woolf retorted, "Of course they do! How will the Phoenix take advantage of their noble martyr unless the Bonds know who to answer to—the *Phoenix!*"

Galinin rose, a monolithic shape looming through an inexplicable haze.

"Phillip, you're making a serious error."

Woolf faced him defiantly. "Mathis, if you're fool enough to believe him—" he seemed incapable of pronouncing Rich's name, "—I'm not! If you let him go through with this, you'll give the Phoenix a weapon to blow the Concord apart. You know the inevitable results of this execution, and yet—"

"No, I do not *know* the results, and I don't accept the inevitability of a bloodbath arising from his execution. I'm considering the risks to our Houses if he's denied this . . . martyrdom. I'm weighing those risks against the possibility that his death *will* serve a positive purpose."

Alexand was dimly aware of a pale shape floating in some ambivalent space. His mother's face. She was looking directly at him, her eyes wide with unmasked fear.

"You believe him!" Woolf took two strides toward Galinin, coming between Alexand and his mother. "You believe all that—"

"I believe," Galinin said firmly, "that Rich may be correct in his assessment of the results of his decision. I believe that it's within our power to counteract any use the Phoenix might make of his martyrdom; we are, at least, forewarned. Or have you some alternative to offer that would magically negate the risks involved in trying to stop him?"

"I have the only obvious alternative. If Richard Lamb's arrest can't be prevented, so be it. He *will* be arrested—but there will be *no* execution."

"Holy God, are you suggesting that Rich simply be kept under detention for an indefinite period of time?"

"Yes! That execution must not take place!"

"Phillip, even *I* can't keep this quiet indefinitely without attracting attention, and we can't risk that."

"Not indefinitely. Only—only until . . ." And he finally faltered; silence closed in.

Rich's voice came softly into its void. Alexand turned to look into that luminescent, mystically beautiful face, and he saw something there he recognized as dread.

"Grandser, he means, *only until I die*—of my illness."

The chemistry of rage reached critical mass. Alexand felt the accumulated despair and anger suddenly unleashed within him, pooling with every heartbeat in the pounding cavity of his skull. He had a distinct awareness of the pressure within his head pushing against the delicate interlacings of the sutures in the bone. He wasn't aware of moving, but now he was on his feet, facing his father, close enough to touch him, but seeing him at an unfathomable distance. The room seemed washed in a white glare that drove off the color, and the sound was unbearable. Yet some part of his mind recognized the quiet outside the exploding pile of his brain, and against the outer silence he heard his own voice and its measured tones.

"Let me understand you, Father," his voice said, "your intention is to surrender Rich to the SSB and let them hold him until he dies of natural causes?"

"Yes, that's my intention. We can't allow—"

"You can't *believe* him—your own son. Rather than believe him, you'd put the House in jeopardy and your son in the hands of the SSB indefinitely. Are you aware of the quality of the medical facilities in SSB Detention Centers?"

"I don't see what bearing—"

"Then you've suddenly lost sight of the fact that Rich is ill." His voice was still quiet, but the pressure was out of control, the heat-flash whiteness fading until he was peering down a long tunnel of blackness at his father's face. "And are you aware that the SSB will undoubtedly try to break his Phoenix conditioning? He'd be a prime candidate for them. And are you aware of the SSB's methods of interrogation? The pulsed charges? And their latest development, the neuron sensitizing injections? Perhaps you haven't had time to concern yourself with such trivia; perhaps I should bring you up to date. The sensitizing injections increase pain susceptibility tenfold. Think about it! Your son laid out on—"

"He's *not* my son! Not now!"

"You can't deny your genes in every cell of his body. *He is your son!* And you're condemning him to—how long in hell? Maybe he'll live a month; maybe two weeks. Maybe he'll be lucky and die in *one* week. How many hours in a week, Father? How many minutes? How many seconds?"

"Damn it, he chose the Phoenix! This is a risk he—"

"How long is a *second* when you're in pain? And with Rich, they might not have to resort to their refined methods to reduce him to abject agony. All they'd have to do is cut off his morphinine and let nature take its course."

"I can't help that!"

"You *can* help it, but you won't because of the fear. The fear that's eating at the guts of this holy Concord of ours. It's the *fear* that will destroy the whole rotting pile, and it's reached you, too, Father. You're afraid—"

The sound was a stunning crack, and in its wake came a paralyzed silence.

He had seen his father's hand draw back, seen it move across his body, but it didn't make sense until he felt the smashing impact of the back of that hand against his cheek.

"Afraid?" Woolf's voice was blurred with rage, but still

mordantly cold. "Perhaps *you* should teach me courage! My son, of the delicate stomach and dainty sensibilities, the first Lord of DeKoven Woolf to risk a court-martial for flight from battle. You have no right to speak of *courage*! You're as much a traitor as your brother!"

Woolf didn't need Galinin's sharp, warning command. It hardly registered, and it came too late.

He heard his own words echoing as the torrent of anger dissipated, leaving him empty and intensely aware of the livid mark on his son's cheek and the burning of the skin on his own hand.

That blow, those words, between one Lord and another, were more than sufficient grounds to call a point of honor. He'd seen men killed with far less provocation. But it wasn't that prospect that brought the sick despair. It was what he read in his son's face.

Alexand, forgive me.

Three simple words. They must be said.

Yet his throat constricted on the words, they were gall on his tongue. He could not say them. Then like a signal came the single, sweet-toned chime of the pager. Commander Bary.

The moment had passed. It was too late.

Woolf watched numbly as Alexand turned his back and went to the hearth to stand staring into the red embers. He spoke then, but not to his father; to no one and everyone, in a tone stripped of life.

"I want to speak to Rich. Alone."

And Elise rising, still dry-eyed, reaching out to her father for support. Rich motionless, eyes closed, the dim light catching the glint of tears moving down his cheeks.

3.

The door closed. Whisper slither and click. And Rich was gone. Their last words together had been spoken, were vanished now into the void of the past.

Click. Again. The door closing.

An echo out of the ago only minutes old. It closed again and again in his mind, and every time the cavernous aloneness of the room loomed larger.

There will be no farewells between us, Alex. . . .

And no landing-roof partings. All the words that could be said had been said in this room before the door closed. The choice was made, the plans drawn, the course plotted.

I promised you a cause, Alex. It was always our cause, but now it belongs to you, and you to it. . . .

His eyes held the images of orange coals; his mind layered more images behind them, wraiths that didn't assume solidity, transient as flames.

Alexand looked down at his right hand. He'd picked up his glass. The coals glinted through the amber liquid. He'd picked it up after Rich left, after the door closed. Fallor. This golden distillate of the fields of Alber, an endless sea of harvest-ready gold stretching to the sea-flat horizon, spouting billows of black smoke.

VisLord Richard DeKoven Woolf was dead this night, but Richard Lamb would live to suffer his apotheosis. The Bonds, who recognized the transcendent light in that failing body, would have their saint. The nexus of timelines had been passed, and nothing would ever be as it had been an hour ago, a day ago, a year ago. The choice was made.

Click. Again the door closed. Sealed the silence.

He could still move; could raise the glass, but couldn't taste the whiskey. He could feel the burning of it. A shadow hovered

314

at the edges of his vision. He knew it was there, knew what it was. It would close in soon, the rushing stoop of a predacious bird; a double grief given a ravening edge by regret and guilt, but the choice was made, and by that choice regret and guilt became as inescapable as grief.

On my immortal soul, I take this vow for life and unto death. . . .

And it would be a kind of death. Yet he couldn't fulfill that vow without accepting another kind of death. He was surrounded by death in countless shapes.

Alex, what about Adrien—can you face giving her up?

The door closed. Whispering slide. Click.

At the shattering moment when his father's hand struck his cheek, the first image in his mind was Adrien Eliseer, and he weighed that cost first, weighed it with the grief he would inflict on those he loved, the grief he would bear himself, weighed it against the incalculable grief waiting if he refused his own apotheosis.

Father, I could forgive you that blow, forgive you even your betrayal of Rich, of your son, but the fear. . .

That could be forgiven, too.

But it couldn't be tolerated.

The shadow. It was coming. . . .

Love him; love your husband, Mother. Teach him not to be afraid. A man who would forfeit his life before he recognized defeat, yet he was infected with the plague of fear. Love him, Mother. Give him more sons. Drown your own grief in new sons; time enough for that; years enough.

It was coming. He saw the shadow, a veil dimming the searing lights of the coals.

Adrien, forgive me what is beyond forgiving. . . .

Click, on the pounding silence; again, the closing door. And an emptiness stretching to some infinite vanishing point, a keening rush of loneliness like a wind.

The glass shattered, collapsed into a handful of knife edges. But there was no pain in that ripped flesh. His whole body shuddered with pain. He couldn't feel the cuts.

Darkness moved like smoke around him; his mouth was open, a silent cry straining at his throat. He fell to his knees, convulsed in a foetal knot.

In the Holy Writ the prophet wrestled with the angel of the All-God. . . .

He recoiled, quivering, assaulted with peals of sardonic laughter. And what merciless god sent this clawing beast—the black angel of grief?

The ebony wings pounded the air, the talons locked in his flesh, and if he didn't scream, it was only because his lungs couldn't find air enough. And if he didn't weep, it was only because he hadn't yet surrendered. Tears would be the white flag of defeat.

And death . . . or something like death.

Something he couldn't name.

In the end he lay panting, numbed with ebbing agony, but he called himself the victor, even though he could still hear the distant thunder of black wings. He hadn't killed the beast. It would never die. Not until its host died.

There was in the labyrinths of his mind a steel-barred chamber, and there the black angel was confined, and he had locked and double-locked the door. The beast lived still, but it was enough of a victory that it had been forced into that cell, the locks had been set.

It was enough.

He pulled himself to his knees, and the effort was consuming, but there were no tears. There would never be any tears. He looked down at the welling cuts in his hand; he still couldn't feel the pain.

At length, he could stand without support. He crossed to the 'spenser for a towel and wrapped it around his hand, watching the red stains blossom against the white.

He felt nothing. Not even the weight of his footfalls as he left the salon. He negotiated the silent corridors blindly, and, when he emerged on the landing roof, he didn't feel the bite of the winter wind.

"My Lord?"

He looked around; the guard had repeated his inquiring salutation several times, staring at him, half afraid.

"Ket, call for my 'car."

"Yes, my lord. Do you wish a chauffeur?"

"No."

Ket spoke briefly into his pocketcom.

"A few minutes, my lord. Will you be going far?"

Alexand gazed at him with unfocused, still eyes, and Ket paled, expecting a rebuke for his inquisitiveness.

But Alexand's gaze moved past him and away.

"I don't know."

4.

14:55 Terran Standard Time. 22 July 3253.

The Fountain of Victory was stilled, the Concord's gesture of respect; a life would soon be taken at its command. A custom as old as the Plaza; as old as the ceremonies of execution. Alexand moved through the murmuring crowd, oblivious to the curious whisperings as a path opened before him only to close again in his wake.

The execution stand. That was all his awareness; stark black against the white steps of the Hall of the Directorate, lined on the sides and across the back with golden-helmeted Directorate guardsmen, their uniforms as black as the stand. Black as mourning. More black figures lined the arched promenades on both sides of the Plaza.

The usual guard contingent for an execution had been doubled today, and he didn't have to wonder at whose command. A precaution, Phillip Woolf would call it, and by doubling the number of armed men here, he doubled the risk of bloodshed.

Richard Lamb would have his Testing today, but more than his soul would be tested.

Alexand was here to witness that Testing and to keep a promise made not to Rich, but to himself. His brother would not die, would not endure his Testing, alone. His steps carried him forward, toward that black monolith. He was enveloped in a mantle of numbness; the steel-barred chamber in his mind was still locked, and he held the key. He wore no outward signs of identification, and his face was hidden behind the shadow of his face-screen. If anyone noticed the occasional flash of the scarlet lining of his black cloak, he wasn't concerned.

The execution stand was suddenly before him, filling his field of vision with black. He went to the steps at one end and mounted them without breaking pace. The guardsman there recognized his rank, if not his identity; he made no attempt to stop him.

There was a space of two meters between the end of the

stand and the row of guards. Alexand took up a position a pace from the stairs, behind that grim barricade, feeling out the atmosphere of suspicious wariness here. The guards furtively surveyed the crowd, quiet, totally Bond. The execution had been scheduled for the middle of the daytime work shift when few Bonds would be free to attend it, but there were at least three thousand here. They, too, had come to witness Richard Lamb's Testing.

But there were no reporters or vidicam crews in the Plaza. That would also be at Phillip Woolf's order.

Winter sunlight, clear as white wine, reflected from the mirrored windowwalls of the Hall of the Directorate. Galinin watched from behind one of those sun-glazed walls. Alexand knew his grandfather wouldn't close his eyes to this, and perhaps his father was with him.

Alexand had ignored all Galinin's summonses the last three days, knowing his purpose—to bring him and his father together. Galinin didn't yet understand that it was too late. Nothing would ever be as it had been. Nothing.

A few more minutes. The Testing.

It would also be a Testing for him, for the locks on that steel-barred chamber.

They survived the first test as his gaze moved to the center of the stand and the simple mechanism that was the Concord's instrument of justice: a vertical pole fitted with a padded collar, adjustable to height, to grip the victim's neck and hold his head in place, a framework to hold a stabile laser against his right temple, and a small metal shield to stop the beam once it burned through his brain. And, standing to one side, the red-uniformed, face-screened man who would press the firing lever. The executioner. At the foot of the steps behind Alexand, two men waited with an empty stretcher. The burial detail.

A subdued voice, one of the guardsmen leaning toward the man next to him in the rank. "I don't like it, Harv. Look at 'em."

The second guardsman surveyed the crowd, his head moving in a slow, affirmative nod. "Yeh, I know what you mean. Too damned quiet."

"Something's going on—doubling the guard, and them so quiet."

A Testing. Soon.

Alexand's muscles contracted, reacting before his mind took full cognizance of the sound thrumming from the ampspeakers.

The drum roll.

His mouth was dry, a sudden vacuum under his ribs.

15:00 TST.

He turned toward the steps, nerves quivering with that incessant beat; a sound like a wind moved through the crowd and the black aircar hummed to ground near the stand. Face-screened SSB officers moved silently, methodically, opening the door, forming an entourage around the nulgrav chair, one in front, one behind, one on each side guiding it, marching to the rattling cadence of the drum roll toward the stand.

Phillip Woolf had called up this scene out of his ravening fear; he had named this would-be saint pitiful, and in that, as in so many things, he was in error.

Richard Lamb carried his head high, his graceful, fragile hands resting at ease on the arms of his chair. He wasn't bound, his paralysis was binding enough, and his conditioning was no longer functioning; he was alert and fully aware of his destination, and it engendered no fear in him. The consumptive fire within his frail body emanated from him in flickering waves, his sky-colored eyes were incandescent, and pity was inimical to that light.

Alexand watched the long approach, fighting the urge to close his eyes, yet begrudging the split-seconds lost to blinking, hearing another beating behind the drum roll: the beat of black wings. And another rattling: the locks.

The small procession mounted the steps. It was then that Rich looked up and saw his brother, that lean, straight-backed, mourning-clothed, face-screened figure waiting at the top of the steps. Rich's expression didn't change except for an indefinable shift in the quality of the light burning behind his eyes, something ineffable and intangible.

The guard rank opened to let him and his escort pass, then closed again, and Alexand watched, transfixed, as Rich was brought to the executioner, watched as that red-garbed figure stolidly went about his duties, adjusting the collar and the headpieces. The ampspeakers blared a new tune: the reading of the charges, but Alexand was no more aware of them than were the waiting thousands of Bonds. Words. Sounds. Noises. A background for the executioner's work.

At length, the sounds ceased; the executioner stepped back and faced the ranking guard officer, the captain who stood near Rich, the man who would give the order.

And in that brief silence, Rich crossed his arms, resting his hands on opposite shoulders in the Bond attitude of prayer. His voice moved across the silence like a raindrop in a quiet pool.

"Zekiel and all my beloved, remember me and my words. For my passing, my friends, I ask a sanna."

Zekiel, Elder Shepherd in Galinin's Estate compound, the grayed patriarch who stood in front of the execution stand gazing up at Rich. He sank to his knees and crossed his arms.

"We will remember you, my lord."

At those words the guardsmen tensed in wary bewilderment. Even the executioner paused, scanning the crowd, his uneasy movement echoed by the captain. Zekiel's quavering voice, strangely sweet, began a song, and the captain stared at him as if the sound were utterly foreign. A song with a simple melodic line set in an unfamiliar, minor mode.

"The Lord is my shepherd . . ."

An expanding wave of motion as thousands of arms crossed and every Bond in the Plaza sank to his knees. The words were lost until the voices found a unified cadence.

" . . . He maketh me to lie down in green pastures:
he leadeth me beside the still waters . . ."

The ampspeakers erupted again, but the song burgeoned, thousands strong, against the renewed beat of the drum roll.

" . . . He restoreth my soul: he leadeth me in the
paths of righteousness for his name's sake . . ."

The captain recovered himself and faced the executioner.

" . . . Yea, though I walk through the valley of the
shadow of death . . ."

Rich waited, listening, wrapped in the lambent aura of that consuming light.

" . . . I will fear no evil: for thou art with me . . ."

The captain gave the command; the executioner snapped a salute, his hand moved to the firing lever.

"*...Thy rod and thy staff they comfort me...*"

Alexand, suddenly rigid with terror, stared at his brother's face. *Rich, oh, God, Rich—no!*

"*...Thou preparest a table before me in the presence of mine enemies...*"

The executioner pressed the lever; the drum roll ceased. The white, frail hands fell.

"*...my cup runneth over...*"

Alexand stood motionless, a harp for the wind that plucked at his bones; the wind of flailing black wings.

"*...Surely goodness and mercy shall follow me all the days of my life...*"

The song rode the wind of anguish, and he saw Zekiel's face as if it were a dreaming vision, uplifted, transfixed, tears moving down the gullies of his age-eroded cheeks like spring rain on desert hills.

"*...and I will dwell in the house of the Lord forever.*"

The locks held.

And there was some comfort in the darkness behind his closed eyes. He heard the booted feet on the steps: the burial detail. The comfort was only that he didn't have to watch the cruelly mundane act of the removal of the body of Richard Lamb from the strictures of the execution mechanism.

Richard Lamb had endured his Testing, but another was coming. The voices, one pleading, the other curt and cold. The sea-soothing murmur of the crowd was suddenly ominous; an undercurrent of ferocity, numberless unforgotten frustrations finding focus. And a smell. He recognized it. Fear.

The voices. Zekiel, the pleading, querulous one; and the sharp, impatient one, the captain in charge.

"But, sir, he's a holy man. He *must* be given the Rites of Passing."

"I'm not turning the body over to anybody but the burial detail, old man."

The tension was stifling. Alexand opened his eyes, and his mental focus allowed him no pain, even when he saw the still body on the stretcher at the captain's feet.

"But, sir, it's the law of the Concord—" Zekiel craning back to meet the cold eyes of the captain, his gnarled fists grasping the edge of the stand, his head on a level with the sightless eyes of Richard Lamb. A young Bond wearing the golden skullcap of an acolyte stood beside him, staring with open resentment at the captain.

"Listen, old man, if he was so damned holy, what was he doing up here on this stand?"

Zekiel paled. "But—but it was the Mezion's *will!*"

"Yeh? Well, nobody told *me* about it. Now, get back to your compounds!"

The crowd compressed and the ominous murmur swelled to a warning growl. One of the guardsman's hands moved furtively to his holstered laser.

Zekiel cried, "Sir, we only ask what is *ours!*"

"What's *yours?*" The captain gave a mocking laugh, but there was fear in it, and his eyes moved across the closing crowd that was fast becoming a mob. "What's yours is going to be a laser beam between the eyes if you don't get out of here! *Now, clear the Plaza!*"

The throbbing undercurrent surged to a snarling crescendo of shouts and cries; mouths gaped savagely behind flailing fists. The black ranks, taut and ready, stiffened.

The captain gestured to a subordinate for an ampmike.

"I told you to get out of here, old man! All of you! That's an order! Back to your compounds!"

The amplified words boomed, but the Bonds only pressed closer. The stand had become an island bastion in an angry, clamorous sea. A few Fesh watching from the promenades scurried to the safety of the buildings, leaving the walks empty except for the ranks of guards—the ranks that could trap the Bonds in a three-way crossfire if the captain gave the order.

Alexand saw him take out his transceiver and speak into it, and almost expected the order to be given. But not yet. Under the impetus of the command audible only to the guards through their earceivers, the ranks on the stand shifted position, every other man in the line at the back of the stand marching forward to form a new buttress at the front, those at the side about-facing, the first five moving down onto the steps to defend that access. The captain was speaking into the ampmike again.

"Clear out! All of you! Get back to your compounds!"

But the only response was a raging roar. Zekiel staggered as he was pushed against the stand by the force of pressing bodies,

"This is an order! Get back to your compounds!"

The angry tumult drowned the captain's amplified voice. An assault on the stairs was put down with curses and charged lashes, and Alexand recognized the cloying breathlessness of his own fear. The captain's repeated commands rang futilely against the wall of rage and, along the rigid rows of guards, eyes shifted from the captain to the crowd, waiting. Waiting for the command to open fire.

And finally, slowly, the captain lowered the ampmike and brought up the transceiver.

Zekiel.

Alexand stared at the old man and saw his tear-burned eyes fix on Richard Lamb's still face. The captain surveyed the crowd grimly. Another second, perhaps two. Zekiel straightened and spun around, arms flung upward.

"Peace! My children—listen!"

A hush moved out from him; the words moved before it passed from one Bond to another: "Zekiel speaks . . ."

But the quiet wasn't one of resolution; only a pause on the brink of decision. The captain hesitated, the transceiver still ready, and Zekiel's voice soared over the Plaza.

"Richard the Lamb lies dead before you, his body still warm. *Have you forgotten him so soon?*" He paused at the ripple of cries of anger and shouted demands. "The way of the Blessed is peace. As all people are children of the All-God, they are all brothers. Who lifts his hand in wrath against any person, lifts his hand against his brother and reaps the harvest of doom! Have you forgotten him who lies here? He who showed you the way of the Blessed? The immortal soul of Richard the Lamb is in the gentle hands of the Mezion. His mortal remains will be done with as the Mezion wills!"

The silence was palpable. An equilibrium had been struck; the scales rested at an uneasy perfect balance. A call to action from one of the Bonds or a single aggressive gesture by any of the guards would tip the scales to disaster, but Zekiel spoke not another word.

Alexand counted the seconds, waiting for the scales to shift, and perhaps the wordless longing within him was a prayer. When he reached twenty, he felt, rather than heard, a collective sigh, and at the edges of the crowd first one, then another, then groups of three and four, began moving away. The tight-packed agglomeration loosened, fragmented, and the exodus was under way. The only sound in the wide white Plaza was the soft shuffle of footsteps. Alexand felt the tension slip away with the retreating footfalls, felt the black lines sag. The captain lowered his transceiver, his hand fell away from his holster.

Alexand's gaze moved down to the lifeless, emaciated body on the stretcher. He steeled himself, putting yet another lock on that chamber within his mind.

They had not failed Rich; he could not fail them.

He switched off his face-screen as he strode toward the center of the platform.

"Captain!"

The guardsman's head jerked around, eyes going to impatient slits, then widening.

"My lord?"

The men of the burial detail had been bending over the stretcher, but now they retreated a few steps, making tentative bowing motions, but Alexand's level gaze never left the captain's face as he closed the distance between them.

"Captain, dismiss the burial detail."

"Dis——but, my lord . . ."

"Dismiss them." He didn't wait to see the order carried out; it would be. He turned to the retreating crowd. A few had stopped to watch this new development, among them Zekiel and the acolyte.

"Zekiel——" He saw the Shepherd stiffen, and softened his tone. "Zekiel, bring your acolyte and another man and come to the stand." He turned to the guards at the steps. "Let them pass."

Again, he didn't wait to see his order carried out; he fixed a cold eye on the captain.

"You are aware, Captain, that you've broken a cardinal law of the Concord?"

He went white. "I——I don't understand, my lord."

"The Galinin Rule, part of the Civil Standards Code formulated by the Lord Benedic Galinin. No agent of the Concord will interfere with Bond religious practices and rites unless they constitute a threat to the security of the Concord. I fail to see that giving them the body of this unfortunate man presents any kind of threat. It would normally be surrendered to anyone who claimed it without a thought."

Alexand didn't look down as he spoke of the body; he hadn't allowed himself to look at Rich from the moment he made his presence known. He heard Zekiel approaching with the acolyte and another Bond, but he didn't turn.

The captain's eyes shifted uneasily. "I—I didn't realize—"

"You didn't *think*. This is exactly how the Alber uprising in Canadia began, and you almost had another here. It was this man—" He glanced back at Zekiel, "—this man whom you treat with such contempt, Zekiel—a Bond—who averted a disaster here, not you." He paused to give the captain a few seconds more to consider his fate, then, "Ignorance is no excuse, Captain, but I'll give you the benefit of the doubt, assuming you'll take a lesson from this experience. Clear the guards from the Plaza; they're hardly necessary now."

"Yes, my lord." It came out with an audible sigh of relief. He hurriedly took out his transceiver, and Alexand turned away. Zekiel was gazing at him as if he were witnessing a miracle. No doubt they would call it that, this unexpected intervention. The will of the Mezion.

And, finally, Alexand looked down at the motionless figure on the stretcher. He heard again the echoing rattle of locks.

Like a sea bird lying on some forsaken beach with the seeking edges of the waves, embroidered with foam, curling around its sand-burdened wings. Yet even in this ruin—the *remains*—that ugly and bitterly accurate word—of Richard DeKoven Woolf, there was an echo of the beauty he wore in life, as the graceful contours of the sea bird's wing echoes a remembrance of flight.

"Zekiel, who was he?"

"He is called Richard the Lamb, my lord. He abides now in the Beyond Realm with the Blessed. Perhaps he's only gone home."

"Was he in truth a holy man?"

"Yes, my lord. It is said the holy light of the Mezion burned in him. Too much of a burden for a mortal man, I think; it took all the strength from his body."

Alexand swallowed against the searing dryness in his throat, his eyes moving again to that silent flesh. He pulled off his cloak and knelt by Rich's body and carefully crossed his frail hands on his chest. There was none of that paradoxical strength in those hands now.

Rich—dear God, Rich, I loved you. . . .

He unfurled the cloak, black side outward, scarlet flashing briefly, and draped it over that still form, feeling the dull snap of yet another lock closing on the chamber in his mind as he drew the black cloth over his brother's face.

"My *lord!* What are you—"

Alexand rose abruptly, silencing the captain's perplexed objection with a cold look. Then he turned to Zekiel.

"I suffered a loss of my own only a few days ago. There's grief enough in that to share." He felt his mental focus shifting dangerously and squared his shoulders. "Take him, Zekiel. Take . . . your saint."

"Yes, my lord." The Shepherd nodded to the other Bonds, and they lifted the shrouded stretcher, the acolyte pausing long enough to gaze at Alexand, amazement vying with gratitude, before they moved away hurriedly.

Alexand watched them, the gulf of loneliness widening with their every step, and he was entirely unprepared when Zekiel, his eyes glistening with unnoticed tears, sank to his knees and took his hand, then pressed it to his forehead.

"You are of the Blessed, my lord. Peace be."

Alexand stared at him, past comprehending that gesture or the words, shaken and literally shaking, as the Shepherd rose. Finally, he found his voice.

"Peace be, Zekiel."

The old man turned, following in the wake of Rich's body off the stand and through the silent, awed remnants of the crowd. As the spare procession worked its way out of the Plaza, the last of the guards filed back into the Hall of the Directorate.

And at the other end of the Plaza, the Fountain of Victory came to life, a renascent tracery of white against the blue winter sky.

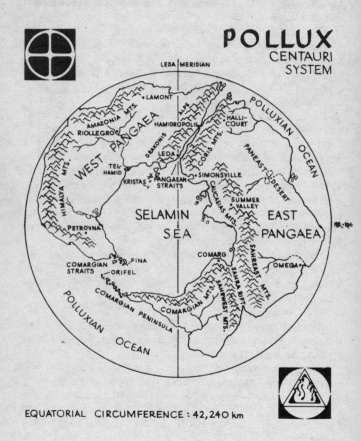

EQUATORIAL CIRCUMFERENCE: 42,240 km

PART 2: METAMORPHOSIS

●■○■●

PHOENIX MEMFILES: DEPT HUMAN SCIENCES:
                    SOCIOTHEOLOGY (HS/STh)
SUBFILE: LAMB, RICHARD: PERSONAL NOTES 10 AVRIL 3253
DOC LOC #819/19208–1812–1614–1043253

I've just returned from a pleasant hour spent on the observation deck on Level 14. I wonder that the Communications personnel don't get weary of seeing me pass the camouflaged antennas (and how much like prehistoric creatures they seem, stranger to my eyes than the inhabitants of this alien world) to reach the deck where I can look north, east, south, and west for such a long and refreshing distance from the lofty apex of Fina.

Yet it's a rather limited view, really, confined almost entirely to water. Our island makes up the foreground, and if weather conditions are right, you can see the nearer islands off the West Pangaean continent to the northwest, the Comarg Archipelago to the south, with fiery little Orifel spewing impatient sparks on its southwestern extremity. But the Selamin Sea makes up most of this vista, and I'd be satisfied with that if no land were visible at all.

A scrap of a poem has lodged in my memory, while its writer's name is forgotten.

> Our mother sea, fair mother sea,
> Cradle of life, inventor of death,
> Who makes no ceremony for either. . . .

I always think of those lines when I look out at that vast, flat panorama—flat, yet sometimes I think I can discern the curve of the planet—and I always think of the Pacific Ocean on Terra as I remember it from a similar high vantage point looking east toward the Barrier Reef.

And sometimes I wonder if a large percentage of the other members who seek out this vantage point aren't Terran. I think it must be especially true when Fina is in Pollux's night. Then the subtle differences of color in the sea and atmosphere are masked; then only the scents from the island foliage and one's consciousness of the lighter gravity are all that makes this sea alien, and one becomes accustomed to the scents, and the body adjusts to the slight difference in gravity within a week.

Tonight our arbitrary Terran Standard Time night was in phase with Pollux's night, and the sky was clear with only a few billowy clouds to make shadows and reflections on the immense, shimmering span of the sea, silk and silver all in one, never in two instants the same, yet profoundly constant. On the island's shores the surf breaks in long sighs, each comber trailed by a lacy train of foam.

There, indeed, is comfort for the displaced children of Terra. Until we look up at the sky.

If humankind had been born on Pollux, I wonder if we'd ever have voyaged to the stars. They're so rarely visible here, except as a vague powdering, with Alpha Centauri B dominating the night sky half of every year. That's a sight my Terran senses still balk at: a pinpoint that lights the entire sky, making the nights dim imitations of day. Even when B is in Pollux's day sky, it's "moon" Castor brightens a good part of the remainder of Pollux's nights. I find myself longing for clear Terran nights when the sky is a well of incredibly distant suns, and you feel that if you look into it too long, you'll fall upward into that glittering abyss, and the thought holds no fear, only vaulting elation.

Tonight Castor set early near Orifel, but B still lighted the western sky. I searched for Proxima, and I've been told where it should be, but I've never been able to find that dim, red dwarf with my unaided eye. I've never been able to find the Sun—*my* Sun—either in Pollux's bright nights.

But all that is the mewling complaint of a homesick Terran. I wish sometimes I'd been born on Pollux so I might appreciate it properly.

I remember my first glimpse of Pollux when my ship emerged from SynchShift and hurtled toward the twin crescents of Pollux and Castor. Our course was such that for a while Pollux seemed to rise over Castor, and it was one of those awesome images that fix themselves indelibly in memory. Then, as we left Castor behind and approached Pollux, I thought how beautiful it must have seemed to the men who first saw it nearly two centuries ago, a blue world with its white calligraphy of cloud. Like Terra.

It's so hard not to think of it that way. Like Terra. I remember thinking of it from a cartographer's point of view, thinking how convenient it was that all its land masses were in one hemisphere except for a finger of the West Pangaean continent and three plume series of islands in the huge midst of the Polluxian Ocean. And I remember thinking of the two continents of East and West Pangaea as echoes out of Terra's geologic history, megacontinents not yet split by the massive shifts of internal convections, but showing incipient rifts in the Pangaean Straits, the Caucasias Mountains, and the Sahra Rift, with the Selamin Sea indicating a rift already accomplished. But obviously the men who named the two continents "Pangaea" had the same thought, and that, like so many of Pollux's place names, demonstrates the Terran proclivity for drawing parallels with Terra.

Yet this is an extraordinarily beautiful planet in its own right, and as unique as Terra. The stellar explorations beyond Centauri taught us that. To be sure, I've seen very little of it except for Fina and views from the cities where my work takes me. Via MT. That's one thing I fear about the MT, it tends to isolate us from awareness of our physical world. But I've seen enough of Pollux and its flora and fauna to delight me: the singing trees, the delicate airriders of netvines, the flying blossoms of floroptera, the iridescent glory of glassgrass in the spring in the Paneast Deserts, the solemn groves of rockwood on the Comarg Peninsula that dwarf even the huge karri trees of Conta Austrail. I've watched the migration of sporowhales through the Comargian Straits, the phosphorescent breeding frenzy of the spidery seanova on Fina's beaches, and the homing flight of flocks of dipnoptera from sea to mountain forest. I've seen the awesome tidal bores in the Pangaean Straits and the black, wind-honed monoliths of the Needles rising out of the endless white saltpans near Omega, felt the ground tremble at the Cataracts of the Amazonia near Riollegro, and walked in the lacy shadows of the fernarbor forests around Hallicourt. It's a beautiful planet, and I can only hope those born to it will feel for this new Eden what I feel for Terra. It is as much a home and sanctuary for humankind as Terra, and those who live on it should feel the same reverence for it.

Terra's children didn't always show that reverence, and I hope Pollux's children won't forget Terra's history, won't forget the cost of irreverence. That's also part of my ambivalence for Pollux. I look at it and see the Eden that Terra once was, and I remember the hideous scars on her fair face left by the Disasters and the century preceding them: the scars of war—the least of them, really—the scars of exploitation, the willful fouling of what was then our only nest; the dead rivers and lakes, the poisoned plains, the sterile valleys, the razed forests, the numberless species— entire *species*—indifferently or rapaciously snuffed out; the mindless multiplication of population with no concern for its demands on the planet, or for the suffering of the billions of human beings thus condemned to die horribly of disease and starvation.

Terra rid herself by the cruel processes of nature of the worst of the burden imposed on her by human ignorance and avarice simply by ridding herself of most of the human population. Terra is still our blue, watery, fertile mother world, but she'll never be the same. Pollux is figuratively still a virgin, and I hope her human inhabitants won't forget Terra's history, or forget that planetary rape is a crime that will, inevitably and inexorably, be punished.

Thus I looked out over the Selamin Sea tonight, sought in vain in the twilight night sky for my Sun, and longed for Terra, for a scarred Eden, and I thought, Oh, you children of this new Eden, honor your mother. She deserves your reverence, and in the end will tolerate nothing less.

CHAPTER VI: July 3253

1.

Dr. Erica Radek's gray eyes moved in a circuit, taking in the five people seated with her at the round Council table. The seventh chair was empty; Ben Venturi was at the other end of the room hovering over the monitors.

This meeting was an error, but neither she nor Ben had succeeded in convincing Andreas Riis of that. He didn't understand the capacities of the human mind in the pursuit of power.

Dr. Radek understood them; she was trained for that. Now, as Andreas outlined the situation, she studied the other councilors, analyzing eye movements, gestures, postures. Yet she seemed to be listening attentively, just as she seemed entirely at ease. She wore the practical slacsuit that was standard garb in Fina, and indulged her feminine vanity only in the arrangement of her silver hair: thick, shining braids coiled at the crown of her head, emphasizing her long neck and the patrician features that hinted at uncommon beauty in her youth.

Her gaze rested briefly on Andreas Riis, and she sighed. She couldn't be angry with him, even recognizing the dangers he courted in calling this meeting. As chairman of the Council, the decision was his to make, and this development was not only unprecedented, but vitally important to the future of the Society. It was reasonable enough that the full Council should be apprised of it.

At least she'd argued him into asking contingency conditioning of the councilors. That would limit their capacity to talk about, or act upon, anything transpiring here.

Half a saint, Rich had called Andreas, and all a scientist in the fullest meaning of the word; the face of an ascetic, his hair white—although it had been dark when Erica first came to Fina, as hers had been—his eyes startlingly black, quick, questioning, yet gently naive; a genius who regularly dealt in concepts far beyond the scope of most minds, yet he didn't understand something so simple as ambition.

Her eyes shifted to the man who sat on Andreas's right, separated from her by Ben Venturi's empty chair. Predis Ussher, Chief of Communications. And perhaps a Lord's son. She watched Ussher, noting the tight lines around his mouth, the narrowing of the indigo eyes that provided a striking color contrast to his long, red hair. He was on his guard; there was little to be read in his face.

Her gaze moved to Andreas's left, to Emeric Garris, Commander of Fleet Operations, whose features were all too readable. He was skeptical; a wily old soldier whose face bore the scar of a past battle in a white line angling across his right eye.

On Emeric's left, John M'Kim sat frowning, arms folded, narrow shoulders tense. The eternal accountant, head of Supply and Maintenance. His thin face displayed suspicion and vague bewilderment. Andreas was talking about something that couldn't be reduced to orderly columns of figures, and M'Kim was uncomfortable.

They were all uncomfortable, even Marien Dyce, Chief of Computer Systems, whose sturdy figure and matronly features always made her seem immune to uncertainty. A charter member like Andreas and Emeric Garris; half a century in Fina, but the old thinking habits still held. She could only regard this development with misgivings, but no doubt she'd respond with some awe in the Lord's presence. They were all Fesh at heart. Even Predis Ussher.

Erica looked toward the monitors at Ben Venturi. He stood with the weight of his rangy body balanced equally on both feet. Tense. She'd long ago become accustomed to seeing *Major* Venturi's black SSB uniform in this stronghold of the Phoenix—he didn't always have time to change on his way to or from his SSB duties in Leda—but at the moment he looked very much the part: the short-cropped dark hair, the broad, tough face with the slightly flattened nose, the gray-green eyes with their habitual squint of suspicion.

Ben was worried, and with good reason. But it was his nature to worry; it was one of the attributes that made him so successful at his double life. Major Venturi was also Com-

mander of Security and Intelligence for the Phoenix. Erica saw
the reactive tightening of his shoulders, the unconscious tilt
of his head toward the 'ceiver in his ear.

"Andreas, he's in contact with the flagship. Emergency
frequency."

Erica said, "Switch it to the room speakers, Ben."

His hand moved to the console, and the speakers came to
life with a shirr of static. It wasn't necessary to ask for silence;
the only sounds emerged from the speakers, a disembodied
dialogue interspersed with dots and dashes of static. She listened intently, eyes closed against visual distraction.

The flagship was still in SynchShift, but the Scout was in
another continuum, plummeting toward the night-shadowed
face of Pollux's Selamin Sea. It would touch down at a point
near the equator, out of range of Fina's radar screens. Only
one of the voices interested her, although she automatically
assessed Commander Todd's for any suspicion or doubt. There
was none. Captain Woolf's performance was faultless, and she
smiled to herself, thinking that Master Jeans would grasp avidly
at such talent for his theater group.

"Scout to flagship. Are you *receiving?*"

"Yes, Captain. Can't you hear me?"

"The ejection switch. Commander, it—it's jammed."

Not too much fear displayed yet; there was more anxiety
in Todd's voice.

"Your altitude—what's your altitude?"

"Altitude twenty thousand meters. Dropping. I'm . . . it's
nineteen-five—"

"Captain, you've got to establish an orbital attitude."

"The steering vanes are out. I *can't.*" The fear was surfacing
now. For perhaps thirty seconds, the signal from the Scout was
drowned in static, and Todd's voice became higher pitched
with every one of those seconds.

"Captain? Captain Woolf, are you receiving? *Captain?*"
And finally the voice from the Scout. "Yes, I—I'm receiving.
Reception weak."

"The 'chutes! Hit the 'chute lever!"

"No, I've tried that. It won't move!"

There was desperation in his voice now. Still, Erica found

herself thinking how much like Rich's it was. She forced the memories back; they disrupted her concentration. Yet they were hard to put down.

Erica, a death pledge. See to my brother. If he needs an alternative, he must have it. . . .

". . . ten thousand meters. Commander, the heat shields—they aren't holding!"

"The auxiliary guidejets, my lord. You *must* slow your entry speed!"

My lord. The Commander was forgetting himself. But that wasn't surprising. He was listening helplessly to the death of the first born of Phillip Woolf.

"I *can't!* The controls—" A burst of static, then the blurred voice, "The controls—they're all out. *All* of them!" There was a chilling hopelessness in his voice, but with it a defiant rage. What came next was a command, not a plea.

"Commander, tell my father—*sabotage!* I've been—"

"My lord!"

"*Tell* him! Selasis!" The name was vicious in its bitterness. "Selasis did this! *Karlis Selasis*—" Abruptly, the transmission ended, but not before the beginning of a cry of agony could be heard.

Erica Radek let her breath out in a long sigh. He had cut it off at exactly the right point. That aborted cry left a great deal to the imagination.

Rich's words echoed in her mind. *I promised him a cause, but he could be a key for you, a key to unlock closed doors.*

He *would* be a key.

The objective tests of screening would still be necessary, but she knew that data would only support her conviction. It was rooted in that accusation against Karlis Selasis. That hadn't been in the script.

Ben Venturi switched off the speakers, his quiet words loud in a stunned silence.

"I've got a subtug waiting in the touch-down area. I'll trans out to it and be back within half an hour."

No one moved except Andreas, and he only nodded.

"Very good, Ben. Bring him directly here."

Erica caught Ben's eye. Another error. But Andreas thought

it reasonable to let the councilors question this unusual recruit.
And again, it *was* reasonable—on the surface.

Erica glanced at her watch. Twenty minutes. She wondered
if something had gone wrong. The pickup would be difficult
in midsea, and the Scout would have to be sunk, but its ejection
capsule kept intact in case it was needed, and it would all have
to be done quickly to avoid Confleet observation. But she was
most concerned about the stunner. Ben insisted on giving Alexand a short-term stunner for the return trans; he refused to
risk revealing the MT to any nonmember, even if he professed
to have faith in memory blocks. The stunner was safe enough,
and the usual recovery period for this particular drug was less
than five minutes. But there was always the possibility of
allergic reaction.

Then she forced the thought out of her mind. Nothing had
gone wrong. Ben would have let them know.

There had been a period of confusion in the Council room
after Ben's departure. The councilors had been caught up in
the drama played out in the skies above the Selamin Sea, even
knowing it was a ruse, and she had no doubt it would be
entirely convincing to the Concord. A spate of almost aimless
querying marked the councilors' recovery. Emeric Garris was
especially interested in the fact that *Captain* Woolf was a Confleet Academy graduate, which didn't please Ussher, who was
cultivating Jan Barret, Emeric's obvious successor in Fleet
Operations. Andreas answered their questions patiently, but
when Ussher began dominating the inquiry, he unobtrusively
surrendered the floor to Erica.

He had promised her that. She had some leverage; Lord
Alexand had asked that only those members who knew Rich's
identity should know his. The only members in Fina who knew
about Rich were Andreas, Ben, and herself. Andreas felt a
little guilty about revealing Alexand's identity to the other four
councilors, and she'd played on that, forcing on him the demand for contingency conditioning and the promise that he'd
let her deal with Predis Ussher.

At first there were a few more questions from the others,
but finally it became a dialogue. They talked across Ben's

empty chair, Ussher outwardly cool, Erica noting the indices of tension under the facade. She would not reveal Alexand's entroit into the Phoenix. Ussher probed and pried, but she wouldn't give him Richard Lamb's name. Instead, she concentrated on the voluminous data available in the memfiles on Lord Alexand, noting that he had been under close observation for years and given a CP-One rating.

"He *asked* for an alternative," she said, meeting Ussher's direct gaze, "of someone he knew to be a Phoenix member. In fact, he knew of this person's association with us for the last three years." She paused to let that sink in. "He didn't betray this person partly because he hoped the Phoenix *did* offer an alternative to a third dark age; he wanted to find out if there was any truth in that hope. We aren't dealing with the usual shallow-minded Lordling here. His attitudes are diametrically opposed to those of most of his peers. In that, he's very much Galinin's grandson."

She left the opening purposely, knowing Ussher would leap into it. He raised an eyebrow, sending Marien Dyce and John M'Kim a faint, almost conspiratorial smile.

"I'm gratified that his attitudes are so liberal, considering he *is* Galinin's grandson." He turned on Erica, the smile gone. "Not only his grandson, but heir to the Chairmanship, as well as the First Lordship of DeKoven Woolf. Why would a First Lord want to join the Phoenix?"

"Because he *isn't* yet a First Lord, nor is he Galinin's heir. Phillip Woolf is Galinin's heir."

"Well, it's the same thing in the end."

"No, it isn't. I might note," she went on, glancing at Marien, who was frowning and on the verge of a question, "that we've taken into consideration the fact that Alexand is presently sole heir to DeKoven Woolf. However, Lady Elise is still within her child-bearing years, and we have no evidence that she's incapable of having more children. We checked that as thoroughly as possible. Otherwise, we couldn't accept Alexand, nor, judging from his responses to his contacts, would he consider joining us. That 'dying' accusation against Karlis Selasis is evidence of his concern for his House. It will put Orin Selasis, the greatest threat to DeKoven Woolf, on the defensive. Woolf and Galinin can keep him reeling for a good year with that. By then the Woolfs can have another heir on the way."

Marien nodded absently, and Erica turned to Ussher.

"Back to your question. The Lord Alexand is neither First Lord nor heir to the Chairmanship; he's heir to Phillip Woolf. Unfortunately, he and his father have come to an irreversible parting of the ways. This makes him politically impotent. We knew he wouldn't accept that. The question we had to consider was *how* he would establish his political potency. Obviously, if he strikes out on his own, he could be a disastrously disruptive factor."

A tinge of red moved across Ussher's face.

"And are we reduced to acting as agents in family vendettas now?"

"That certainly isn't our intention," Erica replied soberly. "If Lord Alexand expects that of us, it will be apparent in the screening tests. In that case, we can't accept him, despite the potentials he offers. We'll have to find other means of dealing with him as a disruptive factor."

"What do you mean by the potentials he offers?"

"At this point, we can't even be sure of his acceptability." She paused; Ussher was waiting for a more specific answer, but she chose not to oblige him.

It was Emeric Garris who said in an awed tone, "Holy God, an heir to the Chairmanship for Phase I."

Leave it to Emeric to spell it out. Dyce and M'Kim were equally awed, but made no comment. Nor did Ussher.

Erica smiled. "Emeric, as I said, we can't even be sure of his acceptability yet."

"No, of course not. Still . . ."

Ussher didn't move except to turn his head toward Andreas. He wanted an answer from him, not from Erica.

"Dr. Riis, if this . . . latest recruit does prove to be acceptable, what about the Peladeen Alternative?"

She was amazed he put it so baldly, and so were the others. At this point, the available alternatives for Phase I were never discussed, and few members outside the Council were aware of them; it was too early to focus the hopes of the members on any one plan—or person. Perhaps Ussher hoped to catch Andreas off guard, but he was never *on* guard, and the question didn't even seem to surprise him.

"I don't know, Predis, but that decision can't be made now. First, as Erica pointed out, we aren't sure of his acceptability. Secondly, we don't know if the Directorate would reinstate him in his present position even if we force them to the bargaining table. And we can't begin to bargain until we have the long-range MT. That decision is years in the future, and it's fruitless to consider it now."

The voice of reason; that phrase so often came to mind with Andreas. A simple statement of fact spoken with no hint of impatience, and no awareness of the overwhelming importance of that answer to Predis Ussher.

The door chime sounded, and Erica felt her muscles go tight. Ben was back with their latest recruit.

She had to make a choice: whether to concentrate her attention on the reactions of the councilors, or on the new recruit. The latter took precedence. For one thing she was only interested in one councilor's responses, and when she turned to face the door, Ussher was behind her.

She noted with some relief that there was no hint of adverse reaction to the stunner. She also noted that the Lord Alexand didn't wait for Ben to lead the way, but walked into the room with no hesitation, as if he were entirely familiar with his surroundings, leaving Ben to follow in his wake. He didn't stop until he stood less than two meters from the table, then he removed his black, gold-striped helmet and held it under his right arm. Ben moved quietly to his chair, but Erica didn't turn; like the others, she was too intent on this young Lord. And he was that to his fingertips.

She almost smiled at the uneasy silence of the councilors; undoubtedly, some of them were wondering whether they should rise. But their uneasiness went beyond that. They were seeing the Society's future in this black-uniformed man; at least a potential beyond their most optimistic imaginings. And most of them were hoping the potential was there.

He waited silently, assessing them as they assessed him, his posture so firmly erect he seemed to be standing at attention. But that regal stance was a product of training, and so well ingrained it was entirely natural to him. He was, by every index, confidently at ease.

Erica's analytical mindset wavered. There was so much of Rich in his face, particularly in the clear blue of his eyes. She hadn't considered the reminders of her own grief that she would encounter in Rich's brother. But he would find reminders of Rich here in Fina, too. It occurred to her that the Confleet black was a symbol of mourning for him, not just a uniform.

Then she frowned. His right hand was bandaged, but that wasn't what attracted her eye. It was the ruby and black jade ring; the ring given him by Adrien Eliseer.

On his left hand was a star sapphire that she knew to be a gift from his mother. She wondered if he'd brought anything of Phillip Woolf with him into this new life.

The process of mutual assessment occupied only a few seconds. It ended as Andreas rose. Erica remained seated, and perhaps the others took their cue from her; they didn't rise, but they seemed uncomfortable. Fesh, she thought, again; Fesh at heart. And, as she expected, they were all a little awed in the Lord's presence.

She glanced at Ussher, finding his eyes veiled to her scrutiny. If this young man represented an unparalleled hope for the Phoenix, he was also a potential catalyst.

Andreas said, "My lord, I'm Andreas Riis. Welcome to Fina."

There was a subtle tension around his mouth as he replied, "Thank you, Dr. Riis. But my name is Alex Ransom." He paused, then, "The Lord Alexand is dead."

2.

Erica Radek led him through the corridors, seeing them, as she always did with a new member, through his eyes. He would note the economy implicit in the lack of moving pedways, and might even deduce Fina's origin in a series of caves in the winding course of the halls, which conformed to the natural rock passages as much as possible. He would count the levels they ascended and read the signs posted beside the S/V screened doorways. She heard a slight break in his step as they passed the one marked MATTER TRANSMITTER; TERMINAL 1. He would also study the people they passed, but there were few members in the halls at this hour; Fina ran on Terran Standard Time, and it was nearly midnight.

He made no comments, and his only question concerned the gold-and-blue triangle-flame motif emblazoned over the directories at the main corridor junctions. She explained the symbol as that of the Phoenix, the equilateral triangle representing both permanence and equality, the flame symbolizing enlightenment and hope.

His uniform attracted no attention from the members they passed, but he'd seen Ben Venturi in his SSB black, and would realize Concord uniforms weren't entirely out of place here. He wore his helmet, which effectively shadowed his face, and made identification unlikely. She'd advised him against using his face-screen; that would attract more attention than his unscreened face.

He didn't voice his questions, but she knew he was taking in every detail and formulating questions in his mind. She would have to be careful when he started asking them; he was adept at drawing out information without seeming to make an inquiry.

She looked back on the Council meeting and almost smiled. She'd been concerned about his being subjected to questioning when he was unfamiliar with the situation or the people involved; Rich hadn't had time to give him any information of that nature. And she'd been concerned because he was so close to Rich's death. Only yesterday. She expected his reactions to be below optimum. But after a half hour of questioning, she was sure Alexand had learned a great deal more than the councilors, and if they expected to sit in judgment of him, they were made aware, subtly but clearly, that they were also being judged.

At length, they reached the doorway marked HUMAN SCIENCES 1: RADEK. He noted the fact that she held the screen-control switch while he passed through. Once inside, he surveyed the small room, a wary tilt to his head as he looked up at the low ceiling; he would need time to adjust to the confined spaces. Three of the walls were composed of a ripple-textured, mirror-finished plasex used extensively in Fina and designed to reduce the sense of confinement; it made the walls seem less solid. He noted the sparse furnishings, only a low table in the center of the room flanked by two armchairs, and he concentrated for some time on the wall to the left, a wall taken up entirely with screens, memfile, datanalysis, and computer consoles. He studied it with an expert eye, no doubt recognizing the components that were neither of Delai Omer nor DeKoven Woolf origin. Finally, he turned to the space between the console wall and the corridor entrance, to the tiered shelves banked with luxuriant foliage and exotic blossoms: the orchids. He looked around at her, a faint smile relaxing his features.

"You were born on Terra."

She laughed. "Yes, I was. Is it so obvious?"

"No. Perhaps it's only the orchids." He walked over to examine them. "These are your hobby?"

"Yes. My little bit of Terra." She joined him by the orchids, but didn't approach too closely. "I've been here for thirty years, and Pollux is beautiful, really; more Terra's twin than Castor's. But I still miss Terra."

He didn't feel that loss yet; his eyes went cold. She studied him clinically, noting the pallor and the shadows under his eyes, and wondered when he'd last eaten or slept.

"This is HS 1, Alex, your home for the next week while I subject you to my black arts: screening and testing. This I call my work room. My office and apartment are through there." She pointed to the doorway on the wall opposite the corridor entrance, then indicated the opening on the right-hand wall. "Your quarters will be in there, and perhaps that's a grandiose term for a single small room and bath, but you'll find life a little spartan in Fina."

"No more than in Confleet, I'm sure."

"Well, that experience might help you adjust to Fina." She noted his quick glance at the corridor entrance; the typical shimmer of the shock screen was evident against the darkness of the S/V screen. "Yes, that door is equipped with a shock screen, and you'll be a virtual prisoner here for a few days, but I'm afraid that's necessary for security reasons. Besides, until you learn the layout of Fina, you might get lost."

He gave a short laugh. "I quite understand."

He was on the edge of physical collapse, and yet she wondered if he realized it. She'd seen this often enough in new recruits; all of them reached Fina through some emotional trauma, but there was in this young man a defiant containment that refused to recognize the price he paid to stand in this small, mirror-walled room. Alex Ransom would present problems for her.

Ransom. An interesting choice.

"Sit down, Alex, if you'd like." As he went to one of the chairs flanking the table, she opened the autospenser compartment by the hall doorway. "This is our source of sustenance here in HS 1; there's a menu and code numbers on the door. Would you like something to eat?"

"No. Thank you, Dr. Radek."

Of course not. She watched him put his helmet on the table and drape his cloak over the back of the chair, then sink into it, unfastening the stiff collar of his uniform. She turned to the 'spenser and touched out a number sequence, waited until a plasex cup slid out of the slot, then took it with her when she went to the other chair.

"I call you Alex because we tend toward first names here, and because I know I must get used to calling you that, as you must get used to hearing it, but you embarrass me with that formal *Doctor* Radek. Please—just Erica."

He smiled politely. "Erica it will be, then."

"Good. Now, you probably have a few questions, but I can't answer them all tonight. For one thing, you'll need some rest. I understand you mustered out at 06:00. It's nearly midnight now, and that makes for a long day. Alex, among other things I'm a qualified physician and, as such, I'm *prescribing* this for you." She leaned forward and handed him the cup. "It's a liquid concentrate. The flavor isn't exactly up to gourmet standards, but it has other attributes, such as enough food value to keep the average man going for a full day. And it stays down more easily than solid food."

His eyes flashed up to hers, then he laughed softly. "A good recommendation. Thank you."

"It will be up to me to assess your acceptability and potential as a member. I don't like my data distorted by factors such as physical depletion. Anyway, I have a few frustrated maternal instincts that surface occasionally. Now. I'll give you a chance to ask some of those questions."

A direct gaze; a speculative scrutiny, then, "I won't burden you with too many questions tonight. I realize you won't be sure of my acceptability until I've passed your screening, and I don't expect you to answer the real questions now, so perhaps I should start with the usual questions, such as, Exactly where am I? Geographically, that is."

"You're in the southern hemisphere of Pollux, latitude about twenty-five degrees, longitude thirty degrees west of the Leda meridian. You're on—or, rather, under—the island of Fina, a name which also applies to our little community. It's one of a number of small islands at the southern tip of the West Pangaean continent. We're near the Comargian Straits between the Selamin Sea and the Polluxian Ocean."

He eyed her obliquely. "That suggests more questions, such as how did I get from my touch-down point near the equator to twenty-five degrees south in the ten minutes in which I was drugged? But I assume that's one of the questions you can't answer now, or I wouldn't have been drugged." He smiled in response to her brief laugh, then, "At least I'm oriented spatially now. Can you tell me what I have to look forward to in the near future?"

"In the near future, yes. I'll oversee the necessary testing and screening here. I have an assistant, by the way: Val Severin. But she'll only help with the objective tests. Any area where your identity might be even indirectly exposed, I'll handle myself. I'll also give you your basic conditioning and some initial orientation. When I'm through with you, you'll go on to General Training, which lasts from one to three months, depending on a new member's background and prior experience. In GT you'll learn the Phoenix in detail, its history and goals, the functions of every department and unit—every aspect of it. You'll study survival arts, role-playing and disguise, physical and mechanical defense, memorization and conditioning techniques, and we have a number of technical devices for defense or intelligence work you'll have to master. You'll have plenty to keep you busy."

His smile was forced. As he leaned forward to put down his empty cup, she saw a flash of gold at the open collar of his uniform. Rich's medallion. So many reminders.

"And after General Training?"

"You'll be assigned to a particular department."

He laughed, and she heard the brittle edge in it. "No doubt Confleet's training will serve me in good stead there. You *do* have some use for a Confleet-trained . . . soldier." He spoke that last word with bitter irony.

"Yes, we have some use for soldiers. Rich told you about the military engagement in the General Plan ex seqs. We're building our fleet in preparation for that, and your training may be useful there. We don't attract many people skilled in military arts. In fact, you're the first Confleet Academy graduate we've had."

He seemed to consider that a moment, then turned his chair and studied the console wall. "My contacts in Concordia told me the possibility always exists that I might fail the screening."

It was a question, and she answered it without forcing him to be explicit.

"If you should fail, we'll know within two or three days. In that case, your ejection capsule will turn up on an island near your 'crash' site, having miraculously functioned at the last minute. Your radio equipment will be burned out, and you'll be in a state of mild shock with a total memory lapse covering the last few days. We always consider the possibility that an applicant might have to be returned, so to speak, and plan his disappearance with that in mind."

"Returned." He seemed to study the word, the mask of containment slipping, exposing a bleak dread. "If I'm *returned*, how will you deal with me as a potential Mankeen?"

That came from Rich. She met his intent gaze calmly.

"I don't know. But you won't fail the screening."

"How can you be so sure?"

"I've quite a fund of information on you. You and the Phoenix are working toward the same goals and can establish a mutually beneficial symbiosis. My only concern was a negative reaction on your part toward your father."

A cold, fleeting light behind his eyes; she recognized the pain in it and found that reassuring. It hadn't been translated into hatred.

"You speak of that concern in the past tense."

"Yes. You've already virtually eliminated it with your accusation against Karlis Selasis."

He smiled, apparently pleased that she recognized the implications in that.

"For nearly four years I've had Karlis's company forced on me by Confleet. Call it retribution."

She laughed. "I'll call it an adroit political maneuver; one designed to protect DeKoven Woolf, and that assures me that you haven't turned completely against your father."

He nodded, and his long breath seemed an effort. "My 'demise' will put enough of a strain on the House. My purpose in joining you isn't revenge against my father. I understand him and his motives. I simply can't accept them. Rich said, or hoped, that I wouldn't have to join a secret society to work for our . . . cause. But he was wrong. He blazed this path for me; I'm here for the same reasons he was." The control was slipping again, and he rose, turning to study the console wall, putting his face in profile to her. "Tell me, what's the function of an ex-Lord in the Phoenix—other than playing soldier, thanks to custom and Confleet?"

"I can't answer that now, but Rich told you enough of our plans, and you are, in a very pragmatic sense, a student of politics. You can guess what we hope for you."

"Phase I. I could be the foothold in the existing power structure, in which case the Phoenix will find it necessary to resurrect the Lord Alexand as its namesake resurrects itself." He seemed for a moment even more weary and tense, then his mouth tightened. "Of course I'll accept nothing less. Unfortunately, except for my Confleet training, I'm suited for no other function than Lordship, and perhaps that sort of ambition will make me unacceptable here, in spite of your apparent faith."

Again, a question with no questioning inflection. She smiled a little at that.

"Do you intend to make yourself Lord of the Phoenix?"

"Ah. A point, and accepted. No. Rich called the Phoenix a tool; one that would serve his purpose by allowing him to become its tool. I'll accept those terms."

"No doubt the Society will also accept them. You realize, I hope, that it's entirely possible that we may not be able to resurrect you."

It was a test of sorts, even if it was a truth. His eyes glinted with amusement, recognizing both.

"The Lord Alexand *will* be resurrected. I was born to that. And there's irony for you; born to resurrection or—"

Death.

He didn't say the word, but she knew it, as she sometimes knew Rich's thoughts. She studied the pale, tense features of this brother Rich had loved so deeply, her own grief encompassing his. Alexand would never be a saint like Rich. There were qualities in Rich that were absent in his brother, but the opposite was also true, and those qualities would be vital to the Phoenix in the next few years, to the Concord.

A silence was growing; she realized he was watching her and felt curiously defensive.

"Alex, you certainly gave the other councilors no hint of your determination to be resurrected. How do you explain your openness with *me?*"

He returned to his chair, seating himself with a little more care than would be normal for a man of his youth, and that couldn't entirely be laid to the fact that he wasn't used to Pollux's lighter gravity.

"Didn't I? I said I was willing to serve the Phoenix in the capacity for which I was best suited."

"Ah, yes." She smiled in retrospect.

"I doubt I'll have any secrets from you after this screening process, so it would be futile for me to be less than honest with you. But the truth is, I can speak openly with you because you

were a friend of Rich's. I know that even if he never spoke
your name. And I trusted his judgment; that's why I'm here."
Then he added, "As for my reticence with the Council, there
was a reason, although I doubt I'd have been less cautious
under any circumstances. Before Rich—on that last night at
the Estate—Rich said something that I could only regard as
a warning. He said I might find it necessary to . . . '*save* the
Phoenix as well as serving it.' He also said that certain political
principles pertain in any social context, and one is that power
vacuums will always be filled." His eyes were fixed intently
on her. "When he first told me about the Phoenix he called it
a power vacuum. Andreas Riis doesn't fill that vacuum; he
isn't emotionally suited to the role. Who does fill it, Erica?
Or, rather, who *wants* to fill it?"

She came close to smiling at that accurate assessment of
Andreas, but his question quelled the inclination. She wasn't
ready to answer it yet. Alex Ransom had been in Fina less than
an hour; he had a great deal to learn and a total personality
reorientation to accomplish. She wouldn't discuss that particular problem with him yet.

"Do *you* want to fill it, Alex?"

Briefly, a chill, *Lordly* impatience flashed in his eyes. Then
he relaxed and laughed.

"Yes, I suppose so, but I don't regard myself as the threat
to the Society Rich implied, and perhaps I'm deluded in that.
You don't wish to pursue the subject of power vacuums."

"No, Alex. Not yet."

He nodded. "I'm capable of patience, although some people
might not believe it, and I'm well aware that I can't be a tool
for the Phoenix, or it for me, unless I have the support of a
majority of its members. That will take time; years, perhaps.
Meanwhile, the Lord Alexand is dead." He looked down at
the ring on his right hand, and Erica wanted to weep, not at
any evidence of grief elicited by that reminder of Adrien Eliseer, but at its absence.

"Alex, the Phoenix will do everything possible to keep the
Lady Adrien free to honor the existing Contracts of Marriage
with Woolf if we succeed in resurrecting you."

He turned paler, and for a long time didn't move; his eyes
were turned on the ring, but they seemed incapable of sight.
Finally, he looked across the table at her and said levelly, "I'm

sure the Phoenix will bend every effort to keep Adrien free. The Woolf-Eliseer union was obviously important to you; you helped bring it about. But, from a personal point of view, I can only hope it will never be finalized."

Erica was taken by surprise, and that was rare.

"Why?" she asked flatly.

"Because the Lady Adrien, unfortunately, loves me. I'm sure you're aware of that, and equally aware that I love her. Yet I've inflicted the agony of grief for my death on her."

"You might have told her your plans. We couldn't monitor or control all your communications."

"Yes, but I had a taste of that these last three years with Rich—of knowing; of wondering every day if he was alive or in the hands of the SSB. And I had personal contact with him periodically. That wouldn't be possible for Adrien and me. Would the Phoenix risk setting up a line of communication with her simply to indulge my needs or desires? Of course not. So Adrien would be in limbo, worse than mine with Rich because there would be no end to it." His eyes closed, but only briefly. "With Rich my terrors were limited by his inevitable death, but for Adrien there would be no end. I considered this the lesser of two unforgivable evils."

A terrible decision to be forced to make, Erica thought bleakly, and a worse decision to live with once made. But few members reached HS 1 without making similar decisions. She'd made her own.

"That doesn't tell me why you hope the marriage won't take place."

He frowned distractedly. "Love turns to hatred so easily. Betrayal is usually the agent. I saw it in my father. He was wrong in thinking himself betrayed by Rich, but I *have* betrayed Adrien. Yet I still love her and always will. Consider our marriage, Erica, if it should take place. She can only despise me for my betrayal, and I can only love her and be daily stretched on the rack of my guilt and her contempt. Not a pleasant prospect."

Erica started to protest that he might be underestimating the Lady Adrien in thinking her incapable of forgiveness, but the protest died on her lips.

Why? From all the evidence available to her, and that from Rich was dependable and detailed, Alex had *never* underestimated Adrien Eliseer. He recognized her potential from the moment they met. Why did he underestimate her now?

She sighed, feeling suddenly weary to the bone.

It was simple enough, and she knew beyond a doubt he believed every word he said. He *had* to. It was the lesser of evils for him, too. He couldn't tolerate maintaining a virtually hopeless hope over months and years, as he was afraid Adrien couldn't tolerate the uncertainty about his fate, and so he killed that hope as he killed the Lord Alexand for Adrien, in one clean, compassionate, agonizing blow.

His reactions to Adrien Eliseer would have to be studied, but only under deep conditioning. She wouldn't challenge his solution to this problem on a conscious level, or say anything that might revive the hope he'd killed. For the Phoenix, it was a workable solution to a potential problem: a division of his loyalty. For Alex Ransom, it was the only merciful solution, because the odds were very high against that hope ever being realized.

"Alex, I'm sorry."

He seemed to weigh those words, and finally nodded mutely. Then he methodically removed Adrien's ring and the sapphire his mother had given him.

"I'm not willing to give these up, but I can't wear them. The one is obvious identification; the other—" He studied the sapphire briefly before he put it on the table. "It's a little ostentatious for a Fesh 'Fleeter." He noted the direction of her glance and touched the medallion at his throat. "This I won't part with. It can't identify me; the symbolism is too personal."

She nodded as she took the rings and put them in her pocket, out of his sight.

"All members are assigned voice-lock boxes for personal valuables. Until that's done, I'll keep these in my office; they'll be safe there."

He looked down at his naked hands, in that drawing her eye to them. Strong hands, she thought, unusual in a man who never had, and never would, earn his living by manual labor. She noted the bandage again, but didn't ask about it because those strong hands were trembling; she saw that before he folded them together to hide that indication of his physical and emotional state.

But his voice was still level; under control. Everything under control.

"Will I have access to vidicom newscasts here?"

"Of course. You aren't that much of a prisoner. You'll also have access to our viditape library, as well as five music bands."

"Life isn't so spartan here, after all."

"We have to make life bearable or the confinement becomes overwhelming. We also have means of entertaining ourselves—a theater group, choral and instrumental ensembles—and we've some talented artists and poets in our ranks."

His interest in that was only polite; he was gazing at the doorway of the room she always referred to as the "guest room," his temporary quarters. She knew even before he started to rise that he had said all he intended to tonight, and it was a great deal more than she had expected.

He pulled himself to his feet, pausing as Erica rose.

"You've been very patient with my questions, Erica, and your answers should suffice for tonight. Thank you."

They would suffice because he was finding it too difficult to maintain that studied calm; he wanted to be alone. She nodded and led the way into the guest room, waving on the light as she entered.

"You'll have more questions, and the answers will come in time. Oh—there's a tape on your comconsole that will provide some of the answers; at least, about Fina and to a degree the Society. There's not much to show you about your quarters; it's all rather self-evident." She frowned slightly. "Alex, perhaps you should have a sedative tonight."

"No." The response was too quick, open overtones of fear in it. He called up a smile. "Thank you, Erica, but I don't take sedatives."

She didn't question that; not now. She rested her hand lightly on his arm, feeling his tension at that touch. It wasn't a reaction to her personally, she knew; he simply wasn't accustomed to casual physical contact with relative strangers.

"Alex, all of HS 1 is open to you, including my office and apartment. I mean, when I'm there, and I'm there most of the time."

He smiled at that. "You're very kind, Erica. You offer aid and comfort without embarrassing me with verbal recognition of a need for it."

"*I'm* supposed to do the analysis around here." She laughed, then felt it slip away from her. "Alex, I loved Rich, too, even if it couldn't be to the degree you did. I made a death pledge that should you need an alternative, you'd be offered one. That pledge has been met sooner than Rich expected. But I made another pledge that should you need a friend, you'd have one." She stopped, seeing him tighten. "Tomorrow we begin the screening. Rest well."

He nodded mutely, then reached out and took her hand for a moment, and she was amazed and moved.

"Erica . . . good night."

"Good night. Welcome to Fina, Alex Ransom."

PHOENIX MEMFILES: DEPT HUMAN SCIENCES: SCREENING/
                    ORIENTATION (HS/S/O)
SUBFILE: PRESCREENING ORIENTATION
                    (AUTHOR: E. RADEK)
DOC LOC #819/19/15–161915–518

I've prepared this tape to answer some of the pragmatic questions new members ask—or should ask—in order to orient themselves in terms of their future personal existence. My purpose is simply to give you a general idea of what kind of place you've come to, and what day-to-day life is like in Fina, which is not only the headquarters of the Phoenix, but a community in which you may spend most of your life.

I say *may*. Over half our members are double idents based outside Fina. The breakdown in round numbers: total membership is fourteen thousand, of which six thousand are based here in Fina. Of the eight thousand double idents, six thousand function as agents in the Houses with as many as a hundred in each of the Directorate Houses. The remaining two thousand work in various branches of the Concord bureaucracy.

But you're in Fina now, whatever your future assignment.

Even with your brief acquaintance with it, you've probably guessed that Fina was built in a series of natural caves. Originally, it was a geophysical research station operated

under the auspices of the Peladeen Republic University.
Soon after the Society's founding in 3200, work began on
enlarging the existing facilities to serve as our HQ, but most
of the construction was carried out during the War of the
Twin Planets, and the success of the project and the efficacy
of the security shield surrounding it, we owe entirely to
Elor Ussher Peladeen, last Lord of the House. He and his
wife, Lady Manir, were from the outset staunch supporters
of the Phoenix, and his last lettape was addressed to Andreas
Riis. You'll have an opportunity to read it later. It's an
eloquent document.

Fina is built within a limestone uplift dominating the
island, which we facetiously call Mount Torbrek. There are
fourteen levels, although they aren't as neatly arranged as
that suggests; the builders had to take advantage of natural
chambers and passages as much as possible.

Beginning at the bottom, Level 1, a hundred meters
below sea level, is Fleet Operations (FO), our military
branch, with its three hangars and undersea access locks.

Level 2 is the domain of Supply and Maintenance, specifically our storage and manufacturing facilities. Level 3,
which is at sea level, also belongs to SM, and is devoted
primarily to food and power. Here our power generators
are located. We depend entirely on hydroelectric power
generated by the channelization of tidal bores. The tides on
Pollux are much higher than those on Terra, incidentally,
with Castor impelling them.

Level 3 also houses our food processing facilities, which
include hydroponic gardens, plankton screens, and docking
facilities for our submarine fishing fleet. Most of our protein
derives from Pollux's seas, and with our processing procedures is identical to Terran-produced protein. However,
we don't recommend eating Polluxian "fish" straight from
the water.

On the next seven levels are the living quarters. Level
7, midway in the housing levels, is the Service, Medical,
and Recreation—or SMR—level. Here you'll find the supply distribution center, our source for all personal and
household necessities, and the Medical Center, consisting
of a three-hundred-bed infirmary, diagnostic center, phar-
macy, and a permanent care unit for patients with chronic
or terminal diseases or disabling injuries. For recreation,
we offer, among other things, a gymnasium complex. There

are usually informal interdepartmental competitions in progress in various sports. These are entirely voluntary, but double idents and members in FO and Security and Intelligence are required to pass annual fitness tests.

SMR also houses the Basic School for our Second Gen (that is, second generation) youngsters, workshops for crafts and hobbies, meeting rooms, and a small auditorium. These are used by musical, theatrical, or other mutual interest groups, most of whom present concerts, plays, vididramas, lectures, or exhibitions periodically. Also in SMR is the General Training unit, as well as the Council room and offices.

Each of the six living-unit levels houses about a thousand, with two dining halls on each level. The basic living-unit room module is four meters square. The one-person unit consists of two rooms and bath, the two-person unit of three rooms and bath, and so on up to a four-person unit. You may think that extra room in all the units extravagant, but we've had to weigh demands on our resources and space against the detrimental psychological effects of long confinement. This is one of many concessions we consider necessary.

Our recreational facilities exist for the same reason, and if it all sounds a bit frivolous, be warned that members in Fina have only one day a week free—and many don't even take one—with five days devoted to assigned duties, and the remaining day to "SM duty," also known as "drudge duty." That is, the necessary cleaning, maintenance, and kitchen tasks that SM isn't staffed to contend with alone.

A comment here: Rank has its privileges even in Fina. For instance, department heads are provided apartments adjoining their offices, although not all of them choose to use them. Department and unit heads, and members deemed by them to be on priority assignments, are exempt from drudge duty. The privilege is not abused, however; we recognize, out of necessity, our mutual responsibilities here.

The choice of living arrangements—where, with whom, or with how many—is yours, and you may change your mind at any time. A note on related choices: We don't discourage sexually based relationships, hetero- or homosexual, nor do we discourage marriages, although only ten percent of our members are married. The only limitations the Society imposes is in the matter of children. Paired—

that is, unmarried—couples may not have children. If a pregnancy results from a pair relationship, the couple has the choice of marrying (and accepting assignments in Fina if they are double idents) or abortion, or, if the mother wishes to bear the child, surrendering it to a Sisters of Faith orphanage. If married double-ident couples wish to have children, they will be reassigned to Fina. This is to protect the children—who deserve a more secure life than double idents can offer—and to protect the parents; children are, unfortunately, high security risks. Our birth rate is very low: .1 percent per year. Most members feel their psychic energy is totally absorbed in a consuming cause. Others, however, consider bringing up a second generation literally born to the cause a commitment to its future.

To continue with the physical description of Fina: There is an inadvertent symbolism in its construction, since the first ten levels support the next four. The real work of the Phoenix is carried out on those top levels, but it would be impossible without the practical foundation of the other levels.

Level 11 is divided between two major departments, Computer Systems and Physical Sciences. The former is in a sense the brain of the Phoenix; certainly it is as vital to our work. The latter includes research, teaching, and library facilities for sciences ranging from astronomy to zoology. CompSystems, by the way, also includes a comprehensive library of human knowledge that in depth and detail surpasses even the Concord University Library and the Archives.

Level 12 is devoted to Human Sciences, which includes medicine, psychoscience, history, all aspects of sociology, and the sociohistorical trend-monitoring systems. This is where you are now, specifically HS 1.

On Level 13 is the Security and Intelligence Department, and in its intelligence functions it is a particularly vital part of the Phoenix. SI agents are much more than spies; they are data gatherers providing information necessary to the functioning of every other department. If CompSystems is the brain of the Phoenix, SI is its eyes and ears.

The nerve system, to continue the metaphor, is Communications, which occupies Level 14, the topmost in Fina. There is no comparison in the Concord for our communications network. It is and must be the best ever devised.

Not only does the transmission of the information so essential to our existence and purpose depend on our communications system, but so do the lives of our eight thousand double idents. And one thing I can promise you about the Phoenix: we are few in number and we care very much about each other; we look after our own.

I'll conclude this at the top of our Mount Torbrek. You have many more questions, I know, some of which I can't answer now, but I offer the assurance that eventually most of your questions will be answered. At least, those the Phoenix has the answers for.

3.

"Good morning, Erica." Ben Venturi paused at the office door, a cup of coffee gripped in one hand, and looked back into the empty work room, then crossed to her desk and perched on the edge. "Your guest still sleeping?"

"No." Erica Radek frowned. She'd be relieved if her "guest" were asleep at 08:00 in the morning. "I sent him to the infirmary for a physical examination."

"A physical? What's wrong with him?"

"Nothing, really. The Woolfs are great believers in physical fitness." A brief sigh escaped her. "Grief, Ben. That's what's wrong with Alex Ransom."

"Oh." He frowned down at the floor. "Rich?"

And Adrien Eliseer, she added to herself, but that was one problem she didn't intend to discuss with Ben.

"Yes. Of course the infirmary can only treat some of the side effects, such as loss of appetite and insomnia. Dr. Calder probably won't have any more luck on the latter than I did."

Ben was silent, thinking of Rich, she knew, the sadness in his eyes out of character in that tough face that usually epitomized so fully the SSB major, even when he was out of uniform, as he was now. He took time to finish his coffee, and when he tossed the cup into the syntegrator by the desk, he was in character again.

He asked, "What about Predis?"

"That's a vague and very broad question."

"I thought you might know the specific questions to ask. Like, what's he going to do about Alex Ransom?"

"Nothing, probably, for the time being." She paused, frowning. "But when Alex is free to leave HS 1, you might keep him under protective surveillance until we're sure of Predis's reaction."

"It's already set up. What do you mean about Predis doing nothing?"

"He's under no immediate threat; he's had time to think it through, and no doubt he's even considering how useful Alex might be to him. Inadvertently, of course. Emeric Garris has been talking about retiring from Fleet Operations for years. His problem has been finding a competent successor. Curious, isn't it, we seem to be able to attract or produce such excellent spies, but so few really good soldiers."

"What about Emeric? Do you see Alex as his successor in FO? That leaves Jan Barret out of the running, and Predis won't be happy about that. The Council seat goes with command of FO, and Predis wants Jan on the Council."

She nodded. "Of course, but Jan won't be out of the running; he'll probably end up as Alex's second-in-command. Meanwhile, Alex is a Confleet Academy graduate—who tested out in the top five percent of his class, incidentally—and Predis will realize that he can bring our military program to optimum level for Phase I far sooner than Jan could. That's what I mean by Predis considering Alex useful, and he'll tolerate him until he ceases to be useful or becomes an imminent threat."

Ben rose and propped his fists on his hips, his mouth tightening irritably.

"Well, we can't go to the bargaining table without the long-range MT, no matter what shape FO's in."

"I know, and I don't think we have to worry about Alex until Andreas gets a breakthrough on the MT."

"So why are you asking me to keep an eye on him?"

She shrugged. "For the same reason you'd already set it up. Predis can be unpredictable."

Ben sighed and glanced at his watch. "True. I have to go now. But, Erica, we've got to get through to Andreas about Predis and this whole damned situation."

"I'm working on it. I've set up a series of extrapolation sequences. Andreas will accept it more easily in the form of data-based potentials."

"Good luck." He turned and started for the door. "I'm on duty at the Cliff in an hour. I'll talk to you when I get back."

"Take care, Ben."

"I always do. Later."

PERSONAL FILE: E. RADEK   CASE NOTES: 24 JULY 3253
SUBJECT: ALEX RANSOM

I've assumed personal supervision of Alex's screening with Val Severin assisting on the objective tests. We've completed the Tchekov Sensory Apperception series, the Aptitude-Motivation correlations, and the Barzoni Modal Intelligence tests. We also recorded for voice print analyses today using the Luxe Connotative list, but I'll take more VP samples during analytic screening with the Comodo series.

I began the initial analytic screening today, and Alex is consciously cooperative, but has set up strong preconscious inhibitory systems. They seem to be directed against expression of normal grief reactions. He has refused sedatives; possibly fears losing emotional control. He obviously suffers nightmares, which isn't unexpected or unusual. He's also reluctant to take inhibition-reducing drugs. I've limited the use of drugs to allay his anxiety about them and will work through conditioning techniques. He's highly resistant, even in consent, but that's consistent with his ego-function indices.

Note: Try HF modulated light conditioning; he is apparently more sensitive to visual than to aural stimuli. Also, investigate associations with the word "locks." Unusual theta pattern on VPs.

Alex has shown a strong interest in public reaction to his "death" that is in no way obsessive, and I consider it positive. We discussed newscasts relating to his accusation against Karlis Selasis today. A special Directorate Investigative Board has been assigned to look into Lord Alexand's death, and negative reaction to the Selasids is strong on both Elite and Fesh levels. Karlis was transferred to Concordia and is being kept under "protective guard."

I'm gratified at Alex's reactions to his father. I'll investigate it further, but there seems to be little deep-seated hostility. He'll have difficulty resolving his guilt responses toward his mother, but he's capable of recognizing them and has already begun a process of channelization independently and will need little outside direction.

There is no indication of perception warp or disruption resulting from his brother's death, but repressive systems are strong. This and one other factor may require Level 3 conditioning if I can achieve it: the extreme repressive systems associated with Adrien Eliseer. This may still be a negative factor.

4.

Erica Radek put her coffee cup down and switched off the table vidicom when she heard the click of the guest room doorscreens, then turned her chair and smiled up at Alex Ransom, noting the comfortable fit of the name. Alex in a brown slacsuit, showing already on his second morning in Fina a remarkable capacity for blending into his milieu. On the surface, at least. He was still pale, his eyes ringed with dark shadows, but his smile was warm and seemed to come without too much effort.

"Good morning, Erica."

"Good morning." She rose and crossed to the 'spenser. "What would you like for breakfast?"

"Nothing, thank you."

"Alex, must I start making doctorly noises again?"

He laughed at that. "All right, just don't ask me to make any decisions about it."

"Well, we don't have that much choice, anyway." She touched out a number sequence and waited for the covered tray to slide from the slot. When she carried it to the table, he took it from her and put it on the table himself. She sat down, watching him as he gingerly removed the cover from the tray.

"It's as close as we can come to steak. Very high in protein and all that." Her gray eyes glinted with amusement as he tasted it and made a polite effort at appreciation.

"It's a . . . close approximation." He glanced at the vidicom. "You were watching a newscast."

"Yes." She picked up her cup. "Selasis is still squirming. Of course, your father is making sure your dying accusation against Karlis gets a good vidicom play."

"One of the advantages of the PubliCom System franchises. Anything new from the Directorate?"

"Robek and Honoria Ivanoi are spearheading a movement to unseat Selasis, which will undoubtedly fail, but Lord Orin hasn't had time to take advantage of Woolf's temporary weakness."

He nodded, then still staring down at his tray, "Was anything said today about my mother?"

"Yes, of course, and no reporter can resist waxing maudlin in a situation like this, but your mother is the Lady Woolf and a daughter of Galinin. Don't underestimate her strength or resilience."

"I don't, Erica. And my father?"

"Ben had a report from Fenn Lacroy last night. Your father is dealing with his grief very well, and as you'd expect him to, by channeling the emotional charge into protecting the House. Alex, this isn't easy for either of them, but they'll survive it, and so will DeKoven Woolf."

She saw the ambivalent light in his eyes resolve into something close to resignation as he turned his attention to cutting his steak.

"They'll survive and the House will survive. I had no doubt of that." And the subject was closed.

Erica leaned back, waiting for him to ask about Adrien Eliseer. But he didn't, and she wasn't surprised.

He worked at his breakfast, pausing at length to ask lightly, "Well, Erica, what black machinations have you in store for me today?"

"More of the same, with variations, but I'll give you a few minutes to finish your breakfast."

"For that I'm grateful, and perhaps you'll humor me by answering a few more questions."

She smiled faintly. She'd given him few opportunities for questions yesterday, but he had taken advantage of every opening.

"I'll answer any I'm free to at this point."

"The Society's ultimate aim for the Concord is a representational form of government. Do you practice what you propose?"

"No. We're not in a position to enjoy the ideal we hope to make possible. For an organization officially classified as subversive, representational government is far too unwieldy. Still, we have vestiges of it in our Code of Law. For instance, we've provided for the removal of any councilor by a majority vote of the total membership. That rule has never been invoked, however."

He studied her a moment, then, apparently having reached

his limit of protein-enriched approximation, crossed his knife and fork on his tray and pushed it aside. "In all your half century of existence, there have been no major disagreements?"

She shrugged. "Of course there have, but none serious enough to force a confrontation. The harmony derives from the nature of the membership in part—generally upper-class, well educated Fesh, and all of us are here because we share certain convictions and believe in them strongly enough to make the necessary sacrifices. And all of us have survived the screening process, which eliminates any radical elements we might attract. Beyond that, we're forced into harmony to a great degree. We're outlaws in the eyes of the Concord, and totally dependent on good organization and tight security. We depend on one another for our very lives."

He nodded, frowning slightly, then rose, and she'd learned by now that no discourtesy was intended in this tendency to leave a conversation to begin pacing the room.

"Haven't you other HQs comparable to this one?"

"Only small comcenters. Our outside chapters are rather loosely knit."

His pacing took him to the orchids; he stopped to study them as he asked, "Over half your membership is in the outside chapters, isn't it—the double idents?" He looked around to catch her nod, then, "I can see why representational government would be so unwieldy with the members so scattered."

Back to the original question. She smiled to herself. "Our government, Alex, is similar to that of a House hierarchy. Our chain of command works down from the major department chiefs to unit and subunit heads. For instance, I'm Chief of Human Sciences; I have jurisdiction over several units, including History, Sociology, Medicine, and Psychoscience—which happens to be my specialty. I have ten unit chiefs responsible to me, and each of them has three to twelve subunit heads responsible to them."

He walked back to his chair but didn't sit down, instead resting his elbows on the back.

"The Council is at the top of this chain of command."

"Yes. All major decisions come from the Council. It's analogous to the Directorate, except Andreas doesn't wield as much power as Galinin."

"Is he precluded from that by your Code of Law?"

"No, only by his nature. Andreas guides the Phoenix as he has from its birth by consent, and by virtue of the profound respect he commands among the members."

He nodded acceptance of that, but there was a brief narrowing of his eyes at the word "guides." He straightened and began pacing again.

"Can you tell me more about the Council? I mean, is that one of the questions you're free to answer now?"

He also meant, can you tell me about the *councilors,* but that unasked question she chose to ignore.

"Yes. The Council is made up of the chiefs of the seven major departments, and by custom the successor to a major department head also assumes the Council seat. The original Council was elected by majority vote of the charter members. There were about fifteen hundred of them; around four hundred are still with us, and three of our present councilors were on the original Council." She paused, then added, "New members usually don't meet the Council until they've completed GT, but you're a special case."

He seemed to consider that, and she wondered if it displeased him; his oblique smile offered no revelation.

He asked, "Is that why you've taken personal charge of my screening?"

"Partly, yes, but I often take personal charge of at least part of the screening of new members. We seldom accept more than twenty applicants a year. We're a very exclusive organization. We have to be. Our survival depends on it, and a great deal depends on our survival." She smiled wistfully. "Perhaps even the survival of the Concord."

He returned to his chair, and his scrutiny took on a cast of curiosity ameliorated by a solicitude that was unexpectedly personal.

"Erica, how did you become one of the chosen few?"

She smiled. "Well, that's a long story, but I think I can make it fairly succinct. But I should warn you that in Fina— or in the outside chapters, for that matter—a tradition has developed over the years that makes it . . . well, a breach of etiquette to inquire about a member's past before the Phoenix."

He hesitated, then, "Thank you for the warning, and you needn't answer my inquiry about *your* past."

"I don't share most members' reticence on that, perhaps

because my pre-Phoenix past is so many years behind me; the wounds have long ago healed." She sipped at her coffee, noting the transient veiling of his eyes. "To begin at the beginning, I was born in Na'saki, allieged to the House of Matsune, although I wasn't much aware of that allegiance in my childhood. My parents were teachers in the University on indefinite allegiance grants to the Concord. In other words, Independent Fesh. Mother was a psychosociologist, Academicians Guild third degree; Father was an anthropologist and a GuildMaster. After Basic School I entered the University, of course—my parents spoiled me, really; they were in a position to open almost any academic door for me—and I dabbled in sociology, anthropology, history, even theology, which explains why I'm so useful here in what we so cavalierly lump under the heading of 'Human Sciences.' I think I was about twenty when I decided I'd found my life's work in medicine. I stayed with that exclusively for four years, and my error was in not stopping there and going into Conmed."

"Why your error?"

"Because I became fascinated with psychology, and my doting father managed to get me a continued studies leave so I could enroll for an advanced degree in psychohygiene research. Within a year, a call went out from Conpol for psychocontrollers and, with my training and aptitude quotients, I became valuable to Lord Henri Matsune. In fact, worth ten conscript Fesh in that year's tax levy. That's when I learned the real meaning of independence as applied to *Independent* Fesh, and that's when I was inducted into the training program for SSB psychocontrollers."

His breath came out in a long sigh with the words, "Holy God . . ."

She nodded, feeling the old tension in her stomach; perhaps the wounds healed, but some scars, however old, never seemed to lose their capacity to ache.

She said lightly, "My story is rather typical, really. Many of our members were driven into our fold by conscription. Ben Venturi is another conscript recruit, by the way."

He raised an eyebrow, but refrained from questioning her. She answered this unasked question because Alex Ransom and Ben Venturi must of necessity come to terms with each other in the future; it was important that Alex have some insight into Ben.

"Twenty years ago," she said, "Ben was just beginning a promising career as an executech in the Neeth Cameroodo estate in Leda when he was conscripted into Conpol. Like me, he was well educated, with equally well educated parents, although they were strictly House Fesh. A year after his conscription, Ben saw his father arrested on charges of treason simply because he was a friend of a man who went berserk one day and nearly killed Lord James's younger brother, Luther. The man's grievance, incidentally, was that Luther had raped his daughter, which the ever moral Cameroodo refused to believe. He called it a revolutionary conspiracy. Ben's father died of a heart attack the day after his arrest, and his mother was taken in by the Sisters of Solace—as a patient. And here's the long arm of coincidence for you: one of the nuns on her ward is Andreas's sister."

Alex frowned at that, but after a moment his surprise gave way to a brief laugh. "Strange, I hadn't thought about Dr. Riis having a family."

"I know. I always find it hard to believe he wasn't simply created whole in Fina. His sister is the only other member of his family who survived the Fall. She was a charter member of the Phoenix, but after Elor Peladeen's defeat, she opted for the Sisters of Solace. But Amelia Riis is another story. To go on with Ben's story, a short time after his father's death, he was offered a promotion into the SSB by Conpol, and an alternative by the Phoenix. He took both. He's one of the few members who were double idents from the beginning. Now he's ranked a major in the SSB and is in charge of the comcenter at the Cliff in Leda."

Alex's eyebrows went up. "In Leda?"

No doubt he was considering not only the difficulty of maintaining two demanding jobs, but the practical problem of commuting on a regular basis across half a world from Fina to Leda.

But she didn't give him a chance to ask about that.

"I don't know how much longer Ben can keep up both identities, but he has a high energy quotient and excellent organizational capacities." She added with a sigh, "He also has ulcers, but we manage to keep that under control. Anyway, one thing Ben and I have in common is that we were both offered the alternative of the Phoenix at crisis points precipitated by conscription. My alternative was presented by a friend from the University. I'd known him for several years, and knew we agreed on certain basic social concepts, but of course he'd never said a word about the Phoenix. Even after he offered it, I tried to find another alternative, another way out of my Bondage to the SSB, and my vain efforts to escape into Conmed, into the University, into my comfortable *independent* past, finally brought everything into focus in my mind." She was looking at Alex, but for the moment she was seeing the face of a man, a young man then, who waited patiently and in faith for her to come to the most important decision of her life; a man who was dead now, who stayed too long in his double ident assignment.

Then she roused herself, finding a similar patience in Alex's eyes as he waited for her to go on.

"It certainly wasn't the plight of the Bonds that drove me into the Phoenix. It was *my* plight as an educated, sensitive human being forced to turn my talents and training to refined techniques of torture for a secret police that is in itself a symptom of the internal decay of the social system. I don't know what I'd have done if I hadn't been offered the alternative of the Phoenix, but I do know I was seriously contemplating suicide. And in that I wasn't unique. I've done some stat correlations on Fesh suicides. A large percentage occur soon after conscription into Conpol and Confleet, and the percentage has risen in the last twenty years in direct ratio to the increasing incidence of Bond uprisings. Both are red-alarm indices, but I doubt the Concord is even aware of the first, and it refuses to recognize the significance of the second." She stopped, then lifted her cup to finish her coffee, adding matter of factly, "But that's why I'm here. That's why we're all here."

He recognized, she knew, the signal in the change of her tone, but at first he didn't move, still studying her with that solicitous interest.

At length, he said, "Thank you, Erica."

"For what? My life story?"

"Yes." Then he looked at his watch and rose. "But now I suppose you're ready to delve further into *my* life story—at least as it applies to the workings of my mind." A pause, then, "Will Val be assisting you today?"

A guarded question, but it was clear that he wasn't anxious for Val Severin's assistance, and that was unusual in the young men who passed through HS 1.

"No, not on this part of the screening." Erica went to the console wall to set up the recording and mod-stim systems. He watched over her shoulder as she explained each operation. She'd have assuaged his curiosity under any circumstances, and she'd learned that it reduced his preconscious inhibitions when he knew exactly what to expect.

Finally, she said, "Well, now we're ready to get to the workings of your mind. If you'll just sit down and turn your chair this way."

He started to comply, then hesitated, frowning.

"One more question, Erica—or, rather, a request. I'd like to find out more about Rich's work here."

It seemed natural enough; Alex had always been interested in Rich's work. Yet she read a purpose behind it, something more than interest.

"Why?"

He responded with a self-conscious shrug. "I don't know. Because it was Rich's, I suppose."

She let the evasion stand. "All his reports are in the mem-files. I'll get you clearance later today."

"Thank you." He went to his chair and turned up his palms in mock helplessness. "Now—I'm at your mercy."

She laughed. That would be the day the sun didn't rise.

PERSONAL FILE: E. RADEK   CASE NOTES: 27 JULY 3253
SUBJECT: ALEX RANSOM

Alex's screening is progressing faster than I anticipated, considering his resistance to conditioning and aversion to drugs. He's recovering physically, but still suffers insomnia. I've had some success under Level 2 conditioning in reaching the sources of his nightmares, but no success with

Adrien Eliseer. A cathexis exists there, and I doubt it's susceptible to manipulation short of Level 4, and I'm reluctant to attempt anything so drastic.

Despite this one negative factor, I'm entirely satisfied with his acceptability. However, my time with him may be limited now. The Phoenix has been struck twice by lightning in two unusual recruits; first Alex Ransom, and today a young man from another extreme of the Concord's social spectrum—an Outsider. His name is Jael, and he comes to us from Helen. We have little background information, but Harv Vandyne of the Helen chapter recommended screening. I've decided to take Jael under personal supervision, too, at least for the analytic screening. Dr. Hamlin can begin the objective tests, which will give me more time with Alex.

5.

"I have a double surprise for you today," Erica said, looking back at Alex as they left the lift. "A reward of sorts after your grueling week in HS 1."

He didn't comment, perhaps because he was too intent on their destination. The door was only a few paces down the corridor; the door marked MATTER TRANSMITTER: TERMINAL 1. It was a small room dominated by a plasteel cubicle two meters in height, a meter and a half square. The side toward them was open, but the other sides and the roof were braced with dense, ominously humming metal coils. There was just enough room at one side of the chamber for the control console and the tech seated in front of it, a man of middle age who gave her a warm smile, and Alex a curious scrutiny.

She said, "Good afternoon, Chan. Are you clear to give us a ride to the surface?"

"The park? Sure, Dr. Radek." He faced the console, his fingers moving deftly across the controls. "Just step into the chamber."

They did, Alex still offering no comment, and as she expected, he was notably cool about his first MT trans. Outwardly, at least. Like the Second Gens, who had all but grown up with the MT and took it very much in stride. But to Erica, it would always seem something close to a miracle to stand in this humming box that seemed to vibrate with unfathomed power on a frequency almost beneath the range of her senses, then that curious inward jar—a sensation she'd never been able to define because it was so fleeting—and suddenly to find herself elsewhere, to feel the dispersive wind of that materialization.

The elsewhere now was the surface of the island, and the hum vanished to be replaced by the distant rumbling of surf, the MT chamber was replaced by a canopy of lacy foliage with a heavy, sweet scent, and the sunlight filtering through it was momentarily blinding.

Alex looked around a little dazedly, then sent her a slanted smile. "That's . . . quite a surprise."

She laughed and stepped down off the small platform and followed a narrow path that led them out of the foliage.

"Come, Alex. There's more."

They crossed an open area of dune netted with a low-grow-
ing, grayish plant with spidery tendrils. When they reached the
crest of the dune, she stopped. Beyond a span of white beach,
the sea lay before them, the sun glinting on the molten curves
of the breakers, the white foam dancing jubilantly. She heard
him catch his breath, but he didn't speak, and she understood
his silence. It was a vista that asked a little time, a little silence;
a vista that was for Terrans poignantly connotative.

She knew some of the memories this sun-gleamed scene
would call up for him. He would watch the people lounging
on this beach, especially the children, and remember another
beach on another planet; remember childhood days at the Woolf
beach estate learning the water and sand secrets of the sea with
Rich.

Erica always enjoyed introducing new members to the Society's private spa, and inevitably she found herself seeing it
through their eyes, and through the eye of memory, remembering her first taste of the alien, yet paradoxically familiar
beauties of the Selamin Sea and Pollux's surface. The light
wind carried scents that were almost familiar, but still strange;
the cloud-studded sky seemed a spring Terran sky, except for
the pinkish cast and for the pale crescent of Castor in its "new
moon" phase—too eerily large a moon for the Terran eye accustomed to Luna—and except for the beacon of Alpha Centauri B bright on the horizon. The flora of the island had a
tropical look, but the wind was cool, although Fina was in its
summer; a mild summer by Terran standards at this latitude,
and Pollux's twelve-degree axis tilt made seasonal changes
almost imperceptible. She closed her eyes, listening. There
were plants in the dense foliage behind them that sang in the
wind, falling into delightful accidental harmonies, but that song
wasn't meant for human ears; it was a siren song to entice
small, flying, insect-like creatures to their deaths.

She heard the distant shouts of children dancing with the
waves and smiled. This area of the island was veined with
paths and sprinkled with picnic areas, and it always seemed
perilously foolhardy to new members. Fina was assumed to
be uninhabited by the Concord, and these obvious signs of
human existence *would* be dangerous except for the infrared

and visual frequency camouflage screens. But, like all new members, Alex would come to understand that this apparent extravagance was a psychological necessity for human beings confined indefinitely to underground life.

Now he looked up at Castor's crescent, then back to the sea.

"Do you ever get used to it? Everything seems so familiar until you take a close look or a deep breath."

She laughed. "The oxygen ratio is lower than you're accustomed to, and so is the gravity level, of course. No, you never get used to it. I wonder if it wouldn't be easier to adjust to a *really* alien environment."

He turned, surveying the exotically forested slopes of Fina's Mount Torbrek.

"How large is the island?"

"About ten kilometers long and five across. It's a remnant of an old marine uplift, but most of the islands to the southwest are volcanic. There—" She pointed to her right. "See that plume of smoke on the horizon? That's Orifel. It's part of an archipelago stringing off the Comarg Peninsula. Pollux as a whole has more volcanism in progress than Terra. Makes for colorful sunsets."

He smiled at that. "And earthquakes?"

"Yes, and tidal waves. But Fina—our community, I mean—was built to withstand disasters of that kind. At least as far as is humanly possible." She pulled in a deep breath as the wind gusted off the breakers carrying a faint salt scent with it; that more than any other was closest to a Terran scent. Then she started down the bank to the beach. "Come, we may as well get some sand in our shoes."

They began walking along the bank, Alex letting her determine their course. She chose to avoid the concentration of people near the water, preferring to maintain their privacy.

"We're at midtide now," she noted. "At high tide the beach is virtually nonexistent, and at low tide it's a kilometer's walk to the water." Then she stopped, distracted by a movement in the surf off the farthest point of land. "Look, Alex—see those long-necked things out in the water?"

He followed the direction of her pointing finger toward a cluster of slender, weaving objects that with their bulbous ends always reminded her of small-headed, long-necked beasts. He frowned slightly, apparently impressed with the size of the organisms, if nothing else.

"What are they?"

"Now, here's a bit of Terracentrism. They're called kelp, and in fact they *are* closer to plants than animals. But they're carnivorous. When I first saw them, I was convinced it was a herd of plesiosaurs, but in that I betray my own Terracentricity."

She resumed her slow pace, and he walked along beside her, hands clasped loosely behind his back.

"Erica, how long are you going to put me off with Polluxian natural history?"

She sent him an oblique glance. "Aren't you interested in your fellow inhabitants on the island?"

"Intrigued, but at the moment I'm more interested in what brought me within sight of them."

They reached a pile of sea-worn boulders and she sat down on one, waiting for him to seat himself on another.

"The matter transmitter is a reality, Alex, and it will be our strongest lever on the Concord, as a weapon, a threat, and once we force the Directors to the bargaining table, as an offering."

He was silent for a while, apparently fascinated with a spring-ball game going on near the water's edge.

"I suppose information on the matter transmitter is restricted to full-fledged members."

"Yes, but you *are* a full-fledged member now."

He glanced at her, then shrugged. "Perhaps I need some sort of initiation rite to convince me of that."

"Unfortunately, we don't have a proper initiation rite. As for the MT, I'll tell you what I can, but Andreas is the only one qualified to explain it fully."

"I'm not interested in how it works. Physics isn't my forte. I want to know its capabilities in practical terms—and its limitations."

"Its capabilities are potentially enormous, but you're right, there are limitations. We're limited now in terms of equipment and energy. Still, we've had MTs in operation for fifteen years and can trans up to a ton, but we use it primarily for moving people. We have stationary terminals scattered around both Systems, and a return terminal can be established almost anywhere by carrying or leaving a homing device or 'fix.'"

Alex smiled faintly. "That explains those stories about Phoenix agents vanishing into nothing."

"Some of them, at least. Some SI agents can achieve nearly the same effect with disguise, but the MT has been quite useful in escape and rescue operations. Another limitation is the necessity of the fix. We can't transmit to an 'unfixed' point; at least, not people. The coordinates could be off a fraction, and we'd trans someone into a wall or piece of furniture, which is highly fatal."

He nodded. "But in transing something like explosives you wouldn't have to be so concerned with exactness. How unwieldy is this homing device?"

"It's very compact. Usually, two are embedded in the soles of the shoes. They're shielded on the bottom and set up a conical field extending upward about two and a half meters. There's some leeway within the field, but it's a good idea to have your feet firmly under you when you trans."

He leaned forward, elbows on his knees. "With more powerful energy sources, would there be any practical limit to what you could . . . trans?"

"No. Of course, no matter how you move an object, it takes a specified amount of energy to move it across a specified distance. The MT doesn't reduce the basic energy requirement, but the movement is instantaneous, which saves the time spent on acceleration and deceleration for SynchShift. But more important, it means you don't have to package the object to protect it from space vacuum, radiation, etc. A Selasid First Line freighter—empty—weighs about a thousand kilotons. Think how much energy you'd save if you didn't have to move a package weighing that much with the goods."

He smiled, and there was an introspective cast to it. "What about . . . moving objects beyond Centauri?"

"That's Andreas's real hope for the MT. The stars. He's thinking in terms of exploration primarily, but the MT could also make colonization more feasible." Then she sighed. "It's one of those inventions that will change the course of history, Alex, and the face of civilization. I'm not really sure I'll like all the changes. Of course, I won't live to see all of them, and maybe it's a sign of old age, but I'm rather glad of that."

"Erica, old age is something you don't have to worry about

yet. But what about the MT for commercial transport?"

She smiled at that compliment and at the impatience that impelled the question so quickly on its heels.

"With more efficient energy sources—beamed solar power, for instance—the MT would be much cheaper than present modes of commercial transport. At least for distances over ten thousand kilometers. Under that, it's either a luxury or an unavoidable necessity. That's really something of a relief for us; it will have no appreciable effect on Robek's Planetary Transystem franchises, and Robek is one of the liberal Houses we try to protect."

"What do you mean by its having no appreciable effect?"

"I mean it won't offer Robek any real competition. You see, we intend to offer the MT to the Concord in the bargaining process, but we'll put a precondition on it. The MT will be controlled exclusively by an agency of the Concord; we won't let it fall into the hands of any single House."

A speculative pause, then, "That would put Orin Selasis in a very uncomfortable position. The MT *will* offer him real competition."

"That's been an important factor in our calculations." She gave a short laugh. "And the MT won't just make Selasis uncomfortable, it will bankrupt him."

"But not yet. You aren't ready to take this to the bargaining table yet."

"No. We aren't ready for the military confrontation that must preface negotiations, and beyond that, the MT has . . . other limitations."

"What are they?"

"Well, we haven't found a way of negating high-energy field interference. We can't risk transing people within five meters of a shock screen, for instance. That's a minor drawback, though; we usually manage to work around it."

"And the *major* drawbacks?"

"There's only one. The MT presently functions only within Einsteinian spatial limits. Andreas hasn't worked out a way of tying it into Drakonian equations. I can't explain the mathematics of it, but at this point transmissions fall under Einsteinian limits. A trans to Terra now would take four and a half years. That's not only impractical, but the transing limit for organic life is a maximum of sixty seconds before cellular damage can occur. The negative effects aren't cumulative, by the way, but when we trans people, we play it safe with a ten-second limit."

Erica saw the slight sag of his shoulders.

"That does constitute a major problem."

"It isn't hopeless. Andreas Riis is a Drakonian physicist—the best since Orabu Drakon himself—and he has two more on his staff who may not be his equals, but they aren't numbskulls: James Lyden and Caris Bruce. Andreas could get a breakthrough any day, or any year; these things can't be scheduled. We can only push the program to the full extent of our resources. And hope."

A sigh escaped him. "Hope. My alpha and omega. Have you any more surprises like the MT hidden away?"

"It's the main attraction. We have a number of minor attractions—inventions and improvements on existing devices or processes. Enough for each of the Houses in the Court to be benefited by at least one. They'll be part of the package we'll offer if we can bring the Concord to the bargaining table. It's quite an impressive list."

"I'm sure it is, but you'd be hard pressed to equal the MT, both as a threat and an offering—*if* you can make it function within Drakonian spatial limits."

"We have nothing else comparable, and we've calculated the odds on bargaining successfully *without* the long-range MT. They're not even worth considering. But we *will* have it. It's only a matter of time."

He turned away, looking seaward, but his eyes were unfocused. Erica watched him, listening to the rushing cataracts of the waves.

"So," he said at length, "you have a powerful tool, potentially, at least; a lethal strategic weapon even in the short-range form, and in the long range, an offering of inestimable value. If the Phoenix succeeds in forcing the Directors to the bargaining table, it could ask a great deal in return."

She smiled to herself; the unasked question. Then she leaned down to scoop up a handful of sand and let it sift through her fingers.

"What we'll ask in exchange will also be of inestimable

value. We'll ask for Phase I, for the foothold in the power structure we must have in order to initiate the reforms necessary to keep the Concord alive."

He waited for her to amplify that, and when she didn't, he frowned with a hint of annoyance.

"Erica, you and Rich both called me a key. The Phoenix has quite a lot of leverage to put behind that key, and it may open the door to Phase I for you. But I can't believe the Phoenix has put all this effort into building levers while it waited for a disenchanted Lordling to drop from the heavens—literally, in this case. You must have other alternatives, other candidates for the role of key or foothold."

"That's a logical assumption." She paused, casting another handful of sand into the wind. "We do have another candidate, as you put it; someone who could reasonably be accepted by the Directors and could step into the Concord hierarchy at the level of the Court of Lords. We must begin at that level in order to build an effective power base."

"Will you tell me more about this candidate of yours, this potential Lord in your ranks?"

"Not yet. Bear with me, please. In time nothing about the Society will be closed to you."

He hesitated, and she knew acceptance didn't come easily, but finally he nodded.

"I told you I'm capable of patience."

"I know, and I'm sorry to try it so." Then she frowned at her watch as she came to her feet. "And I'm sorry to say our brief taste of untrammeled space and unfiltered air is at an end. I have an appointment with John M'Kim in a few minutes. I'll try not to let him detain me too long. I've another outing planned for you today."

He fell into step with her as she started back along the bank.

"What kind of outing?"

"A tour of Fina. It's time you learned your way around. By the way, you're cleared on the MT memfiles, and you're also free to enjoy our park at any time."

He looked out at the plunging breakers and pulled in a deep breath of salt-laden air.

"That's welcome news."

6.

Valentin Severin smoothed her tawny hair, an unconscious mannerism indicative of preoccupation or uneasiness. She looked up when she reached HS 1 and touched the doorcon, then frowned absently at the spool case in her hand—the compiled test results on one Jael, an Outsider, and a candidate for membership in the Phoenix—and she was wondering at her own ambivalent reactions. The doubts derived from the fact that Jael was an Outsider, not from the test results, which were impressive, nor the man himself, who was also impressive in his own way. No doubt he'd be very useful to the Society. And she found herself personally impressed with him; she had to admit that.

"Oh—hello." She expected the work room to be empty, and she was surprised to see Alex Ransom at the holojector. At first, he seemed equally, and atypically, startled.

"Hello, Val." That reserved smile, the surprise entirely masked now.

She glanced at the closed doorscreens on the office. "Is Erica in?"

"No, she had an appointment with Fer M'Kim."

Val felt an unexpected tension in him as she walked over and looked curiously at the subject of his interest.

"Boning up on the Council?" she asked. The hologram image was that of Predis Ussher.

He shrugged. "I decided I might as well start at the top. Do you know the councilors, Val?"

"Not really well, except for—what's this?" She frowned at the reading screen beside the holojector, and her question stopped him from turning it off.

The memfile heading was "History, Centauran: Peladeen Republic. Subfile: Lord Elor Ussher Peladeen." Her eyes moved automatically across the section framed in the screen.

". . . Elor Ussher Peladeen and his wife, Lady Manir, had only one child, a son, Predis, who was two years old at the time of the Fall. After the Battle of Helen, Lord Elor was buried in an unsanctioned ceremony at the Leda estate, but the bodies of his wife and son were never..."

Val looked up at Alex and knew she'd paled.

"How much did Erica tell you about the Peladeen Alternative? That's Pri-One information. In fact, *I* know very little about it, and I have access to nearly all the memfiles."

His laugh was as easy as that smile, reserved and impersonal. "Dr. Radek is very circumspect in what she tells me, Val. You know that. Actually, all I know about it is that Predis Ussher is the key to the Peladeen Alternative."

"Yes. The Concord assumed that Lord Elor's son died—" She stopped, looking up at him. The words slipped out so easily, as they often did with him. She glanced down at the spool case. "Well, I...Erica wanted these tapes; I'll leave them for her." She crossed to the office door and inserted the case in the compartment beside it, opening it with her name spoken into the voice lock.

Alex moved to one of the chairs, but didn't sit down. He was waiting for her to leave. She smiled at that. An introvert, it would seem; totally goal-oriented, Erica called him, a man who wouldn't permit himself to be distracted, or made vulnerable. Val would leave him to his studies and privacy, but she wouldn't let him be entirely undistracted by the people around him. She walked toward him, smiling.

"I understand you had your first taste of pure Polluxian air this morning."

He nodded. "It was refreshing. And surprising."

"You mean the MT?" She stopped a few paces from him. He wouldn't retreat if she moved closer, but it would make him uncomfortable; he had a low proximity tolerance. It was curious that Jael, the Outsider, had the same low tolerance.

"Yes, the MT *is* surprising," she agreed. "We're so used to it, we hardly give it a second thought. But it's convenient." She checked her watch as she asked, "Did Erica say when she'd be back?"

"Only as soon as possible."

"Mm. Well, if she's with Fer M'Kim, that may be a while. He believes in putting everything in quadruplicate." She started for the hall door. "Tell her I'll be in HS 9. We have another new member, you know."

One eyebrow came up slightly. "No, I didn't know."

"You'll meet him in a few days. Anyway, you'll have company in General Training. Goodbye, Alex." She smiled, not only as a parting gesture, but because she was sure he wasn't particularly pleased at having company in GT.

But as she walked down the corridor, her preoccupied frown returned. She was wondering how much Erica had told him about the Peladeen Alternative. It wasn't like her to discuss Pri-One information with a new member.

PERSONAL FILE: E. RADEK   CASE NOTES: 29 JULY 3253
SUBJECT: ALEX RANSOM

Alex's basic conditioning is completed and I've nearly finished the initial orientation. He'll go on to General Training day after tomorrow. Jael will join him there within the week, and I'll be interested in Alex's assessment of our Outsider.

I've completed the ex seqs on what I call the Ransom Alternative. I've been dubious for some time about the Peladeen Alternative, not only because of certain personality patterns I've seen in Predis Ussher, but because it would take so many years to achieve an effective power base, and stress factors in the Concord are building faster than the General Plan ex seqs predicted. SocioAnalysis brought me the latest seqs today, and they indicate a crisis period in the Concord in the next five to twenty years.

The time factor in itself makes the Ransom Alternative a better choice, and the personality factors make it our only rational choice. I've voiced no objections to the Peladeen Alternative simply because we had no other real choice, but now we do, fortunately.

However, the Ransom Alternative has its dangers. It could very easily catalyze a polarization. The General Plan ex seqs warn of a crisis period within the Society in the next five to ten years, which could coincide with a crisis in the Concord. I'm particularly concerned about certain attitude trends among the Second Gens.

I'm drawing up Alex's schedule for GT, and it will be demanding. I intend to maintain contact with him, however, at least through GT, even if I can only work with him on conscious levels. The metamorphosis of Lord Alexand into Alex Ransom—without destroying Alexand—is an ego-balancing act that would try anyone's emotional equilibrium. He's made the transition seem all too easy, but there are still latent disruptive factors he refuses to recognize. His interest in Rich's work will give me the necessary rationale to see him while he's in GT. I'm still doubtful about his motivation on that. He said this much under Level 2 conditioning: Rich opened a door that can't be allowed to close. There's more to this than aimless interest, but I haven't succeeded in uncovering his real purpose.

Our two new recruits have much in common, including this ability to resist mental manipulation under conditioning. Jael has presented me with the first block I've ever encountered that isn't susceptible to Level 3. It isn't important in itself, but unsettling as a phenomenon. It concerns his mother; specifically, her name. He's willing to talk about her, but not to reveal her identity. He said she was "uppercaste," which translates as Elite. No doubt one of the survivors of the Purge who took refuge in the Outside after the Fall of the Republic. I'm sure there's a lot of blue Elite blood in the Outside in the Centauri System.

Jael's mother died several years ago; there was no hint of subterfuge on the brainwave readings or VP analyses on that. My only concern is that he said it was she who first told him about the Phoenix, and I wonder how she knew about it. But of course there are few secrets in the Outside.

7.

No one else could tell him.

Ben had offered to do it, but Erica refused. She called Alex a friend, as she had his brother. There are certain obligations in friendship. But meeting this one was searingly painful.

The Lady Elise Galinin Woolf is dead—by her own hand.

This was to be his last morning in HS 1; he'd shown more animation than she'd ever seen, asking intent questions about GT, his schedule, the staff. Then the call from Andreas. A private conference. Immediately.

Alex had turned on the reading screen on the table even before she left the room, and she knew what 'files he'd be calling. He wasn't concerned at her leavetaking. But he hadn't heard Andreas's voice or seen his face in her 'com.

No one else could tell him.

Your mother was physically incapable of bearing more children. . . .

The reading screen was still glowing with the words of Richard Lamb. Erica went to the table and switched it off, noting absently that her hand was trembling. Then she looked around, toward the orchids.

He was standing there, his back to her, his image reflected in a pebbled blur in the wall behind the orchids.

She had told him. It seemed bitterly ironic that it had taken so few words. And he had listened in a terrible, contained silence, finally turning away, drawn to the orchids. Terra was in every leaf and fragile bloom.

She moved closer to him, coming around toward the wall so she could see his face, at least in profile. He might have been thinking of nothing more than the white blossom that provided a point of focus for his gaze. His fingers traced the contours of the petals, his touch so light the flower didn't move. Such fine manual control would be difficult for anyone at any time, and she found herself chilled. The steadiness of his hand didn't deceive her. She could also read the beat of his pulse in his throat and the pace of his breathing, and she wondered if he thought he could hold back the tears all his life.

She waited silently, watching him, and when at length he spoke, his voice was as lifeless as his eyes.

"My father, is he . . . all right, Erica?"

"Yes, as far as we know. Ben told Lacroy to stay as close as possible to him."

He nodded and pulled in a breath that caught in his throat. "Harlequin. Poor Harlequin. This will kill him."

He almost seemed to lose control, and somehow it sharpened the edge of her own pain that it was an old Bondman's grief that shook that iron constraint. Then his hand fell away from the orchid and he looked at her.

"What was the official cause of death?"

"Cerebral hemorrhage."

"Of course. Why didn't you simply give me the official version? I'd have no way of knowing the truth."

"Perhaps not. I didn't think you'd accept anything less than honesty from me, even if it's more painful."

"It's more painful for you, too. I know that." His hand moved to the orchid, again tracing the petals with that precise, delicate touch. "She was exquisitely beautiful, Erica. The imagraphs never came close to it. Beautiful to the bone; to the soul. It occurred to me that such beauty should be spared the process of aging." He stared fixedly at the flower. "Of withering. But she would never have been less than beautiful, however old she was. A paradox that I loved her so much, and yet I killed her."

Erica flinched, clenching her hands unconsciously.

"Alex, if that's the case, we're also guilty because we allowed you to join us, to 'die.' Even Rich is guilty because he opened your way into the Phoenix."

"I'm not talking about guilt. Only cause. Regret and guilt are different entities, both equally painful."

"Oh, Alex, you must believe me—we didn't *know*."

"I believe you," he said softly, "for a number of logical reasons, but more for the illogical ones. I know in my soul you wouldn't lie to me." Then his eyes closed, his hand dropped to his side, and she tensed, realizing he was on the fine edge of giving way.

But he didn't slip over the edge. She watched the struggle behind his closed eyes, and knew the battle had finally been won when he took a deep breath and opened his eyes.

But she wondered who had really won.

He turned and took a few steps toward the table, his hands resting easily on his hips, and she knew the physical movement was possible only because he felt himself fully under control, body and mind. He paused, staring at the blank reading screen, then finally looked around at her.

"Erica, you're crying." He seemed vaguely bewildered.

She hadn't been aware of her tears, and it put her off balance. She wiped her cheeks with shaking hands.

"A feminine prerogative," she said, trying to smile.

His hand came up as if to reach out to her, then he turned away abruptly, folding his arms across his chest.

"I'd like to go outside; to the beach."

She nodded numbly. "Would you prefer to be alone?"

"Yes."

"Alex, you can reach me at any time."

He went to the doorway, seemingly driven by an overwhelming need for escape, but there he stopped.

"Erica, don't waste your tears on me. I can't even offer . . . words. Nothing."

"I need no words."

He hesitated a moment longer, then he was gone; the S/V screens snapped on. Erica pressed her hands to her eyes and in the empty silence wept.

PERSONAL FILE: E. RADEK   CASE NOTES: 30 JULY 3253
SUBJECT: ALEX RANSOM

This morning I learned of the death of the Lady Elise Galinin Woolf. We're fortunate in having Fenn Lacroy in the House of Woolf; he had an opportunity to plant a minicorder in Lord Woolf's clothing, and the information garnered from that explained what would otherwise be inexplicable.

The cause of death as reported on the newscasts was cerebral hemorrhage, but rumors are already rampant that she took her own life out of grief for her sons. It was in fact suicide, but I couldn't accept grief as her sole motivation, although it was undoubtedly a contributing factor. Elise Woolf was too cognizant of her responsibilities to the House, and too deeply in love with her husband. Fenn found the answer in a conversation between Woolf and Dr. Marton Stel.

Elise Woolf was incapable of bearing more children, but only her husband and Stel knew it. It was understandably a well kept secret. So well kept even Rich and Alex didn't know about it. The Lady Elise didn't abdicate her obligations to her husband and House; she took her life so that Phillip Woolf would be free to remarry and sire new heirs.

The bitterest aspect of this for me—and for Alex, I'm sure, although he hasn't spoken of it—is that it was really custom that killed her, the senseless, intransigent custom dating from Pilgrim's Holy Confederation that precludes divorce for any reason in Elite marriages. How many Houses have fallen, heirless, because of that custom, and how many barren wives have died, by someone else's hand or their own, like Lady Elise?

Except for what Alex said when I told him about her death, he has refused to discuss it, even when we had a report this evening on Woolf's collapse. Alex's concern for his father was obviously sincere but, once assured of Woolf's recovery, he would say nothing more about his mother's death.

I succeeded earlier in learning the meaning of the word "locks" as a verbal symbol in association with Rich's death, and I assume Alex intends to lock this away, too. I've seen too many similar repressive mechanisms fail, and the results are always disastrous, but unfortunately its immediate success tends to sustain it, and I have no hope of unlocking that "steel-barred chamber" under conditions where the beast within can be dealt with sanely.

I'll send Alex on to GT tomorrow as planned. He needs the emotional diversion, and no purpose would be served in detaining him here. I've given out some hints in Psychosociology that he's shown an aptitude for PS, which will explain my continued interest in him. It's more imperative than ever that I maintain contact with him the next few weeks.

A light has gone from the Concord with the Lady Elise's death. She was an extraordinary woman who mothered two

extraordinary sons, one a saint, and the other—
But that can't be predicted now. He'll make his mark.

PHOENIX MEMFILES: DEPT HUMAN SCIENCES: BASIC SCHOOL
(HS/BS)
SUBFILE: LECTURE, BASIC SCHOOL 23 JANUAR 3252
GUEST LECTURER: RICHARD LAMB
SUBJECT: POST-DISASTERS HISTORY:
WARS OF CONFEDERATION (2876–2903)
DOC LOC #819/219–1253/1812–1648–2313252

The Wars of Confederation was a time of turmoil and
change in every part of Terra, including Conta Austrail,
and Lord Patric Eyre Ballarat in the course of his imperial
campaign of conquest came very close to breaking down
the restrictions of the Holy Confederation's class system.
Bonds were given an opportunity to achieve Fesh status by
volunteering for military service, where a minimum of education and training were given them of necessity, and Fesh
who demonstrated unusual ability as officers or administrators might be advanced to Lordship of one of the conquered domains. The term "VisLord" was introduced at this
time and applied to these new Lords; only when Fesh ad-
vancement later became curtailed by custom did the term
come to apply simply to any male Elite past Age of Rights
who was not a First Lord or the first born of a First Lord.

Shek Mashet provided the only incident in the imperial
campaign even resembling a defeat in its first seven years,
and Ballarat accepted that in order to push forward to new
victories. His brother Bryan's Noramerikan campaign was
also successful, but less impressive simply because again
Bryan had difficulty finding inhabited domains to conquer;
so much of the west coast of Noramerika was rendered
incapable of supporting any kind of life during the Disasters.
He did encounter seafaring-fishing cultures in Alask and
south to just below the forty-fifth parallel, and added to
Ballarat's subject territories the holds of Ancorage, Seaward, Victoria Isle, and Coosbay, which proved valuable
producers of marine protein and timber, as well as some

ores. Bryan continued down the coast (and his meticulously kept journals, as well as those of scientists accompanying him, have since been treasures for historians, archeologists, biologists, and zoologists) past the Coastal Wastes and the ruins of Francisco and Ellay into Mexamerika. He met strong resistance in the domains of Lapaz and Mazelan, and in an inland thrust to the stronghold of Durang, and further south a particularly recalcitrant tribal coalition centered in Ozaca, but none of these appreciably delayed his rather leisurely campaign. He and his officers and scientific staff recorded in photograms Mexamerikan ruins predating not only the Disasters, but the First Dark Age. They also discovered the ruins of the fabled Panam Canal, which—and many ecotechs assure us Terra should be grateful—was not destroyed during the Disasters, but simply silted in afterward and was eventually reclaimed by jungle; the ancient locks held until opening them became impossible.

Patric Ballarat's campaign was anything but leisurely as he continued westward and found that the strongest rulers in Sahrafrika had united in two alliances, one centered in the Nile cities of Zandria, Aswan, and Kartum, the second in the southern Medit enclaves of Asmar, Tunis, Algir, and Tangir. These two groups later formed an even more imposing alliance with the northern Medit domains of Valenz, Marsay, Napolis, and the ancient cities of Athens and Stanbul. I wonder why some sites seem destined for cities whatever the historical vicissitudes. Another such stubborn site is Zandria, of course, and Hamadan, Mashet's relinquished city, which under the name of Ecbatana was the capital of the precursors of the ancient Persians.

Ballarat was undoubtedly interested in the history of these sites, but he had more immediate concerns, and he spent five years subduing Sahrafrika and the Medit. At that point, Bryan had reached the northwestern coast of Sudamerika and there in a naval battle off Quador, the Holy Confederation first encountered the Allienza Salvador under the leadership of the Doms Victorio DelCampina and Duardo Iquito, and its first major defeat.

Bryan retreated with the remnants of his fleet across the Pacific to Conta Austrail, and only then did he send a message to his brother informing him of the defeat. Ballarat, it is recorded, flew into a towering rage when the news reached him. The time factor in communication was not appreciably slower than we're accustomed to, thanks to radio communication, but the time factor in the movement of troops and fleets was very appreciable. Ballarat left the Noreuropan campaign to his second-in-command, Lord Aram Barth Andrasy, and returned via airship to Sidny, but by the time he had marshalled his forces for a renewed assault on Sudamerika, the Allienza—whose Lords (or "Doms") represented every civilized enclave on the continent, including Lima, Sudlapaz, Rio Dejanero, Sopallo, Bonaires, and Cracas—was ready and waiting for him.

Andrasy meanwhile found a similarly solid front in Noreurope in the Coben Alliance, which included the holds of Dublin, Edboro, Pars, Essn, Bohn, Bergen, Gotberg, and Vaasa. The Coben Alliance, however, had no strong leadership, and those territories so devastated in the Disasters offered scant resources to support the counterassault. The Alliance ultimately splintered before Andrasy's armies, and one by one its leaders surrendered to him. He then moved into western Ruskasia, where he met no organized resistance in the holds of Varsaw, Karkaw, Rostaw, Astrakan, Taskan, and Samarkan. Andrasy found an ally in the ruler of the domain centered in Mosk, incidentally, and the Holy Confederation demonstrated its gratitude by making Andray Mankeen Lord of a new House, which a few generations later produced Lionar Mankeen.

With Noreurope and western Ruskasia subdued, Andrasy was free to join Ballarat in the Sudamerikan campaign, and finally DelCampina and Iquito were forced to surrender. They did so in 2896 on the twentieth anniversary of Ballarat's election to the Chairmanship of the Directorate of the Holy Confederation.

Those were a fateful twenty years that changed the course of history and made the Holy Confederation the dominant power in the civilized world. Those years were also the prime of Patric Ballarat's life, and I wonder if at fifty-seven he wasn't beginning to feel a little weary. And I wonder if it didn't occur to him that during his twenty years as Chairman, he had spent very little time in Conta Austrail, instead delegating his duties there to his brother Hugh under the title of VisChairman. His long absences from Conta Austrail were perhaps his greatest error. But the campaign wasn't over, and the worst was still to come.

Ballarat had yet to meet the Minister-Keffe (as he styled himself, although the "Keffe" is often translated as "Chief") Tsane Valstaad. And Tsane had had twenty years to prepare his Sudafrikan Union for that encounter.

CHAPTER VII: Augus 3253

1.

"Oh—your guest room is empty again."

Erica nodded, looking up at Valentin Severin as she paused at the open doorway of the office.

"Yes, that bird has flown. I think I'll move our other bird in now so I can get to know him better."

"Jael?"

"Yes. Our very rare bird." She switched off the reading screen on her desk and leaned back. "Would you bring me a fresh cup of coffee, Val?"

"Of course." She went to the 'spenser by the door, and Erica watched her with almost maternal pride.

A born leader. Erica had recognized that special quality without the aid of personality profiles, even though it was still in potential; she was only twenty-five. Val Severin had the physical attributes: she was tall, and some atavistic need in the human psyche was satisfied with height. And she was attractive, with long tawny hair, quick green eyes, strong features that made an indelible imprint on the memory. Val had attracted the Society's attention while exercising her talent for leadership—and betraying her dangerously liberal ideals—by attempting to organize what she brazenly called a "social protest" group among the Fesh in the House of Hamid, where she was a stattech. Fortunately, the Phoenix reached—and recruited—her before she attracted Lord Lazar Hamid's attention.

She crossed to the desk with two cups, handed one to Erica, then sipped at the other.

"Alex has started GT?"

"Yes, but we'll be seeing him occasionally. He's shown an inordinate interest in psychosociology, and far be it from me to discourage that. We need a good field man in PS."

Val frowned. "But I thought he was going into FO."

"Really?" Erica tasted her coffee, adding nothing to that vague inquiry.

"Well, I suppose I thought since he was a Confleet Academy graduate, he'd naturally go into FO."

"Emeric Garris probably will steal him away from me, unfortunately." She gave a rueful laugh, keeping her tone light. "Did Alex tell you he was in Confleet?"

Val hesitated. "Well, no, I guess it *wasn't* Alex who told me."

Erica studied her expression and tone; there was no hint of subterfuge.

"Val, if Alex didn't volunteer that information, I'd like to know where you heard it. It's no great secret, but I wouldn't want him to think *everything* he said here could become public property in Fina."

"No, of course not." Her frown relaxed into a smile. "Oh, now I remember. It was Fer Ussher. About five days ago I was at Jan and Nina Barret's apartment when Fer Ussher dropped in. He said something about how fortunate we were to have a Confleet captain *and* an Academy graduate. I guess he didn't know how tight-lipped Alex is. He assumed I knew, since I was helping with his screening."

Fer Ussher had undoubtedly made other assumptions about what Val Severin might know concerning their new recruit— if it were likely that he would pass the screening and prove acceptable for membership, for instance.

Erica only nodded absently, commenting, "As a councilor Fer Ussher has access to basic background information on new members, of course. What did he think of our Outsider?"

"Mm. Well, I don't know. He didn't mention him."

"By the way, you can go down to HS 9 and tell Jael he'll be moving into new quarters. I've already talked to Dr. Hamlin. And you may as well bring Jael back with you."

"You seem especially interested in this new member, too. Another PS recruit?"

"No, Ben will probably grab him for SI, but he might be interesting as a source of data for PS."

Val smiled. "If you can translate the jargon. He's . . . quite amazing, though."

Erica's eyes narrowed. Val's tone indicated a very personal response. "He *is* amazing, Val. An Outsider with convictions of a nature to induce him to join us is nearly unbelievable."

"Maybe he's really a spy for old Amik, the Lord of Thieves."

Erica laughed at that; there were ironies in it only she could appreciate.

"I'll give that possibility some thought, Val."

"Not much, I'll bet." She started for the door. "I'll go down to HS 9 and retrieve our rare bird."

PERSONAL FILE: E. RADEK   CASE NOTES: 6 AUGUST 3253
                        SUBJECT: ALEX RANSOM

Alex has completed his first five days in GT, and he's made the program I thought would be so demanding pale in comparison to his demands on himself. I've talked with him three times: the first two were rather inconclusive, but yesterday's conversation was more satisfying, although he's still blocking on his mother's death. He was particularly interested in the rumors of a match between his father and Sandro Omer's daughter, Olivet. Omer is the only one of the Directorate fence riders not yet aligned by marriage, and a Woolf-Omer alliance would tend to tip the balance of power in favor of Galinin and Woolf.

Alex regarded the match as a solid probability on the basis of Omer's tie-breaking vote yesterday on the Woolf succession to the Chairmanship. He's convinced that Omer voted with the Galinin-Woolf faction because he'd like to see a grandson of his in the Chairmanship eventually. That isn't guaranteed him, however. The Directors actually only voted on the question of whether to demand a *new* Declaration of Succession to the Chairmanship. That proposal was turned down, thanks to Omer, which means Galinin's Declaration still stands as written—a relief to us, but less than a total victory for Woolf. *He* is still heir apparent to the Chairmanship, but there's no provision in the present Declaration for any heirs of his *not* born of Galinin's eldest daughter. The Directors are simply leaving the matter open to be decided at a future date, which will be when either of the factions is confident of a solid majority. Shang and

Fallor, despite their marriage commitments to Selasis and Robek, would still be fence riders if the issue were forced at this point, and neither faction wants to risk an irremediable loss, so a tacit truce is in effect. We can only hope Lord Alexand's resurrection can be accomplished before the truce is broken.

Alex discussed all this with no overt emotional reaction. His mother's death has given impetus to the submersion of Lord Alexand. He's fallen into the habit of referring to his father as "Lord Woolf," and his grandfather as "Lord Galinin" or "the Chairman." This isn't studied; the impersonal forms of address seem to come most naturally to him now. That depersonalization hasn't extended to Rich, but I don't expect it to, and I'm grateful for that. Without Rich I'm not sure it would be possible to keep Alexand alive in Alex Ransom.

2.

Except for Leon Sarnov, the instructor, Jael was the last to leave the classroom, but not because of any reluctance to depart. His ten classmates were all Second Gens, the oldest no more than sixteen, and undoubtedly the imminent opening of the dining rooms sped their exodus. Maybe Sarnov was hungry, too, or just glad to get loose from his youthful class. He made his exit with a minimum of words, even if they were friendly enough.

But they were all friendly, all the members, and on this his first day in GT, Jael the Outsider was having a hard time getting used to that. Where he came up, a new face pulled nothing but long looks, and wariness was a fundamental state of mind.

He leaned against the wall by the doorway and the sign reading BASIC SCHOOL/GENERAL TRAINING 12: MEMORIZATION AND RECALL TECHNIQUE. That ingrained wariness was implicit in his posture, and even though he considered himself entirely relaxed, there was in his lean body the ready grace of a predator, quiescent, but ever potential. That watchful readiness was also evident in his dark features—features that revealed his negroid heritage in the flared nostrils, dark hair, and heavy-lidded eyes, opaquely black, reflective, giving a misleading impression of somnolence.

He looked at his watch: 17:10. Val was late. He shifted his weight, frowning slightly as he watched the people passing him in the corridor, most sending him curious but open glances. The walls redoubled their images in vague reflections. He understood the purpose of the textured, mirror-finished walls so ubiquitous in Fina, but they only plucked at his nerves. He didn't like constantly catching shadows at the edges of his vision only to find they were his own reflections.

Then he straightened, a smile pulling at his lips. Val was hurrying down the hall toward him. He watched her, enjoying the sweep of her long strides. A green-eyed Fesh sweet, straight as a rule; top-grade goods, and an eye-holder. And perhaps a heart-holder. He thought with a sigh that it was just as well he'd be out of Fina soon.

"Jael, I'm sorry I'm late," she said a little breathlessly when she reached him. "Come on, we'd better get to the gym. Jobe said he'd wait for us." Then, as they started down the corridor together, "Oh—you'll get to meet Alex, too."

Another group of Second Gens was leaving the gymnasium as they entered. A mixed group, Jael noted, both boys and girls, and he knew they'd just finished a hand-to-hand combat class. The gym was obviously a converted cave chamber, a big room with the rock walls sprayed with white plasment. The last of the Second Gens were nobbing with a middle-aged man going a little thin and gray in the hair. But he moved well; he kept himself on top. That would be Jobe Howe, head of Physical Training, and once SportsMaster in the House of Drakonis.

Val confirmed the guess with her introduction, although she left off any name dressing that went with Howe's pre-Phoenix life. For Jael, the only name dressing was "our newest member."

Howe offered a smile and a hand. "Jael, glad to meet you. As soon as your partner gets here, I'll put you through a few paces. No use starting you with beginner's exercises if you're ready for advanced level."

Jael was a little put off by the term "partner," but decided Howe must mean Alex Ransom, the other newest member.

"Alex should be here in a few minutes," Val assured Howe, "but I've got to get back to HS 1. Jael..." Her eyes met his, then moved away, but her smile stayed with him. "Let me know if you need anything."

"Thanks, Val. You'll be hearing from me."

She walked to the door, which wasn't at all unpleasant viewing. There she met a man coming in and stopped to talk with him briefly before she departed.

"Here he is," Jobe said. "He's way past beginner's level, by the way. I've worked him in with a special SI review class."

Jael studied his "partner" curiously, and at first that's all it was: mild curiosity. Fesh, he read, from a distance; maybe that was just the regulation slacsuit and his manner with Val— reserved, polite, friendly with no ulterior motives. Jael didn't change his mind until after Howe made the introductions, although something about Ransom's face was hackling him even then.

Howe, oblivious to Ransom's slight frown, called him *ex-Captain* Alex Ransom, and that was one on with the haircut, a little short for most Fesh.

Jael asked, "You were a 'Fleeter?"

Ransom raised an eyebrow and laughed. "Yes, as a matter of fact." He was going to add a question, but Howe cut that off.

"All right, you two go get stripped down, and I'll run you through a practice match to see what you can do. You'll find sports trunks in the dressing room. Alex, you know where they are."

Jael followed Ransom, and before they reached the dressing room door, Jael had suddenly tallied it; he knew who Alex Ransom was. At first he doubted the tally; his mind was playing games on him. But while they undressed and put on the close-fitting trunks, Jael watched him—without once getting caught out at it—and finally he had to believe. Yet neither Val nor Howe had given any sign that they had it tallied.

Jael knew he was getting an eye-over, too, but Ransom wasn't getting caught out, either. He asked casually, "How did you know I was an ex-'Fleeter, Jael? Does it show?"

"Yes." He folded his slacsuit on a bench, smiling at Ransom's questioning look. "I knew you weren't a Pole or Shad, so that leaves Confleet. House guard ranks don't carry any heft; Jobe wouldn't tie the rank with you if it was just House power."

Ransom laughed. "Logical. What's a 'Pole'? Conpol?"

"Yes. Sometimes they're called 'Polers.' 'Shad' is tongue for SSB. I'm an Outsider, Alex; you've caught that."

"I've caught it, and your reputation preceded you."

Jael crossed his arms, eyeing Ransom obliquely. "Did it? Well, I don't mind if people here know about me. It's easier, really; I don't have to watch my mouth so much. Anyway, I lined in on you early on." There was nothing in Ransom's steady gaze to hint at whether he was wondering how far Jael had lined in on him. "I mean, I was sure you weren't a Pole or Shad. I can smell them out ten meters underground. That's part of survival training in the Outside."

"Now you have me worried about the rest of Outside survival training." Alex was smiling with that, and as he started for the door he added, "I have a feeling Jobe doesn't know what he's getting me into."

The gym was empty now except for Howe, who was waiting for them at the far end by the mats, each five meters square, designed to break the hardest fall, even if they were only ten centimeters thick.

"This'll be a practice match," Jobe said. "That means you stop short of actual injury. Otherwise, there aren't any rules. We aren't in this for the sport of it. When you have to use anything you learn here, there won't be any referees counting points. This match'll be two falls out of three, and a fall means a throat hold. I don't care how you get it. Oh—there *is* one rule: When I call stop, you'd damn well better stop. I don't want anybody getting hurt. Any questions? All right—have at it!"

Jael had already sized Ransom for heft and reach, and he knew he was up against top training. Better than Jobe ever dreamed, probably. And Jael was still wondering if Jobe didn't realize—

Ransom didn't waste time circling. He moved in fast, backing his body hold with a hooking motion of his foot that nearly sent Jael flat when he twisted free of the body hold. But the foot hook put Ransom off balance, and Jael doubled over, rolling to the mat, slamming into his legs. And it should have worked; Ransom should have gone to the mat on his back, open for Jael's next move. Instead, Jael found himself on his back, and Ransom on top of him. But he didn't get a throat hold. Not then. Jael pulled his chin down, his elbows up in front of him, and wrenched his body around under Ransom's, then, before Ransom could try for a hold on the back of his neck, Jael arched his back upward, pushing from his toes, and that threw Ransom just enough to give Jael a chance to twist out from under and get to his feet.

But that was an error, and it came from reading his opponent wrong. Most Insiders would automatically try to get upright, too, and on equal footing, but Ransom didn't bother. He got a lever point behind Jael's knee, and again they were both down on the mat, and again Ransom was on top, but this time his hands were locked on Jael's throat, thumbs pressed lightly against his larynx.

"Stop!" Howe was hovering close, concerned perhaps that either of them might get too enthusiastic, but he was worrying over air. Ransom backed off and got to his feet, a laughing light in his eyes that Jael liked. He wasn't laughing at Jael, or with triumph; it was simply pleasure in meeting a challenge, and as he pulled himself to his feet, Jael was thinking that the old Ser would enjoy this. Jael the Outsider wrestling, all holds on, with—

But this was one of many ironies Jael had encountered in Fina that his father would be deprived of enjoying.

"First fall to Alex," Howe said. "So, show me what else you can do. Ready? Go to it!"

The second fall was longer in coming; they had each other sized better now. Jael lost count of the number of times they went down, and he was feeling the strain, breathing with his mouth open, sweat threatening his vision. But he was getting a feel for Ransom's moves, noting the pace and style of them, noting occasionally the flat-handed slices that could have broken bones if this weren't a practice match. Jael didn't get him in a floor clinch. They were both on their knees in a straining embrace when Jael finally slipped in with a back-of-the-neck hold, and Howe shouted, "Stop!"

They disengaged while Howe acknowledged the second fall to Jael, both using the time to catch their breath.

"Even on," Howe noted. "Ready? Go to it!"

It was an education, Jael was thinking, and they both had learned each other's weaknesses and strengths by now. The third fall was even longer coming than the second. They had reached an apparent impasse—circling warily, lunging for a hold, going down to grapple on the mat, pulling free to start circling again. Jael's muscles ached unremittingly, and there seemed no end in sight; they were too evenly matched, both physically and mentally. But Jael recognized one advantage that neither his opponent nor their erstwhile referee did: Alex Ransom was a gentleman born; he played by the rules, even when the game had no rules.

Jael let himself be drawn into another grappling session on the mat, then lowered his guard just enough for Ransom to get in a flat-palmed blow to the head. Jael gave a choked cry of pain and abruptly went limp.

Ransom could have had him then, but he pulled back, and

Jael, eyes closed, had to imagine his momentary chagrin.
That's all he was allowed. Before Howe could call a stop, Jael
moved, and Ransom was caught entirely off guard. In a few
seconds, Jael had him on his back, his hands at his throat, and
Howe finally got out a startled, "Stop!"

For a moment, Ransom stared up at Jael blankly, then he
began laughing aloud. All three of them were laughing, the
combatants sagging wearily on the mat, and at length Howe
shook his head and said, "Hell, there's nothing I can teach you
two. You want to come to the SI class for practice, that's fine.
Otherwise, no use wasting your time or mine." He looked at
his watch. "Time for supper. Go on, get yourselves a shower
and get out of here."

Jael and Alex had supper in the SMR-level dining hall. It
wasn't one of the main halls, but there were at least fifty
members using it, and a good number of them took time to
introduce themselves. Friendly. And half blind, one and all.
They didn't read Alex Ransom.

Still, someone in Fina had to be lined in on him. Radek
definitely, and probably Venturi and Riis. But the nonranked,
average member? The answer almost made Jael laugh. None
of them; not one. They didn't look past the name and standard
slacsuit, or that easy manner that deftly put a little space between him and anyone else without making them feel excluded.
They didn't even really look at his face.

Fesh. A nest of tooks.

Jael shrugged mentally; he had no intention of interfering
with Alex's gim. The only question in his mind was whether
Alex knew he read the gim. Nothing said during the meal
suggested he did; he might be suspicious, but he was in some
ways as much at a disadvantage as a Fesh.

Finally, they took their empty trays to the disposal chute,
then retired to the GT quarters, which consisted of four bed-
room/bath units opening onto a small sitting room, a comfortable room by Fina's standards, furnished with cushioned
chairs, a low table, a vidicom console, and a 'spenser by the
door. Jael sagged into one of the chairs and leaned back, flexing
his legs.

"Damn, I hope every day won't be as hard as this one. The

strain on the brain's enough of a down go without the strain on the body."

Alex laughed. "Wait till Master Jeans starts on you."

"Jeans? Oh, your disguise man. That one doesn't hackle me. I might line *him* in on a few garb gims."

"I don't doubt that." He went to the 'spenser. "Coffee?"

"Yes, I could use it." He nodded his thanks when Alex handed him a cup and sat down in another chair. "You know, you didn't pick up on all your hand-to-hand from Confleet."

A distant smile and a veiled look; but Jael didn't expect Alex Ransom to strip himself for anyone, especially not for someone he'd only known a few hours, and an Outsider at that. He wondered if the latter carried much weight with him.

"Oh, I've picked up a few nonregulation techniques—here and there." Alex tried his coffee, relaxed and at ease—and on full alert. "I suppose you're something of a rarity here, Jael. What induces a soul Outsider to join a group like the Phoenix? That suggests you're as much an anomaly in the Outside as you are here."

Jael gave him a slow, wry smile. "I thought it was considered bad taste to ask about a member's past, pre-Phoenix."

Alex only shrugged. "It is, and it's your prerogative to tell me to mind my own business."

"Well, I'm not as strung up about taste as some, and I probably tied in for the same reasons you did. I don't like what's coming on out there, and I don't see anyone doing anything about it except the Phoenix."

"A logical and simple explanation. Too simple."

Jael nodded. "Well, maybe I *am* an anomaly in the Outside. For one thing, my old Ser does all right for his own; money's never been short, and money buys education, if that's where you're turned. Of course, it's not so easy in the Outside. The old Ser could lay hands on a kilo of diamonds any time, but teachers—that's another gim. But he managed, and we have inputs to almost any Concord memfiles, including the University's. Mostly, there was my mother." He paused, frowning into his cup. "She was different. A fringer, really; born uppercaste. Anyway, she had it in her head I should be educated, and she was no illit dodder herself."

Alex frowned slightly, his gaze direct now.

"You speak of her in the past tense."

"Yes. Well, my lady mater died a few years ago. Viral cancer. We've got the medical facilities to handle the rips and burns the Brothers pick up on the line, but we aren't set up for anything like that, and she couldn't walk into a Conmed hospital. Her survival odds would've been nil."

Alex turned away, and Jael saw the small, spasmodic tensing of muscles along his jaw.

"I'm . . . sorry, Jael."

It was a straight say, and Jael understood it. But he didn't pursue it; he recognized a screened area when he ran into it.

"Anyway, my mother made the error of seeing I got educated, and I guess that tends to be an eye-lifter always. And then . . ." He hesitated, searching for the words. "Maybe the view from the Outside gives you a sharper focus. You see the derelicts, and the poor tooks on the slip looking for a door, and the survivors—the ones who live to come out of the DCs—and the little men in the big uniforms, and the fat Fesh smugs praying with one hand, digging the other into someone else's pocket. And the Lords—they let the Outside stay in business so they'll have a place to go to buy off boredom with excess. You never get disillusioned when you come up in the Outside; you never *learn* any illusions. And you see everyone on the quiv. When the ones wearing the black get scared, they start squeezing the lowcaste Fesh, or the Outsiders, but mostly the Bonds. The ones on the bottom blow off now and then, but nothing comes up from that except they get burned and everyone starts squeezing harder." He took a long breath and let it out slowly. "Nothing will change the basic nature of the human animal, but you have to lay certain lines and hold them or the whole system spins out. Maybe I don't cleave deep to the old Concord, but I keep wondering what happens when it spins out altogether."

Alex was silent for some time, his eyes shadowed, and Jael recognized in that silence a kinship.

"Jael, the view from the Inside isn't so different."

"No, I guess it isn't." He leaned back, clasping his hands behind his head. "I thought it would be. These people here are all Insiders, but they see the same picture, even if the angle's different. And they really knock me blind, you know. I mean, I didn't have anything to lose and maybe a hell of a lot to gain tying with the Phoenix, but they tossed off everything—careers, homes, families. Like you, brother. You tossed it all."

The pale eyes were cool, probing, but there wasn't a hint of suspicion; it was there, but well hidden.

"Sacrifices are relative, and I can't believe you haven't made your own. What do you hope to *gain* from the Phoenix?"

Jael shrugged. "Maybe just something to hope for, or to believe in. That runs short where I came up. Religion is for Insiders, and the Concord doesn't pull any believers in the Outside. The Brotherhood isn't something you *believe* in; it's just something you're cleave to for survival's sake."

"The Brotherhood? You mean the Brotherhood of Amik the Thief?"

"That's the only Brotherhood there is in the Outside. You'll find a few independent clans, but most of them are cleave one way or another to the Brotherhood, and there aren't many soul Outsiders who don't line with it."

One eyebrow came up a millimeter. "Does your 'old Ser' know about you and the Phoenix?"

"Yes, but he's been conditioned. Besides, he wouldn't turn the Shads on me; not on a blood son. Nor on anything I lay edict for."

"What does he think of your joining the Phoenix?"

Jael laughed, remembering his father's initial reaction.

"Well, he doesn't hold much faith in the Phoenix, but he doesn't in anything, and he feels some kinly since it's Outside, too, for the Shads. Maybe he has it in his head there might be some fringe divvies in a blood tie in the Phoenix, and in that, he's doomed for a go-down. But he wouldn't try to stop me. I take my own way."

Alex concentrated on his coffee. "There might also be some advantages for the Society in that blood tie."

"Don't count *that* in your calculations. I won't use the old Ser or the Brothers; I lined that out from the first."

Alex met his eyes, and his laugh was indicative of satisfaction. "I'm relieved to hear that."

"You should be. Any tie-up with the Brothers would be asking fate for the Phoenix. The Brotherhood will be around when the Phoenix and the Concord take the last fall. Again, the nature of the human animal." He picked up his cup, then, finding it nearly empty, rose and went to the 'spenser. He filled his cup, but didn't return to his chair. He'd said enough for tonight, and he didn't expect Alex Ransom to reciprocate that self-revelation.

"I'm going to put in some time with the memfiles. You have a lap on me. How far behind am I, anyway? How long have you been here?"

Alex rose. "About two weeks, but no one's clocking us to the finish line."

Two weeks. Jael almost laughed. If he had any doubts, the timing would still them.

"I'm not asking for a race." He went to his bedroom door, then turned to give Alex a sidelong smile. "Tomorrow night I'll give you another lesson in Outside hand-to-hand techniques—if you're up to it."

Alex laughed. "Any time, Jael. Any time."

"Rest up, brother."

Jael switched on the doorscreens and went to the desk console, but for some time he only stared at the blank reading screen.

Alex Ransom. That one was a walking time charge here, and perhaps for the Concord as well. And he might make light of the price he paid to join the Phoenix, but Jael doubted anyone else here had paid a higher price. And he wondered what he asked in return.

PERSONAL FILE: E. RADEK   CASE NOTES: 7 AUGUS 3253
                 SUBJECT: ALEX RANSOM

I had an opportunity for a short conversation with Alex this evening—he's taking full advantage of my offer to use my inputs on the Richard Lamb files and prefers to have me on hand to augment them with personal comments and assessments. It's sometimes rather exhausting. And that impersonal attitude is evident now even in his approach to Rich's work, if not to Rich himself.

Alex's immersion in the Phoenix is becoming a borderline obsessive tendency. He has ceased to refer to his family by familiar names entirely, and when he refers to himself as "Lord Alexand," it is in no way synonymous with "I." This is consistent with the identity reorientation demanded of him, but he's using that to buttress his repressive systems. I suppose I should be pleased with the success of the reorientation, and for the Society I am, but I'm concerned about the cathexis associated with Adrien Eliseer. It's indicative that from the time of his arrival in Fina, he showed a healthy interest in his family and House, but has yet to ask what effect his "death" had on the Lady Adrien.

I haven't discussed the latent schism within the Phoenix with him yet, and I won't until after he's completed GT. However, the potentials haven't escaped him. In anything related to politics, he's a sensitive observer.

Jael joined Alex in GT today, and I learned of their first encounter from Jobe Howe in Physical Training. Jobe was a SportsMaster before he joined us, and I was concerned when he said Alex's style showed elements of formal karatt, which he wouldn't learn in Confleet. But Jobe has created his own rationale for this apparent anomaly: Alex was training to be a SportsMaster before being conscripted into Confleet. It's interesting, of course, that he was aware of Alex's Confleet experience. I doubt Predis intended to broadcast that so widely when he let it "slip" to Val and the Barrets.

Jobe is jubilant, thinking he may have found a fencing partner in this supposed fellow SportsMaster. Jobe's been trying to interest someone in the Sport of Lords since he joined us. I must warn Alex. For him to show unusual skill at fencing could be too revealing, and Jobe is so outgoing and aggressive, he might box him in.

I'm pleased, however, that Alex has discovered our gymnasium, and I've no doubt he'll take full advantage of it. Adjusting to the confinements of Fina hasn't been easy for him. Beyond that, physical preparedness is important to his ego percept. I only hope he never suffers a serious disability; he'd find it difficult to tolerate.

3.

The sign by the doorway read SECURITY AND INTEL-LIGENCE 10: WILLS.

Jael glanced at Alex and touched the doorcon. The door-screens went off, and the man behind the desk inside the small room pushed his chair back and rose.

"Come in. I'm Haral Wills. Most people call me Willie."

Jael studied him—wiry, tight-knit, dark eyes that didn't miss anything.

Alex said, "I doubt we need to introduce ourselves to you, Willie. I'm sure you know everything worth knowing about us."

Wills nodded, answering Alex's smile with his own.

"Right, Alex, I probably do. At least, from SI's point of view." Then he glanced around the austere room—which Jael noted did not have the usual mirrored walls—and said, "Well, this may not look like a classroom, and it isn't. This is my office, and all you're going to get from me is a sort of intro-duction to SI and some of the things you'll be learning about when I turn you over to Marg Conly."

Jael put in, "And maybe a close eye-over?"

Wills laughed. "What did you expect, Jael? But this is going to be a short session; I've got a meeting in a few minutes. You won't mind, though, when you meet Marg. But I warn you, she's happily married, and her husband's big enough to take on both of you at once."

Jael gave that a laugh as Wills came around to the front of the desk, hands on his hips in a ready stance that seemed to come naturally.

"All right, first I'll show you some of the mechanical de-vices you'll need to know about, either for protection, acquiring information, or maintaining contact with other Phoenix agents or your HQ, wherever that happens to be. In SI we deal with situations pertaining outside Fina primarily, but even if you're assigned to Fina, you're expected to know how to handle your-self as a double ident. The people you'll have to watch out

406

for—House security, other House agents, and the SSB—use a lot of the same kind of equipment, so one of your problems is to learn how to recognize it as well as use it. I've set up a demonstration for you. A test, really, to see how good your eyes are."

Alex asked, "What are we looking for?"

"That's the test." He moved a pace away from the desk. "But I'm making it easy; what you're looking for is all on me. I want you to tell me what I'm carrying on my person that wouldn't be considered normal wearing apparel."

Alex glanced at Jael. "I think this is going to be *your* kind of gim." Then, to Wills, "How close an inspection are we allowed?"

"Close as you want, but visual only. I'll give you one minute; that's more than you'll usually get under real working conditions." He looked at his watch. "Beginning now."

While the two of them circled him, Wills stood patiently, hands still on his hips, feet a little apart. The slacsuit was skimp for cover, but there were pockets, the waistband, shoes. And there were enough subtle bulges and anomalies so that Jael knew if he met Haral Wills in the Outside, he'd give him a long look and maybe a little space.

Finally, Wills checked his watch, gave them a few seconds, then said, "All right, time's up. What did you find?"

Jael asked of Alex, "You want first go?"

He laughed briefly and shook his head. "It's all yours, Jael."

He nodded and turned to Wills. "Well, off the top, I don't know exactly what that ring does, but it's part of your arsenal."

"What makes you think so?"

"You aren't a body-decker. Some kind of memento ring, maybe, but that rock—what is it, anyway? If it's supposed to be a moonstone, it's a sad synth."

Wills laughed at that. "You're right about it being part of my arsenal, and it is a synthetic."

"May I see it?"

He nodded and took it off, and when Jael reached for it, it slipped and fell to the floor. A try at catching it deflected it under Wills's feet, and that left it to him to go for it. Wills bent to retrieve it, then handed it to him, accepting his apology with a hint of skepticism.

"It has more than one function," Wills commented as Jael

inspected it, then passed it on to Alex. "That 'sad synth' of a stone is a lens. The ring puts out a modulated light frequency as well as an audio mod-stim. It's a conditioning aid. This particular ring also carries a spring-activated stun dart, so be careful with it, Alex. We use standard Conpol or SSB drugs, plus a few we've developed ourselves. The effects range from a short blackout to instant fatality. You'll learn more about the available drugs later. All right, Jael, what else caught your eye?"

Jael gave him another quick survey, noting the way he perched on the desk, looking fully relaxed, and he was, but he unconsciously kept the leverage right in case he had to move fast. A straight blade; he'd be that in the Outside.

"Well, you're wearing body armor under your clothes, you've got a 'ceiver in one ear, a laser in a spring sheath in your right sleeve, which tells me you're a right-hander. You have an underarm sheath—flat; probably a blade. That watch has a hidden compartment and probably a few other special features; it's not a standard Concord product. Your 'com probably isn't either, but I haven't seen it, so that's just a guess. And your shoes—the seam isn't standard. I don't know what you have in hide there, but if we were facing off in unfriendly stats, I'd keep an eye on your feet."

Wills studied him, then laughed heartily.

"Not bad. Anything else?"

"Not on a fast scan."

"Alex? Any observations to add?"

He smiled obliquely. "No. I know when I'm outclassed."

Wills said, "That's always a good thing to know. All right, I'll tell you more about these items—and show you the ones you missed, Jael." He straightened and pulled his shirt out of his waistband to display the dark, gleaming fabric underneath. "Not that you missed much. And you were right about the body armor—*and* the fact that it limits your movements to some extent. Especially in bending over."

Jael shrugged. "I'll admit the finger-slip's an old gim."

"But you're damned good at it. Anyway, we use spun borasil for body armor; the same stuff we use on our ships as a protective and insulating coating. It's even more flexible than flexsteel, and there's no metal to read on detectors." He stuffed his shirt back under the waistband, but with enough care to alert Jael to what else might be hidden there. But he didn't comment; he'd done enough flashing off.

Wills snapped his right arm down, and a small, flat X^1 sprang from the sheath under his sleeve into his hand.

"Jael, you're probably familiar with the spring sheath. What about you, Alex?"

"No. That's not exactly Confleet's style."

"Well, you'll be issued a sheath and gun, but make sure you practice with it. If you don't catch the gun when it pops out, you're in trouble." He reached inside the breast pocket of his shirt and pulled out a thin-bladed silicon knife. "This is a false pocket to make it easier to get at the underarm sheath."

Jael hefted the knife, thinking that he'd want more weight behind it if his life were up for stakes.

Wills continued, "The watch *is* special, Jael. We have different models for different functions, some with microwave transceivers or conditioning aids." He touched the rim of the watch face; it flipped up, revealing an empty chamber. "This is handy for hiding things like minicorders or microtape spools. And this earceiver—" he took a tiny disk from his ear, "—is useful for one-way communications, but it has drawbacks. Obviously, it shows up on a close inspection, and it limits your hearing to some degree. We have another earspeaker that's handy for making contacts. The con-rad. It sets up a signal tone when you get close to another one on the same wavelength. You were right about the shoes, too, Jael." He hit the back edge of one heel against the floor, and at the toe a sliver of a needle appeared.

"Another stunner?" Jael asked.

"Right." Wills didn't try to remove the needle, but simply kicked his toe against the floor and broke it off, then leaned down to pick it up, handling it carefully as he put it on the desk. "If you ever have to use one of these, be damned sure you don't get tangled up in your own feet and stab yourself. The soles of the shoes have hidden compartments, too; we usually use them for MT fixes." He reached into his pants pocket for his 'com, then flipped the back open to show them a flat chamber. "Another handy hiding place. We also have 'coms equipped with spring-fired stunners, conditioning aids, and some modified for long-range microwave frequencies. Those have built-in sigmod circuits for signal encoding and decoding. You'll be issued a personal 'com, by the way, and personal call seqs. Those are clear lines keyed to your voice; they can't be monitored without your knowledge, and no one else can use them."

Wills put the 'com down on the desk, then reached under his waistband and pulled out a small cylinder about one centimeter in diameter and four long; one end was slightly flared. He handed it first to Jael.

"That's something else you missed. Stunner injector. Careful—don't put any pressure on the wide end. They're only good for close-range encounters; they require direct skin contact. But they're handy on occasion."

Jael passed the injector on to Alex while Wills went around to the back of the desk and began pulling various items out of a drawer. "A lot depends on your mission, your location, and your role. If you're going upper-class Fesh, you can use jewelry—rings or medallions like these. Women have an advantage with jewelry and koyfs and some hair styles. In fact, a lot of our male agents with the build for it prefer to take female roles. That has its problems, too, of course. Some of these things are equipped with transceivers, stunner ejectors, or conditioning aids. This medallion has an imagraph lens." Next, he took out a handful of small, nearly transparent disks. "These are adhesive minicorders. They'll stick to almost any surface, and they're hard to see once they're in place. We have plants down to half a centimeter in diameter. This sort of thing you can carry whatever your role, and unless you're assigned duty here in Fina, you'll be playing a role of one kind or another all the time. But that's getting into Master Jeans's department."

Jael smiled. "We've already had a taste of Jeans's department."

Wills nodded, meeting his eye with an answering smile.

"He's a real bastard for detail—right? Well, just see that you don't miss any of it. The disguise angle—the plasimask, wigs, iris lenses, costume—all that's part of it, but his talent, and I should probably say his *genius*, is acting. A disguise isn't worth a damn unless you can play the role that goes with it." He took a flat, black rectangular object small enough to fit in the palm of his hand from the drawer. "Here's another handy item. A jambler. Good insurance for private conversations. And this—" he brought out a similar box-like object, slightly larger, with a thin loop antenna at one end, "—this is a montector. Any monitor puts out an emission on some wavelength, no matter how weak it might be. This thing can locate any plant we've come up with, and certainly anything the SSB has to offer." He paused, and for a moment studied the equipment scattered on the desk, then looked up, first at Jael, then at Alex.

"Quite an array, right? And this is only a sampling. But the most important item in our arsenal is conditioning." He picked up the ring he'd worn for the initial test, slipped it on, then stood with his arms folded, the ring turned upward.

The light was barely visible, the flash frequency so fast it didn't even read as a flicker, but it was aimed directly at Jael's right eye, and what he felt in his head ran a chill down his spine. He looked away from the ring, but felt the drag in it; his eyes didn't want to move.

Wills turned his hand slightly and let Alex have a feel of it, and he obviously didn't like it either. Then Wills's thumb moved under his palm, against the shank of the ring, Jael realized, and he became aware of a high whine that was more a sensation than a sound. He didn't like the feel of that, either, and he couldn't turn his ears away.

Wills switched off both the light and sound, smiling faintly.

"I'm not trying to condition you. Anyway, you're both resistants. If you weren't, I'd have you close to a Level 1 by now. Of course, Erica put you through conditioning, but she always starts with low intensities and works up to something like this. If you ever have to use conditioning in a working situation, you won't have time for that." He took off the ring and put it down on the desk. "We call these mod-stim devices. That's for 'modulated frequency stimulus.' What these visual or audio frequencies do is induce synergistic resonances with the subject's brainwaves. That creates the receptivity state, then you set up the conditioning verbally. There's an art to that, but you'll have plenty of practice on it later. And you'll learn more about the different types of conditioning. Some of it *you're* the subject for; that's the basic conditioning Erica gave you. Sec-con, for instance; security conditioning. That covers everything associated with the Phoenix. The memory-lapse phenomenon. You probably haven't experienced it yet, but if you tried to tell an outsider—" He stopped, and with a

wry glance at Jael amended, "I mean a non-Phoenix member
where our main HQ is, you'd find that every time you tried
to say the word 'Fina,' you just wouldn't be able to remember
it. You've also been given a set for contingency conditioning,
which means that if any Phoenix member asks consent and you
grant it, they can set up a conditioned command."

"But it takes consent," Alex put in.

"Yes, and there are safeguards. We don't make any member
vulnerable to nonconsent conditioning; not from anyone. Another type SI agents use a lot is recognition conditioning. For
instance, if you're trying to make an initial contact with an
agent you don't know, and electronic contact devices aren't
feasible, then you can be conditioned to recognize a voice. It's
as sure as VP ident. Then, of course, there's the TAB. That's
the one all of us hope we never have to use. It goes into effect
automatically if you're arrested. Actually, it's not literally a
total memory block; it leaves you with the memory you need
to function. Essentially, it strips you of personal identity. Anything pertaining to you, past, present, or future, is gone. That
includes everything you know about the Phoenix. Sometimes
the TAB is modified for various reasons so it won't go into
effect unless you're interrogated. Fortunately, arrest doesn't
always mean interrogation. The SSB knows Phoenix conditioning when they see it, and generally they won't waste time
trying to break it. But the PCs give it a try occasionally. All
we can do is get prisoners out of their hands as fast as possible.
We've got agents in the SSB and we're usually successful at
that. One thing you can count on: we take care of our people."

That was a straight say; something in Wills's eyes put muscle into the words. Jael looked down at the desk.

"What if a member gets pulled down carrying any of this?
Some of it might look tice to the Shads."

Wills gave a short laugh. "Yes, but most of our equipment
has self-destruct mechanisms. If anyone tries to open it up to
see how it works, all they'll get is a handful of dust and singed
fingers." Then he frowned and glanced at his watch. "You
probably have more questions, but I'll have to leave it to Marg
to answer them. Come on, I'll take you to the supply room.
That's her department."

Jael noted that Wills put all the equipment back in the desk
and set the print locks before he left the room; he also locked

the doorscreens behind them. A careful man, and it was all habit; he didn't have to think about it.

As they started down the hall, Jael said, "Willie, if they give me a say, I'll opt for SI. Will I get a choice?"

"You always get a choice, but I'm glad to hear you're leaning toward SI; we can use a man with your—uh, unusual training." Then, as if he thought Alex might feel excluded, "I'm afraid your training will make you more useful in another department, Alex."

Alex only nodded and said, "Yes, I'm afraid so."

Jael was giving Wills a close eye. He was talking about Alex's Confleet training. Nothing more. He was lined in on that, which was standard stat for his department, but he wasn't lined in beyond it.

And he hadn't read a glim of it in Alex Ransom's face. Wills was a careful, ready man with a quick eye, but even he didn't tally the gim.

PERSONAL FILE: E. RADEK   CASE NOTES: 13 AUGUS 3253
SUBJECT: ALEX RANSOM

Alex has been in GT two weeks, and he continues to demand more of himself than his instructors ever could. Ben tells me both our new recruits are adept with Security and Intelligence devices and techniques, especially Jael. In fact, SI has picked up a few pointers from our Outsider. Alex has shown particular skill with conditioning techniques and even achieved a Level 3 on one of the volunteer subjects. This is in consent, of course, but still remarkable.

I saw Edgar Jeans yesterday, and he's fairly dancing with frustration over his new students. He calls them natural talents, which isn't entirely true in either case; they've both had stringent training of one sort or another in the art of acting. Master Jeans wants both of them for his theater group, but neither has shown any interest in it. Jael will undoubtedly be assigned outside Fina, and Alex is too goal-fixated to indulge in the frivolities so vital to the sanity of less single-minded mortals. His only recreation is a nightly session in the gym. Jobe apparently backed him into a corner on the fencing, but perhaps I'm being overanxious about that. Certainly it's a useful identity reference and probably should be encouraged if the Lord Alexand isn't to be completely buried.

Ben and Andreas and I discussed the Ransom Alternative last night. Andreas is still reluctant to believe that Predis would put his personal ambition before the best interests of the Phoenix, but Ben is, of course, more pragmatic. He's been watching Predis closely. And Predis has been watching Alex. But so far he's made no overt moves.

4.

When Jael left the dressing room, it was nearly 23:00, and that surprised him. He'd stayed in the pool longer than he intended. But he'd had good company there. Val Severin had a way of making time slip.

At the open door of the gym he stopped, hearing the clash of foils echoing in the cave chamber. He relaxed against the doorjamb to watch. He didn't know the rules of this game, nor did he care; he found it interesting enough without knowing the fine points.

Both combatants were stripped to the waist, open-mouthed and pulling for air. Behind the clear plasex mask, Jobe Howe was grinning exuberantly, showing amazing quickness for all his heft and fifty-on years. Alex Ransom didn't have his heft, but he had reach on him. And he was a dancer. The term was ambivalent in the Outside, but in this case it was no insult. The play was too fast for the eye, the blades throwing off blurred showers of sparks. Jael saw Jobe's foil strike home against Alex's ribs, and Jobe was jubilant as they disengaged.

Alex said, "A point, Jobe, and accepted." He touched the guard of his foil to his mask, then brought the blade down to his side in a flashing arc.

"And that gives me one to your two," Jobe replied, making an absent imitation of the salute, "and a fighting chance. Ready? Garde!"

Alex laughed and brought his foil up. "Garde and allon!"

The mock battle resumed, and Jael was thinking that this would be an eye-lifter for the Brothers. They nosed up at the Sport of Lords; the knife was the weapon of choice and honor in the Outside. But if they thought the foils too dainty, it was because they hadn't seen them properly used. This face-off was less than lethal only by mutual consent and because of the soft tips and low charges. But Alex was holding back—Jobe would never get a point otherwise—and maybe he thought that was enough to turn any long looks. For most of the tooks here, it would be. Jobe had supplied the gim line himself: Alex had been training for a SportsMaster's spot. If Jobe swallowed it, then it would it would go down with most of the members, and Alex Ransom was no dodder; he kept a side eye out and never indulged himself or Jobe except at late hours when the gym was deserted.

Jael didn't hear the hall doorscreens open—the sound was lost in the clash of blades—but he felt a change in the emptiness of the vault-like room. He turned his head slightly to look along the wall to the door, and perhaps it was only habit that made him adopt that attitude of inner stillness learned from childhood, a process of melting into the background. The man entering the gym wouldn't even be aware of him unless he moved.

Jael searched his memory as the man paused, then folded his arms, settling himself to watch the fencing match. Alex had his back to him, and if Jobe saw him, he gave no indication of it; he was too intent.

A tall man, who would have weight and power behind him, but not quickness. For age, that had to be somewhere just past forty. The features were Noreuropan: a high forehead, long, chiseled nose, strong mouth, a little thin-lipped, and eyes of dark, brilliant blue.

A name came to mind now. For some reason Jael considered warning Alex, but satisfied himself with watching the man and trying to analyze why he felt it necessary to give Alex a backup eye.

Predis Ussher, Chief of Communications.

Jael knew nothing about Ussher except what was in the memfiles, and he wasted no mental energy sorting that information. His uneasiness wouldn't be explained by facts. In the Outside, they called it reading a man's shadow.

Predis Ussher had the power; he was a mover. Imagraphs and holograms never caught it; a vitality that couldn't be computed. Such men needed watching.

And Ussher wasn't here on an idle pass-through. His attitude might be that of a man briefly attracted by an interesting phenomenon, but he didn't know he was being watched, and his face was slipping. He was only interested in one thing: Alex Ransom. And his interest wasn't friendly.

Jael let himself be distracted by a change in the pace of the blades and saw Alex's foil make a spiraling loop, then spring into an arch against Jobe's chest.

"Point!" Jobe stepped back with a wry grin and saluted him. "And match. Next time let me see that last maneuver again, but slow so I can tell what's happening."

Alex laughed as he took off his mask. "The old feint to the eyes. I learned that one the hard way. A good match, Jobe. Thanks." He wiped his forehead, pushing back the wet strands of black hair, and as he turned toward the dressing room, he saw Jael.

But Jael didn't smile; his head moved in a quick nod toward Ussher, and he thought again that Alex Ransom picked up fast. His gaze moved smoothly past Jael on to Predis Ussher. But there, a tensing, a narrowing of his eyes.

Jobe took Alex's foil and mask with his own and started for the case on the wall.

"I'm the one to give out the thanks, Alex. These foils have been waiting—" He stopped, his smile fading to be replaced by another that was set and polite. "Hello, Predis."

Ussher crossed the room with long strides, his smile as contrived as Jobe's, but more skillfully; a strong voice, rich and deep, that would be as facile as those foils.

"Jobe, how are you?" Then an easy laugh. "As if that needs answering after watching you in action."

Jobe shrugged, and his smile wasn't so forced now. "Well, I'm doing all right for an old man. You're looking good."

"I'll never keep up with you. Damn, I haven't been down here for weeks, and I miss it. But everything keeps piling up in the office. You know how that goes."

Jobe nodded his sympathy. "They're keeping the old in-file stacked up, huh?"

Alex waited silently as Jobe took the foils and masks to the case. Jael recognized that almost indifferent expression; there was more here than met the eye.

"We're putting in some new equipment," Ussher was saying. "SynchCom transmitters; a new model, as a matter of fact. Lord Woolf's finest."

Jael frowned. Ussher had glanced at Alex with that. It was either a test, a challenge, or some kind of reminder. But he

gave more than he got. Alex didn't so much as blink, and Jael
found the byplay informative. Ussher was lined in on Alex
Ransom.

Ussher still addressed himself to Jobe. "How are Laura and
Davy? But I suppose it's 'Dave' these days. He's practically
a young man by now. Seventeen, isn't he?"

Jael almost laughed. A tooth man, and gifted with a good
memory, a prerequisite for the gim. But any inclination to
laughter died when Jobe, his initial reserve dispelled, beamed
proudly as he turned from the foil case.

"Seventeen just last month. He and Laura are fine, Predis,
and Dave's half a head taller than I am already."

Ussher laughed appreciatively. "I'll be damned. He's a fine
boy, Jobe. You're a fortunate man." He glanced around the
gym, nearly losing his smile when he saw Jael. "I was looking
for Jan Barret, but I got so fascinated with your display of
fencing skill, I all but forgot my purpose. That's something
I never expected to see in Fina. Who's your fencing partner,
by the way?"

"Oh—sorry, Predis," Jobe said, "I forgot you hadn't met
my worthy opponent."

Alex took the initiative with a disarmingly open smile.
"Councilor Ussher, isn't it? I've encountered you in the memfiles." He extended his hand. "I'm Alex Ransom."

Ussher hesitated only a split second before he reached out
to give him a firm, vigorous handshake.

"Well, Fer Ransom, I'd like to extend a personal welcome
to Fina and the Phoenix. We need young men of your caliber.
We've a long struggle ahead of us, but let me assure you we
will win our battles. There's a saying among the Bonds, you
know: Might makes its Rightness. But *I* say, Rightness makes
its Might."

Alex absorbed that without a flicker of expression, nor did
he respond. He simply ignored it, leaving Ussher slightly off
balance.

"Fer Ussher, have you met our latest recruit?" He glanced
at Jael, who took the cue and walked over to them, giving
Ussher a straight eye. Ussher could only meet it for five seconds
at once.

"Councilor Predis Ussher," Alex said, "this is Jael."

The broad smile snapped on again and the hand went out. A skin presser.

"Welcome, Fer Jael. This is an unexpected pleasure; I don't often get to meet our new members until they've completed GT. I can see the Phoenix is doubly fortunate in its two newest members. With young men like you in our ranks, we can't fail."

Jael played to the gim with a self-conscious smile. "Thanks, Fer Ussher. I hope you're right."

"I know I am. And, Jobe, you seem to have found a fencing partner at last. I'm sure Fer Ransom is especially welcome to you."

Jobe gave Alex a crooked grin. "Maybe too much of a partner for this old man. He really keeps me stepping."

"Now, Jobe, you make most of the young sprouts around here look pretty decrepit. But I'll admit Fer Ransom seemed to be giving you a good run. Of course, I don't know the first thing about the Sport of Lords."

Again, a test or a challenge. Jael caught a cold, hidden light behind Ussher's eyes.

Alex only smiled politely. "It's a fine sport, Fer Ussher. Excellent for developing good reflexes."

"I'm sure it is. Well, Jobe, it's late and high time for you to get on to your apartment. Oh—was Jan here this evening?"

"Commander Barret? No, I didn't see him, and I've been here since 19:00."

Ussher shrugged. "He said he was coming up for a workout tonight. Well, say hello to Laura and Dave for me." He turned to Alex and Jael, offering each a handshake. "Fer Ransom, Fer Jael, it's been a pleasure meeting you. If I can be of any assistance, don't hesitate to call on me." He emphasized that with a decisive nod, then started for the door. "Good night, Jobe. Keep up the good work."

"Thanks, Predis. Good night."

Jael was watching Jobe. There was still a hint of that initial reserve, but only a hint. His gaze shifted, meeting Alex's. He read Ussher; he was no took.

But Jobe Howe didn't, and there were more of Jobe's ilk in Fina than Alex Ransom's.

A tooth-gimmer, Jael thought bleakly; a second-rate charm-

gaffer who wouldn't pull a look in the Outside, but here he had six thousand potential tooks.

Alex started for the dressing room. "I'll take a quick shower, Jael. I'll only be a few minutes."

He nodded. "I'll wait."

Jobe joined Alex in the dressing room; Jael heard their voices in a casual exchange. Alex was good at that, as he was good at camouflage and at calling other people's paces.

Power, Jael was thinking grimly. That was the gim Predis Ussher was running, and he wouldn't be satisfied, like the tooth-gimmers in the Outside, just to pick the fruit and spook. He'd go after the whole damned tree.

Jael sighed. There was a snake in every garden; he wasn't surprised to find Ussher here. Now he had him sighted, and he intended to do some sniffing around, but he'd waste no time in the memfiles. Nor with Alex. He might read the tooth-gimmer, but he wouldn't open up.

But Jael wondered if Alex Ransom read Ussher all the way. Alex was a gentleman born, but Ussher wasn't; he wouldn't play by the rules.

PERSONAL FILE: E. RADEK   CASE NOTES: 23 AUGUS 3253
                             SUBJECT: ALEX RANSOM

If Alex were so inclined, he might celebrate an anniversary of sorts today: a full month in the Phoenix. I talked with him this afternoon, but only briefly; he was scheduled for fingerprint removal. He won't have larynx alteration, and there's some risk in that in the unlikely—I hope—event of his arrest, but the SSB is so accustomed to finding print removal accompanied by larynx alteration—and for that we can thank the Outsiders—they seldom bother to check VP once they see the print removal. At any rate, he must have some means of identifying himself beyond a doubt if the Lord Alexand can be resurrected.

He'll finish GT in five days and has been officially assigned to Fleet Operations. I've set up an appointment for him with Emeric Garris this evening and suggested to

Emeric that Jan Barret give Alex a tour of FO's facilities. Jan will respond to Alex, and perhaps Predis's hold over him can be negated to some degree.

I talked with Alex about Jael again today, and he's still obviously impressed with our Outsider. Out of curiosity, I did a comparison overlay of their personality profiles and motivational matrix patterns, and they coincide to a remarkable degree. That would seem impossible in view of the difference in their formative experience, but the Outside is closer to the highest circles of the Elite than one might think, and they are, of course, both sons of Lords in one sense or another.

5.

Fleet Operations; Level 1, a cavern world a hundred meters below sea level.

The builders of Fina had used the natural chambers, flooring them and coating the walls with plasment that left the rock contours still visible. The scale of the hangar vaults was so vast, it made the black-hulled ships berthed within them look like miniatures.

Commander Jan Barret took some pride in reeling off dimensions as he conducted this private tour. Hangar 1, the main hangar, was roughly rectangular, two hundred by three hundred meters, and eighty meters high at the apex where a bank of helions flooded the vault with light. The comcenter was set into one of the long walls, a semicircular chamber fronted with a sound-screened windowall and a narrow deck raised a meter above the hangar floor. From the deck, one had a clear view of the entire hangar and the lock tunnel across the vault.

The other two hangars, which were each about half the size of the main one, but still impressive enough, were used for storage and maintenance. The tour included a survey of the maintenance, docking, and loading facilities, an inventory of the fleet—five Troop Carrier Corsairs, ten Corvets, and forty-two Falcons—as well as the comcenter and introductions to its staff. There were never fewer than thirty techs on duty, none rated under Grade 6, and FO's comcenter would make the average Confleet equivalent look crude by comparison.

Now they crossed Hangar 1 to the lock tunnel, their footfalls echoing in the quiet. It was the dinner hour; the hangars were nearly deserted.

Jan Barret was one of five men in FO ranked leftant commander, but he wore no uniform; no one in Fina wore a uniform. The only indication of his rank was the insignia with the triangle-flame symbol above a single star on his collar. He wore it proudly. He was only thirty, and often enough people judged him to be even younger; he had a freckled, boyish face and sandy hair that defied a comb. But neither the men under him nor Commander Garris were put off by that, and he was well aware of the rumors that Garris might name him first commander when he retired.

Barret frowned, watching Alex Ransom, and wondering why Predis seemed so uneasy about him. He might be a Confleet Academy graduate, but he wasn't looking down his nose at the Society's fleet; his questions were serious and pertinent.

And there was something about him—Barret sighed, finding that special quality elusive. He had the feeling Ransom was used to uniforms and would wear them well. Boots. He'd probably worn boots most of his life. For Barret, a Second Gen, the life style associated with uniforms and boots was foreign and in no way attractive, but there were some aspects of it he could respect. Like training and discipline. Ransom's carriage conveyed both.

Ransom paused, looking up at a Falcon whose hull bore a long, scorched gash, the borasil coating blistered around it.

"She's acquired her battle scars."

Barret nodded. "Yes, and so did some of her crew. We lost two men aboard *Imp*."

Ransom was silent for a moment, black brows drawn, but he made no comment on the casualties.

"Commander, your ships don't carry the Phoenix symbol."

Barret shrugged as they continued down the row of Falcons. "I guess Commander Garris doesn't think we should advertise ourselves. Why? Do *you* think we should carry insignia?"

Ransom glanced at him and laughed. "I wouldn't presume to say. For one thing, that isn't the best way to get on good terms with your commanding officer. I was just thinking of it from Confleet's point of view. The Phoenix gets blamed for a great deal of piracy we have nothing to do with. But perhaps that's all to the good."

Barret nodded. "If the Concord knew what a small fleet we really have, they might not be at all impressed. Fortunately, size isn't everything."

They walked on in silence for a while, Ransom examining the ships as they passed.

"Your total manpower is about sixteen hundred, isn't it? How is that divided between flight and ground crews?"

"Very roughly, Captain. Most of our personnel are trained for both flight and ground duty."

Ransom's pale eyes narrowed, and Barret realized he'd slipped, using his rank. Garris had introduced him as *Fer* Ransom. But Ransom only looked away as if he were embarrassed.

"I'm not entitled to that rank here. That was my Confleet rank, and I don't know where Commander Garris intends to start me in FO—probably base private. And I wouldn't mind that. I want to make my own way here."

Barret paused, feeling out the tone of that, and he found himself pleased with it.

"Look, we don't put much stock in ranks or last names, except on duty. Call me Jan and, if it's all right with you, I'll call you Alex."

Ransom smiled at that. "Thanks, Jan."

Barret slowed his pace as they approached the mouth of the lock tunnel.

"Anyway, I doubt you'll be starting out at base private. That'd be a hell of a waste. I mean, you're the only Confleet Academy graduate we've ever had. You have more training behind you than all the rest of us put together."

He laughed. "The Academy program isn't *that* good, and I thought Commander Garris had Confleet training."

"He did, but he worked his way up through the ranks. Besides, that was a long time ago."

"Confleet hasn't changed its methods that much."

"Maybe, but there've been a lot of technical changes." He cocked his thumb over his shoulder. "Like those new Falcons we picked up a couple of weeks ago. They carry new guns—modified X^6s—more firepower than any Falcon's ever carried before. But you probably know all about those little cannons."

"Not really. I wasn't a gunnery officer. What I know about the new X^6s is out of the manuals or word of mouth."

"Well, you'll get a chance to learn about them firsthand. I don't think this is what Confleet had in mind for you, though."

Ransom was surveying the lock tunnel. "Confleet wouldn't approve of the use I'll be putting to any of their training. I'm only glad it will finally be put to good use."

"It will be, Alex, and we'll put *you* to good, hard use. There'll be times when you get used so hard, you won't be able to put one foot in front of the other."

Ransom was still looking down the tunnel, his eyes veiled as if he were focusing on some bitter memory.

"Jan, I've been searching all my life for a cause I could work at to the point of exhaustion; something I could believe in and care about that much." He stopped abruptly, as if he'd said more than he intended, but there was a ring of conviction in those words that stirred some indefinable excitement in Barret.

"You've found it here." Then he laughed, feeling a need to dispel the sober mood. "Both a cause and an opportunity for exhaustion. We're small, so we have to work damn hard to keep the enemy on his toes."

"The enemy?" Ransom looked directly at him, a probing gaze that made him vaguely uncomfortable.

"Well, I mean the Concord."

"Oh. I guess I've been out of a military milieu too long. That's the first time I've heard the Concord referred to as the enemy. But I suppose it's a matter of habit for someone like Commander Garris with his military background."

Barret was silent, wondering about the word that came so easily to his lips. It wasn't Emeric Garris who habitually referred to the Concord as the enemy.

"What about the lock, Jan? How many ships will it accommodate?"

He roused himself and looked down the tunnel toward the huge, segmented doors.

"It'll take one of the Corsairs, or three Corvets, or six Falcons. That's the lock itself. We can stack quite a few ships in the outside approach tunnel."

"It's ingenious, the underwater access."

"It works well enough. We're screened against observation on any wavelength for five hundred kilometers around Fina. Our ships always surface or submerge at irregular intervals and at random points within the screened area. Of course, we have to do some structural reinforcement on the ships so they can take the inward pressure from the water."

Ransom nodded, turning as Barret did and keeping pace with him back across the hangar toward the corridor entrance.

"Jan, are any of your ships equipped with MTs?"

"No, and we're not really using the MT strategically yet. The equipment's expensive and hard to come by, and they're put together practically by hand; we're not set up for heavy manufacturing. And they're a big energy drain." He sighed

"I'd like to see all the Corvets equipped with MTs, but John M'Kim says it just isn't feasible now." They reached the wide double doors at the corridor entrance, and Barret stopped. "Well, that about covers it. I'll leave you here. I have to check with TacComm on a recon run I'm taking out tomorrow."

"Thanks for the tour, Jan." Then Ransom gave him an easy smile. "Maybe I'll end up in your command."

"I'll put in a word with Garris, but with your training and experience, it may work out that I'll end up in *your* command."

Ransom paused, his gaze direct. "Jan, if by any chance you did eventually end up in my command, would it bother you?"

Barret's inclination was to pass that off with a noncommittal reply, but he didn't; he couldn't. And again he was thinking that Predis was worrying too much about Alex Ransom.

"No, it wouldn't bother me; not as long as I was sure you were qualified."

Ransom smiled. "Well, I don't think we need to worry about that contingency now. I'm sure Commander Garris will give me a hard run before he's satisfied with my qualifications for anything."

"He knows how to give a man a run, too. TacComm is setting up a series of raids in the Solar System in a couple of weeks, so don't count on much rest."

"I don't need much. You don't have a permanent FO base in the Solar System, do you?"

"No." Barret's mouth tightened irritably. "It'd be handy for diversion, among other things. Besides, every time we move a ship in or out of here, there's a risk; it could lead Confleet to Fina. Another good reason is that a lot of our missions take us into the Solar System, and that means SynchShift both ways. Takes a lot of power. But again, the problem is expense and matériel. We're working toward it, though. We've had our eye on Rhea. That would put us near the middle of the Solar System in the Saturn orbit. Rhea's only an overgrown rock, really, just big enough to hide a good-sized underground hangar, but too small to interest the Concord for mining or anything else."

Ransom nodded. "We'll have our Rhea base, sooner or later. Jan, thanks for the tour."

"Sure. I'll see you around the hangars in a few days." He put out his hand. "And, Alex, welcome to Fleet Operations."

PERSONAL FILE: E. RADEK   CASE NOTES: 27 AUGUS 3253
SUBJECT: ALEX RANSOM

I'll be making my last report on Alex tonight. Tomorrow
he begins his career in Fleet Operations. In retrospect, I can
call the metamorphosis of Lord Alexand into Alex Ransom
entirely successful. Almost too successful, except for the
persistent warp associated with Adrien Eliseer.

The test of Alex Ransom's emotional equilibrium comes
later this evening when I show him the ex seqs: the Ransom
Alternative. I've asked Ben and Andreas to come to my
office, too, but we'll have to be circumspect in this and in
subsequent meetings. Andreas objected to the late hour and
the "sneaking about," but not too strenuously. Even he
recognizes the necessity of it.

Alex will also recognize it, and won't be as reluctant
to face it. In a way, I'm also reluctant, because I must tell
him that a threat exists that may shatter all his hopes and
make his sacrifices meaningless. But we've all made sacrifices, and any of us who didn't recognize the high risk
of failure were deluded.

6.

It took nearly half an hour to cover all the sequences, including the subalternatives and contingency variables, a time of taut quiet broken only when Erica explained each new sequence, then subsided into silence while Alex studied it. He asked few questions.

The screen was on the compconsole at one end of her office; their backs were to Ben Venturi and Andreas Riis, who were seated in front of the desk. But Erica was aware of them and their part in the silence. Waiting as she was.

And now she watched Alex as he studied the last seq, absorbing the information as if he were himself a computer, analyzing and sorting, drawing instantaneous probability curves in his mind.

"Is that all of them?" Even his voice had a flat, mechanical tone.

"Yes."

He turned off the screen, but when it went dark, didn't look up, apparently still concentrating on the graphs and figures in memory. But his blink rate was too fast. He was concentrating on her, and he didn't look at her because he wanted privacy.

She left him and crossed to the 'spenser. "Coffee, anyone?"

Ben and Andreas seemed to find it difficult to shift their attention from Alex long enough to give her the expected murmured declinings. She punched for coffee for herself, then took the cup to her desk and sat down. Alex turned, and she was reminded of the first time she saw him on his arrival in Fina: the regal posture, a lifetime of training behind it; a child taught from infancy to hold his head high as his father did, and his before him. In his month at Fina, he'd become more relaxed, blending into his background, into his new identity. But his posture now wasn't a reversion to his former identity, only indicative of a state of mental alertness.

He looked at Andreas and Ben, but the silence remained unbroken. Still calculating. She felt something chilling in that cybernetic mindset. It wasn't new, or a product of thirty-two days in Fina. It was only, like his posture, in some sense different.

He was calculating potential opposition now; that's why his attention was focused on Andreas and Ben. He was confident of her support. This she could have predicted, this establishment of a mandate of command at the outset. She watched as his gaze met and held Ben's. Ben didn't look away any more than he would back down, but he would accept leadership he could believe in; he was waiting for proof.

There was a slight relaxation in Alex's posture as he asked, almost casually, "Erica, why didn't you elaborate on the Eliseer line in those ex seqs? Weren't you sure I was capable of dealing with it objectively? You may all put your minds at ease on that score. Of course, if these ex seqs are implemented, we must try to keep the Lady Adrien free to honor the existing Contracts of Marriage with Lord Alexand. The political advantages of the union are obvious. However, the maximum time range in these ex seqs is ten years. It's highly unlikely that Lady Adrien could be kept free so long, and that contingency is a very minor factor in the Ransom Alternative."

He crossed to the desk, his eyes moving slowly, with the leisure of confidence, from one face to another, but when he came to Erica, she wasn't capable of meeting his gaze. She turned to Andreas, who was looking up at Alex in stricken bewilderment. A paradox, Andreas; so much a scientist, yet he counted the cost of every decision first in subjective terms.

And Ben Venturi, the pragmatic idealist—his eyes were narrowed to slits, but the suspicion was gone. He found his proof in Alex Ransom's ability to speak of the Eliseer match as if it were only a factor to be computed, from his denial of himself as Alexand. Exactly what Alex intended.

"Dr. Riis," Alex said, "I assume you're prepared to act on the basis of these ex seqs?"

Andreas answered, "Yes. The Ransom Alternative will put us in a stronger position far sooner than any other alternative available to us."

Alex began pacing a circle in the open area between the desk and the doorway, hands clasped behind his back, eyes apparently focused on the floor, yet she doubted he'd have missed it if Ben or Andreas so much as raised an eyebrow.

Then he stopped and faced Andreas. "I must take exception

both to the assertion that the Ransom Alternative will put us in a stronger position, and to the primary objective delineated in those ex seqs."

Andreas frowned questioningly. "I don't understand."

"The primary objective is the reinstatement of the Lord Alexand with all powers intact *as of his death*. But the Lord Alexand will be your representative in the Concord; your tool. No amount of force will make a bladeless knife cut. If you simply reinstate Alexand, reestablish the old status, you'll find yourself with an impotent tool. It isn't enough."

Ben's mouth was tight. "What *is* enough?"

"The Chairmanship. Lord Alexand must be made *direct* heir to Galinin. It isn't unreasonable. Alexand was in fact the real heir thanks to the blood link through Lady Elise."

Andreas frowned. "Still, Galinin named Phillip Woolf his immediate successor, and at this point the Directors are holding to that in spite of your 'death.' But to make you a direct heir—that would mean putting a known Phoenix member in the Chairmanship within a few years. They won't be ready to accept that so soon; it's too much to expect of them. And we'll only get one chance at bargaining."

Alex remained clearly unimpressed and unconcerned with that argument.

"If you consider it a lost cause, Dr. Riis, I advise you to give up the Ransom Alternative and concentrate on the Peladeen Alternative."

Erica stared at him. The Peladeen Alternative was Pri-One information, and Alex didn't have access to those files. Then she almost laughed. She'd been foolish to think she could conceal that from him for a full month. At least she no longer had the problem of how to tell him about it and the threat it represented. Once he recognized the Peladeen Alternative, the threat would be obvious.

Ben was shaken, too, and no doubt wondering about Alex's source of information, but that didn't concern Andreas.

"Alex, do you consider your father that much of an impediment?"

She saw a flicker of coldness, an ambivalent reaction outside calculation. But it wasn't evident in his tone.

"The Lord Woolf might have a change in attitude in the future. We know he's been profoundly affected by the losses he's suffered. But he may *not* change, or he may be driven to even more reactionary attitudes by his grief. In that case, he'll be not only an impediment, but an insurmountable barrier. Except for Lord Phillip's father, the Woolfs have been notably long-lived. Can the Phoenix afford to wait thirty or forty years before Alexand can even sit in a Directorate meeting? The next twenty years will be crucial for the Concord. Can you afford to wait that long to *begin* to initiate reforms? Consider it, Dr. Riis. Perhaps you should stay with Predis Ussher as your focus for Phase I."

Ben glanced at Erica, a question in his eyes: How much have you told him? But she ignored both his gaze and the question. She was wondering why Alex had chosen to use Ussher's name. He might have used the term "Peladeen Alternative" again.

Alex was looking intently at Andreas, and that was the answer. He wanted Andreas's reaction to the name. And Andreas obliged him with an uneasy, uncertain frown.

Alex said tightly, "Dr. Riis, I will not suffer this apotheosis or allow the Phoenix to waste its time and resources simply to reestablish a situation I know to be untenable. We must aim for the Chairmanship or give up the Ransom Alternative."

It was an ultimatum, and Erica saw Ben bridling at it, but Andreas stopped him before he could voice an objection.

"He's right, Ben. We aren't in a position to assess Woolf's attitudes or their results." Then, as Ben subsided, he said to Alex, "We'll have to take the chance that we can force the Directors to go beyond reinstating you. The Peladeen Alternative has too many disadvantages for us to consider it seriously now. We have no choice but to aim for the Chairmanship, as you suggest."

Alex's expression didn't change, although this was the recognition of leadership he wanted.

He looked at Ben. "Commander, are you in agreement?"

"I'd go with Andreas under any circumstances." He hesitated, then nodded decisively. "But in this case, I go willingly. Yes, I'm in agreement."

It was a statement of faith that went further than Erica expected, and Alex seemed to realize that. It stopped him for a moment and even called up a hint of a smile.

"Thank you, Commander. Erica?"

That inquiry was only a matter of courtesy; he knew where she stood.

"I'm in agreement."

He nodded and turned away to resume his pacing.

"It would be a waste of time to make detailed plans for implementing the Ransom Alternative now. We're faced with two major obstacles. First, we can't go to the bargaining table until we have the long-range MT."

Andreas sighed. "Unfortunately, I can't predict when we'll have it. The ex seqs were based on the assumption that we'll get a breakthrough within five years, and that's within the limits of probability, but I can't pinpoint it."

Alex took another slow turn, showing no dismay at that.

"At any rate, we need time to prepare both Alex Ransom and the Phoenix. I can't be foisted on the members as their tool or representative without their support. Perhaps we should be grateful to Confleet for equipping me so well for FO. It's a natural springboard. I've studied the staff and matériel, and if I can't work my way up to First Commander by the time Garris retires, I'll fail you in my apotheosis." He stopped and turned to face them. "We can also dismiss that problem for the time being, but there's one problem we can't dismiss: the second major obstacle to the Ransom Alternative, and the problem that brings us together in this clandestine meeting."

Andreas shifted uncomfortably, eyes averted.

"Clandestine? Alex, we . . . simply thought you should be apprised of the ex seqs privately."

"No, Dr. Riis, 'clandestine' is the proper term, and this meeting marks the formation of a conspiracy. If it's to be successful, we must be honest with one another. And with ourselves. Tell me, why isn't the full Council considering these ex seqs?"

"I didn't think it wise to discuss them with the other councilors at this time."

"Especially not with Fer Ussher?" Then, at Andreas's silent nod, "At least we've named the problem. Am I correct in assuming the main thrust of the Peladeen Alternative is to induce the Directors to restore the House of Peladeen with Predis Ussher as First Lord?"

"Yes, that's correct."

"And Ussher claims to be Elor Peladeen's son?" Andreas

only nodded again. Alex paused, then, "*Is* he Peladeen's son?"

Andreas pulled in a deep breath, frowning slightly.

"Well, we're as sure of that as we can be. The bodies of Lady Manir and Predis Peladeen were never found, of course, and there's some physical resemblance to Lord Elor. Predis had some jewelry known to belong to Lady Manir, and related a few childhood memories. Not too much along that line, but he was only two at the time of the Fall."

"How did he survive it?"

"A Fesh nursemaid took him in tow and later claimed him as her own child. She died a year before he joined us, so we couldn't question her, but we have evidence that she *was* a nurse for the Peladeen child, and we couldn't find any record of her marrying or having a child of her own. But very few records survived the Fall. That's one problem we had in investigating Predis. For instance, there's not a single fingerprint or VP record on Predis Peladeen to be found. Actually, we can't prove his claim beyond a doubt. We only know it can't be *dis*proved, and for our purposes that was sufficient."

Alex asked Ben, "Are you convinced of the validity of his claim?"

"*His* claim isn't important now. We'll have no trouble proving *your* claim."

"It might be important in terms of his responses and the loyalty he can command among the members. You've created a power vacuum in the Phoenix and it's attracted a man of strong personal ambition. That's inevitable. What makes him dangerous is that you'll have to crush his ambitions, and he's not the kind of man to willingly toss aside his own aspirations for Lordship in order to make someone else a Lord. Commander, how will he react if he knows the Peladeen Alternative is to be set aside?"

Ben sighed. "He could be very dangerous. He's unpredictable when he's crossed."

Alex's gaze shifted. "Erica?"

"Predis was screened twenty years ago, and the information in the screening files isn't too conclusive; our methods have improved considerably since then." She paused, her fingers drumming on the arm of her chair. "My opinion is based on little more than day-to-day observation, but I do consider him dangerous. He could be highly disruptive, and we're so vulnerable in terms of security and morale. I don't know how far he'd go if he knew his ambitions would be crushed, but I'm sure he won't accept it passively."

Alex walked back to the end of the desk and sat down on the edge, arms folded loosely, and only Erica was alerted by his casual tone.

"So, Dr. Riis, here is a man capable of wreaking havoc within an organization vulnerable to betrayal from within and totally dependent on mutual trust. One dissatisfied member could destroy the Phoenix, either outright by betrayal, or slowly by fostering dissension. Predis Ussher is a threat to the very existence of the Phoenix. Perhaps you should give some thought to removing that threat."

Andreas stiffened, his eyes seeming to sink back into their sockets.

"*Removing* him? What are you suggesting?"

"There are always ways of removing a threat."

"We've considered all available means, and most of them involve the risk of engendering a schism in the membership—and that *would* destroy the Phoenix. He has a loyal following, Alex; remember that. There is no feasible alternative short of assassination, and we will not be reduced to that. The Phoenix never has and never will resort to bloodshed to solve its problems. When we go to the bargaining table, we'll go with clean hands. And for any of us to sink to murder would be more damaging to the mutual trust that binds us than Predis could ever be. If he does represent a serious threat, we'll have to deal with it as best we can, but we cannot resort to murder."

Alex studied him, eyes veiled, then turned to Ben, and the same conviction was in his face as in Andreas's. Finally, he looked around at Erica and smiled.

"Your survival is remarkable." Then, to Andreas, "Dr. Riis, I will be guided in this by you."

Andreas needed a moment to recover, and Erica had to smile; he was only now aware that he'd been tested.

"I'm . . . gratified, Alex."

Then Alex rose, frowning, hands propped on his hips. "The problem, however, isn't solved. The question now is, if we're stymied at doing anything about the Ransom Alternative for the time being, is Ussher also stymied?"

Erica answered that. "Yes, I think he is, and I think the

Ransom Alternative will just have to be our secret until you're established in the Phoenix, and especially until we have the LR-MT."

He considered that, still frowning. "But the other councilors know my identity. Won't some of them be a little curious?"

"Undoubtedly, but Andreas can salve their curiosity without encouraging speculation or discussion. Before your potential in the Phoenix can be assessed, you must prove yourself as a working member." She paused, giving him a slow smile. "And you'll be proving yourself for a long time to come."

"Besides," Ben put in, "Predis will help discourage any speculation about you in the Council. He doesn't want them comparing the Peladeen and Ransom alternatives, because he'll come out on the short end. And the Peladeen Alternative hinges on the LR-MT, too. He can't do a damn thing until we have it."

Alex raised an eyebrow. "Can't he? You mean he *probably* won't do a damn thing until we have it." Then he shrugged. "But I suppose a positive probability is better than a negative certainty. So, now we must work out some plans for the survival of our conspiracy. Tomorrow I begin my career with FO, and it will be some time before we can meet again without attracting undue attention."

He clasped his hands behind his back as he resumed his pacing. Calculating again, computing the variables. Erica felt herself relaxing as if a burden had been lifted from her shoulders. Perhaps it was only that the lines had been drawn and there could be no turning back.

And she was thinking of Rich. Alex Ransom had come to Fina to finish his brother's work, and that was one more reason to be grateful for having known and loved a saint.

27 Augus 3253
Fina

Alex:

Call me a quiv for spooking and leaving you with nothing but a lettape, but I don't like wave-offs. You know about my SI assignment. Venturi gave me a fast pass on the special training, and I've opted for the Helen chapter. Helen is home to me, and I know the ground; I have in-lines there no one else can tap.

I can't say the same of Fina, but I don't like the smell of what's going down here. You know about it; you're neck deep in it. I have a good nose and I'm good at addition, but I can only guess out the real stat. I'm crossing your lines to say this much anyway. But I have a word of wise to leave you. No, I have two. First, I read the tooth-gimmer clear; I know his ilk. You know politics; that's your gim, and I hold faith you can take him down at that. But he's no gentleman born, and he needs watching.

What I'm trying to say is don't ever turn your back on Predis Ussher. You'll end up with a blade in your heart, and I mean that literally. I came up foot to foot with killers; I can smell them out as easy as the Shads. And my kins have a saying: You read a man by what you see in the mirror. I've pulled a few down, one way or another, and I read Ussher. You do, too, but I don't think you have it in you to read him all the way. Maybe you do. Anyway, keep him in your line of sight.

The second word I'll leave is this: If it comes to a face-off and you need a little backup or just a sharp side-eye, you'll know where I am, or you can find out.

That's all. Just hold me in faith. I'm cleave to you, brother, because I have you smelled out, too. I'm cleave for personal reasons, but I'm also seeing long, and I'm thinking about the Phoenix and everything past that.

You and I will meet again sooner or later, and until then we'll both have plenty to track. I expect to see you in Garris's chair before the year comes around twice. Just keep your eyes open and, remember, all I need is a sign.

> Fortune, brother—
> Jael

EXCITING SCIENCE FICTION BESTSELLERS!

____ **STRANGER IN A STRANGE LAND**
Robert A. Heinlein   08094-3 — $3.95

____ **THE MOON IS A HARSH MISTRESS**
Robert A. Heinlein   08100-1 — $3.50

____ **GOD EMPEROR OF DUNE**
Frank Herbert   08003-X — $3.95

____ **CHILDREN OF DUNE**
Frank Herbert   07499-4 — $3.95

____ **DUNE**
Frank Herbert   08002-1 — $3.95

____ **DUNE MESSIAH**
Frank Herbert   07498-6 — $3.95

____ **THE BOOK OF MERLYN**
T. H. White   07282-7 — $2.95

____ **THE ONCE AND FUTURE KING**
T. H. White   08196-6 — $4.50

____ **WIZARD**
John Varley   07283-5 — $2.95

____ **TITAN**
John Varley   06386-0 — $2.95

Prices may be slightly higher in Canada.